MENACE
of the
MONSTER

Classic Tales of
Creatures from Beyond

edited by

MIKE ASHLEY

This collection first published in 2019 by
The British Library
96 Euston Road
London NW1 2DB

Cataloguing in Publication Data
A catalogue record for this book is available from the British Library

ISBN 978 0 7123 5269 7
e-ISBN 978 0 7123 6496 6

Frontispiece illustration by Warwick Goble, originally published in *Pearson's Magazine*
August 1897 to accompany the serialization of *The War of the Worlds* by H. G. Wells.

Front c͏͏   dden
appearanc **GREENWICH**   veeping
men out of **LIBRARIES**   originally published in *Pearson's* *Magazine*
July 1900 to accompany the article "How Will the World End" by Herbert C. Fyfe.

ELT   Cover design by

3 8028 02413677 9	
Askews & Holts	18-Oct-2019
AF ASH SCF	£8.99
6162945	

MENACE
of the
MONSTER

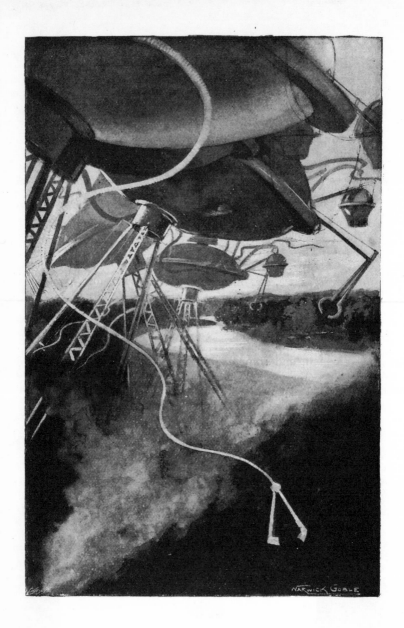

WARWICK GOBLE

CONTENTS

INTRODUCTION

MONSTERS AND ALIENS

There have always been monsters.

From our infancy we are told tales of strange creatures—dragons, sea serpents, ogres, giants, trolls, elves. We learn about the possibility of the Abominable Snowman, or Yeti, and its North American cousin, Bigfoot. We are told about the Loch Ness monster and sea monsters like giant squids or krakens. The Bible tells us how Jonah was swallowed by a "big fish". The Bible also tells us, in *Genesis*, that "there were giants in the earth in those days…"

The earliest known significant work of literature, the *Epic of Gilgamesh*, dating from around 2100 BC includes a battle between Gilgamesh and the monster Humbaba described variously as having the head of a lion or a bull, the claws of a vulture, and a tail that ends in a snake's head. It shares with the Greek legend of Medusa, whose hair was also writhing snakes, that its glare can strike people dead or turn them to stone.

The Greek legends are full of monsters—centaurs, the Chimera, the many-headed dog Cerberus, the Hydra and, most famously, the Minotaur—half-man, half-bull.

And then there are the dinosaurs.

Oh yes, there have always been monsters.

It seems we can't live without wanting to believe in monsters of some kind or another, whether fearful or wonderful. As children we are told that if we don't behave ourselves the Bogey-man will get us or the Monster under the Bed. And who can forget King Kong or Godzilla!

The fear of monsters is such a part of our psyche, so primitive, that it must date from our earliest ancestors who struggled to survive at a time when there were genuine land monsters that no longer survive—the mastodon, the woolly mammoth, the megatherium, the sabre-toothed smilodon, and the elasmotherium or giant rhinoceros, to name but a few. These creatures became extinct perhaps twelve thousand years ago, some earlier, but certainly within the time of our hunter-gatherer ancestors. The giant bird, the moa, survived in New Zealand until it was hunted to extinction by humans in the mid-1400s.

All these creatures were native to the Earth. It may also be possible that millennia ago the Earth was visited by aliens from other worlds. Although the theories about ancient astronauts proposed by researchers Erich von Daniken, Zecharia Sitchin and others have been dismissed by academics, it is still fascinating to speculate that our earliest ancestors may have witnessed alien explorers, and have been influenced by them.

Monsters and other strange creatures have been part of science fiction from the start and this anthology brings together examples from the classic period, the 1890s to the mid-1960s. Here you will find Earth-bound monsters, alien invaders, and creatures on other worlds, showing the diversity of beings that writers can create. The success of *The War of the Worlds* (1898), in which H. G. Wells gave powerful impetus to the idea that intelligent creatures on another world would be so different to humans, to all intents created the alien monster genre. Soon many writers were exploring the idea of monsters from either elsewhere on the Earth or from space.

Monsters were usually portrayed as violent and must be destroyed, as in the stories here by Ranger Gull and A. E. van Vogt. But over time writers gave more thought to the nature of alien creatures and in two stories here, those by James White and Eric Frank Russell, consideration is given to how we might care for the health and well-being of aliens and consider their rights. Alongside the incomprehensibility of some beings, as in the stories by Nelson Bond and H. P. Lovecraft, or the inability to cope with them, as shown by Coutts Brisbane and John Martin Leahy, we also explore the very idea of what constitutes a monster, alien or human, as brought to life by Idris Seabright and Marcia Kamien.

It was impossible to cover all the diversity of aliens and creatures that science fiction has created and though these stories are representative of the genre, I'd also like to explore the emergence of the monster in classic science fiction to cover other works you may wish to track down.

None of these monsters is supernatural. There are no witches or vampires or zombies or werewolves. All these monsters have a grounding in science and just because you haven't encountered any of them yet, it doesn't mean that they're not out there, waiting to be found.

HERE THERE BE MONSTERS!

Although this anthology deals with animals rather than humans, it is worth starting with a sobering thought about our attitudes towards people who, for whatever reason, seem abnormal. Humans with any type of deformity were once portrayed as monsters or freaks.

It was rare for any such human to be portrayed sympathetically. William Shakespeare managed it to some degree with his portrayal of Caliban in *The Tempest* (first performed, 1611). Caliban is described as half-man, half-fish and was the sole human inhabitant of an island before it was taken over by the mage Prospero who harshly enslaved Caliban.

It is much the same in one of the pioneer works of science fiction, *Frankenstein, or the Modern Prometheus* (1818) by Mary Shelley, where the creature brought to life by the eponymous Baron is never named but is referred to as "the monster". It is because it is treated badly by its creator, who is horrified at what he has achieved, and is abandoned and shunned by the public, that it seeks revenge upon its creator. Throughout the book Shelley wants the reader's sympathy to be with the creature, telling part of the story from its viewpoint.

Victor Hugo also encouraged sympathy for Quasimodo, the hunchback in *The Hunchback of Notre Dame* (1831), but the readers' fear of what Quasimodo might do remains a crucial plot element of the novel. It is the same in Gaston Leroux's *Le Fantôme de l'Opéra* (1910). It is shameful that many with deformities were displayed as freaks in travelling sideshows, such as happened with Joseph Merrick, the so-called Elephant Man, in the 1880s. The public loved to peer and gloat at such individuals whilst keeping a safe distance.

Whilst one hopes that attitudes have changed, it is this combination of fear and fascination that keeps our interest in all forms of unusual creations alive.

So it was with the dinosaurs. People had long known of fossils, usually ammonites or trilobites or large individual bones, but rarely of entire big specimens. In 1811 Mary Anning, who lived in Lyme Regis in Dorset, discovered an entire fossilized skeleton of what is now called an ichthyosaur, though at the time was believed to be a crocodile. Anning found further fossils including those of a plesiosaur and a pterosaur. Her discoveries helped expand the new science of palaeontology, exploring the concept that there were once animals that had become extinct, thus refuting the then long-held belief that not only had all animals been saved by Noah in the global flood, but that the Earth was barely six thousand years old. The biologist Richard Owen was able to inspect several of Anning's discoveries and it was he who coined the word "dinosaur", meaning terrible lizard, in 1841.

One of the first large land dinosaurs to be identified was the iguanodon and the name was coined in 1824. Other prehistoric beasts discovered at that time were the Megalosaurus in 1824 and the glyptodon in 1823, though not recognized as a distinct species or named until 1837. The process of discovery and identification grew steadily throughout the nineteenth century, though it was not until the late 1890s that the best known of all the giant dinosaurs, the tyrannosaurus, was identified. Until then the iguanodon, mistakenly believed to be a carnivore rather than a herbivore, took centre stage and featured amongst the group of dinosaur sculptures unveiled at the Crystal Palace park in South London in 1854.

The concept of huge reptiles having lived on Earth aeons ago was not easily accepted by Victorian society but it gathered pace with the publication of Charles Darwin's *On the Origin of Species* in 1859 with his theory of evolution through natural selection. The author Charles Kingsley was intrigued by the idea. Not only did he model *The Water Babies* (1863) on the theory but he made a point within the novel that men had scoffed at the idea of a dragon being real and yet, they had now discovered the bones of a real flying dragon, the pterodactyl. Kingsley was one of the first to incorporate ancient creatures in a novel. In *Alton Locke*, published in 1850, he includes a dream sequence in which the narrator has a vision of the evolution of life on Earth with an episode where he becomes a mylodon, or giant sloth.

It wasn't long before dinosaurs became a feature in science fiction. In *Voyage au centre de la terra*, published in 1864, Jules Verne has his explorers encounter marine dinosaurs, such as a plesiosaur, in a vast subterranean sea. Verne realized that if humans are going to encounter dinosaurs the creatures must have survived in places humans had not previously visited and others took up that idea. In "The Iguanodon's Egg" (1882), the Scottish-born American journalist Robert Duncan Milne has his iguanodon surviving in a remote part of New Guinea. In *A Strange Manuscript Found in a Copper Cylinder* (1888), James De Mille locates his dinosaurs in a warm climatic anomaly in the Antarctic as does Frank Savile in *Beyond the Great South Wall* (1899). Both Edwin J. Webster in "The Slaying of the Plesiosaurus" (1903) and Clotilda Graves (writing as Richard Dehan) in "The Great Beast of Kafue" (1917) place their last surviving dinosaurs in remote parts of the African continent.

Starting in 1897 Robert W. Chambers wrote a series of stories later collected as *In Search of the Unknown* (1904) in which a zoologist at the newly established Bronx Zoo in New York travels to remote parts of the Americas and beyond in search of strange creatures encountering giant auks, a merman, a "dingue", the ux bird and a nautical monster, the thermosaur. Although written somewhat tongue-in-cheek, Chambers's work reflects much of the fascination of the period with frequent real discoveries of the fossils of ancient creatures.

Others chose more distant settings. One of Ambrose Bierce's cynical satires on the American state, "For the Ahkoond" (1888), is set millennia in the future where the iguanodon has reappeared in a remote part of North America. Gustavus W. Pope has the planet Venus the home of just about every dinosaur, sea serpent and monster imaginable in *Journey to Venus* (1895). For the next seventy years Venus became the go-to planet for dinosaurs until space probes revealed that the surface of Venus is so hot that there is no water, no tropical jungles and no hope of primeval monsters. In 1965 Roger Zelazny published "The Doors of His Face, the Lamps of his Mouth" as a romantic homage to the watery, dinosaur-ridden Venus of our imagination.

The classic story of dinosaur survival is *The Lost World* (1912) by Sir Arthur Conan Doyle where his monsters exist on a virtually inaccessible mountain in South America. Edgar Rice Burroughs invented the island of Caspak, situated in the south Pacific near Antarctica, with unassailable high cliffs, not unlike Doyle's lost world, to house his dinosaurs, primitive men and other creatures in "The Land That Time Forgot" (1918) and its sequels.

Another way of restoring dinosaurs to life was to discover an egg, which hatches, as Milne had done in "The Iguanodon's Egg". H. G. Wells did the same in "Æpyornis Island" (1894), set on an island off Madagascar, where a giant bird, previously believed extinct, hatches and is raised by its discoverer. In "The Dragon of St. Paul's" (1899) by Reginald Bacchus and Ranger Gull, which is reprinted here, the egg was discovered in the Arctic.

The love affair with dinosaurs continues throughout the period of classic science fiction and well into today, especially in the cinema. Doyle's *The Lost World* was first adapted for film in 1925, directed by Harry Hoyt, with the creatures brought to life by the remarkable (for its day) stop-motion photography of Willis O'Brien. The success of that film generated a host of monster movies of which surely the best known and most influential was *King Kong* (1933). The story, set on an unspecified remote island, includes not only the eponymous giant ape but an impressive array of dinosaurs and is perhaps the epitome of the monster story. Willis O'Brien once again brought the creatures to life. The original story was the idea of film director and producer Merian C. Cooper. Early in the process he brought in the famous thriller writer Edgar Wallace to help develop the script. Unfortunately, Wallace died of pneumonia in February 1932. Cooper later claimed that Wallace did not write any scene or dialogue for the film but Wallace's surviving draft scenario suggests that it was he who developed the "beauty and the beast" theme. Just before the release of the film a novelization was completed by Delos W. Lovelace in December 1932, and a few months after the film's release, writer and editor Draycott Dell, wrote his own version. That story is reprinted here.

The fascination with dinosaurs revived interest in fiction with other monsters, especially sea monsters. These had been the stuff of legend and sailors' yarns for centuries. The Carthaginian trader and navigator Himilco, who lived around the sixth century BC, and plied the route from Carthage to Britain, may well have recorded the first reports of a sea monster. Similar monsters (probably whales or basking sharks) were reported in the travels of St. Brendan some time in the sixth century but not written down until around the year 900AD. It was the belief in sea monsters that caused early cartographers, such as Gerardus Mercator, to enter *"Hic Svnt Dracones"* ("Here be dragons") on maps.

Sightings of sea monsters became so numerous that the Norwegian Bishop of Bergen, Erik Pontopiddan, listed many in his *Natural History of Norway* (1752). He was the first to describe the *kraaken*, later popularized by Lord Tennyson in his poem "The

Kraken" (1830). Victor Hugo vividly described an encounter with a kraken, or *poulp*, near the Channel Islands in *Les Travailleurs de la mer* (1866).

Frederick Marryat included a hundred-foot long sea serpent in his "Fourth Voyage of Huckaback", part of his *Arabian Nights* style collection *Pacha of Many Tales* (1835). But it was Jules Verne, again, who opened the portals of science fiction to the sea monster in *Vingt mille lieues sous les mers* (1870). Captain Nemo's submarine *Nautilus* is itself initially believed to be a sea monster, and on its travels it encounters many creatures from giant crabs and lobsters to huge squids which attack the vessel.

For several decades after Verne there was a flurry of sea-monster stories, so much so that they started to parody themselves and became predictable. The sightings of sea serpents became so numerous that in October 1871 the London *Times* noted it was "sea-serpent season"! In "A Matter of Fact" (1892) Rudyard Kipling has a journalist, who witnessed two sea-serpents driven to the surface following an underwater eruption, unable to sell the story because editors thought it is another hoax.

There was one author, though, who made the sea monster very much his own and that was William Hope Hodgson. His first, "A Tropical Horror" (1905) describes an enormous serpentine sea creature with tentacles that end in giant claws. Hodgson had spent seven years at sea during the 1890s and he let his imagination run riot in many stories. In "The Stone Ship" (1914) an ancient, now petrified, sunken ship is blown to the surface by an underwater eruption and brings with it giant eels and sea caterpillars. Other stories feature massive crabs and things covered in an almost sentient fungus. He brought many of these nightmares together in *The Boats of the "Glen Carrig"* (1907), a novel set in 1757, telling the perils faced by survivors on a wrecked ship, which becomes trapped in weed-clogged waters, and encounters giant octopuses, tentacled humans and pulpy trees with whip-like branches.

Most sea-monster stories are variations on a theme and can become too formulaic. I included some of the best in my anthology *From the Depths*, also published by the British Library. One other author who established his own original concept about denizens of the sea was H. P. Lovecraft. Several of his stories developed a concept around ancient cosmic beings one of which, Cthulhu, is imprisoned on Earth in the sunken city of R'lyeh deep in the Pacific Ocean. The earliest story to set down this idea was "The Call of Cthulhu" (1928) which describes the monster as being hundreds of feet tall with an octopoid head but an anthropoid body. It has hundreds of worshippers who believe that one day Cthulhu will return. As Lovecraft developed what was later dubbed the Cthulhu Mythos, earlier stories were incorporated into the narrative including "Dagon" (1919), which is included here, and which tells the fate of a stranded mariner who finds himself on an island recently thrown up from the sea-bed.

Apart from the depths of the oceans or remote parts of the Earth another, and somewhat less obvious place for monsters, was in the air, the upper atmosphere. In "The Horror of the Heights" (1913) Sir Arthur Conan Doyle created a vivid picture of giant jellyfish far up in the stratosphere which menace early aeronauts. But he wasn't the first to explore the idea. There was a flurry of such stories at that time. The first to appear in English was "The Strange Case of Alan Moraine" (1912) by Bertram Atkey where a pioneer aeronaut is captured by a UFO. However, the previous year, in *Le Péril Bleu* (1911), the French author Maurice Renard told of an invisible alien airship which orbits the Earth in the upper atmosphere and captures animals and humans from Earth to study—this is where the idea of alien abductions by UFOs really began. The idea was adapted, with permission, by John Raphael as *Up Above* (1913) and was reworked again by George Allan England in *The Empire in the Air* (1914). By the time E. R. Punshon used the idea in "The Last Ascent" (1916) it was already old hat.

At this same time, the phenomenologist, Charles Fort, was working on *The Book of the Damned* (1919), the first of several books that brought together actual bizarre events, such as it raining frogs, and suggested that there may indeed be life in the upper atmosphere. He went further and suggested that "We are property", meaning that aliens are watching over us as if we were the product of an experiment. Before long the early ideas of Renard and Doyle were explored again in the science-fiction magazines. In "The Earth Owners" (1931), for example, Edmond Hamilton has Earth menaced by weird black gaseous clouds that suck the life force from humans but are destroyed by globes of light who are the "protectors" of Earth. In "Exiles of the Stratosphere" (1935) Frank Belknap Long has a race of beings living in the upper atmosphere that occasionally casts its rejects down to Earth.

The classic of this sub-genre is *Sinister Barrier* (1939) by Eric Frank Russell. He reveals that Earth is co-occupied by a race of aliens visible only in the far infrared and which feed upon human emotions. These aliens are large blue spheres, not unlike ball lightning.

In the Middle Ages, with the power of the Catholic church throughout Europe, it was dangerous to speculate too much about life on other worlds. It hadn't always been so. The German theologian, Nicholas of Cusa, firmly believed that there must be life elsewhere in the Universe. In his treatise, *De docta ignorantia* ("Of Learned Ignorance", 1440) he wrote:

> Rather than think that so many stars and parts of the heavens are uninhabited and that this earth of ours alone is peopled— and that with beings perhaps of an inferior type—we will suppose that in every region there are inhabitants, differing in nature by rank and all owing their origin to God, who is the centre and circumference of all stellar regions.

To think any less, he reasoned, would be to cast doubt on God's creativity.

His views were not challenged at the time and they became assured reading to many forward-looking thinkers, but when Giordano Bruno reiterated these thoughts and others in the late sixteenth century he was arrested as a heretic and burned at the stake in 1600.

Thereafter writers exercised considerable caution in expressing any views about life on other worlds. Few published such works during their lifetimes. Johannes Kepler's *Somnium* was not published until 1634, four years after he died. Francis Godwin's *The Man in the Moone* (1638), appeared five years after his death, and Cyrano de Bergerac's *Histoire Comique* (1657), two years after his death and even then heavily edited. Kepler took particular note of the lunar environment and was the first to seriously consider how life would have developed in relation to its surroundings. He argued that any life forms would be short-lived, because of the extreme heat and cold of the lunar day and night, but that also they needed to grow to a large size in order to benefit from any heat. He describes lunar life as serpentine, some having wings. Cyrano de Bergerac imagined that the Sun was inhabited by intelligent birds.

Yet, only thirty years after Cyrano's death, Bernard de Fontenelle met with much acclaim following publication of *Entretiens sur la pluralité des mondes* ("Conversations on the Plurality of Worlds", 1686). He revisited the proposal that, because God is infinite, then the universe must also be infinite and therefore life on other worlds is infinite. It was still some while before authors felt they could be totally free in imagining aliens. Even the French philosopher Voltaire kept his aliens in *Micromegas* (1752) humanoid, albeit gigantic. The eponymous Micromegas was an inhabitant of a planet orbiting Sirius and was eight leagues or 24 miles (39 kilometres) tall! As he travels to our Earth he befriends a native of Saturn who was, by comparison, a dwarf, at a mere thousand fathoms (or just over a mile) tall.

One of the first to let imagination go wild on life forms was Miles Wilson, a curate and schoolmaster at Halton Gill, tucked away in the Yorkshire Dales. Fascinated with the potential wonders of the solar system he wrote a story to educate his pupils. In *The History of Israel Jobson* (1757) the eponymous cobbler (who is also the Wandering Jew and is thus already over 1700 years old) is taken to the Moon by an angelic chariot where he encounters creatures of metal. He is taken to the other planets and encounters red Martians who are rooted like trees and Saturnians who are without sin but are in the process of building their equivalent of the Tower of Babel, and have one giant eye in the front of their head and a smaller one at the back. Unfortunately for Wilson his pupils' parents thought that what he was telling the children was true and Wilson had to apologize and destroy all copies of his book. It is now extremely rare.

For decades, though, authors still treated intelligent life on other worlds as either humanoid or angelic. In *Lumen* (1872) the French astronomer Camille Flammarion explored the universe and the nature of life on many planets and although in most cases they are humanoid he does occasionally think outside the box. On one planet, for example, the inhabitants are intelligent trees, on another they are a blend of animal and vegetable that can barely retain a fixed form.

In Flammarion's wake came a Belgian-born writer with considerable imagination who created some highly original aliens, but because his work was not translated into English at that time it failed to have the wider impact it deserved. This was J.-H. Rosny *aîné*, the alias used by Joseph-Henri Boëx, regarded by many as the natural successor to Jules Verne in the *roman scientifique*. Amongst his early stories were "Les Xipéhuz" (1887) and "Un autre monde" (1895) both of which explore the impact of alien creatures on Earth. These creatures are not necessarily extraterrestrial; part of their fascination is in not fully knowing what they are. In "Les Xipéhuz" (also translated as "The Shapes"), set in prehistory about 10,000BC, they seem to be trans-dimensional beings which, in our world, are visible only as odd shapes such as cones, slabs or cylinders. In "Un autre monde" the narrator, due to an affliction in his eyesight as a child, is aware of other beings all around him, invisible to everyone else. They take all shapes and sizes.

Had Rosny's work been better known in the English-speaking world, there might have been a more significant development in the imagination of aliens. Instead it was down to H. G. Wells to make the major advance in the portrayal of alien life. In *The War of the Worlds* (1898) he created Martians who are so hideous that it totally changed our concept of extraterrestrials and has remained a landmark work of fiction. Wells's novel is essential reading for any devotee of science fiction. However, it is little known that in 1920, in response to some new illustrations created by the Dutch artist

Johan Briedé, Wells produced an abridged version of the novel as a short story, and that version is reprinted here.

Wells created other types of monsters, though none so memorable as his Martians. In "The Sea Raiders" (1896) there are giant amphibious octopuses, in *The Island of Dr. Moreau* (1896) there are the beast-men, the results of Moreau's attempts to turn animals into humans, and in *The Food of the Gods* (1904) experiments with a new chemical lead to a rapid growth in several animals including chickens, rats, wasps and eventually humans. The idea of giant insects became a science-fiction staple in the pulps, despite the fact that the square-cube law means that if an insect doubled in size its volume would quadruple and it would soon be impossible to fly.

The War of the Worlds was a gamechanger and thereafter writers had a much freer rein in creating alien beings—though not all took the opportunity. Initially, it was more of a trickle. The British civil servant Sir Joshua Flynn, who wrote as Owen Oliver, was heavily influenced by Wells. In "The Black Shadow" (1903) attempts are made to discover whether there is life on the Moon and it is realized too late that lunar life exists as a psychic force which can be transmitted electro-magnetically and can take control of humans. In "The Plague of Lights" (1904) a passing planetoid makes contact with humans in the form of strange, apparently sentient lights which can kill but which also affect human emotions. In "The Cloud-Men" (1911), which is included here, a strange form of nebulous being almost wipes out life on Earth.

For many years, however, most aliens were humanoid. They may have had an extra set of arms or their skins may have been a different colour, they may have been telepathic or able to fly, but they were still humanoid in form and in culture, often able to converse without any problems. Edgar Rice Burroughs, the creator of Tarzan, contributed significantly to the humanoid alien in his long-running series about John Carter on Mars which began with "Under the Moons of Mars" (1912; expanded as *A Princess of Mars*, 1917) and which popularized the sub-genre of planetary romance. On Burroughs's Mars, or Barsoom to give it its native name, there are two races. The more senior is red skinned, completely humanoid, has some telepathic skills and is scientifically advanced. The other is green-skinned with an extra pair of arms, over twelve-feet tall and although essentially humanoid, they lay eggs. There are other lesser intelligent races such as the vampirical plant men and the kangaroo-men, but Burroughs did not extend himself in creating anything totally alien.

That was left to Abraham Merritt who, in the years just after the First World War vied with Burroughs in popularity amongst readers of scientific adventures in the American pulp magazines. Most of Merritt's work was fantasy but he occasionally ventured into science fiction or, more often, the murky area in between. One of his earliest stories, "The People of the Pit" (1918), which clearly influenced H. P. Lovecraft, tells of a previously undiscovered land in an unfathomably deep valley in far northern Canada wherein live a race of huge tentacled, transparent slug-like creatures which generate a psychic light.

Merritt's most remarkable alien appears in *The Metal Monster* (1920), another lost-world story set somewhere between Afghanistan and Tibet. Here the explorers meet a host of sentient metal shapes, cones, spheres, pyramids, which can combine into various forms and even merge into a city, ruled by a giant sphere, the Metal Emperor. The metal beings wish to reshape the world into their form and rid it of organic beings.

Merritt was as big an influence as Burroughs on extravagant fiction, encouraging writers to stretch their imagination in creating exotic worlds and bizarre creatures. Edmond Hamilton's first sale, for example, "The Monster-God of Mamurth" (1926), has an explorer stumble upon an ancient city with its guardian giant invisible spider. In other stories we encounter aliens such as giant cockroaches ("The Dimension Terror", 1928), giant tentacled globes ("Crashing Suns", 1928), toad-men ("The Polar Doom", 1928), intelligent slugs ("The Sea Horror", 1929), turtle-men ("The Other Side of the Moon", 1929), disk-men ("The Universe Wreckers", 1930) and vampiric frogs ("The Second Satellite", 1930). Jack Williamson's first story, "The Metal Man" (1928), with its gigantic crystalline beings like snowflakes, was also inspired by Merritt and though he created his various aliens, like Hamilton—giant crabs in "The Lake of Light" (1931), and a giant serpentine butterfly in "The Moon Era" (1932)—he pulled in the reins after a few years, though not until one final extravaganza. "Born of the Sun" (1934) has perhaps the largest monsters of all when it is discovered that the planets are really cosmic eggs that hatch to give birth to enormous dragons.

Clark Ashton Smith, who was as much a devotee of Lord Dunsany as he was Abraham Merritt, created many exotic creatures such as the moth-beings in "The City of Singing Flame" (1931), the multi-tentacled, two-headed metal beings in "The Eternal World" (1932), the dark angels and beings of pure chance in "The Dimension of Chance" (1932) and the tentacled slug-like monster in "Dweller in Martian Depths" (1933). When Smith submitted that last story to *Wonder Stories*, the editor, David Lasser, was so horrified by the viciousness of the alien monster that he toned-down the story, much to Smith's annoyance.

There are aliens aplenty in the pulp magazines of the 1930s, mostly exotic, and almost always dangerous. One author chose to turn this round. Starting with "A Martian Odyssey" (1934), which I reprinted in *Lost Mars*, Stanley G. Weinbaum created a diversity of creatures which seemed to relate to their environment (unlike most previous monsters) and were only violent if provoked. Weinbaum's trademark became unusual, intriguing, often humorous aliens, going about their lives regardless of humans. Weinbaum did ring the changes in a short series he wrote about Ham Hammond and his future wife Pat. The first two, "Parasite Planet" and "The Lotus Eaters" (both 1935) are set on an inhospitable Venus with parasitic fungi, giant amoebas and the screeching trioptes, who are semi-intelligent but vicious. The second story includes an intelligent telepathic vegetable which cannot fight back against the trioptes and so is content to accept life and death the way it is.

Weinbaum's work was revolutionary at the time, and he became one of the most popular contributors to the American sf pulps. Today the stories are strong period pieces, somewhat dated but which remind us of a short-lived writer who made his name by creating aliens with which we could sympathize and even relate.

He hadn't been the first to do this. The Australian-born but British-resident R. Coutts Armour, who wrote variously as Coutts Brisbane and Reid Whitley, had been writing stories, rather like fairy tales, about humorous and at times sympathetic aliens since "Take it as Red" and "Earthwise" (both 1918) set respectively on Mars and Venus. Over several stories he worked his way through most of the solar system. His Venusians were gigantic spiders, his Martians giant crabs but also intelligent kangaroos, on Mercury they are like frogs, whilst on Neptune, which is almost entirely covered by water, with abundant sea-worms, the main form of life is like an aquatic rodent. He saved his most creative beast for Saturn, as the following description from "Under the Moons" (1919) reveals.

Having described them as "more vegetable than anything else", he continues:

> ...though Retipuj had knobby things that served him for eyes, he wasn't limited to a single pair, but had them set singly or in clusters at convenient points all over his trunk, as well as on the great bulge in the midmost thereof, which, if not precisely his head, was the headquarters of his intelligence system. At the lower end of this trunk were a number of flexible tentacles, which served him for legs and feet; at the upper end, and at several places betwixt and between, were other groups like unto arms and fingers, strong and delicate, equal to all sorts of complicated manipulation. That he might communicate with his fellows, he was furnished with a box of tricks almost comparable to a harp, a series of taut tendrils played upon by pluckers. This extraordinary apparatus was placed at his trunk top, nearly hidden by a mantle of leathery, spiky leaflets that served at once as an umbrella against fervent sun and as lungs.

The description continues and we learn Retipuj is over thirty-two feet high and is like an intelligent tree with bug-eyes.

The "bug-eyed monster" or BEM was a phrase commonly used in the 1940s and 1950s to describe many of the creatures portrayed on the covers of the sf magazines. The term was coined in 1939 by leading sf fan Martin Alger who protested (light-heartedly) about such covers on recent issues of *Thrilling Wonder Stories*, but such illustrations went back for over a decade. Possibly the first was drawn by the legendary Frank R. Paul for the October 1926 *Amazing Stories* showing the intelligent crustaceans of the Antarctic in A. Hyatt

Verrill's "Beyond the Pole", but since these creatures were giant shrimps and lobsters they would inevitably be bug-eyed. A more appropriate starting place is Hans Wessolowski's cover for the May 1931 *Astounding Stories* depicting a scene from "Dark Moon" by Charles W. Diffin. In that story a rogue planetoid has passed near to Earth causing tsunamis and other disasters. Three daring adventurers go to the world, which they call the Dark Moon, and confront many giant insect-like creatures including a huge bug-eyed spider.

The science-fiction pulps never abandoned the BEMs, though monsters became less bug-eyed as writers, artists and (to a lesser degree) publishers, sought to produce more sophisticated science fiction in the 1950s.

At the same time the British philosopher, Olaf Stapledon, sent his imagination on a cosmic journey resulting in *Star Maker* (1937), a remarkable tour-de-force. It's a travelogue through time and space encompassing the whole span and history of the universe, and in his travels the narrator encounters many life-forms which he seeks to understand in relation to their environment. Thus, as he ventures further from Earth, and thereby further from humanoid creatures, he discovers much stranger forms, such as six-limbed beings that evolve into centaurs, or humanoid echinoderms which evolved from starfish and developed a communal culture. There are nautiloids, or intelligent tentacled ships, and there are two symbiotic races, the fish-like ichthyoids and the crab-like arachnoids. The psychic voyage continues into breath-taking realms eventually moving towards the ultimate Cosmic Being, the Star Maker itself, and en route we learn that the stars and galaxies are themselves sentient. It's impossible to summarize *Star Maker*, and it remains the single most astonishing work to consider life forms on a cosmic scale. Arthur C. Clarke called it "probably the most powerful work of imagination ever written", whilst Brian Aldiss claimed it was the most wonderful novel he had ever read.

The idea of a sentient galaxy had been considered by others, perhaps surprisingly in the American pulps. Laurence Manning's "The Living Galaxy" appeared in 1934, ahead of Stapledon's work. It is set millions of years in the future and considers how our universe is under threat from a living galaxy whose atoms are stars. Around this same time Ross Rocklynne wrote "Into the Darkness" though was unable to get it published until 1940. It was the first of four stories which eventually saw book publication as *The Sun Destroyers* (1973). Each story tells the adventures of a vast living galaxy and its descendants. They were certainly the most extreme creatures ever to appear in the pulp magazines.

Amongst smaller aliens in the sf pulps was the progenitor of the monster in the movie *Alien* (1979) and its many sequels. In "Discord in Scarlet" (1939), the second of A. E. van Vogt's stories about the voyage of the *Space Beagle*, his explorers encounter a monster somehow surviving in space which finds its way into the spaceship and begins hunting down the crew, laying eggs inside them. Although Dan O'Bannon, who produced the original story for *Alien*, denied having been inspired by van Vogt's story, the author brought a lawsuit against 20th Century Fox and it was settled out of court. That original story is included here.

The editor who bought van Vogt's story was John W. Campbell, Jr., and he wrote another classic story of an alien, which was later made into the film *The Thing from Another World* (1951). Campbell's original story was "Who Goes There?" (1938) set in the Antarctic where scientists have discovered an ancient spacecraft and succeed in reviving its pilot. This being is a shape-shifter and can take on the form of anything it eats. Before long it is assuming the bodies of various of the research team. In creating the story Campbell had drawn upon the childhood unease of not being able to distinguish between his mother and her twin sister who would sometimes deliberately confuse him. That uncertainty of who is who gives the story a formidable atmosphere of terror.

Horrors in the frozen north or the Antarctic had been the focus of several earlier stories most notably "The Thing from—Outside" (1923) by George Allan England, where an unseen creature is gradually killing a group of individuals in a remote part of Labrador, and "In Amundsen's Tent" (1928) by John Martin Leahy, which is included here, where a team trying to beat Amundsen and Scott to the South Pole encounter an abandoned tent with traces left by some unseen but very tangible horror. Both these stories may have sown seeds in the imagination of H. P. Lovecraft whose novella "At the Mountains of Madness" (1936) is set in the Antarctic and depicts several ancient life-forms and provides a history of the Old Ones who had settled on Earth aeons ago and had set in chain life on Earth. Amongst the horrors they created were the amoeboid protoplasmic shapeshifting shoggoths.

The idea of aliens taking over humans, as in Campbell's novella, has been a frequent concept in science fiction, with two landmark works. In *The Puppet Masters* (1951), Robert A. Heinlein has a flying saucer land on Earth in which are slug-like aliens that attach themselves to humans and take control. In *The Body Snatchers* (1955) by Jack Finney, alien spores take root on Earth and grow into pods in which are reproduced exact copies of individual humans. Both these books were published around the time of the McCarthy witch-hunts in the United States which fuelled the fear about communist infiltration. The movie version of Finney's novel, *Invasion of the Body*

Snatchers (1956) ends with the character Dr. Miles Bennell, played by Kevin McCarthy, screaming directly into camera at the audience warning them about aliens (or communists), shouting "They're here already! You're next! You're next!"

The idea of life coming to Earth via spores from space, a theory called panspermia, had been considered by scientists for decades but was brought into its final form by the Swedish chemist Svante Arrhenius in 1903. P. Schuyler Miller incorporated the idea in his story "The Arrhenius Horror" (1931) where spores have accumulated around a deposit of radium and bursts into crystalline life. Laurence Manning also used the idea in "Seeds from Space" (1935) where alien seeds grow into intelligent trees which methodically try to sew their spores across space onto other worlds. The cover of the June 1935 *Wonder Stories* by Frank R. Paul illustrating Manning's story shows these trees looking remarkably like another alien plant that would become synonymous with a fearful monster—the triffid.

The triffid was not from outer space. It was a product of botanical experiments/genetic engineering in Russia. In *The Day of the Triffids* (1951) John Wyndham evades describing their origin. The triffids, which are tall, carnivorous and venomous, are initially contained within various research facilities, but after most of the human race is blinded by a vivid meteor shower, the triffids escape and rapidly take over most of Europe and Britain.

John Wyndham was the alias of British writer John Beynon Harris who had been contributing to the science-fiction pulps since 1931. In one of his early stories, "Spheres of Hell" (1933) the West Country is overrun with a fungus that forms into a globular plant that is poisonous to the touch. Harris/Wyndham would go on to create many alien monsters. Some are invisible, as in "Invisible Monsters" (1933) and "...And the Walls Come Tumbling Down"

(1951) where, in fact, the aliens are benign and it is humans who are murderous. "Phoney Meteor" (1941) is the first story where aliens turn out to be considerably smaller than first believed, an idea developed further by Katharine MacLean in "Pictures Don't Lie" (1951). Wyndham's later novels include *The Kraken Wakes* (1953) in which aliens establish themselves deep in our oceans and begin to melt the ice-caps to turn Earth into a water world, and *The Midwich Cuckoos* (1957) in which all women in a small English village are impregnated by some unknown alien form of xenogenesis and the children born are human in form but utterly alien in their outlook, attitude and abilities.

The popularity of Wyndham's work meant that the word triffid passed into the English language initially to mean any unusual plant but soon to mean anything that multiplies at an alarming rate and takes over. Thanks to Wyndham, classic British science fiction had created an all-purpose monster.

MIKE ASHLEY

THE WAR OF THE WORLDS

H. G. Wells

H. G. Wells (1866–1946) is rightly seen as one of the founding fathers of science fiction, a term that had not been invented at the time that he produced the majority of his work. His early stories and novels established the nature of a genre that hitherto had had many seeds but no established flowering. Remembering those days Wells later recalled that he was producing stories that caused "the vivid realization of some disregarded possibility in such a way as to comment on the false securities and fatuous self-satisfaction of the everyday life." That he achieved with profound effect with his novel The War of the Worlds, *serialized in* Pearson's Magazine *during 1897. It created a considerable reaction amongst critics and public alike, especially when Wells remarked to an interviewer that it could well come true. There was already a growing fear in Britain that it was ill prepared for any foreign invasion, especially from France or Germany, but the idea that it might come from Mars with scientifically superior beings added a new and worrying dimension. If there was any work of science fiction that established the idea of the threat of the alien in people's imagination it was* The War of the Worlds.

Wells was fascinated with the way the book encouraged artists. Warwick Goble had illustrated the original serial, whilst in 1906, a French edition ran drawings by the Brazilian artist, then resident in Belgium, Henrique Alvim-Corréa. After the First World War, Wells was attracted by the work of the Dutch artist Johan Briedé and was encouraged to produce a "compact summary" of his original novel, which is reproduced here.

A Falling Star

THE FIRST STAR WAS SEEN EARLY IN THE MORNING RUSHING over Winchester eastward, high in the atmosphere. Hundreds must have seen it, and taken it for an ordinary falling star. For in those days no one gave a thought to the outer worlds of space as sources of human danger. At most, terrestrial men fancied there might be other men upon Mars, perhaps inferior to themselves and ready to welcome a missionary enterprise. Yet across the gulf of space, minds that are to our minds as ours are to the beasts that perish, intellects vast and cool and unsympathetic, regarded this earth with envious eyes, and slowly and surely drew their plans against us.

No one seems to have troubled to look for the fallen thing that night. But early in the morning it was found, almost entirely buried in the sand, among the scattered splinters of a fir-tree on the common between Horsell, Woking, and Ottershaw. The uncovered part had the appearance of a huge cylinder, caked over, and its outline softened, by a thick, scaly, dun-coloured incrustation. It had a diameter of about thirty yards. A stirring noise within the cylinder was ascribed at first to the unequal cooling of its surface, for at that time it did not occur to anyone that it might be hollow.

When, about sunset, I joined the crowd at the edge of the pit the thing had dug by its impact with the soil, the end of the cylinder was being screwed out from within. Nearly two feet of shining screw projected. Somebody blundered against me, and I narrowly missed being pitched on the top of the screw. As I turned to avoid the fall the lid of the cylinder fell upon the gravel with a ringing concussion. For a moment the cavity seemed perfectly black, for I had the sunset in my eyes.

I think everyone expected to see a man emerge—possibly something a little unlike us terrestrial men, but in all essentials a man. I know I did. But, looking, I presently saw something stirring within the shadow—greyish, billowy movements, one above another, and then two luminous discs like eyes. Then something resembling a little grey snake, about the thickness of a walking stick coiled up out of the writhing middle, and wriggled in the air towards me, and then another.

A big, greyish, rounded bulk, the size, perhaps, of a bear, was rising slowly and painfully out of the cylinder. As it bulged up and caught the light, it glistened like wet leather. Two large, dark-coloured eyes were regarding me steadfastly. It was rounded, and had, one might say, a face. There was a mouth under the eyes, the lipless brim of which quivered and panted, and dropped saliva. The body heaved and pulsated convulsively. A lank, tentacular appendage gripped the edge of the cylinder, another swayed in the air.

Those who have never seen a living Martian can scarcely imagine the strange horror of their appearance. The peculiar V-shaped mouth with its pointed upper lip, the absence of brow ridges, the absence of a chin beneath the wedge-like lower lip, the incessant quivering of this mouth, the Gorgon groups of tentacles, the tumultuous breathing of the lungs in a strange atmosphere, the evident heaviness and painfulness of movement, due to the greater gravitational energy of the earth—above all, the extraordinary intensity of the immense eyes—culminated in an effect akin to nausea. There was something fungoid in the oily brown skin, something in the clumsy deliberation of their tedious movements unspeakably terrible. Even at this first encounter, this first glimpse, I was overcome with disgust and dread.

Suddenly the monster vanished. It had toppled over the brim of the cylinder, and fallen into the pit with a thud like the fall of a great mass of leather. I heard it give a peculiar thick cry, and forthwith another of these creatures appeared darkly in the deep shadow of the aperture.

At that my rigour of terror passed away. I turned, and, running madly, made for the first group of trees, perhaps a hundred yards away; but I ran slantingly and stumbling, for I could not avert my face from these things. There, among some young pine trees and furze bushes, I stopped, panting, and waited further developments. Once a leash of thin black whips, like the arms of an octopus, flashed across the sunset, and was immediately withdrawn, and afterwards a thin rod rose up, joint by joint, bearing at its apex a circular disc that spun with a wobbling motion.

Suddenly there was a flash of light, and a quantity of luminous greenish smoke came out of the pit in three distinct puffs, which drove up, one after the other, straight into the still air. At the same time a faint hissing sound became audible. Beyond the pit stood a little wedge of people, a little knot of small vertical black shapes upon the black ground. As the green smoke rose their faces flashed out pallid green, and faded again as it vanished.

Then slowly the hissing passed into humming, into a long, loud droning noise. Slowly a humped shape rose out of the pit, and the ghost of a beam of light seemed to flicker out from it. Forthwith, flashes of actual flame, a bright glare leaping from one to another, sprang from the scattered group of men. It was as if some invisible jet impinged upon them and flashed into white flame. It was as if each man were suddenly and momentarily turned to fire.

Then, by the light of their own destruction, I saw them staggering and falling, and their supporters turning to run.

I stood staring, not as yet realizing that this was death leaping from man to man in that little distant crowd. All I felt was that it was something strange. An almost noiseless and blinding flash of light, and a man fell headlong and lay still, and as the unseen shaft of heat passed over them, pine trees burst into fire, and every dry furze-bush became with one dull thud a mass of flames. It is still a matter of wonder how the Martians are able to slay men so swiftly and so silently. Many think that in some way they are able to generate an intense heat in a chamber of practically absolute non-conductivity. This intense heat they project in a parallel beam against any object they choose by means of a polished parabolic mirror of unknown composition—much as the parabolic mirror of a lighthouse projects a beam of light. But no one has absolutely proved these details. How ever it is done, it is certain that a beam of heat is the essence of the matter—heat, and invisible, instead of visible, light. Whatever is combustible flashes into flame at its touch, lead runs like water, it softens iron, cracks and melts glass, and when it falls upon water incontinently that explodes into steam.

That night nearly forty people lay under the starlight about the pit, charred and distorted beyond recognition, and all night long the common from Horsell to Maybury was deserted, and brightly ablaze.

II

Fighting Begins

It was in a storm that I first saw the Martians at large, on the night of the third falling star. How can I describe the thing I saw? A monstrous tripod, higher than many houses, striding over the young pine trees, and smashing them aside in its career; a walking engine of glittering metal, striding now across the heather, articulate ropes of steel dangling from it, and the clattering tumult of its passage mingling with the riot of the thunder. A flash, and it came out vividly, heeling over one way with two feet in the air, to vanish and reappear almost instantly, as it seemed, with the next flash, a hundred yards nearer. Can you imagine a milking-stool tilted and bowled violently along the ground? That was the impression those instant flashes gave. But instead of a milking-stool, imagine it a great body of machinery on a tripod stand.

Seen nearer, the thing was incredibly strange, for it was no mere insensate machine driving on its way. Machine it was, with a ringing metallic pace, and long flexible glittering tentacles (one of which gripped a young pine tree) swinging and rattling about its strange body. It picked its road as it went striding along, and the brazen hood that surmounted it moved to and fro with the inevitable suggestion of a head looking about it. Behind the main body was a huge thing of white metal like a gigantic fisherman's basket, and puffs of green smoke squirted out from the joints of the limbs as the monster swept by me.

All that night the creatures were busy—communicating, I suppose, and maturing their plans. It was not until the next morning that our resistance began. The fighting I saw took place at

Shepperton Wey, where a crowd of fugitives were waiting their turn to cross the river by the ferry.

Suddenly we saw a rush of smoke far away up the river, a puff of smoke that jerked up into the air, and hung; and forthwith the ground heaved under foot, and a heavy explosion shook the air, smashing two or three windows in the houses near, and leaving us astonished.

Quickly, one after the other, one, two, three, four of the armoured Martians appeared, far away over the little trees, across the flat meadows that stretch towards Chertsey, and striding hurriedly towards the river. Little cowled figures they seemed at first, going with a rolling motion and as fast as flying birds.

Then, advancing obliquely towards us, came a fifth. Their armoured bodies glittered in the sun as they swept swiftly forward upon the guns, growing rapidly larger as they drew nearer. One on the extreme left—the remotest, that is—flourished a huge case high in the air, and the ghostly terrible heat-ray I had already seen on Friday night smote towards Chertsey, and struck the town.

"Get under water!" I shouted, unheeded. And, as the first Martian towered overhead scarcely a couple of hundred feet away, I flung myself under the surface.

When I raised my head, it was on the bank, and, in a stride, wading halfway across. The knees of its foremost legs bent at the further bank, and in another moment it had raised itself to its full height again, close to the village of Shepperton. Forthwith the six guns, which, unknown to anyone on the right bank, had been hidden behind the outskirts of that village, fired simultaneously. The sudden near concussions, the last close upon the first, made my heart jump. The monster was already raising the case generating the heat-ray as the first shell burst six yards above the hood.

Simultaneously two other shells burst in the air near the body as the hood twisted round in time to receive, but not in time to dodge, the fourth shell.

The shell burst clean in the face of the thing. The hood bulged, flashed, was whirled off in a dozen tattered fragments of red flesh and glittering metal.

"Hit!" shouted I, with something between a scream and a cheer.

I heard answering shouts from the people in the water about me. I could have leapt out of the water with that momentary exultation.

The decapitated colossus reeled like a drunken giant, but it did not fall over. It recovered its balance by a miracle, and, no longer heeding its steps, and with the camera that fired the heat-ray now rigidly upheld, it reeled swiftly upon Shepperton. The living intelligence, the Martian within the hood, was slain and splashed to the four winds of heaven, and the thing was now but a mere intricate device of metal whirling to destruction. It drove along in a straight line, incapable of guidance. It struck the tower of Shepperton church, smashing it down as the impact of a battering-ram might have done, swerved aside, blundered on, and collapsed with a tremendous impact into the river out of my sight.

A violent explosion shook the air, and a spout of water, steam, mud, and shattered metal shot far up into the sky. As the camera of the heat-ray hit the water, the latter had incontinently flashed into steam. In another moment a huge wave, like a muddy tidal bore, but almost scalding hot, came sweeping round the bend upstream. I saw people struggling shorewards, and heard their screaming faintly above the seething and roar of the Martian's collapse.

Then again I ducked, for the other Martians were advancing. When for a moment I raised my head to take breath and throw the hair and water from my eyes, the steam was rising in a whirling white fog that at first hid the Martians altogether. The noise was deafening. Then I saw them dimly, colossal figures of grey, magnified by the mist. They had passed by me, and two were stooping over the tumultuous ruins of their comrade.

The third and fourth stood beside him in the water, one perhaps two hundred yards from me, the other towards Laleham. The generators of the heat-rays waved high, and the hissing beams smote down this way and that.

The air was full of sound, a deafening and confusing conflict of noises, the clangorous din of the Martians, the crash of falling houses, the thud of trees, fences, sheds, flashing into flame, and the crackling and roaring of fire. Dense black smoke was leaping up to mingle with the steam from the river, and as the heat-ray went to and fro over Weybridge, its impact was marked by flashes of incandescent white, that gave place at once to a smoky dance of lurid flames.

For a moment, perhaps, I stood there, breast-high in the almost boiling water, dumbfounded at my position, hopeless of escape. Through the reek I could see the people who had been with me in the river scrambling out of the water through the reeds, like little frogs hurrying through grass from the advance of a man, or running to and fro in utter dismay on the towing-path.

Then suddenly the white flashes of the heat-ray came leaping towards me. The houses caved in as they dissolved at its touch, and darted out flames; the trees changed to fire with a roar. It flickered up and down the towing-path, licking off the people who ran this way and that, and came down to the water's edge not fifty yards from where I stood. It swept across the river to Shepperton, and the water in its track rose in a boiling wheal crested with steam. I turned shoreward.

In another moment the huge wave, well-nigh at the boiling-point, had rushed upon me. I screamed aloud, and, scalded, half-blinded, agonized, I staggered through the leaping, hissing water towards the shore. Had my foot stumbled, it would have been the end. I fell helplessly, in full sight of the Martians, upon the broad, bare gravelly spit that runs down to mark the angle of the Wey and Thames. I expected nothing but death. I have a dim memory of the foot of a Martian coming down within a score of feet of my head, driving straight into the loose gravel, whirling it this way and that, and lifting again; of a long suspense, and then of the four carrying the *debris* of their comrade between them, now clear, and then presently faint, through a veil of smoke, receding interminably, as it seemed to me, across a vast space of river and meadow. And then, very slowly, I realized that by a miracle I had escaped.

But it was not on the heat-ray that the Martians chiefly relied in their march on London. The monsters I saw that evening as I fled were armed with tubes which they discharged like guns. There was no flash, no smoke, simply that loaded detonation. Every minute I expected the fire of some hidden battery to spring upon them, but the evening calm was unbroken. Their figures grew smaller as they receded, and presently the gathering night had swallowed them up. Only towards Sunbury was a dark appearance, as though a conical hill had suddenly come into being there, and remoter across the river, towards Walton, I saw another such summit. They grew lower and broader even as I stared. These, as I knew later, were the black smoke. It was heavy, this vapour, heavier than the densest smoke, so that, after the first tumultuous uprush and outflow of its impact, it sank down through the air and poured over the ground in a manner rather liquid than gaseous, abandoning the hills, and streaming into the valleys and ditches and watercourses, even as I have heard the carbonic acid gas that pours from volcanic clefts is wont to do And the touch of that vapour, the inhaling of its pungent wisps, was death to all that breathes.

One has to imagine the fate of those batteries towards Esher waiting so tensely in the twilight, as well as one may. Survivors there were none. One may picture the orderly expectation, the officers alert and watchful, the gunners ready, the ammunition piled to hand, the limber gunners with their horses and wagons, the groups of civilian spectators standing as near as they were permitted, the evening stillness, the ambulances and hospital tents, with the burnt and wounded from Weybridge; then the dull resonance of the shots the Martians fired, and the clumsy projectile whirling over the trees and houses, and smashing amidst the neighbouring fields.

One may picture, too, the sudden shifting of the attention, the swiftly spreading coils and bellyings of that blackness advancing headlong, towering heavenward, turning the twilight to a palpable darkness, a strange and horrible antagonist of vapour striding upon its victims, men and horses near it seen dimly running, shrieking, falling headlong, shouts of dismay, the guns suddenly abandoned, men choking and writhing on the ground, and the swift broadening out of the opaque cone of smoke. And then, night and extinction—nothing but a silent mass of impenetrable vapour hiding its dead.

III

Dead London

So you understand the roaring wave of fear that swept through the greatest city in the world just as Monday was dawning—the stream of flight rising swiftly to a torrent, lashing in a foaming tumult round the railway stations, banked up into a horrible struggle about the shipping in the Thames, and hurrying by every available channel northward and eastward. By ten o'clock the police organization, and by midday even the railway organizations, were losing coherency, losing shape and efficiency, guttering, softening, running at last in that swift liquefaction of the social body.

All the railway lines north of the Thames and the South-Eastern people at Cannon Street had been warned by midnight on Sunday, and trains were being filled, people were fighting savagely for standing-room in the carriages, even at two o'clock. By three, people were being trampled and crushed even in Bishopsgate Street; a couple of hundred yards or more from Liverpool Street station revolvers were fired, people stabbed, and the policemen who had been sent to direct the traffic, exhausted and infuriated, were breaking the heads of the people that they were called out to protect.

And as the day advanced the engine-drivers and stokers refused to return to London, the pressure of the flight drove the people in an ever-thickening multitude away from the stations and along the northward-running roads. By midday a Martian had been seen at Barnes, and a cloud of slowly sinking black vapour drove along the Thames and across the flats of Lambeth, cutting off all escape over the bridges in its advance.

If one could have hung that June morning in a balloon in the blazing blue above London, every northward and eastward road running out of the infinite tangle of streets would have seemed stippled black with the streaming fugitives, each dot a human agony of terror and physical distress.

Directly below him the balloonist would have seen the network of streets far and wide, houses, churches, squares, crescents, gardens—already derelict—spread out like a huge map, and in the southward *blotted*. Over Ealing, Richmond, Wimbledon, it would have seemed as if some monstrous pen had flung ink upon the chart. Steadily, incessantly, each black splash grew and spread, shooting out ramifications this way and that, now banking itself against rising ground, now pouring swiftly over a crest into a new-found valley, exactly as a gout of ink would spread itself upon blotting-paper.

And beyond, over the blue hills that rise southward of the river, the glittering Martians went to and fro, calmly and methodically spreading their poison-cloud over this patch of country, and then over that, laying it again with their steam-jets when it had served its purpose, and taking possession of the conquered country. They do not seem to have aimed at extermination so much as at complete demoralization and the destruction of any opposition. They exploded any stores of powder they came upon, cut every telegraph, and wrecked the railways here and there. They were hamstringing mankind. They seemed in no hurry to extend the field of operations, and they did not come beyond the central part of London all that day. It is possible that a very considerable number of people in London stuck to their houses through Monday morning. Certain it is that many died at home, suffocated by the black smoke.

I have not space to tell you here of my adventures during the days that followed—of how I saw men caught for the Martians' food, of how the third falling star smashed the house where I was resting, and of what I saw while I was hiding there. When I came out into the air again I found about me the landscape, weird and lurid, of another planet. Everywhere spread the red weed, whose seed the Martians had brought with them. All round were red cactus-shaped plants, knee-high, without a solitary terrestrial growth to dispute their footing. The trees near me were dead and brown, but further, a network of red threads scaled the still living stems. I went on my way to Hampstead through scarlet and crimson trees; it was like walking through an avenue of gigantic blood-drops.

IV

How the Martians Were Slain

It was near South Kensington that I first heard the howling. It crept almost imperceptibly upon my senses. It was a sobbing alternation of two notes, "Ulla, ulla, ulla, ulla," keeping on perpetually. I stopped, wondering at this strange, remote wailing. It was as if that mighty desert of houses had found a voice for its fear and solitude. It was not until I emerged from Baker Street that I saw, far away over the trees in the clearness of the sunset, the hood of the Martian giant from which this howling proceeded. I watched him for some time, but he did not move.

I came upon the wrecked handling machine halfway to St. John's Wood Station. At first I thought a house had fallen across the road. It was only as I clambered among the ruins that I saw, with a start, this mechanical Samson lying, with its tentacles bent and smashed and twisted, among the ruins it had made. The fore part was shattered. It seemed as if it had driven blindly straight at the house, and had been overwhelmed in its overthrow.

A little beyond the ruins about the smashed handling machine I came upon the red weed again, and found Regent's Canal a spongy mass of dark red vegetation.

The dusky houses about me stood faint and tall and dim; the trees towards the park were growing black. All about me the red weed clambered among the ruins, writhing to get above me in the dim. Night, the mother of fear and mystery, was coming upon me.

London gazed at me spectrally. The windows in the white houses were like the eye-sockets of skulls. About me my imagination found a thousand noiseless enemies moving. Terror seized me, a horror of my temerity. Far away, I saw a second Martian, motionless as the first, standing in the park towards the Zoological Gardens, and silent.

An insane resolve possessed me. I would die and end it. And I would save myself even the trouble of killing myself. I marched on recklessly towards this Titan, and then, as I drew nearer and the light grew, I saw that a multitude of black birds was circling and clustering about the hood. At that my heart gave a bound, and I began running along the road. Great mounds had been heaped about the crest of the hill, making a huge redoubt of it. It was the final and largest place the Martians made. And from behind these heaps there rose a thin smoke against the sky. Against the skyline an eager dog ran and disappeared. The thought that had flashed into my mind grew real, grew credible. I felt no fear, only a wild, trembling exultation, as I ran up the hill towards the motionless monster. Out of the hood hung lank shreds of brown at which the hungry birds pecked and tore.

In another moment I had scrambled up the earthen rampart and stood upon its crest, and the interior of the redoubt was below me. A mighty space it was, with gigantic machines here and there within it, huge mounds of material and strange shelter places. And, scattered about it, some in their overturned war-machines, some in the now rigid handling machines, and a dozen of them stark and silent and laid in a row, were the Martians—*dead!*—slain by the putrefactive and disease bacteria against which their systems were unprepared; slain as the red weed was being slain; slain, after all man's devices had failed, by the humblest things that God, in His wisdom, had put upon this earth.

Already when I watched them they were irrevocably doomed, dying and rotting even as they went to and fro. It was inevitable. By the toll of a billion deaths man has bought his birthright of the earth, and it is his against all comers; it would still be his were the Martians ten times as mighty as they are. For neither do men live nor die in vain.

THE CLOUD-MEN

Owen Oliver

Owen Oliver was the pseudonym of the author and civil servant Joshua Albert Flynn (1863–1933). Following a privileged private education he entered the Admiralty in 1884 and the next year transferred to the War Office. He continued his studies, graduating from London University in 1891 with first-class honours in mental and moral science. His many skills became obvious during the Boer War when he served as assistant to Lord Kitchener and upon his return was appointed Director of Army Accounts. He had already turned to fiction, writing many stories for the popular magazines from 1898 onwards and a fair proportion of these were science-fiction. His war background meant that he was interested in exploring how Britain might face all manner of disasters and invasions from a variety of monsters and aliens. Surprisingly during his life he did not collect any of these into book-form and it was not until 2012 that the enterprising American publisher, Coachwhip Publications, assembled a volume aptly titled Days of Doom. *It includes the following story, first published in 1911.*

Foreprint from the London News Sheet
of March 9, 1915

T HIS NEWSPAPER IS PUBLISHED UNDER THE AUTHORITY OF the News Act, 1915, which directs the printing of a single newspaper in the United Kingdom. Under the provisions of the act, the paper will be exclusively devoted to the plain statement, without colourable matter, of important events, and to articles useful to the community.

It is provided by Section 3 of the act that the communication of false news is punishable as follows:

First offence—two years' penal labour.

Second offence—five years' penal labour.

Third offence—death.

Readers are reminded that the Unprofitable Employment Act has been repealed only to the extent indicated above. The writing or perusal of fiction, therefore, remains a penal offence.

The census of the United Kingdom, taken under the Act for the Settlement of the Population, has been completed, with the following results:

Males, total	51,504
Males, unmarried (age 20 to 60)	9,212
Females, total	52,214
Females, unmarried (age 18 to 50)	8,901

Under Section 2 of the act, persons between the ages specified who have not arranged marriages by April 1 next will be paired by the local committees appointed under the act.

A list of the centres selected for the concentration of the inhabitants of this country is published on page 4. The inclusion of Edinburgh and Dublin is provisional only, and depends upon sufficient persons desiring to reside in those cities. Choice of residence in the selected centres can be allowed only so far as is compatible with the public welfare. For instance, the necessity of a coal supply will require a certain population for Newcastle. Forms of choice will be distributed during the week.

The consultative committee of the governments of Europe, North America, and Japan has decided that the capital penalty must be enforced for the second offence of wilful idleness, as, in the present crisis, this despicable crime threatens the continued existence of the human race.

LOCAL GOVERNMENT OF LONDON—NOTICES

The weekly train for the North will start at 10.15 on Saturdays in future. Free passes may be obtained at the council offices, on good reason for the journey being shown.

Persons taking possession of vacant houses should affix a notice to the front door, stating that they are in occupation. Otherwise the houses will be liable to be reappropriated.

In consequence of the universal disarmament, a large number of naval and military uniforms are available for conversion into workmen's clothing. Applications should be made at the office of the clothing committee.

A *crèche* has been opened in the building in Whitehall formerly known as the War Office.

EDITORIAL NOTICES

We desire to publish articles describing the experiences of any persons who came into close contact with the so-called Cloud-Men. Photographs will be especially welcome.

The following article is by Mr. John Pender, now superintendent of the Food Bureau. He and his wife, Mary Pender, formerly Melville, are the only persons known to us who have survived first-hand acquaintance with these terrible beings; but it is thought that there may be others.

The Experiences of John and Mary Pender

I

It is common knowledge that a great darkness set in during the later weeks of August, 1914. This was ascribed to the formation of clouds of exceptional thickness, and to their gradual descent toward the earth. At the time this was attributed to abnormal atmospheric conditions, although scientific authorities differed greatly as to the nature of the disturbances.

It is now believed that the clouds contained elements from some extinct world, dissipated in the form of gaseous matter and encountered in the journey of the earth through space. This question will be dealt with in a later article by Dr. John Dodd. I shall confine myself to my personal experience of these elements as reincarnated in terrestrial forms—adopting Dr. Dodd's view—and to the disastrous events which I actually witnessed.

At two o'clock upon the afternoon of Friday, August 30, 1914, I was walking in the Strand, to the east of Bedford Street. Some newsboys were making a great clamour. One placard said, "The Clouds Alive—Descent Upon Paris—Great Slaughter." Another said, "War of the Worlds—Wells Justified." There was a great rush to secure papers, and, consequently, I did not notice what was happening around.

I had just obtained a paper, and was standing under an electric light to read it, when I heard a great shouting. People near me screamed and ran, and I looked up and saw the clouds descending into the roadway, in long, thick rolls. They fell upon the vehicles and their occupants, and upon groups of foot-passengers, and appeared to smother them.

I dropped the newspaper, and turned and ran in the direction of Charing Cross. I was thoroughly unnerved, not only by the shrieks, but by the abrupt manner in which they ceased wherever the clouds fell; and I find myself unable to recall the exact impression which they first produced upon me.

I was soon stopped by a barrier of vehicles which had jammed together, a number having come into collision and overturned, in their attempts to escape. Other vehicles followed till they were brought up by the blockade, and I had difficulty in finding standing space between.

I was one of a group of about ten who took refuge among the debris of two wagons and an overturned motor-bus. A very good-looking young lady, who was one of the party, seemed much distressed, and I talked to her. She said that the clouds reminded her of the unearthly visitants in some of the tales of one Owen Oliver. I had not then heard of him, but I believe him to be one of the persons very properly convicted by the present government for wasting his time in writing fiction.

I suggested that the clouds were only a heavy—and possibly

poisonous—vapour; but the young lady declared that they were alive, and were deliberately killing people; and a white-faced man said that that was certainly so. He had seen a cloud settle on a bus near him, and, when it left the bus, the passengers all had the appearance of having been drowned.

A woman sobbed that she had just bought a new mantle, and it was "so greatly reduced" and "such value in the materials." A loafer tried to snatch my watch, and I knocked him down. A flower-girl started singing and dancing. I think the fright had unhinged her mind.

Then the clouds began to descend on us, and most of our group smashed their way through the overturned motor-bus. I should have gone with them, but the young lady fainted; so I remained, supporting her on one arm.

The clouds were of a blackish-grey colour, and appeared to be of stouter material than vapour. Their size varied. I do not mean merely that they differed from one another in magnitude, but that the same cloud expanded and contracted, rising as it drew out and falling as it drew in. Their proportionate dimensions remained the same, the shape being that of a cylinder with spherical ends, and the length about twice the diameter. When they first hung overhead the diameter was usually about twenty-five feet.

They had a black, diamond-shaped patch in front, which I believe to have been an organ of vision, and eight small circular patches at the sides and the other end, which were, I think, in some mysterious way, the sources of their horizontal movements. From time to time they made a faint whirring sound. Afterward I had reason to believe that this was a kind of musical language, depending upon the pitch and quality of the note, and not upon the articulate sound, which was always the same—whir-r-r-r! At least, it seemed so to me. My wife thinks that there were four kinds of whirs, and three different ways of rolling the r's in each. However, she agrees that the language depended partly, if not wholly, upon the pitch.

The clouds came down one by one upon the vehicles near us, and the knots of people jammed between them. The victims shrieked until they were enveloped; then all sound ceased. When the clouds left them, they had the appearance of drowned persons, as the white-faced man had said.

I will not dwell on the subject. The sight is one which most of my readers have seen. Let those who have not be thankful!

I crawled under a wagon and a cab, dragging the young lady, and reached a shop-window, just as a cloud fell upon us. I had hoped to get to the shop-door and inside, but could not. This was our salvation, probably; for it was clear, afterward, that the clouds searched the houses.

As we were being wrapped all round, I smashed the plate-glass with my fists, cutting myself rather badly, and put our heads through the opening. The cloud did not enter inside the glass, and we were able to breathe. We were enveloped to the necks by what felt like a heavy, wet blanket—a blanket that seemed to be, in some horrible way, alive—for about five minutes. Then we were left.

My limbs were limp and helpless. I slipped down on the pavement, with the young lady's head resting on my shoulder, and stared at the tops of the vehicles, which were all that I could see. The busses were full of "drowned" bodies, lolling against one another. A wagon-driver on a high seat had fallen forward, but his legs still held in the apron, and he hung head downward, leering horribly. A dead horse was at my back. I leaned against it.

It was very quiet now. The shrieks, that ended so suddenly, came from further and farther away.

After a time the girl opened her eyes and looked round. She tried to speak, and could not. Neither could I.

I opened my lips after a quarter of an hour.

"The Lord have mercy upon us!" I groaned.

"Amen!" said the girl on my shoulder.

She had not moved except to clutch at my jacket.

I held out my hand to her. When she was about to take it she saw the gashes that the broken glass had made, and cried out piteously.

"Hush!" I said. "They may have ears!"

For I never doubted that they were alive after the wet monster had touched me. It felt like a blanket that was all fingers!

She nodded, took out her handkerchief, and bound my cuts gently. She asked in a whisper how I had done it, and I told her in a whisper how I had broken the glass, and why.

"Thank you," she said. "That isn't much to say for a life, is it? I mean more."

She looked at me and tried to smile. It was pitiful, very pitiful.

"Life isn't much to be thankful for now," I said; "except—that there is *some one* left. There is no one else, I think. We will help each other."

"We will help each other," she said.

Her voice and look were those of a steadfast woman; and so she proved.

Presently we crawled through the vehicles and the "drowned" people till we got into a restaurant. We found "drowned" waiters and customers there. Mary—that was my companion's name—sank on a seat. She would not have cried, I think, but I put my hand on her shoulder.

"Cry, dear woman," I said. "It will help you."

She sat with her face in her hands, and her body quivering, for a while. Then she wiped her eyes with my handkerchief, and smiled the pitiful smile.

"You are good to me," she said.

We ate and drank, and then we explored the upper rooms. The people in these were "drowned," too; and those in the other houses that we entered, creeping stealthily from one to the next. We heard the whirring sound sometimes, and saw the cloud cylinders pass by. Most of them were high above the houses, and were going toward Whitehall. We noticed a sound of firing from that direction, and guessed that soldiers were trying to defend the War Office—which, as we learned long after, was really the case.

After a few moments the firing ceased. Soon after that, the electric lights went out. They had been going for several days, and probably the power had failed; or one of the cloud-cylinders had fallen on those who controlled it—some brave men who stood at their post till the end. There were many such.

II

We stayed in the house for two nights and a day—a day that was no different from the night—groping about in the dark for food, and sitting on a sofa, leaning against each other, when we slept for a short time. She was afraid to be alone, she said. I did not say that I was afraid, but I was.

After that time—it must have been the forenoon of the 1st of September—the darkness decreased to that of a dull twilight. We peered from the windows, and saw none of the cloud-rolls about, and heard no sounds. So we ventured out.

We got into the side streets, which were less obstructed, and into Whitehall. We then went over Westminster Bridge—it was strange to see the vessels drifting helplessly on the river—and wandered on till we reached Camberwell Green. We saw no sign of life all the way; men, women, children, horses, dogs, cats, even birds, were all "drowned," as I call it. The clouds had fallen upon humanity, and the dependants of humanity, and wiped them out.

The girl cried sometimes; but she was very brave. She told me about herself as we walked along. She was Mary Melville, a mistress at a high-school.

"And I shall never see my little girls again," she said. "They were such dear, naughty little girls, and I loved them so much! I liked to think that some day they would be good women."

We went into a house, the door of which was open. We found meat and drink there. She slept on a sofa while I watched; and then she watched while I slept—after breakfast we went on. We did not know where we were going; but we could not rest.

In the Peckham Road we met a man. He was dusty and travel-worn. His eyes blinked, and he spoke as if he were half asleep. He had walked up from Rochester, he said. The cloud-men—that was what he called them—had "wiped every one out," he told us. He had crept between two mattresses of a bed, and so escaped their search. He was going to Piccadilly Circus to look for his "girl." She was a waitress in a restaurant there.

"We were going to be married next month," he said.

Then he burst suddenly into tears. He was a big, strong fellow—a fitter in the dockyard, he said.

A large party of soldiers had encountered the cloud-men on Chatham Lines, he told us. They had come upon a handful of the survivors running over Rochester Bridge. They had scattered some of the cloud-men, at first, by explosive shells; but the cloud-men had expanded into thin vapour, which the shells did not seem to harm, and advanced upon the army in that form till they had encompassed it in mist. Then they contracted into "things like long balloons," and dropped upon the soldiers and "smothered them."

I suggested that, as we seemed to be all of the world that was left, we should make an appointment to meet again in, say, a week; but the man from Rochester shook his head.

"If I don't find my girl," he said, "and it stands to reason I won't, I'll go into a chemist's and take what comes handy till I hit upon something that settles me. Of course, if I find her, we'll come all right. You'd like her; quite a lady in her way, she is—was, I suppose. She—I'll be making a fool of myself if I start talking about her. So-long, and good luck!"

"God bless you and help you," said Mary, "and—and you will find her here—or there."

She pointed to the sky.

"Here or there," he said. "That's it. Good luck!"

He went on at a tired trot toward the city; and we walked on away from it.

"To be left alone," Mary said. "To be left alone! It is an awful thing. Alone! If you left me!" I looked at her reproachfully. "No, no! I don't mean that, only—if anything happened to you—"

Her lips trembled.

"We are in the hands of God," I said, "my dear. I shall never leave you while I am alive."

"No, dear," she answered.

That was all our love-making in those days—that we called each other "dear."

III

We found our way to Dulwich by the afternoon. At the station we came upon a collection of about thirty people. They greeted us as if we were old friends, and we greeted them so. They had taken refuge in a cricket pavilion, they explained, and the clouds had omitted to search it. Every one else in the place was "drowned," as they too called it. They were lucky to have one another, they said; "so many of us"—and some of the women cried.

One young fellow was an electrical engineer. He had ascertained by the telegraph that the clouds were settling upon all the large towns, and destroying the inhabitants. This applied to the Continent and America, as well as Great Britain. Now he could get no answer from anywhere.

We walked together toward Forest Hill, and found nine survivors in Dulwich Park. A black mist drove upon us there. It was "only mist," we assured one another, clinging desperately together. But it condensed into the infamous cylinders. Our company ran in various directions, crying out till the clouds settled upon them.

Mary and I ran hand in hand, till she dropped exhausted. I sat beside her, and lifted her in my arms. We kissed each other. Then four of the cylinders came up, and one lowered itself upon us. The damp folds were enveloping us; and then a fifth cylinder, with four white bands—which were, I think, the insignia of high rank—made a whirring noise, changing the pitch as if it sang.

This was when I realized that they had a language. The cylinder that was smothering us lifted itself; and the belted cylinder drew near and settled on the ground, and shrank till it was not more than eight feet long. It pressed against us as if it examined us. It felt about as hard as a sofa-cushion in its contracted form; a hard cushion that was all hands and terribly alive. It stared at us with its diamond-shaped eye. Then it "sang" again, and somehow I knew that its song meant that we were spared.

Two other cylinders pushed us on our feet, and held us, and urged us forward. They took us to a large house, and into a long drawing-room; and one stayed by the window, and one by the door, to keep us there.

So far as I have been able to ascertain, we were the only persons who were deliberately spared by the cloud-men; and many conjectures have been made as to their reasons. Professor Dodd holds that we were selected as "specimens" for a museum which the cloud-men proposed to establish; but, if so, I do not know why I was chosen. Mary, indeed, is, in my opinion, a singularly handsome woman; but I cannot claim any distinction of personality, except that I am a good deal above the average in size and strength.

We remained in this house—which, curiously enough, I cannot identify—for nine days, during which we had every opportunity of studying the cloud-men, as we came to call them; for the house and its vicinity seemed to be a kind of *rendezvous*.

I will give a few particulars which we noticed.

Their shape, as I have said, always remained the same, but their size varied greatly, and as it varied they appeared to be composed of quite different substance. At the largest, they seemed to be nothing but dark smoke, and one lost all perception of outline in them, except that the "eye" remained as a little dark cloud floating in the smoky mist. As they contracted, they took definite shape in the cloud-cylinders which I have already described, and which felt like a wet blanket; a blanket which divided and "flowed" round one like water, exerting a discriminating pressure, like that of countless fingers. When they had further contracted to the size at which the belted cloud-man had shrunk when he settled on the ground, they were, as I have said, of the density of a rather hard but springy sofa-cushion; but, in spite of their hardness, a good deal of their pliability remained.

One that was probably not full-grown sometimes played with us, pushing us round the room, and, though firm, he did not hurt like a hard substance. When they were resting, they grew much smaller—at the extreme, not more than a foot in length. They then looked like black metal, and were so heavy that Mary and I together could barely move them. They felt as hard as iron, and we could make no impression on them; but yet they could fold round an object and handle it without crushing or injuring it in any way. I have seen them hold a flower, the metallic substance seeming to divide as they did so.

When they were in this state a hissing sound came from the eight circular disks, which appeared to control their motion, whenever they moved; and their whirring was sharper and clearer. It sounded like the playing of a musical instrument in a chromatic scale. We even learned to understand the meaning of certain series of notes, and especially of one which indicated that we might go out from our room and find something to eat—a privilege only accorded to us after a good while.

We were very near being starved at first. There was no food in the room, and no water, except some in which flowers had stood. We were reduced to drinking that. We tried vainly to get by the sentinel at the door; but he always enveloped us and pushed us back.

After we had fasted for nearly two days, and the last of the foul water was gone, we persisted in trying to get out, and entreated and made gesticulations. At last one of the belted cloud-men came. He watched our gesticulations for some time with his one diamond-shaped eye, and he and our guards talked, or "sang," to one another.

Finally the guard stood aside, and we were allowed to go to the kitchen under escort. We found some stale bread and some good bacon there; also some tea and sugar—the milk was sour. We took back some biscuits and two large jugs of water. After that we were allowed to go there twice a day, and a number of cloud-men came to watch us. So far as we had seen, they did not take food—they appeared to lack mouths—and our custom of eating puzzled them.

We were beginning to lose the edge of our aversion to these extraordinary creatures, and to think that perhaps their cruelty had been due to ignorance of the nature of life and death; and then three things happened which brought back our fears—and worse.

The first was a sight which we saw from the drawing-room window, outside which the cloud-men often held what were evidently assemblies. A vast multitude of the cloud-rolls came along, contracted, and hung in a circle round one who seemed to be a prisoner. After some "talking" in their way, one of the belted men sang a fierce sentence; and then the prisoner wailed miserably. After this they drew back from him, watching him closely. He swelled slowly, wailing all the time, and then suddenly there was a flash, and he was gone! His fellows sang a kind of dirge; then expanded and floated away. Sentence had been executed.

If they punished others, they would not scruple to punish us, Mary said; and so it proved.

The second incident, which brought this punishment, was a frustrated attempt on our part to escape. The guard at the door was talking, in his singing way, to the guard at the window. Mary and I took the opportunity to slip out through the door. They overtook us as we were running down the front path, and pushed us back. One held Mary and the other held me, keeping us at different ends of the long drawing-room. I could feel that my captor was angry by the touch, and in a few moments he folded himself close round me, pressing till my bones ached. Mary screamed and tried to get to me, but could not stir.

After a while my captor covered my head and slowly smothered me, till I was at my last gasp. Then he released my head, but still held me firmly, while his companion treated my poor Mary in the same manner. They repeated this cruelty three times. When they released us it was half an hour before we had strength enough to crawl to each other; and after that they pushed us roughly as we went to and from the kitchen to get our food, and sometimes made as if they would smother us again, though they never actually did so.

We both became very silent and grave after this, and we used to kiss each other good-by before either slept, which we always did one at a time, the other watching—though I do not know what service there was that watchfulness could do; asleep or awake, we were equally in their power.

The third incident came about as a result of the second, I think, though this is merely a conjecture.

I fancy that our warders thought, from our depressed and silent condition, that we were dying—perhaps we were—and they were afraid of being held responsible for the loss of the valuable "specimens" entrusted to their care. Anyhow, they were less rough, and allowed us more freedom in going about the house; and one day we went into the dining-room. It looked out upon great fields, which we had not seen before. A large number of "drowned" people lay there, arranged in orderly rows. They had evidently been gathered together by the cloud-men. But, why? We talked about that for the rest of the day.

The next day we again went into the dining-room, unattended. We saw a number of cloud-men, in the cloud-cylinder condition of existence, come and settle upon the "drowned" people; each upon one. When the cloud-men rose, the bodies upon which they had settled had disappeared.

Mary turned a greenish colour; looked at me; swayed slowly. I held her in my arms. My first thought was to try to make the awful thing seem less awful to her.

"After all," I said, "we eat animals. If I could get you out of this, they might kill me, and welcome. Oh, Mary!"

I sobbed like a little child, and the tears streamed down my face. Mary folded me in her arms and kissed me, as a mother might have done.

"Come," she said, and led me to the open window.

It was about ten feet above the ground. I lowered her down. Then I jumped.

I could have made the jump safely enough a fortnight before—could make it safely now; but I suppose my limbs had grown feeble. The fall damaged one of my ankles, and I could not stand. Mary lifted me up and held me.

"Go," I said. "It will be easier for me if I can hope that you have escaped. Let me say this first—if all the women in the world were back again, I should want only you—dear Mary! Now, go!"

She laughed a strange little laugh, like a child. Then she lifted me up and staggered on with me—on and on. Sometimes she fell. She always laughed that curious little laugh, as a young mother might with a little child.

Presently we heard the whirring sound from the house. We understood that it was a warning of our flight. I cannot tell how we knew this; but we knew. We looked back and saw the cloud-men rising into the air, expanding as they rose.

"Dear Mary," I said, "this is the end!"

She gave a fierce cry, like a mother defending her young, and tried to carry me farther. When she found that she was too much exhausted to bear my weight, she dragged me to a hollow filled with dead leaves that the long darkness and mist had brought off before their time. We burrowed under the leaves, and lay there.

We heard the cloud-men go by, "whirring" loudly. I suppose they did not know that I was hurt, and expected us to have run much farther. Anyhow, they did not search the leaves.

For hours we lay quite still. In the dusk we peeped out and saw a great concourse of the cloud-men; and presently we heard a loud song, which we recognized as the judge's sentence. Two flashes followed. Our negligent guards had met their fate.

We were tired, and we rested softly among the leaves. We fell asleep.

IV

When we woke and peeped out, the sun was shining, for the first time for many weeks. There was a huge gathering of the cloud-men about. They were not flying, but moving over the land. Some were small, like the shots of big guns; others were as big as sheep; others were as big as a bear; others as large as an elephant.

They kept changing from small to large. Sometimes they changed back again, but mostly they expanded and floated up in the air. One or two seemed to dissipate into black mist, and be drawn up in a long spiral into the sky. They whirred continually—"whirs" of anger, or was it despair? It seemed as if they tried to hold to the earth and were drawn away.

"They are going!" Mary cried.

She raised herself out of the leaves. So did I; and then the cloud-men saw us. Several advanced upon us, growing to the size of elongated balloons, and rising.

Most of them grew and grew, and went up into the sky; but one reached us and settled on us. It felt wet and cold. It twitched fiercely as it swallowed us in its embraces, and blotted out sight and sound. My breath was nearly gone; and then the suffocating cloud seemed to grow thinner. I could see through it. I could breathe a little. Suddenly it parted from us with a snap, like the breaking of elastic.

The sun was shining cheerfully, and we breathed God's good air. The cloud-men went up, up, in streamers of black smoke. The time came when the last disappeared. We laughed and cried—laughed and cried.

"I wonder if any of our world is left'" I said.

"All my world is left," said Mary. "All!" She held my hand; and I kissed her hand that held mine. "But we will look for the others," she said. "We will look for them—our own dear people of our own dear world!"

We found none that day. We could not go far, as my ankle was badly swollen; but in the afternoon Mary came upon a little truck. She put me upon it, on cushions, and wheeled me to find the people of the world.

After that we came upon some, day by day; first a mother and her child, who had hidden in a chimney; then a man who had been left for dead, but had revived—the only case of the kind which has come to my notice. It was like drowning, he said.

Then we met a husband and wife.

"We will quarrel no more," they told us; and they told that to all whom we met.

They do not. Even people who love each other do not quarrel now!

At Chatham we found a large assembly, including a train-load who had come down from London. The man who had talked to us in the Peckham Road was among them. Strange to say, he had found his "girl"—a pretty, fair-haired, laughing little thing. She and several other waitresses had hidden in the roof of their restaurant. They were so frightened that they remained there and starved for several days.

"When I heard Will walking about below and calling for me," she said, "I thought I had died, and gone to heaven!"

"How did you know it was heaven?" some one asked.

"Why, I knew Will's voice!" she answered.

"We are going to be married tomorrow," he said. "Every man ought to look after a woman in these times."

I thought so, too; and Mary and I, and many other pairs who have met during the reign of terror, were also married then, promising ourselves a honeymoon in easier days. For at that period we worked eighteen hours daily, moving up to London, and sending rescue parties all round to gather up the remnants of the scattered population.

If we had not done this, I believe that half of those now surviving would have perished. For many were afraid to venture out from their hiding-places in search of food, and others were too weak to do so. Some seemed to have temporarily lost their reason from fright and hardship. A pestilence was threatened from the unburied bodies of men and animals, and was only avoided by our clearing certain districts for habitation, and proscribing other localities until time had removed the danger.

Trade and production had stopped, and machinery rusted. Oversea supplies ceased, and accumulated stocks were left to rust and rot in the abandoned districts.

Through the hard winter which followed, all lived upon a dole; and many a time, as we waited for the return of the spring, we thought that the last day had come to the human race. The despatch of food-ships from America alone saved us, in my opinion. We had just strength to unload them—no more. I shall never forget the pale faces of the tottering men and women who worked at this.

Now, I hope and believe that we are through the worst. There is food enough—on this point I can speak with authority, as I have the honour to be m charge of the department concerned with our supplies—to last us for the rest of the year, with care; and I believe that we can organize husbandry and industry so as to make satisfactory provision for the future.

Practically all domestic animals were destroyed in England, it is true; but, fortunately, a large number of oxen in the Highlands escaped our ferocious visitors; and in Ireland and elsewhere the pigs showed a capacity of recovery from "drowning" which no other animal has exhibited. A few surviving specimens of sheep are being carefully reserved for breeding purposes; and though the horse is extinct, it is hoped to rear a race of superior donkeys from half a dozen which escaped. Moreover, we have plenty of motor vehicles.

The stores of clothing and furniture are sufficient for many generations, so long as we do not allow ourselves to fall back under the absurd dominion of "fashions." I have great hope that we shall escape this, although, even in the best of women, I notice that a tendency to elaboration and decorativeness in dress still unfortunately survives.

I am confident, however, that none will allow such petty vanities to interfere with more solid occupations. For nothing has struck me more than the noble manner in which the women have struggled to help in the reconstruction of a prosperous and united society—a united society of the surviving human race.

"Union" is the key-note of our future. The days of discord and war are over. Each in future will love his neighbour as himself. Each will work for all. Unborn generations, when in more leisured times they come to write the history of the world, will record that the clouds of selfishness and cruelty lifted from the world with the darkest clouds that ever rested upon it; as if the evil passions of humanity were concentrated in and departed with those diabolical spirits of evil whom we have named the cloud-men.

THE DRAGON OF ST. PAUL'S

Reginald Bacchus & C. Ranger Gull

Bacchus and Ranger Gull were fellow journalists who collaborated on several stories of the weird and the strange in the 1890s before going their separate ways. Bacchus (1873–1945) became a theatre critic and, in the spring of 1899, married the actress Isa Bowman who, as a child, had been one of Lewis Carroll's photographic models. The marriage did not last long and Bacchus led a rather desultory life writing a notorious erotic novel, The Confessions of Nemesis Hunt *(1902–6), based to some degree on Isa Bowman.*

Cyril Arthur Ranger Gull (1875–1923) became better known under his alias Guy Thorne, under which name he wrote When It Was Dark *(1903) which considered the social and religious unrest that follows the revelation that archaeological evidence proved that Christ was never resurrected. Gull settled in Cornwall and produced a mass of short fiction and novels, several of which were science fiction such as* The Greater Power *(1915),* The Air Pirate *(1919),* The City in the Clouds *(1921) and* When the World Reeled *(1924). Alas he became alcoholic and developed diabetes, dying in London aged only forty-seven.*

"IT IS CERTAINLY A WONDERFUL YARN," SAID TRANT, "AND excellent copy. My only regret is that I didn't think of it myself in the first instance."

"But, Tom, why shouldn't it be true? It's incredible enough for any one to believe. I'm sure I believe it, don't you, Guy?"

Guy Descaves laughed. "Perhaps, dear. I don't know and I don't much care, but I did a good little leaderette on it this morning. Have you done anything, Tom?"

"I did a whole buck middle an hour ago at very short notice. That's why I'm a little late. I had finished all my work for the night, and I was just washing my hands when Fleming came in with the make-up. We didn't expect him at all tonight, and the paper certainly was rather dull. He'd been dining somewhere, and I think he was a little bit cocked. Anyhow he was nasty, and kept the presses back while I did a 'special' on some information he brought with him."

While he was talking, Beatrice Descaves, his *fiancée*, began to lay the table for supper, and in a minute she called them to sit down. The room was very large, with cool white-papered walls, and the pictures, chiefly original black and white sketches, were all framed in *passe pas Tout* frames, which gave the place an air of serene but welcome simplicity. At one end of it was a great window which came almost to the floor, and in front of the window there was a low, cushioned seat. The night was very hot, and the window was wide open. It was late—nearly half-past one, and London was quite silent. Indeed the only sound that they could hear was an occasional faint burst of song and the tinkling of a piano, which seemed to come from the neighbourhood of Fountain Court.

Guy Descaves was a writer, and he lived with his sister Beatrice in the Temple. Trant, who was also a journalist on the staff of a daily paper, and who was soon going to marry Beatrice, often came to them there after his work was done. The three young people lived very much together, and were very happy in a delightful unfettered way. The Temple was quiet and close to their work, and they found it in these summer days a most peaceful place when night had come to the town.

They were very gay at supper in the big, cool room. Trant was a clever young man and very much in love, and the presence of Beatrice always inspired him to talk. It was wonderful to sit by her, and to watch her radiant face, or to listen to the music of her laugh which rippled like water falling into water. Guy, who was more than thirty, and was sure that he was very old, liked to watch his sister and his friend together, and to call them "you children."

"What is the special information that the editor brought, dear?" Beatrice asked Trant, as soon as they were seated round the table.

"Well," he answered. "It seems that he managed to get hold of young Egerton Cotton, Professor Glazebrook's assistant, who is staying at the Metropole. Of course various rumours have got about from the crew of the ship, but nothing will be definitely known till the inquest tomorrow. Cotton's story is really too absurd, but Fleming insisted on its going in."

"Did he give him much for his information?" Descaves asked.

"Pretty stiff, I think. I know the *Courier* offered fifty, but he stuck out. Fleming only got it just at the last moment. It's silly nonsense, of course, but it'll send the sales up tomorrow."

"What is the whole thing exactly?" Beatrice asked. "All that I've heard is that Professor Glazebrook brought back some enormous bird from the Arctics, and that just off the Nore the thing escaped and killed him. I'm sure that sounds quite sufficiently extraordinary for anything; but I suppose it's all a lie."

"Well," said Trant. "What Egerton Cotton says is the most extraordinary thing I have ever heard—it's simply laughable—but it will sell three hundred thousand extra copies. I'll tell you. I've got the whole thing fresh in my brain. You know that Professor Glazebrook was one of the biggest biologists who have ever lived, and he's been doing a great, tedious, monumental book on prehistoric animals, the mammoth and all that sort of thing that E. T. Reid draws in *Punch*. Some old scientific Johnny in Wales used to find all the money, and he fitted out the Professor's exploration ship, the *Henry Sandys*, to go and find these mammoths and beasts which have got frozen up in the ice. Don't you remember about two years ago when they started from Tilbury? They got the Lord Mayor down, and a whole host of celebrities, to see them go. I was there reporting, I remember it well, and Reggie Lance did an awfully funny article about it, which he called 'The hunting of the Snark.' Well, Egerton Cotton tells Fleming—the man *must* be mad—that they found a whole lot of queer bears and things frozen up, but no very great find until well on into the second year, when they were turning to come back. Fleming says he's seen all the diaries and photographs and everything; they had a frightfully hard time. At last one day they came across a great block of ice, and inside it, looking as natural as you please, was a huge winged sort of dragon creature, as big as a cart horse. Fleming saw a photograph. I don't know how they faked it up, and he says it was the most horrid cruel sort of thing you ever dreamt of after lobster salad. It had big,

heavy wings, and a beak like a parrot, little flabby paws all down
its body like a caterpillar, and a great bare, pink, wrinkled belly.
Oh, the most filthy-looking brute! They cut down the ice till it was
some decent size, and they hauled the whole thing chock-a-block,
like a prune in a jelly, into the hold. The ice was frightfully hard,
and one of the chains of the donkey engine broke once, and the
whole thing fell, but even then the block held firm. It took them
three weeks to get it on board. Well, they sailed away with their
beastly Snark as jolly as sandboys, and Cotton says the Professor
was nearly out of his mind with joy—used to talk and mumble to
himself all day. They put the thing in a huge refrigerator like the
ones the Australian mutton comes over in, and Glazebrook used
to turn on the electric lights and sit muffled up in furs watching
his precious beast for hours."

He stopped for a moment to light a cigarette, noticing with
amusement that Guy and Beatrice were becoming tremendously
interested. He made Beatrice pour him out a great tankard of
beer before he would go on, and he moved to the window-seat,
where it was cooler, and he could sit just outside the brilliant circle
of light thrown by the tall shaded lamp. The other two listened
motionless, and as he unfolded the grisly story, his voice coming
to them out of the darkness became infinitely more dramatic
and impressive.

"Well, Cotton says that this went on for a long time. He had
to do all the scientific work himself, writing up their journals and
developing the photos, as the Professor was always mysteriously
pottering about in the cellar place. At last, one day, Glazebrook came
into the cabin at lunch or whatever they have, and said he was going
to make a big experiment. He talked a lot of rot about toads and
reptiles being imprisoned for thousands of years in stones and ice,

and then coming to life, and he said he was going to try and melt out the dragon and tickle it into life with a swingeing current from the dynamo. Cotton laughed at him, but it wasn't any good, and they set to work to thaw the creature out with braziers. When they got close to it Cotton said that the water from the ice, as it melted, got quite brown and *smelt!* It wasn't till they were within almost a few hours from the Channel—you remember they put into some place in Norway for coal—and steaming for London River as hard as they could go, that they got it clear.

"While they were fixing the wires from the dynamo room, Cotton hurt his ankle and had to go to his bunk for some hours to rest. He begged Glazebrook to wait till he could help, for he had become insensibly interested in the whole uncanny thing, but it was no use. He says the fellow was like a madman, red eyes with wrinkles forming up all round them, and so excited that he was almost foaming at the mouth. He went to his cabin frightfully tired, and very soon fell asleep. One of the men woke him up by shaking him. The man was in a blue funk and told him something dreadful had happened in the hold. Cotton hobbled up to the big hatchway, which was open, and as he came near it with the mate and several of the men, he said he could hear a coughing choked-up kind of noise, and that there was a stench-like ten thousand monkey houses. They looked in and saw this great beast *alive!* and squatting over Glazebrook's body picking out his inside like a bird with a dead crab."

Beatrice jumped up with a scream. "Oh Tom, Tom, don't, you horrid boy! I won't hear another word. I shan't sleep a wink. Ugh! how disgusting and ridiculous. Do you mean to tell me that you've actually gone to press with all that ghastly nonsense? I'm going to bathe my face, you've made me feel quite hot and sticky. You can tell the rest to Guy, and if you haven't done by the time I come back, I won't say goodnight to you, there!"

She left the room, not a little disconcerted by the loathsome story which Trant, forgetting his listeners, had been telling with the true journalist's passion for sensational detail. Guy knocked the ashes slowly out of his pipe. "Well?" he said.

"Oh, there isn't much more. He says they all ran away and watched from the companion steps, and presently the beast came flopping up on deck, with its beak all over blood, and its neck coughing and working. It got half across the hatchway and seemed dazed for about an hour. No one seemed to think of shooting it! Then Cotton says it crawled to the bulwarks coughing and grunting away, and after a few attempts actually flew up into the air. He said it flew unlike any creature he had ever seen, much higher than most birds fly, and very swiftly. The last they saw of it was a little thing like a crow hovering over the forts at Shoe'ness."

"Well, I'm damned," said Guy. "I never heard a better piece of yarning in my life. Do you actually mean to tell me that Fleming dares to print all that gaudy nonsense in the paper. He must certainly have been very drunk."

"Well, there it is, old man. I had to do what I was told, and I made a good piece of copy out of it. I am not responsible if Fleming does get his head laughed off, I don't edit his rag. Pass the beer."

"Is the ship here?"

"Yes it was docked about six this morning, and so far all the published news is what you had today in the *Evening Post*. It seems that something strange certainly did happen, though of course it wasn't that. They are going to hold an inquest, Fleming says. Something horribly beastly has happened to Glazebrook there's no doubt of that. Something has scooped the poor beggar out. Well, I must be going, it's nearly three, and more than a little towards dawning. Tell Bee I'm off, will you?"

Beatrice came back in a minute like a fresh rose, and before he went she drew him on to the balcony outside the window. There was a wonderful view from the balcony. Looking over the great lawns far down below, they could just see the dim purple dome of St. Paul's which seemed to be floating in mist, its upper part stark and black against the sky. To the right was the silent river with innumerable patches of yellow light from the rows of gas lamps on Blackfriars bridge. A sweet scent from the boxes of mignonette floated on the dusky, heavy air. He put his arm round her and kissed her sweet, tremulous lips. "My love, my love," she whispered, "oh, I love you so!"

Her slender body clung to him. She was very sweet. The tall, strong young man leant over her and kissed her masses of dark, fragrant hair.

"My little girl, my little girl," he murmured with a wonderful tenderness in his voice, "there is nothing in the world but you, sweet little girl, dear, dear little girl, little wife."

She looked up at him at the word and there was a great light in her eyes, a thing inexpressibly beautiful for a man to see.

"Love, good-night," he whispered, and he kissed the tiny pink ear that heard him.

After the fantastic story he had been telling them, a story which, wild and grotesque as it was, had yet sufficient *vraisemblance* to make them feel uncomfortable, the majesty of the night gave the dim buildings of the town a restful and soothing effect, and as they stood on the balcony with their love surging over them, they forgot everything but that one glorious and radiant fact.

Beatrice went with him to the head of the staircase—They lived very high up in the buildings called "Temple Gardens"—and watched him as he descended. It was curious to look down the great well of the stone steps and to feel the hot air which rose up from the gas lamps beating on her face. She could only see Tom on each landing when he turned to look up at her—a tiny pink face perched on a little black foreshortened body.

When he got right down to the bottom he shouted up a "good night," his voice sounding strange and unnatural as the walls threw it back to each other. In after years she always remembered the haunting sound of his voice as it came to her for the last time in this world.

Between seven and eight o'clock the next morning Guy, who was on the staff of the *Evening Post*, one of the leading lunch-time papers, left the Temple for the offices in the Strand.

It was a beautiful day, and early as it was the streets were full of people going to their work. Even now the streets were full of colour and sunshine, and every little city clerk contributed to the gayness of the scene by wearing round his straw hat the bright ribbon of some club to which he did not belong.

Guy had been working for about an hour when Gobion, his assistant—the young man who afterwards made such a success with his book "Penny Inventions,"—came in with a bunch of "flimsies," reports of events sent in by penny-a-liners who scoured London on bicycles, hoping for crime.

"There doesn't seem anything much," he said, "except one thing which is probably a fake. It was brought in by that man, Roberts, and he tried to borrow half a James from the commissionaire on the strength of it, which certainly looks like a fake. If it is true, though, it's good stuff. I've sent a reporter down to enquire."

"What is it?" said Descaves, yawning.

"Reported murder of a journalist. The flimsy says he was found at four o'clock in the morning by a policeman, on the steps of St. Paul's absolutely broken up and mangled. Ah, here it is. *'The body, which presented a most extraordinary and unaccountable appearance, was at once removed to St. Bride's mortuary.'* Further details later, Roberts says."

"It sounds all right; at any rate the reporter will be back soon, and we shall know. How did Roberts spot him as a journalist?"

"Don't know, suppose he hadn't shaved."

While the youth was speaking, the reporter entered breathless.

"Column special," he gasped.

"Trant, a man on the *Mercury*, has been murdered, cut all to pieces. Good God! I forgot, Descaves. Oh, I am fearfully sorry!"

Guy rose quickly from his seat with a very white face, but without any sound. As he did so by some strange coincidence the tape machine on the little pedestal behind him began to print the first words of a despatch from the Exchange Telegraph Company. The message dealt with the tragedy that had taken immediate power of speech away from him. The familiar whirr of the type wheel made him turn from mere force of habit, and stunned as his brain was, he saw the dreadful words spelling themselves on the paper with no realization of their meaning. He stood swaying backwards and forwards, not knowing what he did, his eyes still resting on the broad sheet of white paper on which the little wheel sped ceaselessly, recording the dreadful thing in neat blue letters.

Then suddenly his eyes flashed the meaning of the gathering words to his brain, and he leant over the glass with a sick eagerness. Gobion and the reporter stood together anxiously watching him. At length the wheel slid along the bar and came to rest with a sharp click. Guy stood up again.

"Do my work today," he said quietly. "I must go to my sister," and taking his hat he left the room.

When he got out into the brilliant sunshine which flooded the Strand, his senses came back to him and he determined that obviously the first thing to be done was to make sure that the body at St. Bride's was really the body of his friend.

Even in moments of deep horror and sorrow the mind of a strong, self-contained man does not entirely lose its power of concentration. The Telegraphic news had left very little doubt in his mind that the fact was true, but at the same time he could not conceive how such a ghastly thing could possibly have happened. According to the information he had, it seemed the poor fellow had been struck dead only a few minutes after he had left the Temple the night before, and within a few yards of his chambers. "On the steps of St. Paul's" the wire ran, and Trant's rooms were not sixty yards away, in a little old-fashioned court behind the Deanery.

It was incredible. Owing to the great shops and warehouses all round, the neighbourhood was patrolled by a large number of policemen and watchmen. The space at the top of Ludgate Hill was, he knew, brilliantly lighted by the street lamps, and besides, about four it was almost daylight. It seemed impossible that Tom could have been done to death like this. "It's a canard," he said to himself, "damned silly nonsense," but even as he tried to trick himself into disbelief, his sub-conscious brain told him unerringly that the horrid thing was true.

Five minutes later he walked out of the dead house knowing the worst. The horror of the thing he had just seen, the awful inexpressible horror of it, killed every other sensation. He had recognized his friend's right hand, for on the hand was a curious old ring of beaten gold which Beatrice used to wear.

SECOND EPISODE

Mr. Frank Fleming, the editor or the *Daily Mercury*, was usually
an early riser. He never stopped at the office of the paper very
late unless some important news was expected, or unless he had
heard something in the House that he wished to write about
himself. Now and then, however, when there was an all-night
sitting, he would steal away from his bench below the gangway
and pay a surprise visit before Trant and his colleagues had put
the paper to bed. On these occasions, when he was kept away
from his couch longer than was his wont, he always slept late into
the morning. It was about twelve o'clock on the day of Trant's
death that he rose up in bed and pressed the bell for his servant.
The man brought his shaving water and the morning's copy of
the *Mercury*, and retired. Fleming opened his paper and the black
headline and leaded type of the article on Professor Glazebrook's
death at once caught his eye. He read it with complacent satisfaction. Trant had done the thing very cleverly and the article
was certainly most striking. Fleming, a shrewd man of the world
and Parliamentary adventurer, had not for a moment dreamt of
believing young Egerton Cotton, but he nevertheless knew his
business. It had got about that there was something mysterious
in the events that had occurred on board the *Henry Sandys*, and
it had also got about that the one man who could throw any
authentic light on these events was Cotton. It was therefore the
obvious policy to buy Cotton's information, and, while disclaim-
ing any responsibility for his statements, to steal a march on his
contemporaries by being the first to publish them. As he walked
into the pretty little dining-room of his flat, Mr. Fleming was in an
excellent temper.

He was dividing his attention between the kidneys and the *Times*, when his man came into the room and told him that Mr. Morgan, the news editor, must see him immediately.

He could hear Morgan in the *entresol*, and he called out cheerily, "Come in, Morgan; come in, you're just in time for some breakfast."

The news editor entered in a very agitated state. When Fleming heard the undoubted fact of Trant's death he was genuinely moved, and Morgan, who had a very low opinion of his chief's human impulses, was surprised and pleased. It seemed that Morgan had neither seen the body nor been to the scene of the crime, but had simply got his news from some men in the bar of the *Cheshire Cheese*, in Fleet Street, who were discussing the event. Trant had been a very popular man among his brethren, and many men were mourning for him as they went about their work.

"What you must do," said Fleming to his assistant," is this. Go down to the mortuary on my behalf, explain who Trant was, and gain every morsel of information you can. Go to the place where the body was found as well. Poor Tom Trant! He was a nice boy—a nice boy; he had a career before him. I shall walk down to the office. This has shaken me very much, and I think a walk will buck me up a little. If you get a fast cab and tell the man to go Hell for Leather, you will be back in Fleet Street by the time I arrive. I shall not walk fast." He heaved a perfectly sincere sigh as he put on his gloves. As he left the mansions and walked past the Aquarium he remembered that a cigar was a soothing thing, and, lighting one, he enjoyed it to the full. The sunshine was so radiant that it was indeed difficult to withstand its influence. Palace Yard was a great sight, and all the gilding on the clock tower shone merrily. The pigeons, with their strange iridescent eyes, were sunning themselves on the hot stones. The editor forgot all about Trant for some minutes in the pure physical exhilaration of it all. As he advanced up Parliament Street he saw Lord Salisbury, who was wearing an overcoat, despite the heat.

Fleming turned up Whitehall Court and past the National Liberal Club to the Strand, which was very full of people. Fleming had always been a great patron of the stage. He knew, and was known to, many actors and actresses, and you would always see his name after a ten-guinea subscription on a benefit list. He liked the Strand, and he walked very slowly down the north side, nodding or speaking to some theatrical acquaintance every moment.

When he came to the bar where all the actors go, which is nearly opposite the Tivoli Music Hall, he saw Rustle Tapper, the famous comedian, standing on the steps wearing a new white hat and surveying the bright and animated scene with intense enjoyment.

The two men were friends, and for a minute or two Fleming mounted the steps and stood by the other's side. It was now about half-past one.

"Well," said the actor, "and how are politics, very busy just now? What is this I see in the *Pall Mall* about the murder of one of your young men? It's not true, I hope."

"I am afraid it is only too true. He was the cleverest young fellow I have ever had on the paper. I got him straight from Balliol, and he would have been a very distinguished man. I don't know anything about it yet but just the bare facts; our news editor has gone down to find out all he can."

They moved through the swing doors into the bar, talking as they went.

The Strand was full of all its regular frequenters, and in the peculiar fashion of this street every one seemed to know every one else intimately. Little groups of more or less well-known actors and journalists stood about the pavement or went noisily in and out of the bars, much impeding the progress of the ordinary passer-by. There was no sign or trace of anything out of the common to be seen. It was just the Strand on a bright summer's day, and the flower-girls were selling all their roses very fast to the pretty burlesque actresses and chorus girls who were going to and fro from the agents' offices.

About two o'clock—the evening papers said half-past two, but their information was faulty—the people in Bedford Street and the Strand heard a great noise of shouting, which, as far as they could judge, came from the direction of the Haymarket or Trafalgar Square. The noise sounded as if a crowd of people were shouting together, but whether in alarm or whether at the passing of some great person was not immediately apparent.

It was obvious that something of importance was happening not very far away. After about a minute the shouting became very loud indeed, and a shrill note of alarm was plainly discernible.

In a few seconds the pavements were crowded with men, who came running out from the bars and restaurants to see what was happening. Many of them came out without their hats. Fleming and the actor hurried out with the rest, straining and pushing to get a clear view westwards. One tall, clean-shaven man, with a black patch on his eye, his face bearing obvious traces of grease paint, came out of the Bun Shop with his glass of brandy and water still in his hand.

It was a curious sight. Everyone was looking towards Trafalgar Square with mingled interest and uncertainty, and for the time all the business of the street was entirely suspended. The drivers of the omnibuses evidently thought that the shouting came from fire-engines which were trying to force their way eastwards through the traffic, for they drew up by the curbstone, momentarily expecting that the glistening helmets would swing round the corner of King William Street.

Fleming, from the raised platform at the door of Gatti's, could see right down past Charing Cross station, and as he was nearly six feet high, he could look well over the heads of the podgy little comedians who surrounded him. Suddenly the noise grew in volume and rose several notes higher, and a black mass of people appeared running towards them.

The next incident happened so rapidly that before any one had time for realization it was over. A huge black shadow sped along the dusty road, and, looking up, the terror-stricken crowd saw the incredible sight of a vast winged creature, as large as a dray-horse, gliding slowly over the street. The monster, which Fleming describes as something like an enormous bat with a curved bill like a bird of prey, began to hover, as if preparing to descend, when there was the sudden report of a gun. An assistant at the hosier's shop at the corner of Southampton Street, who belonged to the Volunteers, happened to be going to do some range firing in the afternoon, and fetching his rifle from behind the counter, took a pot shot at the thing. His aim, from surprise and fear, was bad, and the bullet only chipped a piece of stone from the coping of the Tivoli. The shot, however, made the creature change its intentions, for it swerved suddenly to the right against some telegraph wires, and then, breaking through them, flew with extraordinary swiftness away over the river, making, it appeared, for the Crystal Palace upon Sydenham Hill. A constable on Hungerford foot-bridge, who saw it as it went over the water, said that its hairless belly was all cut and bleeding from the impact of the wires. The excitement in the Strand became frantic. The windows of all the shops round the Tivoli were broken by the pressure of the crowd, who had instinctively got as near as possible to the houses. The cab and omnibus horses, scenting the thing, were in that state of extreme terror which generally only an elephant has power to induce in them. The whole street was in terrible confusion. The only person who seemed calm, so a report ran in a smart evening paper, was a tall man who was standing at the door of a bar wearing a patch over one eye, and who had a glass of brandy in his hand. A reporter who had been near him, said that as soon as the monster had disappeared over the house-tops, he quietly finished his glass of brandy, and straightway went inside to have it replenished.

Special editions of the evening papers were at once issued. The *Globe*, owing to the nearness of its offices, being first in the field.

The sensational story of the *Mercury*, which had been the signal for increasing laughter all the morning, came at once into men's minds, and, incredible as it was, there could now be no doubt of the truth.

A creature which, in those dim ages when the world was young and humanity itself was slowly being evolved in obedience to an inevitable law, had winged its way over the mighty swamps and forests of the primeval world, was alive and preying among them. To those who thought, there was something sinister in such an incalculable age. The order of nature was disturbed.

The death of young Trant was immediately explained, and at dinner time the wildest rumours were going about the clubs, while in the theatres and music-halls people were saying that a whole foul brood of dragons had been let loose upon the town.

The sensation was unique. Never before in all the history of the world had such a thing been heard of, and all night long the telegraphs sent conflicting rumours to the great centres of the earth. London was beside itself with excitement, and few people going about in the streets that night felt over secure, though everyone felt that the slaughter of the beast was only a matter of hours. The very uneasiness that such a weird and unnatural appearance excited in the brains of the populace had its humorous side, and when that evening Mr. Dan Leno chose to appear upon the stage as a comic St. George, the laughter was Homeric. Such was the state of the public opinion about the affair on the evening of the first day, but there was a good deal of anxiety felt at Scotland Yard, and Sir Edward Bradford was for some time at work organizing and directing precautionary measures. A company of sharp-shooters was sent down to the Embankment from the Regent's Park Barrack, and waited in readiness for any news. Mounted police armed with carbines were patrolling the whole country round Sydenham, and even as far as Mitcham Common were on the alert. Two or three of them rode constantly up and down the Golf Links.

A warning wire was despatched to Mr. Henry Gillman, the general manager of the Crystal Palace, for at this season of the year the grounds were always full of pleasure-seekers. About nine o'clock the chief inspector on duty at the police headquarters received the following telegram.

"Animal appeared here 8.30, and unfortunately killed child. Despite volley got away apparently unharmed. Heading for London when last seen. Have closed Palace and cleared grounds."

It appears what actually happened was as follows:—

A Dr. David Pryce, a retired professor from one of the Scotch Universities, who lived in a house on Gipsy Hill, was taking a stroll down the central transept after dinner, when he was startled to hear the noise of breaking glass high up in the roof. Some large pieces of glass fell within a few yards of him into one of the ornamental fountains. Running to one side, he looked up, and saw that some heavy body had fallen on to the roof and coming through the glass was so balanced upon an iron girder. Even as he looked, the object broke away and fell with a frightful splash into the basin among the gold-fish. Simultaneously he heard the crack of rifles firing in the grounds outside.

He was the first of the people round to run to the fountain, where he found, to his unspeakable horror, the bleeding body of a child, a sweet little girl of six, still almost breathing.

The news of this second victim was in the streets about ten o'clock, and it was then that a real panic took possession of all the pleasure-seekers in Piccadilly and the Strand.

The special descriptive writers from the great daily papers, who went about the principal centres of amusement, witnessed the most extraordinary sights. Now and again there would be a false alarm that the dragon—for that is what people were beginning to call it—was in the neighbourhood, and there would be a stampede of men and women into the nearest place of shelter. The proprietor of one of the big Strand bars, afterwards boasted that the panic had been worth an extra fifty pounds to him.

The Commissioner of Police became so seriously alarmed, both at the disorderly state of the streets, and the possible chance of another fatality, that he thought it wiser to obtain military assistance, and about half-past eleven London was practically under arms. Two or three linesmen were stationed at central points in the main streets, and little groups of cavalry with unslung carbines patrolled from place to place.

Although the strictest watch was kept all night, nothing was seen of the monster, but in the morning a constable of the C Division, detailed for special duty, found traces at the top of Ludgate Hill which proved conclusively that the animal had been there sometime during the night.

THE THIRD EPISODE

The wide-spread news that the terror had been in the very heart of London during the night created tremendous excitement among the authorities and the public at large. The City Police held a hurried consultation in Old Jewry about nine o'clock in the morning, and after hearing Sergeant Weatherley's account of his discovery, came to the conclusion that the dragon had probably made its lair on the top of St. Paul's Cathedral.

A man was at once sent round to the Deanery for a pass which should allow a force of police to search the roofs, and came back in half an hour with an order written by Dean Gregory himself requesting the officials to give the police every facility for a thorough examination.

It was then that the fatal mistake was made which added a fourth victim to the death roll.

About 9.30 a telegram was received at New Scotland Yard from a professional golfer at Mitcham, saying that some caddies on their way to the club-house had sighted the monster hovering over the Croydon road early in the morning. A wire was at once despatched to the local police station on the lower green, directing that strict inquiries should be made, and the result telegraphed at once. Meanwhile Scotland Yard communicated with Old Jewry, and the City Police made the incredible blunder of putting off the search party till the Mitcham report was thoroughly investigated.

It was not allowed to be known that the police had any suspicion that St. Paul's might harbour the dragon, and the fact of Sergeant Weatherley's discovery did not transpire till the second edition of the *Star* appeared, just about the time the final scene was being enacted on the south roof.

Accordingly the omnibuses followed the usual Cannon Street route, and the City men from the suburbs crowded them as usual. In the brilliant morning sunshine—for it was a perfect summer's day—it was extremely difficult to believe that anything untoward was afoot.

The panic of the night before, the panic of the gas lamps and the uncertain mystery of night, had very largely subsided. Many a city man who the night before had come out of the Alhambra or the Empire seized with a genuine terror, now sat on the top of his City 'bus smoking the after-breakfast cigarette and almost joking about the whole extraordinary affair. The fresh, new air was so delightful that it had its effect on everybody, and the police and soldiers who stood at ease round the statue of Queen Anne were saluted with a constant fire of chaff from the waggish young gentlemen of the Stock Exchange as they were carried to their daily work.

"What price the Dragon!" and "Have you got a muzzle handy!" resounded in the precincts of the Cathedral, and the merry witticisms afforded intense enjoyment to the crowds of ragamuffins who lounged round the top of Ludgate Hill.

Then, quite suddenly, came the last act of the terrible drama.

Just as a white Putney 'bus was slowly coming up the steep gradient of the hill, the horses straining and slipping on the road, a black object rose from behind the clock tower on the façade of the Cathedral, and with a long, easy dive the creature that was terrorizing London came down upon the vehicle. It seemed to slide rapidly down the air with its wings poised and open, and it came straight at the omnibus. The driver, with great presence of mind and not a moment too soon, pulled his horses suddenly to the right, and the giant enemy rushed past with a great disturbance of the air hardly a yard away from the conveyance.

It sailed nearly down to the railway bridge before it was able to check its flight and turn.

Then, with a slow flapping of its great leathery wings, it came back to where the omnibus was oscillating violently as the horses reared and plunged.

It was the most horrible sight in the world. Seen at close quarters the monstrous creature was indescribably loathsome, and the stench from its body was overpowering. Its great horny beak was covered with brown stains, and in its eagerness and anger it was foaming and slobbering at the mouth. Its eyes, which were half-covered with a white scurf, had something of that malignant and horrible expression that one sometimes sees in the eyes of an evil-minded old man.

In a moment the thing was right over the omnibus, and the people on the top were hidden from view by the beating of its mighty wings. Three soldiers on the pavement in front of the Cathedral knelt down, and taking deliberate aim, fired almost simultaneously. A moment after the shots rang out, the horses, who had been squealing in an ecstasy of terror, overturned the vehicle. The dragon, which had been hit in the leather-like integument stretched between the rib-bones of its left wing, rose heavily and slowly, taking a little spring from the side of the omnibus, and giving utterance to a rapid choking sound, very like the gobbling of a turkey. Its wings beat the air with tremendous power, and with the regular sound of a pumping engine, and in its bill it held some bright red object, which was screaming in uncontrollable agony. In two seconds the creature had mounted above the houses, and all down Ludgate Hill the horror-bitten crowd could see that its writhing, screaming burden was a soldier of the line.

The man, by some curious instinct, had kept tight hold of his little swagger-stick, and his whirling arms bore a grotesque resemblance to the conductor of an orchestra directing its movements with his bâton. Some more shots pealed out, and the screaming stopped with the suddenness of a steam whistle turned off, while the swagger-stick fell down into the street.

Over the road, from house to house, was stretched a row of flags with a Union Jack in the centre, which had been put up earlier in the morning by an alderman who owned one of the shops, in order to signalize some important civic function. In mounting, the monster was caught by the line which supported the flags, and then with a tremendous effort it pulled the whole arrangement loose. Then, very slowly, and with the long row of gaudy flags streaming behind it, it rose high into the air and sank down behind the dome of St. Paul's. As it soared, regardless of the fusilade from below, it looked exactly like a fantastic Japanese kite. The whole affair, from the time of the first swoop from St. Paul's until the monster sank again to its refuge, only took two or three seconds over the minute.

The news of this fresh and terrible disaster reached the waiting party in Old Jewry almost immediately, and they started for the Cathedral without a moment's delay. They found Ludgate Hill was almost empty, as the police under the railway bridge were deflecting the traffic into other routes. On each side of the street hundreds of white faces peered from doorways and windows towards St. Paul's. The overturned omnibus still lay in the middle of the road, but the horses had been taken away.

The party marched in through the west door, and the ineffable peace of the great church fell round them like a cloak and made their business seem fantastic and unreal. Mr. Harding, the permanent clerk of the works, met them in the nave, and held a consultation with Lieutenant Boyle and Inspector Nicholson, who commanded the men. The clerk of the works produced a rough map of the various roofs, on any one of which the dragon might be. He suggested, and the lieutenant quite agreed, that two or three men should first be sent to try and locate the exact resting-place of the monster, and that afterwards the best shots should surround and attack it. The presence of a large number of men wandering about the extremely complicated system of approaches might well disturb the creature and send it abroad again. He himself, he added, would accompany the scouts.

Three men were chosen for the job, a sergeant of police and two soldiers. Mr. Harding took them into his office, and they removed their boots for greater convenience in climbing. They were conducted first of all into the low gallery hung with old frescoes which leads to the library, and then, opening a small door in the wall, Mr. Harding, beckoning the others to follow, disappeared into darkness.

They ascended some narrow winding steps deep in the thickness of the masonry, until a gleam of light showed stealing down from above, making their faces pale and haggard. Their leader stopped, and there was a jingling of keys. "It is unlikely it'll be here," he said in a low voice, "and anyway it can't get at us quickly, but be careful. Sergeant, you bring one man and come with me, and the last man stay behind and hold the door open in case we have to retreat." He turned the key in the lock and opened the narrow door.

For a moment the brilliant light of the sun blinded them, and then the two men who were yet a few steps down in the dark heard the other say, "Come on, it's all safe."

They came out into a large square court floored with lead. Great stone walls rose all around them, and the only outlet was the door by which they had come. It was exactly like a prison exercise yard, and towering away above their heads in front was the huge central dome. The dismal place was quite empty.

"The swine isn't here, that's certain," said one of the soldiers.

"No, we must go round to the south side," said the clerk of the works; "it's very much like this, only larger. But there's a better way to get to it. Let us go back at once."

They went down again to the library corridor, and turning by the archway debouching on the whispering gallery—they could hear the strains of the organ as they passed—went up another dark and narrow stairway. They came out onto a small ledge of stone, a kind of gutter, and there was very little room between the walls at their backs and the steep lead-covered side of the main roof which towered into the air straight in front.

"Now," said Mr. Harding, "we have got to climb up this slant and down the other side, and if he's anywhere about we shall see him there. At the bottom of the other slope is a gutter, like this, to stand in, but no wall, as it looks straight down into a big bear pit, like the one we went to first. We shall have to go right down the other slant, because if he's lying on the near side of the pit—and it's the shady side—we shan't be able to see him at all. You'll find it easy enough to get up, and if you should slip back this wall will bring you up short, but be very careful about going down. If you once begin to slide you'll toboggan right over the edge and on to the top of the beast, and even if he isn't there, it's a sixty foot drop."

As they climbed slowly up the steep roof, all London came into clear and lovely view—white, red, and purple in the sun. When at length they reached the top and clung there, for a moment, high in the air, like sparrows perching on the ridge of a house, they could only just see the mouth of the drop yawning down below them.

One of the soldiers, a lithe and athletic young fellow, was down at the bottom considerably before the others, and crouching in the broad gutter, he peered cautiously over the edge. They saw his shoulders heave with excitement, and in a moment he turned his head towards them. His face was white and his eyes full of loathing. They joined him at once, and the horror of what they saw will never leave any of the four.

The Dragon was lying on its side against the wall. Its whole vast length was heaving as if in pain, while close by it lay the remains of what was once a soldier of the Queen.

It was soon killed. The marksmen were hurriedly brought up from below, and after a perilous climb, owing to the weight of their rifles, lined the edge of the pit. They fired repeated volleys into the vast groaning creature. After the first volley it began to cough and choke, and vainly trying to open its maimed wings, dragged itself into the centre of the place. The mere sight of the malign thing gave a shock to the experience that was indescribable. It fulfilled no place in the order of life, and this fact induced a cold fear far more than its actual appearance. A psychologist who talked to one of the soldiers afterwards, got near to some fundamental truths dealing with the natural limits of sensation, in a brilliant article published in *Cosmopolis*. In its death agonies, agonies which were awful to look at, it crawled right across the floor of the court, and it moved the line of flags, which still remained fixed to one paw, in such a way that when they got down to it they found that, by a strange and pathetic coincidence, the Union Jack was covering the body of the dead soldier.

In this way the oldest living thing in the world was destroyed, and London breathed freely again.

DE PROFUNDIS

Coutts Brisbane

Coutts Brisbane was one of the pseudonyms used by the writer and artist Robert Coutts Armour (1874–1945). Born in Queensland, Australia but of Scottish descent, Armour settled in England around the turn of the century. He became a prolific contributor to the cheap popular-fiction magazines, those aimed either at juvenile readers or those who looked for simple entertainment. Armour was an early exponent of humorous science fiction, producing many stories in which he created bizarre aliens and their environments or whimsical stories set in the past or future. In addition to the stories mentioned in this book's introduction were such tales as "The Lower Level" (1913), where troglodytes are discovered deep under Earth, "Eden—Limited" (1915) in which civilization reverts to primitivism and "Ultimate Zero" (1916) in which the Earth freezes when something blocks out the Sun. Although Armour wrote many short novels, including a long run of Sexton Blake adventures, he never collected together any of his short stories. In 1984 bookdealer George Locke assembled a volume of twelve of his interplanetary stories as Denizens of Other Worlds *but as this was an edition of just six copies, it's probably even more scarce than the original magazines. The following story finds Armour in rather more serious mood.*

ABOUT THE JUNCTION YEARS OF THE NINETEENTH AND TWEN-tieth centuries, writers of popular fiction were seized by a prophetic fervour of destruction. I think the scientists pointed the way with interesting speculations about such matters as the heat-life of the sun; an eminent French astronomer amused his leisure with a romantic, dithyrambic story of the human race's end; various cheery people of varying authority decreed the speedy exhaustion of the world's coal-fields; and a host of sprightly authors made haste to entertain us with accounts of great cities overwhelmed, and our painfully built-up civilization obliterated by dire and diverse means. Mars warred with Terra, Ocean sent forth her devouring monsters, nation hurtled against nation, the Yellow Peril loomed terribly, new diseases devastated the whole world, leaving only a few choice spirits to the task of re-peopling it—and whilst we enjoyed this feast of speculation, the forces prepared for our undoing were already marshalling. Whether any one of those ingenious scribes anticipated what came to pass I am unable to say, though, for irony's sake, I trust it was so, and that he has had ample opportunity to revise his theories in the face of facts.

It may seem strange, but the calamity came without any warn-ing, the few isolated incidents that might have served being mis-understood or disregarded. I myself was witness, after the event, of one such, in this wise.

I had been making holiday in Cornwall, tramping the coastline or occasionally diving inland, in an irresponsible fashion that would have shocked the laborious writer of itineraries. The weather was unusually fine and warm, so, having a large waterproof poncho, a bag of provisions, and a little kettle, I gipsied very happily till the eve of the inevitable day when I must return to London. Being by then wise in the selection of a camping ground, I got me at sundown to the sheltered side of a little wood, ate my supper, and, wrapped in my poncho, lay down to enjoy a pipe before going to sleep.

It was my last camp in England, perhaps the last I shall ever make there. At the present time, of course, such a proceeding would be stark lunacy even in the most desolate place. In front of me, looking inland, the ground rose with a gentle swell, dipped and rose again to the horizon quite bare of cover, there being no trees of any growth in that part of the West Country. They were all cut down long ago, I have been told, at the time when every Cornishman turned mole and burrowed after tin, and certainly they must have needed forests to prop the workings with which the country is honeycombed. In the field before me was the shaft of one ringed by a high stone wall, and with it for text I speculated drowsily whether, in the far future, the wood underground would have rotted or turned to coal Then an old horse came and looked over the hedge at me in a friendly way, and the tips of his ears twitching against the sky were my last waking memory.

I awoke once in the dark with a confused sound of hoofs and a long, wailing cry ringing in my ears, but all was quiet. I attributed the noise to a trick of dream, sniffed distastefully a faint, acrid odour drifting on the slow night breeze, and, turning over, slept without stir till the sunlight crept into my eyes. Within half an hour I had sluiced myself at a runnel, eaten breakfast, and was ready to face the road, the rail, and the Big Smoke.

My direct route lay through the field in front, and climbing on the gate I stood at gaze, seeing that close beside the walled shaft-mouth lay something which, I was absolutely certain, had not been there overnight—a large skeleton.

I noticed, too, that my friendly horse was nowhere in view, though the boundaries of the field were all in sight, and, exceedingly puzzled, approached the bones. They were fresh, *raw*, though not a particle of meat adhered to them, and unmistakably equine. I went back to the gate, the only exit, examined the ground beyond it, which was soft enough to show a track, and made sure that the beast had not gone out that way.

The conclusion was obvious. Within a few hours a big, strong animal had been done to death, and clean picked! It was incredible, yet there was the skeleton, without a toothmark, still held together by its ligaments, and perfect as an anatomist could desire. I began to be a little afraid, but being of a fairly practical turn set about searching after further facts, and ran against more incomprehensibility.

From the gory patch about the skeleton to the wall around the shaft, ran two tracks, worn through the turf to bare earth, about four or five inches wide and as much apart, one of which continued in a red stain up the perpendicular face of the stones.

Now, I offer no excuse for my conduct in face of the mystery. Certainly the wall was high, and had been effectively pointed no great while before, but I could easily have climbed it. Only—I didn't want to climb. Without weighing matters I concluded instanter that the power which could so deal with a horse might very easily treat me in like fashion, left the unhealthy precinct on tiptoe, and ran till I came to a cart-road. Decidedly the spirit of research was not in me that morning.

At the time I felt I was doing shamefully, but looking back I see that I acted with common-sense. Had I searched further I should have lost my life as vainly as one who throws himself to a school of sharks; yet my self-esteem barometer went down and down, so I mentioned the phenomenon to no one, but got to town, and to work once again, determined to forget an inexplicable incident.

In those days I had just entered on a series of experiments having for object the discovery of some volatile fuel to replace petrol, and my little laboratory contained so many samples of oils, tars, and essences that, despite ventilation, it usually smelt like the interior of a submarine. I suppose, strictly speaking, mine was a dangerous trade, and certainly the top floor of an old-fashioned office building in Fleet Street was scarcely a fitting place in which to distil inflammable liquids. But it happened that the den was my own, the property having belonged to my people for near a century, and with the near prospect of eviction, when the ground lease expired, I didn't wish to squander money on other premises.

I had but few visitors and only one intimate friend, Henry Mayence, a short, broad, immensely strong man, devoted to motoring, and consequently keenly interested in my attempts to cheapen his pastime. He used to bring all kinds of absurdly unsuitable material, ranging from camphor to burgundy-pitch and palm oil, though apart from this foible he was entirely level-headed. I returned from Cornwall at the beginning of June; twelve days later—on Friday, the 13th, to be precise—I heard his familiar step on the landing, the heavy thump of something weighty banged on the floor, and opened to find him in the act of upending a large iron oil-drum which smelt vilely of crude petroleum.

"So you're back," he grunted: "That's a good job. Didn't want to lug this thing home again. Out of the way!"

He pushed past unceremoniously with the ching in his arms, and, depositing it within with another crash, condescended to explain.

"Right stuff at last," he said. "Wales. They've struck it—regular lake. I've got an option. You try it. It's heavy, but—"

"But, confound you, I don't want a hogshead!" I objected. "It'll stink the place out. Phuff!" I had been at work all night, and so was irritable. "Why on earth couldn't you bring a little? A bottleful would have been enough."

He grinned placidly.

"Because this is going to be a big thing, sonny, and you'll need it all. Besides, what does another flavour matter among so many? Open the windows."

"And kill the sparrows? You'll jolly well have to take it away again! Hang it, man, I'll be run in for causing a nuisance!"

"All right," said he soothingly; "perhaps it is a bit too thick. Didn't notice it on the car. Horrid business, that of the policeman, Kingston way!"

"What business?" I asked. "I haven't been out yet."

"Devilish rummy! Found the poor beggar behind a hedge, uniform on—helmet, too. Beastly! And I may have spoken to him—been held up thereabouts more than once. Poor chap!"

"What are you gibbering about? Was he murdered?" I demanded irritably.

Mayence shivered.

"Ghastly, I tell you! Nothing but his clothes, only bones left inside 'em. Ugh!"

"What?" I shouted. "D'you mean to say—Why, down in Cornwall—"

And forthwith I told him briefly what I had seen.

"Same thing," he said, nodding emphatically. "A horse don't matter, but a man! And a lot of other people are missing, too. Wonder you didn't hear the boys yelling the specials outside."

"I did," said I. "But I'm so used to that, I didn't take notice. Hallo! There's another edition, or—"

We sprang together to the window opening streetwards and craned our necks.

Right opposite building operations were in progress, and a great hole had been dug in the earth, from which, as we looked, the workmen came crowding and jostling, howling gigantically, in a frenzied hurry to reach the narrow door in the hoarding along the street-front.

"Lord!" ejaculated Mayence. "What in thunder's up? Look at that chap!"

A man, who had, I suppose, been in the deepest part of the excavation, came clawing frantically up a ladder, reached the level, put his hands to his head with the gesture of one suddenly smitten to death, reeled, and fell backwards into the pit.

A cloud of dust flew up and hid everything for an instant; then something which looked exactly like a wave of treacle—a brownish-black, shiny, wet-looking, lapping tide—flooded up over the edge of the hole, and flowed out towards the men jammed in the doorway.

They must have felt its coming and redoubled their efforts. A section of the hoarding gave way, falling outwards on the front ranks of the swaying crowd that had collected instantaneously, and, as they gave back, the fear-maddened workmen charged forth, tripping, stumbling, and striking out fiercely at everything in their path, driven by blind, panic terror. Close on their heels through the gap, over the hoarding's top and through every crevice of the boards, came that amazing fluid mass.

Everybody shouted, abruptly everybody faced about, turning to fly, and I had an impression of the crowd as a heaving, whirling maelstrom, with pinky-red faces for bubbles and a tossing spray of straw hats adrift for foam. I saw a tall man—a Press photographer, I presume—struggle free and present his camera at the oncoming treacly tide, stagger, fall, and lie motionless.

Subconsciously I wondered if he had got his picture, and whether I should see it in the morrow's papers. The treacle swept on and over him—ay, and over many another. Men faltered and fell in rows, even as they fled. A tubby man, with flashing glasses that stayed miraculously firm on his nose, swarmed half-way up a lamp-standard, lost his hold for no apparent reason, and fell, limp and lifeless.

The street within our view cleared, the din retreated a little, and I could hear Mayence.

"Alive!" he shouted. "Alive! The stuff's alive. I tell you—alive!" He used language quite unprintable. "And deadly—look at that 'bus!"

It had been at a standstill, unable to move through the swift-gathered throng. Its top was crowded. The driver stretched a hand to put in the clutch, drew it back sharply, lifted it to his mouth, and sagged forward over his wheel.

"What is it? Great heavens, what is—"

Somebody sprang into the room behind us, and banged the door. It was Vidal, a quiet, little, oldish man who, in an office on the floor beneath, practised the nearly extinct art of wood-engraving for such scientific journals as needed clearly detailed pictures, instead of the cheaper dot and smudge variety. Usually he was staid and self-contained, but now, and little wonder, he was livid and shaking with terror.

"They're coming up!" he screamed. "Shut that window! We're done for! I saw 'em once before, but nothing like this!"

Mayence grabbed him by the shoulders and shook him roughly. "What?" he shouted. "What the blazes is it?"

"Ants!" quavered Vidal. "Millions of trillions! They're stinging everyone to death; keep 'em out!"

It was well for us then that Mayence had piloted racing automobiles, a practice that breeds quick thinking. He didn't stop to question the truth of the statement, but shook his man a trifle harder.

"Will paraffin, keep them off?" he demanded.

Vidal nodded.

"Perhaps," he said hoarsely.

"Lucky I brought a big 'un, then!" growled Mayence; and leapt at his oil-drum. "Rags, Tom, a brush, paper—anything! Bathe in it!"

In a twinkling he had the bung out and tipped a pool of thick, yellow, evil-smelling, crude petroleum on the floor by the door, spreading it with his handkerchief over every crevice.

"Mother Partington, Atlantic Ocean!" he grunted, snatched a towel, and stuffed a soaked strip beneath the door. "Window, you cripples! Buck up!"

We worked like demons. As a motive-power there is nothing to excel fear; and yet though we wrought swiftly, smearing the sashes and every visible joint in our defences, the ants were already darkening the panes ere we had finished.

"Kill them! Quick!" shrieked Vidal suddenly, pointing. "There!"

From under the skirting-board a score of large ants, near an inch and a half long, came boldly at us, travelling rapidly, halted at the edge of the puddle in which we stood, and sped swiftly back again.

"Don't like it, by jingo!" Mayence shouted exultantly. "Magic circle! Spread it out!"

It was done. Panting, soaked with oil and sweat, hardly able to breathe because of the stink, we stood up, saved; perhaps the sole surviving witnesses of that first outburst, since it would appear that parties of the ants invaded every building, slaying relentlessly every human being they encountered. Us they let alone after the first trial; and presently, when the panes cleared, being nearly suffocated, we ventured to open the window.

Speech became possible.

"Don't lean out!" Mayence warned me. "Some of the brutes might drop on you!"

Standing on a chair well withdrawn from the casement, I looked forth. Within my circumscribed view I could see the dead photographer and several of the others on the further side, the top of the 'bus with its lifeless load, and a taxicab wedged into a shop window, its engine still running, the driving wheels slithering and grinding on the pavement. At several open windows men hung or sprawled. The air reverberated with a vast noise; the voices of fearful thousands roaring from every point of the compass beat painfully on the ears; but silently, the cause of it, the river of ants, still flowed from the excavation, each yard of it an army, dividing into streams, which went their way west and east without pause.

"Jumping Jupiter!" exclaimed Mayence, mounting behind me. "It's unbelievable! It's—it's a hallucination!"

"It isn't," said Vidal. "I saw something like it in Venezuela once, when I went with a collecting expedition. They kept on for a day and a night, and though they weren't so poisonous as these, everything had to get out of their way or perish. Perhaps they've come out in other places, too."

A duty we had neglected came to my mind, and I jumped from my chair and rushed to the 'phone.

"Exchange!" I yelled. "Are you there? Are you there?"

There was no answer, though I called again and again. My belated attempt at warning was useless.

"Death everywhere," murmured Vidal.

"Or else the gels have scooted," suggested Mayence. "Don't be too infernally gloomy."

"Perhaps it's the beginning of the end for the human race," persisted the little man.

"Rot!" cried Mayence. "It's horribly bad, of course, but that couldn't happen. A lot of damned insects!"

"And they'll soon be settled," said I. "Squirt acids or poisons on them, or—"

"Or set a dog at them," sneered Vidal. "D'you think they'd stand still and let you do it? Look at the pace they can go. And they've got brains, I'm certain. What if this has all been arranged? Why, I'll bet they're all over the town—other towns, too; perhaps other countries."

We cried out at this monstrous suggestion, yet—though, of course, we didn't know it at the time—he wasn't far out in his estimate of the abominations. He warmed to his dismal theme.

"Even if they're driven back underground for the moment, how are you going to keep them there. Nice job it'll be to make every house antproof. And walking about in armoured clothes, or soaked with anticide, will be pleasant, won't it?"

"But they die off or go to sleep in the winter, don't they?" I suggested.

"How d'you know this kind will? Anyhow, they've got lots of time before them. How many of us will live till the first frost? How about harvesting, and tending sheep and cattle? We'll all starve if we're not killed. It's a conquest, an arranged business, I tell you. Perhaps some of us will be kept as slaves. There are species who have others to wait on them—"

"Will you shut up?" roared Mayence. "We're in the devil's own pickle, without being driven daft by your maunderings! What d'you reckon we'd better do, Tom? Stay here till the siege is raised?"

"How about the river?" I asked hopefully. "The oil keeps the beasts off. If we soaked ourselves thoroughly, we might get there all right and find a boat."

"Probably a few thousand others have found it already," he chuckled grimly; "and a few billions of our little friends appear to have gone in the same direction. It's risky every way."

We all stared gloomily at that ceaseless torrent of venomous life, pouring, pouring silently, swiftly, with an ordered purpose. Against uncountable myriads so devilishly endowed, what had man to oppose? I could think of no adequate defence.

"Perhaps you're right, Vidal," I said. "One hopes not, of course. But—"

"Have you got anything to eat or drink?" Mayence interrupted. "We must keep our pecker up."

"Biscuits, whisky, soda—that's all," said I, producing them. And we ate and drank unpleasantly, each mouthful being tainted with the all-pervading petroleum, then stared out of the window again.

"The noise is dying down, I think," said Vidal at length. "But what's that racket overhead?"

Mayence listened.

"Somebody breaking the law. An aeroplane coming—over there, see? By jove! It's the old training 'bus, the biplane at Hendon. What the dickens are they after?"

Moving quite slowly, the 'plane hove in sight, skimming dangerously near the housetops, one of the two men in her apparently searching the ground with field-glasses. Mayence snatched up the linen overall I wore when working, tied a sleeve to a walking stick, and thrust it outside, waving till the airman saw it, and, putting a big megaphone to his head, shouted, something which was drowned by the rattle of the engine. Slowly the machine swung about over the pit, a small, dark object fell from it, and—"crash!" a mighty spout of dust flew up, concrete foundation walls and scaffold-poles crumbled and rocked, tinkling glass tell in showers. The man in the plane had dropped a bomb into the ants' portal.

With the explosion their columns broke, thinned, and vanished into doorways, the drains and crevices; in twenty seconds they were all under cover. The 'plane circled out of sight, returned, and this time we caught something of what the megaphone bawled at us:"… in a dozen places… going to shut 'em down… all right soon." We waved an answer, they shot away, and in a few minutes we heard the smack of another bomb, followed at intervals by others, each more distant.

"A dozen places!" exclaimed Vidal. "What did I say? It's an organized invasion. A fat lot of good those chaps have done. See!"

The side of the crater made by the explosion began to heave and crumble, a dark spot appeared and grew larger, and long before the sound of the last detonation came to us the ant river was flowing again, steadily as though it had never been so rudely interrupted.

Mayence mumbled disgustedly, and faced about. "Question is, what are we going to do? Stay and starve, or take the risk of going out?"

"They won't touch us," said I confidently.

"Don't be too sure. Some of them, maybe, will sacrifice themselves on the off-chance of getting a bite home. At all events, I'll go out first and reconnoitre." But at this Vidal and I protested, and in the end we drew lots. The short match fell to me, and I confess to feeling horribly uncomfortable, but I managed to conceal my feelings whilst I was smeared anew with the abominably smelling oil; my boots were soaked till they squelched at every step; face, hair, cap, and gloves, all were saturated, and Mayence finished me off by tying a dripping duster around my neck. "In case they drop on you from aloft," he explained. "Now you're all right. We'll get ready while you're gone."

I opened the door gingerly. At the edge of the landing was a group of ants, several score, big fellows, with their heads turned towards me; simultaneously, they darted forward, came almost to my feet—and retreated. Instinctively I squashed the hindmost. "All serene!" I cried. "They won't face it," and slithered down the first flight to find another and larger vidette, which behaved exactly like the others. I had no more fear after that, but went on confidently as a mediæval knight in armour of proof hewing his way through a mob of peasants.

On the first floor I peeped into the office of Wardell, an advertising agent, and saw what was left of him lying back in his chair, a half-open sample tin of insect killer on the floor beside him; evidently he had bethought him of this defence at the last moment. The ants were swarming all over him, and I turned away hastily, feeling very sick; it is a shocking thing to see a man you have known and swapped drinks with in process of disintegration. Yet the sight served to diminish the shock I received when I found the entry and the lower stairs completely choked with bodies. I went back and reported, and, since there was no other way, we at last let ourselves down by a rope from the window of Wardell's room, after lowering the precious oil-drum, now half empty, and set foot in a Fleet Street transmogrified to the semblance of a battlefield.

Perhaps a soldier hardened to slaughter could have supported the spectacle, but to us it was near overwhelming. Remember that the view from my office was circumscribed by projecting buildings on either side, and that the portion of street it commanded was abandoned at the first outrush, so that what we had seen before was as nothing compared with what confronted us.

Looking westward, the street was filled from side to side with a horrible barricade, vehicles of all sorts piled and wedged together in inextricable confusion, for a base; and over, under, between, shaken together and trembling to the throb of the engines still working beneath, were piled the dead.

From the accounts since collected it would seem that on this fatal day the ants emerged from the earth, not in a dozen, but in scores of places, from each of which they diverged on either hand, killing as they went, till they met the columns of their fellows, and so ringed Central London in a cordon of poison, whilst from other points within the circle other hordes spread devastatingly till hardly a nook or corner remained unvisited.

Of the millions of folks so surrounded, comparatively few escaped, and those, curiously enough, mainly by the underground railways, which were let alone for some time; but the majority of the people fled panic-stricken from one army only to encounter another, and most often met their fate struggling amidst maddened crowds.

Horror left us dumb for a little, then Mayence, hugging his oil-drum, turned towards Ludgate Circus, and we followed in silence. With us, on either hand, marched thousands of ants at a respectful distance, and so we came to Bridge Street, and the first survivor, a telephone linesman, slung in a travelling cradle from the cables crossing the road. Intent upon our steps, we were startled by his hoarse cry from aloft: "Hi! mates!" he called.

"Can you let yourself down?" answered Mayence. "We've got stuff to keep them off. Come along."

The man became frantically busy with a coil of wire.

"Righto!" he yelled. "Just a minute."

There was a sudden commotion amongst our escort, a thin brown thread shot up the façade of the building directly below the poles supporting the telephone wires.

"They know!" exclaimed Vidal. "They're after him. Quick, man, or they'll get you yet."

Mayence stood ready with his oil, the linesman dropped the end of his cable almost to our feet, unbuckled the strap which held him in the cradle, wound his cap about the wire, gave one unearthly scream, and fell smashing to the pavement. I think he was dead before he reached the ground.

We trudged on towards the river without a word; pity, horror, terror, all capacity for emotion seemed numbed to exhaustion, and we moved mechanically. Blackfriars Bridge was choked by another dreadful barricade, the approaches to the stations were impassable. The river was dotted with people swimming or clinging to lifebuoys or fragments of wood, the barges anchored on the further side were hidden by men clustering like swarming bees, the outermost continually dragged down by others who struggled up from the water; the *President*, the old Naval Volunteer training ship, lay low in the water, weighed down by the numbers aboard her, and dozens clung to her cables fore and aft. I saw one man maintaining possession of a packing-case, which barely supported him, with a bloody knife; a dinghy drifted by, laden with women and one man, who threatened any who approached it with a revolver. As they neared the bridge the arch under which they must pass grew black, and though we shouted, the warning was unheard, or unheeded, the insect death rained down, the boat capsized, and we saw no more.

Nearly half an hour we stood there, hypnotized, the petroleum escaping from our saturated clothes and gathering in little pools around our feet, whilst the ants clustered thick in a semicircle behind and darted continually to and fro along the parapet in front, angry perhaps because we had so long escaped them. Then a river steamer, without a living soul aboard, though her deck was piled, came in sight, her paddles revolving slowly, swinging uncertainly from side to side of the river, till she brought up with a crash on the piles of a wharf and began to settle down.

With the noise we awoke to a realization of a new peril; London town was on fire. Heavy smoke clouds were drawing across the sun, rolling south-eastward before a rising breeze.

"Nobody to stop it," said I. "But at least some of those infernal things 'll get roasted."

"They'll go underground till it's over," Vidal said.

"We'll go up with the first spark," said Mayence. "Can you swim?"

He shook his head.

"Not a stroke."

"And Tom is equal to about a hundred yards. We'll have to make a float of some kind and keep under water going through the bridges; we'll get below these for a start, anyhow. Come on."

With our abominable guard still in attendance we turned our backs on the river, and by great good fortune found the roadway underneath the railway viaduct passable, though we had to climb over many vehicles. The smoke grew even thicker, and we could scarce see our way, but it appeared noxious to the ants, who thinned away and had quite disappeared ere luck brought us to the end of a short street and a little wharf.

"Here we are," said Mayence. "And there are planks and rope. We'll make a raft of sorts. Hurry!"

Somehow, in no very workmanlike fashion to be sure, since we groped in pungent semi-darkness, we got our raft together and launched. It was high time; we were half suffocated, and the flames, spreading unchecked with frightful rapidity, roared near at hand as, sitting awash, we started on our voyage, Mayence, sitting aft, paddling with a short board till the mid stream caught us, and we were swept swiftly forward, unable to see more than a yard or two ahead.

Soon a dark mass loomed above us, the raft swerved, we shot through a bridge—Southwark—and never an ant materialized. Either we passed unseen or they had gone before the smother.

"Three more to pass and we're all right," grunted Mayence.

"Look out! Shove off!" A barge drifting beam-on lay in our path. Vidal howled, thrust out a leg, pushing with all his might. We bumped once, and went clear without receiving boarders. I needn't describe what we glimpsed in passing, nor what we presently saw as we circled in the swirl of the Cannon Street railway bridge; suffice it to say that many had sought refuge upon its floating fenders—in vain.

Below was a red flare of flaming warehouses belching showers of sparks, yet none reached us, and we whirled blindly on in the black, smothering smoke blanket, passed beneath London Bridge without seeing it, and narrowly missed running full tilt into an anchored boat, perilously laden with folks, who yelled in chorus as we rasped across their cable; two men with oars out tugged dementedly, another fool struck wildly with a boathook, smote his iron deep into one of our planks and nearly capsized the lot.

"Let go, you idiot!" roared Mayence, whilst the water licked their gunwale, and, fortunately for them, he obeyed, and we parted company, losing sight of them instantly.

Vidal levered the hook clear and crouched ready to fend off from what might come next. With ebb and current together the stream was a race, and we should have fared badly had we encountered anything moored; but our amazing good fortune held, and though we caught sight of many craft, and heard voices all about us, we kept clear of everything till, about the neighbourhood of Deptford, the smoke thinned and we could see our fellow-men once more.

Either margin of the river was lined with people standing in the water, knee-deep, waist-deep, up to the neck; beyond these a floating fringe, then boats and rafts all loaded nearly to sinking; and the voice of their misery was a continuous giant groan, a deep, plaintive note of despair, such as I hope never to hear again. Of the people in boats around, none heeded us, except to curse when we fouled them; but after I had picked up the blade of a broken oar, we kept a better course, and had no more collisions.

"We must get as far down as we can before the tide turns," Mayence explained; and we paddled our best till in the broad reach a little below Greenwich, we met a flotilla of torpedo-boats. Half dead with fatigue, blistered all over by the oil which had saved our lives at the expense of our skins, we were hauled aboard the first, and stowed in the narrow quarters below, already crowded with refugees, whilst the boats steamed into the smoky pall to rescue all they might, and when they were loaded, dropped down river and decanted us into the cruisers, battleships, and liners anchored about Tilbury.

All night the work went on, and all night and for many days thereafter London blazed unchecked. Of a forlorn hope of blue-jackets who went ashore with the intention of blowing up buildings to stop its progress, only two returned, and by the end of a week a great part of the Empire city lay in ruins.

On the night of our rescue, our cruiser set out in company with a fleet of all kinds of vessels, and in the early morning we were landed at Yarmouth, which for the moment was out of the danger zone, and thence we went by train to Glasgow, where I had some friends. The journey took over two days, so you may guess the congestion and confusion that reigned everywhere. I believe that the Norfolk Broads, the Fen country, and many sheltered bays and estuaries grew populous, thousands of people returning to the primitive style of lake dwellings, and building themselves huts upon piles or rafts.

But the most part believed only in flight, and the roads were black with fugitive multitudes who could find no place on the over-burdened railroads; if the ants had followed up their first onslaught with the speed of which they were capable, I think it probable that the whole island would have been depopulated.

Perhaps the burning of London disconcerted them, or they had the strategical sense to reduce the country in their rear before going further; at all events, they made no move northward for over a week, but during that time overran the country to the south of a line between the Thames and the Severn estuary. methodically slaughtering flocks, herds, and those unfortunates who had not escaped over Channel or fortified themselves in some such fashion as we had done.

Then they flooded northward, but by that the country had been cleared before them, and at the Avon-Welland line they were brought to a full stop for a while. Every bridge was defended, and along the banks and in the gap about Naseby, where once a very different battle had been fought, hundreds of fire-engines pumping blazing petroleum went into action, and thousands of men fought right gallantly with hand-pumps and squirts. Surely it was the strangest battle that the world had seen, bloodless but deadly, so potent being the poison, that to be stung meant death before cautery or antidote could be used. For days it continued, the ants tunnelling beneath the rivers' beds at many points, emerging oftentimes amongst thickets or coverts far in the rear of the firing line, and there, ringed about by the reserves, to be driven to earth again.

Across the country from sea to sea was stretched a broad band of fire-scoured earth, miles wide, and by this frontier the invasion is for the moment stayed, at the price of constant, unremitting vigilance, though none knows what the future has in store. Even the most optimistic of our experts, Professor Guy Durham, is gloomy.

"Our real knowledge of the earth's crust is small," he remarks in his report, "and a poor mile the limit of our shafts. What fissures, crevices, caverns, lie beneath us we know not at all, but it may very well be that, in the four thousand miles from surface to centre, many such occur. London, it is surmised, lies in part above a great subterranean lake, and it requires but a small effort to imagine such regions inhabited."

He goes on to details of our enemy's anatomy: *F. Horribilis*, as it has been dubbed, is in many respects entirely different from and vastly superior to its sun-loving brother, having a marvellously complex brain, excellent smelling apparatus, and, a somewhat unusual endowment for a subterranean creature, well developed eyes. In fact, the thing is altogether a super-ant, and he comes to a conclusion not hard to credit under the circumstances:

"I have no hesitation in announcing my conviction that *Horribilis* is an intellectual, a rational creature, able to plan, to reason, and, as we have so terribly experienced, to act in combination. I am of opinion that their aggression is a deliberate attack upon human supremacy, intolerable though such a suggestion may be to our self-satisfaction; but, taking into consideration their means of offence, their proved skill as miners, and the immense fecundity of such allied species as we know, I am forced to the forlorn conclusion that mankind may, at no very distant date, be compelled to struggle hard for very existence. And, lest we grow over-confident in our present defences, I am bound to point out that, if analogy holds good, our feeble barriers of fire and water may presently be passed, if not underground, then by the path of the air. Both the male and female of the ant, at one period of their lives, *are winged!*"

DAGON

H. P. Lovecraft

Howard Phillips Lovecraft (1890–1937) would be astonished at his popularity today. During his short and somewhat reclusive life the majority of his work was published either in amateur magazines (in the decade before science-fiction fanzines began to appear) or in the pulp magazines, most notably Weird Tales. *He had no pretension to establishing a career as a professional writer preferring instead to promote the role of an anachronistic Yankee Gentleman—he had a penchant for Regency phraseology and spelling. Even when he emerged from this in his final years he still produced material which magazine editors found too long and adjectivally extreme, even though it was his very use of language which endeared him to his readers and later ensured his literary immortality. He is best remembered for the creation of a cycle of stories, later called the Cthulhu Mythos, which has as background a pantheon of ancient beings, the Great Old Ones, who once dominated Earth and to whom human beings have little if any relevance. Unfortunately for humans if they encounter any aspect of the Great Old Ones, notably Cthulhu, it is likely to drive them insane. The first story that Lovecraft wrote to explore this concept was "The Call of Cthulhu" (1928) and it was further developed in "The Dunwich Horror" (1929), "The Whisperer in Darkness" (1931), "At the Mountains of Madness" (1936, though written in 1931),* The Shadow over Innsmouth *(1936, also written 1931) and "The Shadow Out of Time" (1936). Other stories reflect different aspects of the Mythos including the following early story, published during Lovecraft's amateur-press days in 1919.*

I AM WRITING THIS UNDER AN APPRECIABLE MENTAL STRAIN, since by tonight I shall be no more. Penniless, and at the end of my supply of the drug which alone makes life endurable, I can bear the torture no longer; and shall cast myself from this garret window into the squalid street below. Do not think from my slavery to morphine that I am a weakling or a degenerate. When you have read these hastily scrawled pages you may guess, though never fully realize, why it is that I must have forgetfulness or death.

It was in one of the most open and least frequented parts of the broad Pacific that the packet of which I was supercargo fell a victim to the German sea-raider. The great war was then at its very beginning, and the ocean forces of the Hun had not completely sunk to their later degradation; so that our vessel was made a legitimate prize, whilst we of her crew were treated with all the fairness and consideration due us as naval prisoners. So liberal, indeed, was the discipline of our captors, that five days after we were taken I managed to escape alone in a small boat with water and provisions for a good length of time.

When I finally found myself adrift and free, I had but little idea of my surroundings. Never a competent navigator, I could only guess vaguely by the sun and stars that I was somewhat south of the equator. Of the longitude I knew nothing, and no island or coast-line was in sight. The weather kept fair, and for uncounted days I drifted aimlessly beneath the scorching sun; waiting either for some passing ship, or to be cast on the shores of some habitable land. But neither ship nor land appeared, and

I began to despair in my solitude upon the heaving vastnesses of unbroken blue.

The change happened whilst I slept. Its details I shall never know; for my slumber, though troubled and dream-infested, was continuous. When at last I awaked, it was to discover myself half sucked into a slimy expanse of hellish black mire which extended about me in monotonous undulations as far as I could see, and in which my boat lay grounded some distance away.

Though one might well imagine that my first sensation would be of wonder at so prodigious and unexpected a transformation of scenery, I was in reality more horrified than astonished; for there was in the air and in the rotting soil a sinister quality which chilled me to the very core. The region was putrid with the carcasses of decaying fish, and of other less describable things which I saw protruding from the nasty mud of the unending plain. Perhaps I should not hope to convey in mere words the unutterable hideousness that can dwell in absolute silence and barren immensity. There was nothing within hearing, and nothing in sight save a vast reach of black slime; yet the very completeness of the stillness and the homogeneity of the landscape oppressed me with a nauseating fear.

The sun was blazing down from a sky which seemed to me almost black in its cloudless cruelty; as though reflecting the inky marsh beneath my feet. As I crawled into the stranded boat I realized that only one theory could explain my position. Through some unprecedented volcanic upheaval, a portion of the ocean floor must have been thrown to the surface, exposing regions which for innumerable millions of years had lain hidden under unfathomable watery depths. So great was the extent of the new land which had risen beneath me, that I could not detect the faintest noise of the surging ocean, strain my ears as I might. Nor were there any sea-fowl to prey upon the dead things.

For several hours I sat thinking or brooding in the boat, which lay upon its side and afforded a slight shade as the sun moved across the heavens. As the day progressed, the ground lost some of its sticki-ness, and seemed likely to dry sufficiently for travelling purposes in a short time. That night I slept but little, and the next day I made for myself a pack containing food and water, preparatory to an overland journey in search of the vanished sea and possible rescue.

On the third morning I found the soil dry enough to walk upon with ease. The odour of the fish was maddening; but I was too much concerned with graver things to mind so slight an evil, and set out boldly for an unknown goal. All day I forged steadily westward, guided by a far-away hummock which rose higher than any other elevation on the rolling desert. That night I encamped, and on the following day still travelled toward the hummock, though that object seemed scarcely nearer than when I had first espied it. By the fourth evening I attained the base of the mound, which turned out to be much higher than it had appeared from a distance; an intervening valley setting it out in sharper relief from the general surface. Too weary to ascend, I slept in the shadow of the hill.

I know not why my dreams were so wild that night; but ere the waning and fantastically gibbous moon had risen far above the eastern plain, I was awake in a cold perspiration, determined to sleep no more. Such visions as I had experienced were too much for me to endure again. And in the glow of the moon I saw how unwise I had been to travel by day. Without the glare of the parching sun, my journey would have cost me less energy; indeed, I now felt quite able to perform the ascent which had deterred me at sunset. Picking up my pack, I started for the crest of the eminence.

I have said that the unbroken monotony of the rolling plain was a source of vague horror to me; but I think my horror was greater when I gained the summit of the mound and looked down the other side into an immeasurable pit or canyon, whose black recesses the moon had not yet soared high enough to illumine. I felt myself on the edge of the world; peering over the rim into a fathomless chaos of eternal night. Through my terror ran curious reminiscences of *Paradise Lost*, and of Satan's hideous climb through the unfashioned realms of darkness.

As the moon climbed higher in the sky, I began to see that the slopes of the valley were not quite so perpendicular as I had imagined. Ledges and outcroppings of rock afforded fairly easy foot-holds for a descent, whilst after a drop of a few hundred feet, the declivity became very gradual. Urged on by an impulse which I cannot definitely analyse, I scrambled with difficulty down the rocks and stood on the gentler slope beneath, gazing into the Stygian deeps where no light had yet penetrated.

All at once my attention was captured by a vast and singular object on the opposite slope, which rose steeply about an hundred yards ahead of me; an object that gleamed whitely in the newly bestowed rays of the ascending moon. That it was merely a gigantic piece of stone, I soon assured myself; but I was conscious of a distinct impression that its contour and position were not altogether the work of Nature. A closer scrutiny filled me with sensations I cannot express; for despite its enormous magnitude, and its position in an abyss which had yawned at the bottom of the sea since the world was young, I perceived beyond a doubt that the strange object was a well-shaped monolith whose massive bulk had known the workmanship and perhaps the worship of living and thinking creatures.

Dazed and frightened, yet not without a certain thrill of the scientist's or archaeologist's delight, I examined my surroundings more closely. The moon, now near the zenith, shone weirdly and vividly above the towering steeps that hemmed in the chasm, and revealed the fact that a far-flung body of water flowed at the bottom, winding out of sight in both directions, and almost lapping my feet as I stood on the slope. Across the chasm, the wavelets washed the base of the Cyclopean monolith; on whose surface I could now trace both inscriptions and crude sculptures. The writing was in a system of hieroglyphics unknown to me, and unlike anything I had ever seen in books; consisting for the most part of conventionalized aquatic symbols such as fishes, eels, octopi, crustaceans, molluscs, whales, and the like. Several characters obviously represented marine things which are unknown to the modern world, but whose decomposing forms I had observed on the ocean-risen plain.

It was the pictorial carving, however, that did most to hold me spellbound. Plainly visible across the intervening water on account of their enormous size, were an array of bas-reliefs whose subjects would have excited the envy of a Doré. I think that these things were supposed to depict men—at least, a certain sort of men; though the creatures were shewn disporting like fishes in the waters of some marine grotto, or paying homage at some monolithic shrine which appeared to be under the waves as well. Of their faces and forms I dare not speak in detail; for the mere remembrance makes me grow faint. Grotesque beyond the imagination of a Poe or a Bulwer, they were damnably human in general outline despite webbed hands and feet, shockingly wide and flabby lips, glassy, bulging eyes, and other features less pleasant to recall. Curiously enough, they seemed to have been chiselled badly out of proportion with their scenic background; for one of the creatures was shewn in the act of killing a whale represented as but little larger than himself. I remarked, as I say, their grotesqueness and strange size; but in a moment decided that they were merely the imaginary gods of some primitive fishing or seafaring tribe; some tribe whose last descendant had perished eras before the first ancestor of the Piltdown or Neanderthal Man was born. Awestruck at this unexpected glimpse into a past beyond the conception of the most daring anthropologist, I stood musing whilst the moon cast queer reflections on the silent channel before me.

Then suddenly I saw it. With only a slight churning to mark its rise to the surface, the thing slid into view above the dark waters. Vast, Polyphemus-like, and loathsome, it darted like a stupendous monster of nightmares to the monolith, about which it flung its gigantic scaly arms, the while it bowed its hideous head and gave vent to certain measured sounds. I think I went mad then.

Of my frantic ascent of the slope and cliff, and of my delirious journey back to the stranded boat, I remember little. I believe I sang a great deal, and laughed oddly when I was unable to sing. I have indistinct recollections of a great storm some time after I reached the boat; at any rate, I know that I heard peals of thunder and other tones which Nature utters only in her wildest moods.

When I came out of the shadows I was in a San Francisco hospital; brought thither by the captain of the American ship which had picked up my boat in mid-ocean. In my delirium I had said much, but found that my words had been given scant attention. Of any land upheaval in the Pacific, my rescuers knew nothing; nor did I deem it necessary to insist upon a thing which I knew they could not believe. Once I sought out a celebrated ethnologist, and amused him with peculiar questions regarding the ancient Philistine legend of Dagon, the Fish-God; but soon perceiving that he was hopelessly conventional, I did not press my inquiries.

It is at night, especially when the moon is gibbous and waning, that I see the thing. I tried morphine; but the drug has given only transient surcease, and has drawn me into its clutches as a hopeless slave. So now I am to end it all, having written a full account for the information or the contemptuous amusement of my fellow-men. Often I ask myself if it could not all have been a pure phantasm—a mere freak of fever as I lay sun-stricken and raving in the open boat after my escape from the German man-of-war. This I ask myself, but ever does there come before me a hideously vivid vision in reply. I cannot think of the deep sea without shuddering at the nameless things that may at this very moment be crawling and floundering on its slimy bed, worshipping their ancient stone idols and carving their own detestable likenesses on submarine obelisks of water-soaked granite. I dream of a day when they may rise above the billows to drag down in their reeking talons the remnants of puny, war-exhausted mankind—of a day when the land shall sink, and the dark ocean floor shall ascend amidst universal pandemonium.

The end is near. I hear a noise at the door, as of some immense slippery body lumbering against it. It shall not find me. God, *that hand!* The window! The window!

IN AMUNDSEN'S TENT

John Martin Leahy

Although never a prolific writer, John Martin Leahy (1886–1967) left his mark on the field of weird fiction with three novels and four short stories, of which the following, first published in Weird Tales *in 1928 is his best known, and probably most influential. It may well have had an impact on H. P. Lovecraft when writing "At the Mountains of Madness" and upon John W. Campbell, Jr., with his "Who Goes There?"*

Leahy lived his whole life in Washington State, USA, where he worked as a basket-maker for a packaging company. He also did some proofreading work for publishers, and though the appearance of new fiction had stopped by 1928, he may well have been planning a comeback in the early 1950s when he readied his 1927 serial, Drome, *for book publication. The novel explores a lost world discovered under Mount Rainer in Washington. Nothing more came from Leahy and it was not until 2015 that an American publisher produced a reprint of* Drome *along with the following story and its prequel, "The Living Death" (serial, 1924–5) as* Travels Through Lost Worlds. *Leahy's one other novel, "Draconda" (serial, 1923–4) was a heavily influenced lost-race adventure in the style of H. Rider Haggard. Had he written nothing else, though, "In Amundsen's Tent" would have been enough to keep his name alive.*

"Inside the tent, in a little bag, I left a letter, addressed to H.M. the King, giving information of what he (sic) had accomplished.... Besides this letter, I wrote a short epistle to Captain Scott, who, I assumed, would be the first to find the tent."

CAPTAIN AMUNDSEN: The South Pole.

"We have just arrived at this tent, 2 miles from our camp, therefore about 1½ miles from the pole. In the tent we find a record of five Norwegians having been here, as follows:

    Roald Amundsen
    Olav Olavson Bjaaland
    Hilmer Hanssen
    Sverre H. Hassel
    Oscar Wisting

16 DEC. 1911.

★   ★   ★

"Left a note to say I had visited the tent with companions."

CAPTAIN SCOTT: HIS LAST JOURNAL.

"TRAVELLERS," SAYS RICHARD A. PROCTOR, "ARE SOMEtimes said to tell marvellous stories; but it is a noteworthy fact that, in nine cases out of ten, the marvellous stories of travellers have been confirmed."

Certainly no traveller ever set down a more marvellous story than that of Robert Drumgold. This record I am at last giving to the world, with my humble apologies to the spirit of the hapless explorer for withholding it so long. But the truth is that Eastman, Dahlstrom and I thought it the work of a mind deranged; little wonder, forsooth, if his mind had given way, what with the fearful sufferings which he had gone through and the horror of that fate which was closing in upon him.

What was it, that *thing* (if thing it was) which came to him, the sole survivor of the party which had reached the Southern Pole, thrust itself into the tent and, issuing, left but the severed head of Drumgold there?

Our explanation at the time, and until recently, was that Drumgold had been set upon by his dogs and devoured. Why, though, the flesh had not been stripped from the head was to us an utter mystery. But that was only one of the many things that were utter mysteries.

But now we know—or feel certain—that this explanation was as far from the truth as that desolate, ice-mangled spot where he met his end is from the smiling, flower-spangled regions of the tropics.

Yes, we thought that the mind of poor Robert Drumgold had given way, that the horror in Amundsen's tent and that thing which came to Drumgold there in his own—we thought all was madness only. Hence our suppression of this part of the Drumgold manuscript. We feared that the publication of so extraordinary a record might cast a cloud of doubt upon the real achievements of the Sutherland expedition.

But of late our ideas and beliefs have undergone a change that is nothing less than a metamorphosis. This metamorphosis, it is scarcely necessary to say, was due to the startling discoveries made in the region of the Southern Pole by the late Captain Stanley Livingstone, as confirmed and extended by the expedition conducted by Darwin Frontenac. Captain Livingstone, we now learn, kept his real discovery, what with the doubts and derision which met him on his return to the world, a secret from every living soul but two—Darwin Frontenac and Bond McQuestion. It is but now, on the return of Frontenac, that we learn how truly wonderful and amazing were those discoveries made by the ill-starred captain. And yet, despite the success of the Frontenac expedition, it must be admitted that the mystery down there in the Antarctic is enhanced rather than dissipated. Darwin Frontenac and his companions saw much; but we know that there are things and beings down there that they did not see. The Antarctic—or, rather, part of it—has thus suddenly become the most interesting and certainly the most fearful area on this globe of ours.

So another marvellous story told—or, rather, only partly told— by a traveller has been confirmed. And here are Eastman and I preparing to go once more to the Antarctic to confirm, as we hope, another story—one eery and fearful as any ever conceived by any romanticist.

And to think that it was ourselves, Eastman, Dahlstrom and I, who made the discovery! Yes, it was we who entered the tent, found there the head of Robert Drumgold and the pages whereon he had scrawled his story of mystery and horror. To think that we stood there, in the very spot where it had been, and thought the story but as the baseless fabric of some madman's vision!

How vividly it all rises before me again—the white expanse, glaring, blinding in the untempered light of the Antarctic sun; the dogs straining in the harness, the cases on the sleds, long and black like coffins; our sudden halt as Eastman fetched up in his tracks, pointed and said, "Hello! What's that?"

A half-mile or so off to the left, some object broke the blinding white of the plains.

"*Nunatak*, I suppose," was my answer.

"Looks to me like a cairn or a tent," Dahlstrom said.

"How on earth," I queried, "could a tent have got down here in 87° 30' south? We are far from the route of either Amundsen or Scott."

"H'm," said Eastman, shoving his amber-coloured glasses up onto his forehead that he might get a better look, "I wonder. Jupiter Ammon, Nels," he added, glancing at Dahlstrom, "I believe that you are right."

"It certainly," Dahlstrom nodded, "looks like a cairn or a tent to me. I don't think it's a *nunatak*."

"Well," said I, "it would not be difficult to put it to the proof."

"And that, my hearties," exclaimed Eastman, "is just what we'll do! We'll soon see what it is—whether it is a cairn, a tent, or only a *nunatak*."

The next moment we were in motion, heading straight for that mysterious object there in the middle of the eternal desolation of snow and ice.

"Look there!" Eastman, who was leading the way, suddenly shouted. "See that? It *is* a tent!"

A few moments, and I saw that it was indeed so. But who had pitched it there? What were we to find within it?

I could never describe those thoughts and feelings which were ours as we approached that spot. The snow lay piled about the tent to a depth of four feet or more. Near by, a splintered ski protruded from the surface—and that was all.

And the stillness! The air, at the moment, was without the slightest movement. No sounds but those made by our movements, and those of the dogs, and our own breathing, broke that awful silence of death.

"Poor devils!" said Eastman at last. "One thing, they certainly pitched their tent well."

The tent was supported by a single pole, set in the middle. To this pole three guy-lines were fastened, one of them as taut as the day its stake had been driven into the surface. But this was not all: a half-dozen lines, or more, were attached to the sides of the tent. There it had stood for we knew not how long, bidding defiance to the fierce winds of that terrible region.

Dahlstrom and I each got a spade and began to remove the snow. The entrance we found unfastened but completely blocked by a couple of provision-cases (empty) and a piece of canvas. "How on earth," I exclaimed, "did those things get into that position?"

"The wind," said Dahlstrom. "And, if the entrance had not been blocked, there wouldn't have been any tent here now; the wind would have split and destroyed it long ago."

"H'm," mused Eastman. "The wind did it, Nels—blocked the place like that? I wonder."

The next moment we had cleared the entrance. I thrust my head through the opening. Strangely enough, very little snow had drifted in. The tent was dark green, a circumstance which rendered the light within somewhat weird and ghastly—or perhaps my imagination contributed not a little to that effect.

"What do you see, Bill?" asked Eastman. "What's inside?"

My answer was a cry, and the next instant I had sprung back from the entrance.

"What is it, Bill?" Eastman exclaimed. "Great heaven, what is it, man?"

"A head!" I told him.

"A head?"

"A human head!"

He and Dahlstrom stooped and peered in. "What is the meaning of this?" Eastman cried. "A severed human head!"

Dahlstrom dashed a mittened hand across his eyes.

"Are we dreaming?" he exclaimed.

"'Tis no dream, Nels," returned our leader. "I wish to heaven it was. A head! A human head!"

"Is there nothing more?" I asked.

"Nothing. No body, not even stripped bone—only that severed head. Could the dogs—"

"Yes?" queried Dahlstrom.

"Could the dogs have done this?"

"Dogs!" Dahlstrom said. "This is not the work of dogs."

We entered and stood looking down upon that grisly remnant of mortality.

"It wasn't dogs," said Dahlstrom.

"Not dogs?" Eastman queried. "What other explanation is there—except cannibalism?"

Cannibalism! A shudder went through my heart. I may as well say at once, however, that our discovery of a good supply of pemmican and biscuit on the sled, at that moment completely hidden by the snow, was to show us that that fearful explanation was not the true one. The dogs! That was it, that was the explanation—even though what the victim himself had set down told us a very different story. Yes, the explorer had been set upon by his dogs and devoured. But there were things that militated against that theory. Why had the animals left that head—in the frozen eyes (they were blue eyes) and upon the frozen features of which was a look of horror that sends a shudder through my very soul even now? Why, the head did not have even the mark of a single fang, though it appeared to have been *chewed* from the trunk. Dahlstrom, however, was of the opinion that it had been *hacked* off.

And there, in the man's story, in the story of Robert Drumgold, we found another mystery—a mystery as insoluble (if it was true) as the presence here of his severed head. There the story was, scrawled in lead-pencil across the pages of his journal. But what were we to make of a record—the concluding pages of it, that is—so strange and so dreadful?

But enough of this, of what we thought and of what we wondered. The journal itself lies before me, and I now proceed to set down the story of Robert Drumgold in his own words. Not a word, not a comma shall be deleted, inserted or changed.

Let it begin with his entry for January the 3rd, at the end of which day the little party was only fifteen miles (geographical) from the Pole.

Here it is.

Jan. 3.—Lat. of our camp 89° 45' 10". Only fifteen miles more, and the Pole is ours—unless Amundsen or Scott has beaten us to it, or both. But it will be ours just the same, even though the glory of discovery is found to be another's. What shall we find there?

All are in fine spirits. Even the dogs seem to know that this is the consummation of some great achievement. And a thing that is a mystery to us is the interest they have shown this day in the region before us. Did we halt, there they were gazing and gazing straight south and sometimes sniffing and sniffing. What does it mean?

Yes, in fine spirits all—dogs as well as we three men. Everything is auspicious. The weather for the last three days has been simply glorious. Not once, in this time, has the temperature been below minus 5. As I write this, the thermometer shows one degree above. The blue of the sky is like that of which painters dream, and, in that blue, tower cloud formations, violet-tinged in the shadows, that are beautiful beyond all description. If it were possible to forget the fact that nothing stands between ourselves and a horrible death save the meagre supply of food on the sleds, one could think he was in some fairyland—a glorious fairyland of white and blue and violet.

A fairyland? Why has that thought so often occurred to me? Why have I so often likened this desolate, terrible region to fairyland? Terrible? Yes, to human beings it is terrible—frightful beyond all words. But, though so unutterably terrible to men, it may not be so in reality. After all, are all things, even of this earth of ours, to say nothing of the universe, made for man—this being (a god-like spirit in the body of a quasi-ape) who, set in the midst of wonders, leers and slavers in madness and hate and wallows in the muck of a thousand lusts? May there not be other beings—yes, even on this very earth of ours—more wonderful—yes, and more terrible too—than he?

Heaven knows, more than once, in this desolation of snow and ice, I have seemed to feel their presence in the air about us—nameless entities, disembodied, *watching* things.

Little wonder, forsooth, that I have again and again thought of these strange words of one of America's greatest scientists, Alexander Winchell:

"Nor is incorporated rational existence conditioned on warm blood, nor on any temperature which does not change the forms of matter of which the organism may be composed. There may be intelligences corporealized after some concept not involving the processes of ingestion, assimilation and reproduction. Such bodies would not require daily food and warmth. They might be lost in the abysses of the ocean, or laid up on a stormy cliff through the tempests of an arctic winter, or plunged in a volcano for a hundred years, and yet retain consciousness and thought."

All this Winchell tells us is conceivable, and he adds:

"Bodies are merely the local fitting of intelligence to particular modifications of universal matter and force."

And these entities, nameless things whose presence I seem to feel at times—are they benignant beings or things more fearful than even the madness of the human brain ever has fashioned?

But, then, I must stop this. If Sutherland or Travers were to read what I have set down here, they would think that I was losing my senses or would declare me already insane. And yet, as there is a heaven above us, it seems that I do actually believe that this frightful place knows the presence of beings other than ourselves and our dogs—things which we cannot see but which are watching us.

Enough of this.

Only fifteen miles from the Pole. Now for a sleep and on to our goal in the morning. Morning! There is no morning here, but day unending. The sun now rides as high at midnight as it does at midday. Of course, there is a change in altitude, but it is so slight as to be imperceptible without an instrument.

But the Pole! Tomorrow the Pole! What will we find there? Only an unbroken expanse of white, or—

Jan. 4.—The mystery and horror of this day—oh, how could I ever set that down? Sometimes, so fearful were those hours through which we have just passed, I even find myself wondering if it wasn't all only a dream. A dream! I would to heaven that it had been but a dream! As for the end—I must keep such thoughts out of my head.

Got under way at an early hour. Weather more wondrous than ever. Sky an azure that would have sent a painter into ecstasies. Cloud-formations indescribably beautiful and grand. The going, however, was pretty difficult. The place a great plain stretching away with a monotonous uniformity of surface as far as the eye could reach. A plain never trod by human foot before? At length, when our dead reckoning showed that we were drawing near to the Pole, we had the answer to that. Then it was that the keen eyes of Travers detected some object rising above the blinding white of the snow.

On the instant Sutherland had thrust his amber glasses up onto his forehead and had his binoculars to his eyes.

"Cairn!" he exclaimed, and his voice sounded hollow and very strange. "A cairn or a—*tent*. Boys, they have beaten us to the Pole!"

He handed the glasses to Travers and leaned, as though a sudden weariness had settled upon him, against the provision-cases on his sled.

"Forestalled!" said he. "Forestalled!"

I felt very sorry for our brave leader in those, his moments of terrible disappointment, but for the life of me I did not know what to say. And so I said nothing.

At that moment a cloud concealed the sun, and the place where we stood was suddenly involved in a gloom that was deep and awful. So sudden and pronounced, indeed, was the change that we gazed about us with curious and wondering looks. Far off to the right and to the left, the plain blazed white and blinding. Soon, however, the last gleam of sunshine had vanished from off it. I raised my look up to the heavens. Here and there edges of cloud were touched as though with the light of wrathful golden fire. Even then, however, that light was fading. A few minutes, and the last angry gleam of the sun had vanished. The gloom seemed to deepen about us every moment. A curious haze was concealing the blue expanse of the sky overhead. There was not the slightest movement in the gloomy and weird atmosphere. The silence was heavy, awful, the silence of the abode of utter desolation and of death.

"What on earth are we in for now?" said Travers.

Sutherland moved from his sled and stood gazing about into the eerie gloom.

"Queer change, this!" said he. "It would have delighted the heart of Doré."

"It means a blizzard, most likely," I observed. "Hadn't we better make camp before it strikes us? No telling what a blizzard may be like in this awful spot."

"Blizzard?" said Sutherland. "I don't think it means a blizzard, Bob. No telling, though. Mighty queer change, certainly. And how different the place looks now, in this strange gloom! It is surely weird and terrible—that is, it certainly looks weird and terrible."

He turned his look to Travers.

"Well, Bill," he asked, "what did you make of it?"

He waved a hand in the direction of that mysterious object the sight of which had so suddenly brought us to a halt. I say in the direction of the object, for the thing itself was no longer to be seen.

"I believe it is a tent," Travers told him.

"Well," said our leader, "we can soon find out what it is—cairn or tent, for one or the other it must certainly be."

The next instant the heavy, awful silence was broken by the sharp crack of his whip.

"Mush on, you poor brutes!" he cried. "On we go to see what is over there. Here we are at the South Pole. Let us see who has beaten us to it."

But the dogs didn't want to go on, which did not surprise me at all, because, for some time now, they had been showing signs of some strange, inexplicable uneasiness. What had got into the creatures, anyway? For a time we puzzled over it; then we *knew*, though the explanation was still an utter mystery to us. They were *afraid*. Afraid? An inadequate word, indeed. It was fear, stark, terrible, that had entered the poor brutes. But whence had come this inexplicable fear? That also we soon knew. The thing they feared, whatever it was, was in that very direction in which we were headed!

A cairn, a tent? What did this thing mean?

"What on earth is the matter with the critters?" exclaimed Travers. "Can it be that—"

"It's for us to find out what it means," said Sutherland.

Again we got in motion. The place was still involved in that strange, weird gloom. The silence was still that awful silence of desolation and of death.

Slowly but steadily we moved forward, urging on the reluctant, fearful animals with our whips.

At last Sutherland, who was leading, cried out that he saw it. He halted, peering forward into the gloom, and we urged our teams up alongside his.

"It must be a tent," he said.

And a tent we found it to be—a small one supported by a single bamboo and well guyed in all directions. Made of drab-coloured gabardine. To the top of the tent-pole another had been lashed. From this, motionless in the still air, hung the remains of a small Norwegian flag and, underneath it, a pennant with the word "Fram" upon it. Amundsen's tent!

What should we find inside it? And what was the meaning of that—the strange way it bulged out on one side?

The entrance was securely laced. The tent, it was certain, had been here for a year, all through the long Antarctic night; and yet, to our astonishment, but little snow was piled up about it, and most of this was drift. The explanation of this must, I suppose, be that, before the air currents have reached the Pole, almost all the snow has been deposited from them.

For some minutes we just stood there, and many, and some of them dreadful enough, were the thoughts that came and went. Through the long Antarctic night! What strange things this tent could tell us had it been vouchsafed the power of words! But strange things it might tell us, nevertheless. For what was that inside, making the tent bulge out in so unaccountable a manner? I moved forward to feel of it there with my mittened hand, but, for some reason that I cannot explain, of a sudden I drew back. At that instant one of the dogs whined—the sound so strange and the terror of the animal so unmistakable that I shuddered and felt a chill pass through my heart. Others of the dogs began to whine in that mysterious manner, and all shrank back cowering from the tent.

"What does it mean?" said Travers, his voice sunk almost to a whisper. "Look at them. It is as though they are imploring us to—keep away."

"To keep away," echoed Sutherland, his look leaving the dogs and fixing itself once more on the tent.

"Their senses," said Travers, "are keener than ours. They already know what we can't know until we see it."

"See it!" Sutherland exclaimed. "I wonder. Boys, what are we going to see when we look into that tent? Poor fellows! They reached the Pole. But did they ever leave it? Are we going to find them in there dead?"

"Dead?" said Travers with a sudden start. "The dogs would never act that way if 'twas only a corpse inside. And, besides, if that theory was true, wouldn't the sleds be here to tell the story? Yet look around. The level uniformity of the place shows that no sled lies buried here."

"That is true," said our leader. "What *can* it mean? What *could* make that tent bulge out like that? Well, here is the mystery before us, and all we have to do is unlace the entrance and look inside to solve it."

He stepped to the entrance, followed by Travers and me, and began to unlace it. At that instant an icy current of air struck the place and the pennant above our heads flapped with a dull and ominous sound. One of the dogs, too, thrust his muzzle skyward, and a deep and long-drawn howl arose. And while the mournful, savage sound yet filled the air, a strange thing happened.

Through a sudden rent in that gloomy curtain of cloud, the sun sent a golden, awful light down upon the spot where we stood. It was but a shaft of light, only three or four hundred feet wide, though miles in length, and there we stood in the very middle of it, the plain on each side involved in that weird gloom, now denser and more eery than ever in contrast to that sword of golden fire which thus so suddenly had been flung down across the snow.

"Queer place this!" said Travers. "Just like a beam lying across a stage in a theatre."

Travers' simile was a most apposite one, more so than he perhaps ever dreamed himself. That place was a stage, our light the wrathful fire of the Antarctic sun, ourselves the actors in a scene stranger than any ever beheld in the mimic world.

For some moments, so strange was it all, we stood there looking about us in wonder and perhaps each one of us in not a little secret awe.

"Queer place, all right!" said Sutherland. "But—"

He laughed a hollow, sardonic laugh. Up above, the pennant flapped and flapped again, the sound of it hollow and ghostly. Again rose the long-drawn, mournful, fiercely sad howl of the wolf-dog.

"But," added our leader, "we don't want to be imagining things, you know."

"Of course not," said Travers.

"Of course not," I echoed.

A little space, and the entrance was open and Sutherland had thrust head and shoulders through it.

I don't know how long it was that he stood there like that. Perhaps it was only a few seconds, but to Travers and me it seemed rather long.

"What is it?" Travers exclaimed at last. "What do you see?"

The answer was a scream—the horror of that sound I can never forget—and Sutherland came staggering back and, I believe, would have fallen had we not sprung and caught him.

"What is it?" cried Travers. "In God's name, Sutherland, what did you see?"

Sutherland beat the side of his head with his hand, and his look was wild and horrible.

"What is it?" I exclaimed. "What did you see in there?"

"I can't tell you—I can't! Oh, oh, I wish that I had never seen it! Don't look! Boys, don't look into that tent—unless you are prepared to welcome madness, or worse."

"What gibberish is this?" Travers demanded, gazing at our leader in utter astonishment. "Come, come, man! Buck up. Get a grip on yourself. Let's have an end to this nonsense. Why should the sight of a dead man, or dead men, affect you in this mad fashion?"

"Dead men?" Sutherland laughed, the sound wild, maniacal.

"Dead men? If 'twas only that! Is this the South Pole? Is this the earth, or are we in a nightmare on some other planet?"

"For heaven's sake," cried Travers, "come out of it! What's got into you? Don't let your nerves go like this."

"A dead man?" queried our leader, peering into the face of Travers. "You think I saw a dead man? I wish it was only a dead man. Thank God, you two didn't look!"

On the instant Travers had turned.

"Well," said he, "I am going to look!"

But Sutherland cried out, screamed, sprang after him and tried to drag him back.

"It would mean horror and perhaps madness!" cried Sutherland. "Look at me. Do you want to be like me?"

"No!" Travers returned. "But I am going to see what is in that tent."

He struggled to break free, but Sutherland clung to him in a frenzy of madness.

"Help me, Bob!" Sutherland cried.

"Hold him back, or we'll all go insane."

But I did not help him to hold Travers back, for, of course, it was my belief that Sutherland himself was insane. Nor did Sutherland hold Travers. With a sudden wrench, Travers was free. The next instant he had thrust head and shoulders through the entrance of the tent.

Sutherland groaned and watched him with eyes full of unutterable horror.

I moved toward the entrance, but Sutherland flung himself at me with such violence that I was sent over into the snow. I sprang to my feet full of anger and amazement.

"What the hell," I cried, "is the matter with you, anyway? Have you gone crazy?"

The answer was a groan, horrible beyond all words of man, but that sound did not come from Sutherland. I turned. Travers was staggering away from the entrance, a hand pressed over his face, sounds that I could never describe breaking from deep in his throat. Sutherland, as the man came staggering up to him, thrust forth an arm and touched Travers lightly on the shoulder. The effect was instantaneous and frightful. Travers sprang aside as though a serpent had struck at him, screamed and screamed yet again.

"There, there!" said Sutherland gently. "I told you not to do it. I tried to make you understand, but—but you thought that I was mad."

"It can't belong to this earth!" moaned Travers.

"No," said Sutherland. "That horror was never born on this planet of ours. And the inhabitants of earth, though they do not know it, can thank God Almighty for that."

"But it is *here*!" Travers exclaimed. "How did it come to this awful place? And where did it come from?"

"Well," consoled Sutherland, "it is dead—it must be dead."

"Dead? How do we know that it is dead? And don't forget this: it didn't come here alone!"

Sutherland started. At that moment the sunlight vanished, and everything was once more involved in gloom.

"What do you mean?" Sutherland asked. "Not alone? How do you know that it did not come alone?"

"Why, it is there *inside* the tent; but the entrance was laced—from the *outside*!"

"Fool, fool that I am!" cried Sutherland a little fiercely. "Why didn't I think of that? Not alone! Of course it was not alone!"

He gazed about into the gloom, and I knew the nameless fear and horror that chilled him to the very heart, for they chilled me to my very own.

Of a sudden arose again that mournful, savage howl of the wolf-dog. We three men started as though it was the voice of some ghoul from hell's most dreadful corner.

"Shut up, you brute!" gritted Travers. "Shut up, or I'll brain you!"

Whether it was Travers' threat or not, I do not know; but that howl sank, ceased almost on the instant. Again the silence of desolation and of death lay upon the spot. But above the tent the pennant stirred and rustled, the sound of it, I thought, like the slithering of some repulsive serpent.

"What did you see in there?" I asked them.

"Bob—Bob," said Sutherland, "don't ask us that."

"The thing itself," said I, turning, "can't be any worse than this mystery and nightmare of imagination."

But the two of them threw themselves before me and barred my way.

"No!" said Sutherland firmly. "You must not look into that tent, Bob. You must not see that—that—I don't know what to call it. Trust us; believe us, Bob! 'Tis for your sake that we say that you must not do it. We, Travers and I, can never be the same men again—the brains, the souls of us can never be what they were before we saw *that*!"

"Very well," I acquiesced. "I can't help saying, though, that the whole thing seems to me like the dream of a madman."

"That," said Sutherland, "is a small matter indeed. Insane? Believe that it is the dream of a madman. Believe that we are insane. Believe that you are insane yourself. Believe anything you like. Only *don't look!*"

"Very well," I told them. "I won't look. I give in. You two have made a coward of me."

"A coward?" said Sutherland. "Don't talk nonsense, Bob. There are some things that a man should never know; there are some things that a man should never see; that horror there in Amundsen's tent is—both!"

"But you said that it is dead."

Travers groaned. Sutherland laughed a little wildly.

"Trust us," said the latter; "believe us, Bob. 'Tis for your sake, not for our own. For that is too late now. We have seen it, and you have not."

For some minutes we stood there by the tent, in that weird gloom, then turned to leave the cursed spot. I said that undoubtedly Amundsen had left some records inside, that possibly Scott had reached the Pole, and visited the tent, and that we ought to secure any such mementoes. Sutherland and Travers nodded, but each declared that he would not put his head through the entrance again for all the wealth of Ormus and of Ind—or words to that effect. We must, they said, get away from the awful place—get back to the world of men with our fearful message.

"You won't tell me what you saw," I said, "and yet you want to get back so that you can tell it to the world."

"We aren't going to tell the world what we saw," answered Sutherland. "In the first place, we couldn't, and, in the second place, if we could, not a living soul would believe us. But we can warn people, for that thing in there did not come alone. Where is the other one—or the others?"

"Dead, too, let us hope!" I exclaimed.

"Amen!" said Sutherland. "But maybe, as Bill says, it isn't dead. Probably—"

Sutherland paused, and a wild, indescribable look came into his eyes.

"Maybe it—*can't die!*"

"Probably," said I nonchalantly, yet with secret disgust and with poignant sorrow.

What was the use? What good would it do to try to reason with a couple of madmen? Yes, we must get away from this spot, or they would have me insane, too. And the long road back? Could we ever make it now? And what *had* they seen? What unimaginable horror was there behind that thin wall of gabardine? Well, whatever it was, it was real. Of that I could not entertain the slightest doubt. Real? Real enough to wreck, virtually instantaneously, the strong brains of two strong men. But—were my poor companions really mad, after all?

"Or maybe," Sutherland was saying, "the other one, or the others, went back to Venus or Mars or Sirius or Algol, or hell itself, or wherever they came from, to get more of their kind. If that is so, heaven have pity on poor humanity! And, if it or they are still here on this earth, then sooner or later—it may be a dozen years, it may be a century—but sooner or later the world will know it, know it to its woe and to its horror. For they, if living, or if gone for others, will come again."

"I was thinking—" began Travers, his eyes fixed on the tent.

"Yes?" Sutherland queried.

"—that," Travers told him, "it might be a good plan to empty the rifle into that thing. Maybe it isn't dead; maybe it can't die—maybe it only *changes*. Probably it is just hibernating, so to speak."

"If so," I laughed, "it will probably hibernate till doomsday."

But neither one of my companions laughed.

"Or," said Travers, "it may be a demon, a ghost materialized. I can't say incarnated."

"A ghost materialized!" I exclaimed. "Well, may not every man or woman be just that? Heaven knows, many a one acts like a demon or a fiend incarnate."

"They may be," nodded Sutherland. "But that hypothesis doesn't help us any here."

"It may help things some," said Travers, starting toward his sled.

A moment or two, and he had got out the rifle.

"I thought," said he, "that nothing could ever take me back to that entrance. But the hope that I may—"

Sutherland groaned.

"It isn't earthly, Bill," he said hoarsely. "It's a nightmare. I think we had better go now."

Travers was going—straight toward the tent.

"Come back, Bill!" groaned Sutherland. "Come back! Let us go while we can."

But Travers did not come back. Slowly he moved forward, rifle thrust out before him, finger on the trigger. He reached the tent, hesitated a moment, then thrust the rifle-barrel through. As fast as he could work trigger and lever, he emptied the weapon into the tent—into that horror inside it.

He whirled and came back as though in fear the tent was about to spew forth behind him all the legions of foulest hell.

What was that? The blood seemed to freeze in my veins and heart as there arose from out the tent a sound—a sound low and throbbing—a sound that no man ever had heard on this earth—one that I hope no man will ever hear again.

A panic, a madness seized upon us, upon men and dogs alike, and away we fled from that cursed place.

The sound ceased. But again we heard it. It was more fearful, more unearthly, soul-maddening, hellish than before.

"Look!" cried Sutherland. "Oh, my God, *look at that!*"

The tent was barely visible now. A moment or two, and the curtain of gloom would conceal it. At first I could not imagine what had made Sutherland cry out like that. Then I saw it, in that very moment before the gloom hid it from view. The tent was moving! It swayed, jerked like some shapeless monster in the throes of death, like some nameless thing seen in the horror of nightmare or limned on the brain of utter madness itself.

And that is what happened there; that is what we saw. I have set it down at some length and to the best of my ability under the truly awful circumstances in which I am placed. In these hastily scrawled pages is recorded an experience that, I believe, is not surpassed by the wildest to be found in the pages of the most imaginative romanticist. Whether the record is destined ever to reach the world, ever to be scanned by the eye of another—only the future can answer that.

I will try to hope for the best. I cannot blink the fact, however, that things are pretty bad for us. It is not only this sinister, nameless mystery from which we are fleeing—though heaven knows that is horrible enough—but it is the *minds* of my companions. And, added to that, is the fear for my own. But there, I must get myself in hand. After all, as Sutherland said, I didn't see it. I must not give way. We must somehow get our story to the world, though we may have for our reward only the mockery of the world's unbelief, its scoffing—the world, against which is now moving, gathering, a menace more dreadful than any that ever moved in the fevered brain of any prophet of woe and blood and disaster.

We are a dozen miles or so from the Pole now. In that mad dash away from that tent of horror, we lost our bearings and for a time, I fear, went panicky. The strange, eery gloom denser than ever. Then came a fall of fine snow-crystals, which rendered things worse than ever. Just when about to give up in despair, chanced upon one of our beacons. This gave us our bearings, and we pressed on to this spot.

Travers has just thrust his head into the tent to tell us that he is sure he saw something moving off in the gloom. Something moving! This must be looked into.

(If Robert Drumgold could only have left as full a record of those days which followed as he had of that fearful 4th of January! No man can ever know what the three explorers went through in their struggle to escape that doom from which there was no escape—a doom the mystery and horror of which perhaps surpass in gruesomeness what the most dreadful Gothic imagination ever conceived in its utterest abandonment to delirium and madness.)

Jan. 5.—Travers *had* seen something, for we, the three of us, saw it again today. Was it that horror, that thing not of this earth, which they saw in Amundsen's tent? We don't know what it is. All we know is that it is something that moves. God have pity on us all—and on every man and woman and child on this earth of ours if this thing is what we fear!

6th.—Made 25 mi. today—20 yesterday. Did not see it today. *But heard it.* Seemed near—once, in fact, as though right over our heads. But that must have been imagination. Effect on dogs most terrible. Poor brutes! It is as horrible to them as it is to us. Sometimes I think even more. Why is it following us?

7th.—Two of dogs gone this morning. One or another of us on guard all "night". Nothing seen, not a sound heard, yet the animals have vanished. Did they desert us? We say that is what happened but each man of us knows that none of us believes it. Made 18 mi. Fear that Travers is going mad.

8th.—Travers gone! He took the watch last night at 12, relieving Sutherland. That was the last seen of Travers—the last that we shall ever see. No tracks—not a sign in the snow. Travers, poor Travers, gone! Who will be the next?

Jan. 9.—Saw it again! Why does it let us see it like this—sometimes? Is it that horror in Amundsen's tent? Sutherland declares that it is not—that it is something more hellish. But then S. is mad now—mad—mad—mad. If I wasn't sane, I could think that it all was only imagination. *But I saw it!*

Jan. 11.—Think it is the 11th but not sure. I can no longer be sure of anything—save that I am alone and that it is watching me. Don't know how I know, for I cannot see it. But I do know—it is watching me. It is always watching. And sometime it will come and get me—as it got Travers and Sutherland and half of the dogs.

Yes, today must be the 11th. For it was yesterday—surely it was only yesterday—that it took Sutherland. I didn't see it take him, for a fog had come up, and Sutherland—he would go on in the fog— was so slow in following that the vapour hid him from view. At last when he didn't come, I went back. But S. was gone—man, dogs, sled, everything was gone. Poor Sutherland! But then he was mad. Probably that was why it took him. Has it spared me because I am yet sane? S. had the rifle. Always he clung to that rifle—as though a bullet could save him from what we saw! My only weapon is an axe. But what good is an axe?

Jan. 13.—Maybe it is the 14th. I don't know. What does it matter? Saw it *three* times today. Each time it was closer. Dogs still whining about tent. There—that horrible hellish sound again. Dogs still now. That sound again. But I dare not look out. The axe.

Hours later. Can't write any more.

Silence. Voices—I seem to hear voices. But that sound again.

Coming nearer. At entrance now—now—

KING KONG

Draycott Dell & Edgar Wallace

Edgar Wallace (1875–1932) was one of Britain's most prolific, popular and best-selling writer of thrillers, crime fiction and adventure stories. In his day he was best known for one of his earliest books, The Four Just Men *(1905) and for the stories collected in* Sanders of the River *(1911) about the exploits of Commissioner Sanders in British West Africa. Statistics about Wallace's output vary but he wrote around 175 books, including 130 novels plus a thousand short stories and twenty-three plays. But his name is also inextricably linked with the classic monster movie* King Kong *even though in the end he had little to do with it and died long before the film was completed. The idea, really a passion, for the film was that of director Merian C. Cooper and he had already developed his own outline before Edgar Wallace was brought over from England to the RKO film studios to work on the script at the end of 1931. Cooper was still thinking through ideas and had not yet decided on the film's title—it was called* The Beast *at the time Wallace delivered his scenario on 5 January 1932. Wallace's work vanished into the whirlpool of material that Cooper was considering, and he heard no more. Unfortunately, soon after, Wallace caught a chill which developed into pneumonia and he died on 10 February. By the time* King Kong *was released in March 1933 the screenplay had been drafted by James Creelman and revised and completed by Ruth Rose. Just how much of Wallace's work remained is open to speculation, but it has been suggested that his idea of the sexual attraction between Kong and Ann Darrow (played by Fay Wray) which led to the classic final line that it was beauty killed the beast, had come from Wallace. Yet because of Wallace's selling power, his name remained associated with the film. When an abridgement of the novelization of the film, by Delos W. Lovelace, was serialized in* Mystery *(February–March 1933), prior to the film's release, the credit went to Wallace, calling it his "last and greatest creation". Somehow Draycott M. Dell (1888–1940), who was then editor of the British boys' magazine* Chums, *secured details of the story and produced this adaptation for* Boys' Magazine (28 October 1933).

A DANK SEA MIST ENVELOPED THE SS *Venture*, AS SHE NOSED through the grey waters like a baffled hound, seeking some elusive prey. To the men who peered expectantly over the rail, fantastic, swirling shapes seemed to appear out of the ghostly white vapour. Men asked each other why Captain Englehorn did not heave-to until the fog cleared: but even as they asked the question they knew the answer—knew that Englehorn was kept going by Carl Denham, the movie-picture man who headed the expedition.

Denham stood beside the skipper, his whole body tense, his keen ears strained to catch any sound. Somewhere in that mist lay an island, an island of mystery—if the story he had heard long ago were true.

"Can you hear anything?" he asked Englehorn.

"Nothing," came from the skipper.

He was listening for the sound of breakers which would tell him he was nearing the reef that surrounded Denham's mystery island. Only the thump of the engines, however, and the lapping of the water broke the ominous and threatening silence. Still Englehorn kept on.

The tension on board increased. Men seemed to lose control of themselves. Jack Driscoll, the young mate, stood at the rail, his knuckles showing white as he gripped the metal work.

Suddenly, he started away as he heard the skipper's voice boom through the fog.

"Let go!" Englehorn bellowed, and there came the rattle of the anchor chain running out. Englehorn dared not go on now, for there came to him out of the cloying fog a sound as of breakers. Breakers he knew must mean the reef—and beyond the reef lay—what?

"That's not only breakers!" Denham jerked out, staring into the mist. "That's drums!"

But Englehorn refused to up-anchor yet, despite all the movie man's arguing. The drumming increased, and it held a note of mystery and impending danger. Tense and pent, Denham was not afraid, however, even when his trained ears told him that the voice of the drums was angry. Were it not for the confounded fog, he would have landed to make a celluloid record of whatever was going on over there.

Suddenly the tension broke. The mist was lifting, Englehorn, gazing through his glasses, flung out an order for the anchor to be weighed. He was going to take a chance at last, and Denham, like a caged lion, could scarcely contain himself.

He, too, could see through the mist now; and what he saw confirmed the story told him, years before, by a Norwegian skipper. It was a story of a strange island, held in terror by some awful Thing that no white man had ever seen—something that the natives called—Kong.

"Can you see anybody on shore?" he snapped at the skipper.

"Not a thing!" was the answer.

"Funny they haven't spotted us," Denham said. "I'd have thought the whole population would be on the beach."

Before them the island showed a dark mass against the spectral grey-white of the mist. Gradually, above the island, loomed a huge sinister shape. It was a towering mountain formed, by some upheaval of nature, like a gigantic skull, adding to the sense of foreboding evil that was produced by the weird, nerve-racking throbbing of native drums.

"Come on, let's go!" shouted Denham.

Englehorn issued tense orders and the vessel moved cautiously forward, while he stood on his bridge, looking for the opening in the reef. Cruel, jagged rocks seemed to be greedy for the ship, but the captain found the open channel and skilfully steered into the calm waters beyond the reef.

Eager now, the men sprang to lower the boats, and within a few minutes were rowing madly towards the island, not a man of them but wondering what lay ahead of them. As they sprang ashore, almost before the boats beached, Denham rasped an order to one of the men.

"Watch your step, Briggs," he said. "There's enough trichloride in that case you've got to put a herd of hippos to sleep!"

"Sure," said Briggs, knowing the case contained gas bombs, though only Denham, the skipper and Driscoll knew why they had been brought.

Denham gathered the men together, and set off towards the village, Driscoll marched steadily beside Ann Darrow, the young actress brought out by Denham, who looked eager and keen. Driscoll was worried about her. It seemed that, with all this air of impending peril, Denham ought never to have brought a woman to the island.

At last they came to the edge of the village, and Denham peered through tall grasses. For a moment he stood there, silent and tense. Then, he turned, and spoke over his shoulder.

"Holy mackerel, come and have a look at this, skipper!" he breathed.

Wonderingly, Englehorn moved up to him. What he saw almost took away his breath. In a wide space, a large number of men dressed in gorilla skins were dancing with barbaric abandon to the thrum of the drums. In the centre was a young native girl, being decked with flowers. Flaring torches, held by scores of natives cast a lurid light on the wild scene. A great double-gateway was built into a massive wall on top of which stood a tremendous metal gong. All eyes were turned towards the gate, while the natives chanted ceaselessly, monotonously. From the fearful din the white men clearly heard one word:

"Kong! Kong! Kong!"

"Hear that?" Denham breathed at the captain, who nodded slowly. Englehorn knew that Denham's fantastic story of something mysterious was true after all. But what was the mystery? What lay beyond the wall?

"It sounds something like the language of the Nias Islanders," he muttered, listening intently to the shouted words. "I think—"

He stopped. Denham followed his gaze and saw a tall native, obviously a chief, marching down some steps from the wall towards the terror-stricken girl. Suddenly, Denham called in a hoarse whisper.

"Hey, you with the camera, come here!" In the excitement of watching things, he had forgotten his all-important work. Now he grabbed the camera to set it up, but at that moment the native chief stopped, leant forward and shouted in a loud voice. Only Englehorn, of all those white men knew what he said and he interpreted it for Denham.

"Stop! Strangers have come!"

Instantly the drums ceased, the dancers came to a standstill, and all natives looked in the direction in which the chief was pointing.

"Too late, I guess!" growled Denham. "They've seen us! No use trying to hide. Come out, everybody!"

When the whites emerged from the tall grass curtain, the attitude of the natives was fierce and menacing. Englehorn stepped boldly forward, however, and addressed the chief.

"Greetings!" he shouted. "We are friends... friends."

"We want no friends," the chief flung back at him. "Go!"

"Talk him out of that," Denham said. "Ask him what's going on, and what that girl's doing?"

Englehorn jerked out his questions. When he translated the reply, Denham stared incredulously.

"He says, the girl is a sacrifice to *Kong!*" Englehorn whispered.

At that moment, a native decorated with the grisly ornaments of a witch-doctor, leapt up to the chief. He shouted and waved his hands fiercely at the whites.

"He says the thing's finished, Denham," Englehorn said, "because strangers have seen it and—"

He broke off. The Chief, his eyes gleaming, suddenly pointed with his staff to where Ann Darrow stood, her golden hair gleaming in the firelight.

"He says he wants to buy the Golden Woman!" the skipper announced. "Says she's a—a gift for Kong!"

"Great Uncle Sam!" Denham gasped.

Things were getting fierce now, the natives were shuffling menacingly towards the white men. At the first hostile move, Jack Driscoll grabbed Ann and started off with her for the beach. Even Denham, foolhardy though he was, saw the wisdom of beating a retreat. He rapped out orders and the little company set off, Denham striding in their wake. He walked jauntily whistling gaily, and turning and laughing at the natives who were following.

Suddenly, the chief barked an order and the pursuit stopped, much to the movie man's relief. But—Carl Denham had no idea what was in the mind of that crafty savage!

Denham's appetite was whetted by what had happened. The story of the Norwegian skipper had received some confirmation. There *was* a mysterious Thing called Kong, to whom human sacrifices were apparently made. And Denham meant to get a film of that ceremony if it was humanly possible.

For the rest of the day and well into the night he sat with the captain and the mate, working out a plan to placate the natives next morning. Englehorn was mildly critical; Driscoll was definitely antagonistic; but in the end Denham won. It was past midnight, when he yawned and got up to look out of the chart-room window. From the dark blot that was the island, he saw lights flickering, as from hundreds of torches.

"Wonder what's up!" he said. "Wish I could take pictures by firelight. I'd sneak ashore and get a scene!"

"We're lucky to be all safe on board tonight," Englehorn growled, and at that moment a cry went up.

"All hands on deck—everybody on deck."

The three rushed from the chart-room, and cannoned into Charlie the Chinese cook. He was yelling excitedly, and in his hand he held a bracelet.

"Look, sir, me find on deck," he chattered at the skipper.

It was a native bracelet! That meant some of the natives had been on board! Driscoll, remembering the chief's offer to buy the Golden Woman, grasped the sinister meaning of it all, and rushed to Ann's cabin. It was empty and although a hurried search was made of the ship, there was no trace of Ann.

It could mean only one thing—she had been abducted by the natives! Englehorn rasped out orders; rifles were issued to the men, boats were lowered and within a few minutes the greater part of the company was rowing feverishly to the island. The insistent throbbing of drums became louder and louder, and the lights were moving and bobbing about like huge will-o"-the-wisps.

The men sprang from the boats almost before they grounded, and tore towards the village, dreading what they would find. In ape-like costumes savages danced wildly as others dragged Ann towards the great gateway in the wall. It was open now and just outside it stood an altar. Despite all her struggles the natives got Ann to the altar and lashed her to it. At a sign from the chief, standing on the great wall beside the enormous gong, the natives fell silent, the drums ceased.

"We call thee, Kong!" the chief's great voice boomed into the darkness, beyond the wall. "Oh, Mighty One, great Kong! Thy gift is here!"

Ann understood the meaning, if not the actual words and she screamed. Her cries were drowned in the great *boom-boom* of the gong as natives struck it, calling the mysterious Kong to come and accept his gift!

And Kong came! He loomed out of the darkness, roaring terrifically, and beating his great chest. Ann flung a horrified look at the gates as she heard the dreadful sounds, and she saw that they were closing.

Bereft of even the power to scream, Ann stared at Kong. He was a monstrous gorilla, towering fully fifty feet, dwarfing the trees and huts. He walked erect, stopping now and then to beat his enormous bare chest with mighty paws, and roar through awful gleaming teeth. He tore down trees, trod tall grasses underfoot as he made steadily towards the altar. When he reached it he stood, neither man nor beast, looking puzzled at the sacrifice set for him.

Suddenly, he tore away the ropes that held Ann, and took her in one of his paws, holding her as an ordinary man would hold a fragile china doll. He looked up at the torch-carrying natives on the wall and roaring at them, then turned to go away; and Jack Driscoll shouted madly.

He had just reached a window in the wall, having outdistanced his companions in the rush through the village. The natives, intent on their ceremony, had taken no heed of the white men. It was only when the sailors rushed to unbar the gate, that their presence was realized. The bar was drawn out and the gates opened. Driscoll rushed through with Denham and half their force at their heels.

By this time, however, Kong had disappeared. But the anxious little band pressed into the jungle following the broad path made by the passage of the tremendous lumbering gorilla. None but Driscoll knew what Monstrous Thing they were pursuing.

Dawn came and the little band of white men had not caught up with Kong. That they were on the right trail, however, was verified by the sudden, startled exclamation of one of the sailors.

"Get a load of that foot!" he breathed.

The others crowded round him and gazed in silent wonder at the huge imprint to which he pointed.

"Yeah, that's his track all right," Denham muttered at last. "Look at the size of it. Come on, fellows, and keep those guns cocked!"

On and on they went, following the enormous footprints until they came in sight of a mist-enshrouded swamp. Suddenly a harsh, ear-shattering roar brought the whole party to a halt. Had they overtaken Kong? Denham peered through the steamy atmosphere, then whispered hoarsely.

"Keep quiet! Give me one of those bombs!"

Then it was that the rest of the men saw what he had found. Right across their path was an enormous three-horned dinosaurus, and its tremendous body, ending in a spiked tail, was covered with horny scales. The brute scented them as Denham took the bomb. Like some nightmare demon the monster charged, and in sheer panic, the men fired, while Denham hurled the gas bomb.

It exploded right at the feet of the beast, which dropped ponderously to the swampy ground. The men, taking no chances, poured in another fusillade, but the brute was tenacious of life. It roared, rose up, tried to make for them, and Denham planted the death-shot in its head.

Once more the intrepid party pressed on to the swamp, filled with unknown and unnameable terrors. To traverse the swamp seemed impossible, until Driscoll, seeing a great many fallen trees, set the men to work making a raft.

Precious time was lost, but at last they were able to pole off. Hardly had the shore disappeared from view when they heard a strange, terrifying roar on their left. Startled they peered into the fog—and their horrified eyes saw a hideous head raising from the water, towering on top of a tall column that they knew was the neck of some other monster.

Denham knew what it was, but before he could tell his companions that it was a brontosaurus, they had fired. Whether they hit the brute or not they could not tell, for, with water pouring from its mouth like twin fountains, it curved its neck downwards and disappeared. A moment later, the raft rose into the air as if lifted by giant hands. Every man on board hurtled into the water, screaming as they went, fear clutching at their hearts.

It was every man for himself. None knew what happened to his companions, except those who saw the brontosaurus pick up another man here and there in its mouth and crush out his life. Some of the men found shallower water and floundered through it on to dry land. Denham and Driscoll were there and, weaponless, except for a revolver or two, they had no alternative but to go forward. They dared not risk returning through that awful swamp.

Driscoll forged ahead, the rest following close on his heels. They crowded up behind him as he came to a halt on the edge of a deep ravine, across which lay an age-old fallen tree. For a moment they hesitated and then Driscoll sprang on to the tree, the rest hard on his heels. Midway across the chasm, however, they stopped, frozen with horror at the sight before them.

Coming towards them from the other side was—Kong! His hands were empty, but as he lumbered up to them Driscoll heard Ann screaming somewhere behind the gorilla. The terrified men, seeing Kong for the first time, tried to back away. In the panic and confusion some of them were hurled into the depths. Driscoll saw a vine dangling down the side and he leapt for it, a split-second before Kong lifted the trunk and sent it, with its human burden, crashing into the abyss.

Horrified at the fate of his companions, yet unable to do anything for them, Driscoll sprang into a cave just below the edge of the ravine. He risked a look out and down and as he did so Kong's arm reached down groping into the cave for him. With fiercely drumming pulses, Driscoll sprang back out of reach.

Again and again Kong's great paw sought for him without success. His hand came so close, however, that Driscoll slashed at it with his hunting knife. Kong jerked the paw up and looked at it in surprise and anger.

At that moment Driscoll saw the vine in front of the cave tauten. Something or someone was coming up from the bottom of the ravine.

Driscoll thought it might be one of his companions, miraculously saved, and he dared to peer over in case he could help. It was no human being coming up the vine, however, but a gigantic polysauro, a mighty prehistoric reptile, and, at sight of it, Driscoll was almost rendered powerless to move.

With a supreme effort, however, he leapt back into the cave, as Kong's paw stabbed down at him. Kong above and the reptile below, he faced death in a horrible form. But he must not be killed.

He sprang for the vine, braving Kong's paw. He gripped the vine with one hand and began to saw at it with his knife, moving this way and that to avoid the groping hand of the monster above. After what seemed an eternity, the vine parted. The reptile crashed horribly, terrifyingly, as Driscoll backed into the cave away from Kong.

To his surprise, however, the giant gorilla's paw jerked away, and then he heard the heavy tread of the brute as it moved away from the ravine edge. And a new sound made itself heard above Kong's angry bark, and then came the din of battle. Kong was fighting—but what?

To Driscoll it seemed a heaven-sent chance to do something for Ann. He began to climb the vine, and, getting near the top, saw Kong and his foe—a prehistoric meat-eater. With teeth and claws they fought, biting, tearing, rending. A mighty blow from the meat-eater's long, powerful tail floored Kong. The giant ape-man was up in a flash and leapt on its enemy's back. Together they crashed into the tree, in which Ann had been left. Horror-stricken, Driscoll saw it topple, and heavy-foliaged branches pinned the girl to the ground.

The two battling brutes were between Driscoll and where Ann lay, and he could only peer at them, waiting for a chance to spring in to her. But the chance did not come. For suddenly Kong, seizing the meat-eater's jaws, wrenched them apart and let his mighty antagonist's body fall limply to the ground.

Kong stood up, beating his chest triumphantly, and looked round for Ann. He saw her, and, heaving away the branches that held her down, took her into his great paw and set off along the trail.

Driscoll, sick at heart, clawed his way on to the top of the ravine, and as he got there he heard Denham's voice calling him. A moment later Driscoll saw the movie man on the other side of the ravine.

"It didn't get you, then?" Driscoll gasped. His body was tense, and he was impatient to be going after Kong.

"No, I got to cover, the same as you did," Denham panted. "Think we're safe now?"

Driscoll did not answer that question. Instead he flung across the ravine the only words that seemed to fit the occasion.

"There are only two of us left alive to save the girl, Denham!"

"Well," the film man said, after a split-second of silence, "I can't get across to you now, so—"

"Don't want you to," snapped Jack. "You've got to go back and get some more bombs, while I stay on Kong's trail!"

Driscoll turned and tore down the trail that Kong had taken, while Denham stared helplessly after him.

Jack Driscoll could never afterwards describe that awful journey through the jungle. He was haunted by the bellowing of Kong, mingled now and again with the shrill screams of Ann Darrow. After a terrible, nerve-racking pursuit, he crept into a vast cathedral-like cave, moist and hot with steam from a boiling pool; and there he saw Kong with Ann Darrow.

Ann was on a ledge high up in the side of the cave and Kong was close by, fighting with a huge water snake, fully sixty feet long, coiled about his neck.

Hope ran high in Driscoll's heart: it looked as if the snake were going to strangle Kong. But the man-ape held the snake's head from his throat, and with amazing strength, dragged its coiled length from around his neck. He smashed the snake's head against a rock, and with a bellow of triumph, flung it from him; next moment he snatched Ann from the ledge and disappeared behind great rocks.

With wildly beating heart, Driscoll crawled after him, and came at last to another entrance to the cave. Peering out, Driscoll saw Kong squatting on the edge of a cliff, holding Ann in one hand, touching her pale, terror-stricken face with the other, stroking the golden hair.

Suddenly Kong put her down and looked around suspiciously. Ann screamed in terror as a pterodactyl, a great flying reptile, swooped for her and seized her in its claws. Kong whirled at Ann's screams, and moving with lightning-like rapidity, snatched the bird as it rose with her. He loosed Ann from its claws, tore the fighting, squawking reptile to bits, and flung the pieces over the cliff.

At last Driscoll saw his chance. Kong's back was to him and Ann, and Jack crawled to where the girl lay. She started to scream, but he clapped a hand over her mouth, lifted her to her feet and tore towards the edge of the cliff. He had seen the root-end of a vine there, and he slithered over the edge, seized the rope, took Ann on his shoulder, and a moment later they started sliding down the vine.

Kong turned to look for Ann. He missed her, and, roaring with fury, looked over the cliff. He saw the girl and, roaring, grabbed the rope and started to haul it up.

As he felt himself rising, Driscoll did the only thing possible. Below was water, and with a reassuring word to Ann, he let go of the vine.

Down, down they dropped, seemingly for an eternity. At last, with a terrific impact, they struck water, and sank deep beneath the surface. They came up again in a few moments, to find themselves in a great pool formed by a waterfall, now thundering behind them. Somehow, they managed to reach the land, and Driscoll got Ann out. Then, staggering, panting, they flung themselves into the jungle growth, with the roar of Kong sounding above the thunder of the falling waters.

On top of the great wall of the native village, men from the *Venture* stood, armed and watching. On the steps leading to the gates sat Denham and Captain Englehorn, waiting for Driscoll and Ann.

Suddenly, one of the sailors on the wall gave a great shout.

"Hey, look!" he bellowed, and there was a rush to the window. "Mr. Driscoll and the lady, they're coming back!"

They were there in time to see Driscoll carry Ann to the gates, which were opened, and then the fugitives were through.

"Jack, you got her!" shouted Denham, and as Driscoll set Ann down she collapsed.

"We'll have you back to the ship in no time," said the captain. "I—"

"Here, wait a minute," snapped Denham, as Driscoll was moving away, supporting Ann. "What about Kong?"

"What about him?" Driscoll jerked back.

"We've got those gas bombs," Denham shouted. "If we can capture Kong alive—"

"You're crazy," Driscoll flicked the words at him. "Besides, he's on a cliff where a whole army couldn't get at him!"

At that moment, out beyond the wall, there came a sound that struck terror in the hearts of all there: Kong was approaching! He was coming back—for Ann!

Denham roared the order for the gates to be closed. Some of the sailors rushed to where the great bar lay, ready to be moved into position when the gates were shut. Others bore on the gates themselves. A sailor on the wall brought his rifle-butt down on the great gong there, and from the village huts poured a horde of natives.

They raced to the gate and threw their weight upon it, closing it. On the wall, men shouted and fired rifles; but Kong came on. He reached the gate, thudded his great fists on it, pressed his weight against it. Even with the bar over, and the hordes of people pushing, the gates swayed inwards to his thrust.

The bar creaked, splintered, and men and women, white and black, streamed away in terror as the great bulk of Kong stood there between the gates, swinging them back with his vast paws. Then he entered—saw Ann, the Golden Woman. He tore down an obstructing hut and threw the wreckage away. He scooped up scurrying natives and hurled them from him.

"Hey, come back with those bombs!" Denham roared at the man who was carrying them; but Briggs had gone, stampeding with the crowd.

Kong charged at some natives on a staging, snatched first one, then another, smashed them, flung them away. He brought a great paw down on the staging and it scattered like a burst bundle of firewood. Fallen natives were crushed beneath his feet, and then Kong was off in pursuit of fleeing men and women.

The whites were swarming into their boats when Kong broke into view. He lumbered down upon them—but came to a coughing, choking halt as Denham hurled a gas-bomb. The bomb went off with a terrific crash at Kong's feet, and he leant back, as if to escape the rising fumes. Kong swayed as he tried to lift a great rock to hurl it at his tormentors, but he could not move it. He staggered again, tried to save himself, but crashed to the beach. He clawed weakly at the ground, trying to rise. But he failed, slumped heavily at full length, and lay still.

"Come on, men," Denham shouted. "He'll be out for hours. Send to the ship for anchor-chains and tools."

The wondering men gathered round him and Englehorn asked the wild-looking movie man what he reckoned he was going to do. Denham snapped the answer. He was going to build a raft and float him to the ship.

"Why," he exclaimed, "the whole world will pay to see this! He's always been King in his world, but we'll teach him—fear! In a few months it'll be up in lights on Broadway... Kong, the Eighth Wonder of the World!"

The incredible had happened. Kong—King Kong—had been subdued, had been brought from the distant South Seas. Thousands of New Yorkers were crowded in the great theatre Denham had rented to exhibit Kong!

"Ladies and gentlemen," said Denham, standing on the stage. "I am here tonight to tell you a very strange story, a story so strange that no one will believe it. But, ladies and gentlemen, seeing is believing, and we, my partners and I, have brought back the living proof of our adventure. I am going to show you the greatest thing you have ever beheld. Look at Kong... the Eighth Wonder of the World!"

People strained forward as the curtain began to rise. At sight of the Beast, chained to a massive steel beam and straining in his shackles, they gasped, spoke, laughed—and some of them wanted to scream.

"Ladies and gentlemen." Silence fell at the sound of Denham's voice. "Now I want to introduce you to Miss Ann Darrow, the bravest girl I have ever known." He took Ann's hand as she stepped up to him, eyes troubled, heart fluttering. "She has lived through an experience no other woman ever dreamed of. And now I want you to meet a very brave gentleman, Mr. John Driscoll!"

As a great roar of applause went up, Driscoll stepped beside Ann, and, at a sign from Denham, Press camera-men came on to the stage. This was showmanship: the papers would be mad over this thing—but not madder than Kong was, as he fought against his chains.

"Wait a minute," Denham cried to the camera-men. "Kong thinks you're attacking the girl."

The warning came too late. Driven to a mighty frenzy by the flashlights, the giant was roaring and struggling, pulling at his shackles. Suddenly, Kong broke one arm loose. With a mighty tug he got the other free, and reached down to tackle the chains at his waist and ankles. The stage cleared as by magic.

Then Kong was free. It seemed that in all that tumult he had had no eyes for any but Ann. He seemed to know the way she had gone. He lumbered into the wings, and found himself in the great foyer, outside which men and women were milling madly. Syrens were howling, and as Kong stepped out of the building, a car smashed into a pillar, its driver paralysed with fright. With a triumphant roar, King Kong started to climb the face of the building.

In a room high up the theatre building, Jack Driscoll was trying to comfort Ann.

"Now, now, it's all right. Don't worry," Jack soothed her. "I'm going to stay right here with you. Anyhow, you know, they're bound to get him and—"

Ann Darrow screamed, and Driscoll spun round—to see the face of Kong at the window. A long arm reached in, a great paw opened and shut—and Driscoll, seizing a chair, smashed it down on the paw. The chair broke into a hundred pieces and the paw struck Driscoll down.

Then it reached for the bed on which Ann was sitting, petrified with horror. It dragged the thing to the window, and Kong snatched the girl up, beginning at once to clamber down.

At sight of his descending figure the crowd broke and ran screaming. Then Kong reached earth: a king, it seemed, in a deserted kingdom. He was towering above an elevated railway. A train roared past him. He swatted at it, missed it, wrenched up the track in a mad fury. Another train came thundering, its headlight nearly blinding him. It swooped up the shattered track, toppled over, and Kong pounded the steel thing and smashed it, picked it up and hurled it from him, spilling men and women from it in a torrent.

And, inside a police station, Denham and Driscoll arrived there to consult the police as to what could be done, heard the voice of a radio announcer:

Kong is climbing the Empire State Building. He is still carrying Ann Darrow. That is all!

Finality… nothing could be done. Suddenly, however, Driscoll leapt to his feet with a great cry.

"Airplanes! If Kong should put Ann down, they might fly close enough to pick him off—"

But already the police officer was at the 'phone. Within a short while, four army 'planes were zooming around Kong, standing on the dome of the Empire Building. One of the machines swooped down on him, guns spewing leaden death. Uttering his awful, deafening cry Kong swatted at it as if it were a fly.

He missed and climbed from the flat roof on to the very top of the Dome. He waved his long arms up and out, and took a machine by the wing with one great paw—and then dropped it into the lighted abyss that was New York.

As the machine crashed to earth, another swooped and a hail of hot lead seared into the great ape's body. Kong clapped a paw to his wounded chest, took it away, looked at the blood on it, moved round a little and tried to snatch at another 'plane as it went past; then clapped a paw to his throat as bullets took him.

His lips curled back with pain. He felt his wounded chest, teetered on unsteady feet. He swayed, tried to save himself, failed, and dropped off the edge, to hit the ground with a crash that came up to the roof of the building as Driscoll opened a door there.

"Ann... Ann, hold on!" Driscoll yelled, climbing the ladder leading to the parapet beneath the Dome. Ann was there, on the edge, seeming as if she must roll over. In the nick of time he reached her.

"Are you—all—right?" he gasped. She clung fearfully to his arm and they looked down into the depths into which the Eighth Wonder of the World had found disaster.

THE MONSTER FROM NOWHERE

Nelson S. Bond

Nelson Slade Bond (1908–2006), who in his later years became a bookdealer and philatelist, spent around twenty years as a professional writer and in that period managed to produce a huge amount of science fiction and fantasy, sometimes humorous, often eccentric, but always polished. He established his reputation early on with "Mr. Mergenthwirker's Lobblies" (1937)—the title is typical of his light-hearted but sometimes freakish fiction—a story about a man with two invisible alien companions, which led to several sequels, a radio series and a television play. Bond enjoyed creating eccentric characters such as Pat Pending, Lancelot Biggs and Squaredeal Sam, and many of these stories are in the vogue of Thorne Smith and Lord Dunsany. Amongst his collections are Mr. Mergenthwirker's Lobblies *(1946),* The Thirty-First of February *(1949) and* Nightmares and Daydreams *(1958). From time to time Bond produced fiction that was more sinister and weird, as the following shows.*

Enough to think such things may be:
To say they are not or they are
Were folly…

ONE NICE THING ABOUT THE PRESS CLUB IS THAT YOU CAN get into almost any kind of wrangle you want. This night we were talking about things unusual. Jamieson of the *Dispatch* mentioned some crackpot he had heard of who thought he could walk through glass. Snipe Andrews of the *Morning Call* had a wild yarn about the black soul of Rhoderick Dhu, whom Nova Scotians claim still walks the moors near Antigonish. Then a guy named Joe brought up the subject of Ambrose Bierce's invisible beast.

You remember the story? About the diarist who was haunted and pursued by a gigantic thing which couldn't be seen? And who was finally devoured by it?

Well, we chewed the fat about that one for a while and Jamieson said the whole thing was fantastic; that total invisibility was impossible. The guy named Joe said Bierce was right; that several things *could* cause invisibility. A complete absence of light for one thing, he said. Or curvature of light waves. Or coloration in a wavelength beyond that of the human eye's visual scope.

Snipe Andrews said, "Nuts!" Winky Peters, who was getting a little tight, hiccoughed something to the effect that "There are more things in heaven and earth than are dreamt of in your philosophy—" and then got in a hell of a fuss with the bartender who said his name *wasn't* Horatio.

I said nothing, because I didn't know. Maybe that's the reason why this stranger, a few minutes later, moved over beside me and opened a conversation.

"You're Hawley, aren't you?" he asked.

"That's me," I agreed. "Len Hawley—chief errand boy and dirt scratcher-upper for the *Daily Blade*. You've got me, though, pal. Who are *you*?"

He smiled and said, "Let's go over in that corner, shall we? It's quieter over there."

That made it sound like a touch, but I liked something about this guy. Maybe it was his face. I like tough faces; the real McCoy, tanned by Old Sol instead of sunlamp rays. Maybe it was the straightness of his back, maybe the set of his shoulders. Or it could have been just the way he spoke. I don't know.

Anyway, I said, "Sure," and we moved to the corner table. He ordered and I ordered, and we just sat there for a moment, staring at each other. Finally he said, "Hawley, your memory isn't so good. We've met before."

"I meet 'em all," I told him. "Sometimes they're driving Black Marias, and sometimes they're in 'em. Mostly they're lying in the morgue, with a pretty white card tied to their big toe. Or, maybe... Hey!" I said, "You're not Ki Patterson who used to write for the Cincinnati *News*?"

He grinned then.

"No, but you're close. I'm Ki Patterson's brother, Burch."

"Burch Patterson!" I gasped. "But, hell... you're not going to get away with this." I climbed to my feet and started to shout to the fellows. "Hey, gang—"

"Don't, Len!" Patterson's voice was unexpectedly sharp. There was a note of anxiety in it, too. He grabbed my arm and pulled me back into my seat. "I have very good reasons for not wanting anyone to know I'm back... yet."

I said, "But, hell, Burch, you can't treat a bunch of newspapermen like this. These guys are your friends."

Now that he had told me who he was, I could recognize him. But the last time I had seen him—the only time I had ever met him, in fact—he had been dressed in khaki shirt and corduroy breeches, and worn an aviator's helmet. No wonder I hadn't known him in civies.

I remembered that night, two years ago, when he and his expedition had taken off from Roosevelt Field for their exploration trip to the Maratan Plateau in upper Peru. The primary purpose of the trip had been scientific research. The Maratan Plateau, as you undoubtedly know, is one of the many South American spots as yet unexplored. It was Burch Patterson's plan to study the region, incidentally paying expenses *à la* Frank Buck by "bringing back alive" whatever rare beasts city zoos would shell out for.

For a few weeks the expedition had maintained its contact with the civilized world. Then, abruptly... silence! A month... two months... passed. No word or sign from the explorers. The United States government sent notes to the Peruvian solons. Peru replied in smooth, diplomatic terms that intimated Uncle Sam might a damn sight better keep his wingding adventurers in his own backyard. A publicity-seeking aviatrix ballyhooed funds for a "relief flight"... but was forbidden the attempt when it was discovered she had already promised three different companies to endorse their gasoline.

The plight of the lost expedition was a nine-days' wonder. Then undeclared wars grabbed page one. And the National Air Registry scratched a thin blue line through the number of pilot Burchard Patterson and wrote after his name, "*Lost.*"

But now, here before me in the flesh, not lost at all but very much alive, was Burch Patterson.

I had so many questions to ask him that I began babbling like a greenhorn legman on his first assignment.

"When did you get back?" I fired at him. "Where's your crew? What happened? Did you reach the Plateau? And does anyone know you're—?"

He said, "Easy, Len. All in good time. I haven't told anyone I'm back yet for a very good reason. *Very* good! As for my men—" He stared at me sombrely—"They're dead, Len. All of them. Toland... Fletcher... Gainelle..."

I was quiet for a moment. The way he repeated the names was like the tolling of a church bell. Then I began thinking what a wow of a story this was. I could almost see my name bylining the yarn. I wanted to know the rest so bad I could taste it.

I said, "I'm sorry, Burch. Terribly sorry. But, tell me, what made you come here tonight? And why all the secrecy?"

"I came here tonight," he said, "searching for someone I could trust. I hoped no one would remember my face... for it *is* changed, you know. I have something to tell so great, so stupendous, that I hardly know how to present it to the world. Or even... if I should.

"I liked the way you kept out of that silly argument a few minutes ago—" He motioned to the bar, where a new wrangle was now in progress—"because you obviously had an open mind on the subject. I think you are the man whose help and advice I need."

I said, "Well, that's sure nice of you, Patterson. But I think you overrate me. I kept my yap shut just because I'm kind of dumb about scientific things. Ask me how many words to a column inch, or how many gangsters got knocked off in the last racket war, but—"

"You're the man I'm looking for. I don't want a man with a scientific mind. I need a man with good, sound common sense." He looked at his wrist watch. "Len, will you come out to my home with me?"

"When?"

"Now."

I said, "Jeepers, Burch, I've got to get up at seven tomorrow. I really shouldn't—"

He leaned over the table, stared at me intently. "Don't stall, Len. This is important. Will you?"

I told you I was snoopy. I stood up.

"My hat's in the cloak-room," I said. "Let's go."

Patterson's estate was in North Jersey. A rambling sort of place, some miles off the highway. It was easy to see how he could come home to it, open it up, and still not let anyone know he had returned. As we drove, he cleared up a few foggy points for me.

"I didn't return to the States on a regular liner. I had reasons for not doing so; reasons which you will understand in a short time.

"I charted a freighter, a junky little job, from an obscure Peruvian port. Pledged the captain to secrecy. He landed me and my... my cargo—" He stumbled on the word for a moment—"at a spot which I'm not at liberty to reveal. Then I came out here and opened up the house.

"That was just two days ago. I wired my brother, Ki, to come immediately. But he—"

"He's working in L. A.," I said.

"Yes. The soonest he could get here would be tonight. He may be at the house when we arrive. I hope so. I'd like to have two witnesses of that which I am going to show you."

He frowned. "Maybe I'm making a mistake, Len. It's the damnedest thing you ever heard of. Maybe I ought to call in some professor, too. But... I don't know. It's so utterly beyond credibility, I'd like you and Ki to advise me first."

I said, "Well, what the hell is it, Burch?" Then I suddenly remembered a motion picture I'd seen some years ago, a movie based on a story by H. G. Wells. "It's not a... a monster, is it?" I asked. "Some beast left over from prehistoric ages?"

"No, not exactly. At least, I can assure you of *this*... it is not a fossil, either living or dead. It's a thing entirely beyond man's wildest imaginings."

I leaned back and groaned. "I feel like a kid," I told him, "on Christmas eve. Step on it, guy."

There were lights in the house when we got there. As Burch had hoped, Ki Patterson had arrived from California. He heard us pull up the gravel lane and came to the door. There was a reunion scene, one of those back-clapping, how-are-you-old-fellow things. Then we went in.

"I found your note," Ki said, "and knew you'd be right back. I needn't tell you I'm tickled to death you're safe, Burch. But why all the secrecy?"

"That's what I asked him," I said. "But he's not giving out."

"It's something," Ki accused, "about the old workshop behind the house. I know that. I was snooping around back there and—"

Burch Patterson's face whitened. He clutched his brother's arm. "You didn't go inside?"

"No. The place was locked. Say—" Ki stared at his brother curiously—"are you feeling okay, Burch? Are you sure you're not—"

"You must be careful," said Burch Patterson. "You must be very,

very careful when you approach that shed. I am going to take you out there now. But you must stand exactly where I tell you to, and make no sudden moves."

He strode to a library table, took out three automatics. One he tucked into his own pocket; the others he handed to us. "I'm not sure," he said, "that these would be any good if... if anything happened. But it is the only protection we have. You *might* be lucky enough to hit a vulnerable spot."

"A vulnerable spot?" I said. "Then it *is* a beast?"

"Come," he said. "I shall show you."

He led the way to the workshop. It lay some yards behind and beyond the house, a big, lonesome sort of place, not quite as large as a barn, but plenty big. My first idea was that at some time it must have been used as a barn, for as we approached it I could catch that animal odour you associate with barns, stables, zoos. Only more so. It was a nasty, fetid, particularly offensive odour. You know how animals smell worse when they get excited? Or when they've been exercising a lot? Well, the place smelled like that.

I was nervous, and when I get nervous I invariably try to be funny. I said, "If they're horses you ought to curry them more often."

I saw a faint blur in the black before me. It was Ki's face. He said, "Not horses, Len. We've never kept horses on this estate."

Then we were at the door of the shed, and Burch was fumbling with a lock. I heard metal click, then the door creaking open. Patterson touched a switch. The sudden blaze of light made me blink.

"In here," said Burch. And warningly, "Stay close behind me!"

We crowded in. First Burch, then Ki, then me. As Ki passed through the door I felt his body stiffen, heard him gasp hoarsely. I peered over his shoulder—

—Then I, too, gasped.

The thing I saw was incredible. There were two uprights of steel, each about four inches in diameter, deeply imbedded in a solid steel plate which was secured to a massive concrete block. Each of these uprights was pierced, and through the eyelets ran a third steel rod which had been hammered down so that the horizontal bar was held firmly in place by the two uprights.

And on this horizontal rod was… a thing!

That is all I can call it. It had substance but it had no form. Or, to be more accurate, it had every form of which you can conceive. For like a huge black amoeba, or like a writhing chunk of amorphous matter, it changed.

Where the steel rod pierced this blob of thing was a clotted, brownish excrescence. This, I think, accounted for some of the animal odour. But not all of it. The whole shop was permeated with the musty scent.

The thing changed! As I watched, there seemed to be at one time a globular piece of matter twisting on the rod, an instant later the globe had turned into a triangle… then into something remotely resembling a cube.

It was constantly in motion, constantly in flux. But here is the curious part. It did not change shape slowly, as an amoeba, so that you could watch the sphere turn into an oblong, the oblong writhe into a formless blob of flesh. It made these changes instantaneously.

Ki Patterson cried, "Good God, Burch, what unholy thing is this?" and took a step forward past his brother's shoulder.

Burch shouted, "Back, you idiot!" and yanked at Ki's arm. Ki moved just in time. For as he quitted the spot to which he had advanced there appeared in the air right over that spot another mass of the same black stuff that was captured on the bar. A blob of shapeless, stinking matter that gaped like a huge mouth, then closed convulsively where Ki had stood a moment before.

And now the fragment on the rod was *really* moving. It changed shape so rapidly, twisted and wriggled with such determination, that there was no doubt whatsoever about the sentience governing it. And other similar blobs suddenly sprang into sight. A black pyramid struck the far wall of the shed, and trembling woodwork told that here was solid matter. An ebon sphere rose from nowhere to roll across the floor, stopping just short of us. Most weirdly of all, a shaft of black jolted down through the floor... and failed to break the flooring!

That's about all I remember of that visit, for Ki suddenly loosed a terrified yelp, turned and scrambled past me to the door. I take no medals for courage. He was four steps ahead of me at the portal, but I beat him to the house by a cool ten yards. Burch was the only calm one. He took time to lock the workshed door, then followed us.

But don't get the idea he was exactly calm, either. His face wasn't white, like Ki's, nor did his hand shake on the whisky-and-splash glass, like mine. But there was real fear in his eyes. *Real* fear, I mean.

The whisky was a big help. It brought my voice back. "Well, Burch," I said. "We've seen it. Now, what in hell did we see?"

"You have seen," said Burch Patterson soberly, "the thing that killed Toland and Fletcher and Gainelle."

"We found it," said Burch, "on the Maratan Plateau. For we did get there, you know. Yes. Even though our radio went bad on us just after we left Quiche, and we lost contact with the world. For a while we considered going into Lima for repairs, but Fletcher thought he could fix it once we were on solid ground, so we let it ride.

"We found a good, natural landing field on the Plateau and began our investigations." He brooded silently for a minute. Then, reluctantly, "The Maratan is even richer in palaeontological data than men have dared hope. But man must never try to go there again. Not until his knowledge is greater than it is today."

Ki said, "Why? That *thing* outside?"

"Yes. It is the gateway for that... and others like it.

"Some day I may tell you all about the marvels we saw on the Plateau. But now my story concerns only one: the one you have seen.

"Fletcher saw it first. We had left Gainelle tending camp and were making a field survey when we saw a bare patch in the jungle which surrounded our landing field. Fletcher trained his glasses on the spot, and before he even had time to adjust them properly he was crying, 'There's something funny over there. Take a look!'

"We all looked. And we saw... what you saw a few minutes ago. Huge, amorphous blobs of jet black which seemed to be of the earth, yet not quite of it. Sometimes these ever-changing fragments were suspended in air with no visible support. At other times they seemed to rest naturally enough on solid ground. But ever and ever again... they changed!

"Afire with curiosity, we went to the open spot. It was a mistake."

"A mistake?" I repeated.

"Yes. Fletcher lost his life... killed by his own curiosity. I need not tell you how he died. It was, you must believe me, horrible. Out of nowhere one of the jet blobs appeared before him. Then around him. Then he was gone."

"Gone?" exclaimed Ki. "You mean dead?"

"I mean gone. One second he was there; the next, both he and the *thing* which had snatched him had disappeared into thin air.

"Toland and I fled, panic stricken, back to camp. We told Gainelle what we had seen. Gainelle, a crack shot and a gallant sportsman, was incredulous; perhaps even doubtful of our sanity. At his insistence we armed and returned to the tiny glade.

"This time it was as if the *thing* expected us, for it did not await our attack. It attacked us. We had barely entered its domain when suddenly, all about us, were clots of this ever-changing black. I remember hearing Toland scream, high and thin, like a woman. I dimly recall hearing the booming cough of Gainelle's express rifle, and of firing myself. I remember thinking subconsciously that Gainelle was a crack shot. That he never missed anything he aimed at. But it didn't seem to matter. If you hit one of those fleshy blobs it bled a trifle… maybe. More likely than not it changed shape or disappeared entirely.

"It was a rout. We left Toland behind us on the plain, dead. A black triangular *thing* had slashed Gainelle from breast to groin. I managed to drag him half way out of the glade before he died in my arms. Then I was alone.

"I am not a good pilot under best conditions. Now I was frantic, crazed with fear. Somehow I managed to reach the 'plane. But in attempting to take off I cracked up. I must bear a charmed life. I was not injured myself, but the 'plane was ruined. My expedition, hardly started, was already at an end."

I was beginning to understand, now, why Burch Patterson had not wanted the world to know of his return. A tale as wild and fantastic as this would lead him to but one spot… the psychopathic ward. Had I not seen the *thing* there in the shed I would never have believed him myself. But as it was…

"And then?" I asked.

"I think there is a madness," said Burch, "which is braver than bravery. I think that form of insanity seized me then. All I could comprehend was that some *thing*, a *thing* that changed its shape, had killed my companions.

"I determined to capture that *thing* or die in the attempt. But first I had to sit down and figure out what it was."

Ki licked his lips. "And... and did you figure it out, Burch?"

"I think so. But the result of my reasoning is as fantastic as the *thing* itself. That is why I want the help and advice of you two. I will tell you what I think. Then you must say what is best to do."

I poured another drink all around. It wasn't my house or my liquor, but nobody seemed to mind. Ki and I waited for Burch to resume. Burch had picked up, and was now handling with a curiously abstracted air, a sheet of notepaper. As he began, he waved this before us.

"Can you conceive," he asked, "of a world of only two dimensions? A world which scientists might call 'Flat-land'? A world constructed like this piece of paper... on which might live creatures who could not even visualize a third dimension of depth?"

"Sure," said Ki. I wasn't so sure myself, but I said nothing.

"Very well. Look—" Burch busied himself with a pencil for an instant. "I draw on this sheet of paper a tiny man. He is a Flatlander. He can move forward or backward, up or down, but he can never move *out* of his world into the third dimension because he has no knowledge of a dimension rectangular to that in which he lives. He does not even dream of its existence."

I said, "I see what you mean. But what has that to do with—?"

"Wait, Len." Patterson suddenly struck the paper a blow with one finger, piercing it. He held the sheet up for our inspection. "Look at this. What do you see?"

"A sheet of paper," I said, "with a hole in it."

"Yes. But what does the *Flatlander* see?"

Ki looked excited. "I get it, Burch! He sees an unexpected, solid object appear before him... out of nowhere! If he walks around this object he discovers it to be crudely round."

"Exactly. Now if I push my finger farther through the hole—"

"The object expands."

"And if I bend it?"

"It changes its shape."

"And if I thrust another finger through Flatland—?"

"Another strangely shaped piece of solid matter materializes before the Flatlander!" Ki's eyes were widening by the moment. I didn't understand why. I said, "I told you I didn't have a scientific mind, Burch. What does all this mean?"

Burch said patiently, "I have merely been establishing a thought-pattern, Len, so you can grasp the next step of my reasoning. Forget the Flatlander now. Or, rather, try to think of us as being in his place.

"Would we not, to a creature whose natural habitat is a higher plane than ours, appear much the same sort of projection as the Flatlander is to us? Suppose a creature of this higher plane projected a portion of himself into our dimension as I projected my finger into Flatland. We would not be able to see all of him, just as the Flatlander could not see all of us. We would see only a tridimensional cross-section of him, as the Flatlander saw a bidimensional cross-section of us."

This time I got it. I gasped.

"Then you think that thing in the workshed is a cross-section of a creature from the—"

"Yes, Len. From the fourth dimension."

Patterson smiled wanly.

"That is the decision I reached on the Maratan Plateau. There confronted me the problem of capturing the thing. The answer eluded me for weeks. Finally I found it."

"It was—?" Ki was leaning forward breathlessly.

"The Flatlander," said Burch, "could not capture my finger, *ever*, by lassooing it. No matter how tight he drew his noose I could always withdraw my finger.

"But he *could* secure a portion of me by fastening me to his dimension. Thus—" He showed us how a pin laid flat in Flatland could pierce a small piece of skin. "Now, if this pin were bolted securely the finger thus prisoned could not be withdrawn.

"That was the principle on which I worked. But my task had just begun. It took months to effect the capture. I had to study from afar the amorphous black *thing* which was my quarry; try to form some concept of what incredible fourth dimensional beast would cast projections of that nature into the third.

"Finally I decided that one certain piece of black matter, occurring in a certain relationship to the changing whole, was a foot. How, it is not important to tell. It was, after all, theory coupled with guesswork.

"I constructed the shackle you have seen. Two uprights with a third that must pierce the *thing*, then lock upon it. I waited, then, many weeks. Finally there came a chance to spring my trap. And... it worked."

Ki asked, "And then?"

"The rest is a long and wearisome story. Somehow I found my way to a native village, there employed natives to drag my captive from the Plateau. We were handicapped by the fact that we could never get too near the trap. You see, it is a *limb* we have imprisoned. The head, with its eating apparatus or whatever it is, is still free. That is what tried to reach you, Ki, there in the shed.

"Anyway, we made an arduous trek to the coast. As I have told you, I chartered a vessel. The sailors hated and feared my cargo. The trip was not an easy one. But I was determined, and my determination bore fruit. So... here we are."

I said, "Yeah... here we are. Just like the man who grabbed a tiger by the tail, then couldn't let go. Now that you've got this *thing*, what are you going to do with it?"

"That's what I want *you* to tell *me*."

Ki's eyes were glowing. He said, "Good Lord, man, is there any question in your mind? Call in the scientists... the whole damned brigade of them. Show them this thing. You've got the marvel of the age on your hands!"

"And you, Len?"

"You want it straight?" I said. "Or do you want me to pull my punches?"

"Straight. That's why I asked you out here."

"Then get rid of it," I said. "Kill it. Set it on fire. Destroy it. I don't know just how you're going to do it, but I do know that's the thing to do.

"Oh, I know what you're thinking, Ki... so shut up! I'm a dope. Sure. I'm ignorant. Sure. I don't have the mind or the heart of a true scientist. Okay, you're right. But Burch said I had common sense... and I'm exercising it now. I say get rid of that damned thing before something happens. Something horrible that you will regret for the rest of your life."

Ki looked a little peeved. He said, "You're nuts, Len. The thing's tied down, isn't it? Damn it, man, you're the kind of guy who holds back the progress of the world. If you'd been alive in his day, you'd have voted to kill Galileo."

"If he'd trapped a monster like this," I retorted, "a monster that had already killed at least three men, I'd have voted just that way. I'm not superstitious, Burch. But I'm afraid. I'm afraid that when man starts monkeying with the unknown he gets beyond his depth. I say... kill it now!"

Burch looked at me anxiously.

"That's your last word, Len?"

"Absolutely my last," I said. I rose. "And to prove it, I'm going home now. I'm not going to write a damned word about what I've seen tonight. I don't care if this is the best story since the deluge, I'm not going to write it!"

Ki said, "You give me a pain in the neck, Len."

"Same to you," I told him, "only farther south. Goodnight, gents." And I left.

I kept my word. Though I had the mimsies all night, tossing and dreaming about that weird, changing black *thing*, I didn't put a word concerning it on paper. I half expected to hear from Burch Patterson some time during the next day. But I didn't. The following morning I saw why. The *Call* carried a front page blast, screaming to the astonished world the news that, "the missing explorer, Burch Patterson, has returned home," and that tonight there would be "a convocation of eminent scientists" at his home "to view some marvel brought back from the wilds of upper Peru."

All of which meant that brother Ki's arguments had proven more persuasive than mine. And that tonight there was to be a preview of that damned *thing*.

I was pretty sore about it. I thought the least they could have done was give *me* the news beat on the yarn. But there was no use crying over spilt milk. Anyway, I remembered that Ki's paper had a tie-up with the *Call*. It was only natural he should route the story that way.

Then I went down to the office, and Foster, the human buzzsaw who is our City Editor, waggled me to his desk.

"Hawley," he said, "I'm going to give you a chance to earn some of that forty per we're overpaying you. I want you to represent us tonight out at Patterson's home in Jersey. He's going to unveil something mysterious."

I said, "Who, me? Listen, chief, give it to Bill Reynolds, won't you? I've got some rewrites to do."

"What's the matter? New Jersey give you asthma?"

"Chief," I pleaded, "I can't cover this. I don't know anything about science or—"

"What do you mean... science?" Foster glared at me. "Do you know what this is all about?"

That stopped me. I didn't want the assignment, but if I ever admitted that I'd known about Patterson's changeable what-is-it and not beaten the *Call* to the streets with the story I would be scanning the want ads in fifteen seconds flat. So I gulped and said, "Okay, boss. I'll go."

Everybody and his brother was there that night. I recognized a professor of physics from Columbia, and the padwar of palaeontology from N. Y. U. Two greybeards from the Academy of Natural History were in a corner discussing something that ended in -zoic, and the curator of the Museum was present, looking only slightly less musty than one of his mummies.

The press was out in force. All the bureaus and most of the New York papers had representatives there. Ki was doing the receiving. Burch had not yet shown up. I got Ki aside and told him what a skunky trick I thought he'd pulled on me, but he merely shrugged.

"I'm sorry, Len. But you had your chance. After all, I had to think of my own paper first." Then he grinned. "Anyway, you were in favour of destroying the *thing*."

"I still am," I told him dourly.

"Then why are you here?"

It was my turn to shrug. "It was either come or lose my job," I said. "What would you do?"

Then Burch put in an appearance, and the whole outfit went genteelly crazy. Flashbulbs started blazing, and all my learned confreres of the Fourth Estate started shooting questions at him. About his trip, the loss of his comrades, his experiences. I knew all that stuff, so I just waited for the big blow-off to follow.

It came at last. The moment when Burch said, "Before I tell my entire story I prefer that you see that which I brought back with me." And he led the way out to the workshop.

Ki and Burch had fixed up the place a little. They had drawn chalk lines on the floor to show the visitors where they might stand.

"And I warn you," said Burch, just before he opened the shed door, "not to move beyond those lines. Later you will understand why."

The crowd began to file in. From my post in the rear I could tell when the first pair of eyes sighted that *thing*… and when every subsequent visitor saw it, as well. Gasps, exclamations, and little cries of astonishment rippled through the crowd as one by one they moved into the room.

The *thing* was still suspended on its imprisoning rod. As before, it was wriggling and moving, changing its shape with such rapidity that the human eye could scarcely view one shape before that turned into another. In view of what Burch had told me I could comprehend the *thing* better now. I could understand how, if that black blob of flesh captured by the bar were really—as Burch presumed—the leg of some ultra-dimensional monster, the movements of that limb, as it sought to break free, would throw continually changing projections into our world.

I could understand, too, why from time to time we would see *other* bits of solid matter appear in various sections of the room. Though these seemed disassociated with the chunk pinned on the bar, I knew them to be actually separate portions of the same beast. For if a man were to thrust four fingers simultaneously into Flatland, to the Flatlander these would appear to be four separate objects, while in reality they were part of a single unit in a dimension beyond his powers of conception.

The amazement of the savants was something to behold. I began to feel a little ashamed of myself. Perhaps I had been wrong to give Burch the advice I had. Perhaps, as Ki had said, this was one of the greatest discoveries of all time.

One of the photographers was dropping to his knee, levelling his camera at the shifting *thing* on the rod. I caught myself thinking swiftly, *"He shouldn't do that!"* Evidently Burch had the same idea. He took a swift step forward, cried, "Please! I would rather you didn't—"

He spoke too late. The man's finger pressed. For an instant the room was flooded with light...

—And then it happened. I heard a thin scream that came from far away. Or it may not have been a sound at all in the true sense of that word. It may have been some tonic wave of supernatural heights, for it tortured the eardrums to hear it.

The thing on the rod churned into motion. Violent motion. It grew and dwindled, shifted from cube to hemisphere, back to cube again. Then a truncated pyramidal form was throbbing, jerking, churning on the steel. Where once I had seen an old, ugly, healed wound, ichor-clotted, now I saw ragged edges of black break open;

saw fresh gouts of brownish fluid well from raw edges in that changing black.

Burch's horrified voice rose above the tumult.

"Out! Get out, all of you, before it—"

That was all he found time to say. For there came a horrible, sucking sound, like the sound of gangrenous flesh tearing away, and where there had been a changing black shape swirling on an imprisoning steel rod, suddenly there was nothing.

And with equal suddenness several of the shapeless blobs of matter from various parts of the room seemed to rush together with frightful speed. Someone screaming with terror bumped against me. I fell to my hands and knees in the doorway, feeling the flood of human terror swarm over me.

But not until I had seen a scimitar-shaped blob of black flesh reach out to strike at Ki Patterson. Ki had not even time to cry out. He went down as though stricken by the sickle of Chronos.

I cried, "Burch!"

Burch had turned to face the coalescing monster. A revolver in his hand was filling the room with thunder. Orange gouts of flame belched from its muzzle, and I knew he was not missing. Still the thing was closing in on him. I saw what appeared to be four jet circles appear in a ring over the head of Burch Patterson. Saw the circles expand and a wider expanse of black, flat and sinister, appear directly over his head. They came together with a clutching, enveloping movement. Then he was gone.

Somehow I managed to struggle out of that shed. Not that it made any difference. For with the disappearance of Burch Patterson, the *thing* itself disappeared.

★

I won't try to describe the terrified group of newsmen and scientists who gathered at the Patterson house. Who trembled and quaked and offered frenetic explanations for that which had transpired. Who finally summoned up courage enough to return to the shed cautiously, seeking the mortal remains of Burch Patterson.

They found nothing of course. Ki was there, but Ki was dead. Burch was gone. The air was still putrid with that unearthly animal stench. Beneath the steel trap Patterson had built for his *thing* was a pool of drying brownish fluid. One of the scientists wanted to take a sample of this for analysis. He returned to the house for a container in which to put it.

Maybe it was the wrong thing for me to do. But I thought, then, that it was best. And I still think so. If he had taken that sample, made that analysis, sooner or later another expedition would have set out for the Maratan Plateau in search of that *thing* whose blood did not correspond to that of any known animal. I didn't believe this should happen. So while he was gone I set fire to the shed. It was an old place, dry as tinder. By the time he returned it was a seething cauldron of flame. It made a fitting pyre for the body of Ki Patterson.

But I don't know. I have wondered often, since. Somehow I have a feeling that Burch Patterson may not be dead, after all. That is, if a human can live in a dimension of which he cannot conceive.

The more I think of it, the more I try to reconcile that which I saw with that which Burch told me, the more I believe that the thing which descended upon Burch there in the shed was not a mouth… but a gigantic paw. I saw four circles appear, you know. Four circles with a flat black spot above. It could have been four huge fingers and a palm descending to grasp the daring tridimensional "Flatlander" who had the audacity to match wits with a creature from a superior world. If that be so... and if the *thing* were intelligent... Patterson might be alive...

I don't know. But sometimes I am tempted to organize another expedition to the Maratan Plateau, myself. I'd like to learn the truth concerning the *thing* from beyond the gateway. The truth concerning Burch Patterson's fate.

What would *you* do?

DISCORD IN SCARLET

A. E. van Vogt

Alfred Elton van Vogt (1912–2000) was a Canadian-born writer who settled in the United States in 1944 and was granted US citizenship in 1952. He started writing in 1933 selling mostly "true" stories to the confession magazines. He had learned to write fiction by consulting a book and for a long while he produced material as if writing by numbers. There remained an almost mechanistic approach to his narratives but at times that was extremely effective. He turned to science fiction in 1939, chiefly because it gave him more freedom of expression, and was soon selling regularly to the leading sf magazine, Astounding, *edited by John W. Campbell, Jr. His first story, "Black Destroyer", about an alien creature (referred to as "pussy" in the following story) stalking the humans who have landed on its planet, was an instant hit and launched the series that became the book* The Voyage of the Space Beagle *(1950). The following story was the second in the series and was the one that the author claimed had inspired the film* Alien *(1979). Van Vogt went on to produce such classics of science fiction as* Slan *(serial 1940) about a population of mutants who have gone into hiding, even from themselves,* The Weapon Shops of Isher *(1951), an intricate novel set through time with an immortal man endeavouring to keep in balance the relationship between galactic empires, and* The World of Null-A *(serial 1945), with its exploration of super-powers and mind control. Van Vogt's stories of the 1940s became extremely complicated and were both venerated by those who determined to understand them, and admired by those who failed to complete them. His constant exploration of the powers of the mind meant it was not surprising that when L. Ron*

Hubbard launched dianetics in 1950 (which later mutated into scientology) it would lure van Vogt into its web, and he practically stopped writing. Of all the great sf writers who emerged under Campbell in his first few years at Astounding, which included Robert A. Heinlein, Theodore Sturgeon and Isaac Asimov, van Vogt is perhaps the least read today but, as the following shows, his work has lost none of its power. The version reprinted here is the original from 1939 and not the revised version used for book publication.

XTL SPRAWLED MOVELESS ON THE BOSOM OF ENDLESS NIGHT. Time dragged drearily toward infinity, and space was dark. Unutterably dark! The horrible pitch-blackness of intergalactic immensity! Across the miles and the years, vague patches of light gleamed coldly at him, whole galaxies of blazing stars shrunk by incredible distance to shining swirls of mist.

Life was out there, spawning on the myriad planets that whirled eternally around the myriad suns. And life had once crawled out of the primeval mud of ancient Glor—before cosmic explosion destroyed a mighty race and flung his—Xtl's—body out into the deeps of space, the prey of chance.

His brain pulsed on and on in the same old, old cycle of thought—thinking: one chance in decillions that his body would ever come near a galactic system. One chance in infinity itself that he fall on a planet and find a precious *guul*. And never, never a hope that his race would live again.

A billion times that thought had pounded to its dreary conclusion in his brain, until it was a part of him, until it was like a picture unrolling before his eyes—it and those remote wisps of shiningness out there in that blackness. And that picture was more real than the reality. He had no consciousness of the spaceship, until he touched the metal.

Hard, hardness—something material! The vague sense perception fumbled into his dulled brain, bringing a living pain—like a disused muscle, briefly, agonizingly brought into action.

The thought slumped. His brain slid back into its sleep of ages, seeing again the old picture of hopelessness and the shiningness in the black. The very idea of hardness became a dream that faded. Some remote corner of his mind, curiously alert, watched it fade, watched the shadows creep with reaching, enveloping folds of lightlessness, striving to re-engulf the dim consciousness that had flashed into such an anguish of ephemeral existence.

And then, once more, his groping fingers sent that dull pulse of awareness tapping its uncertain message to his sodden, hopeless brain.

His elongated body convulsed in senseless movement, four arms lashed out, four legs jackknifed with blind, unreasoning strength. There was a distinct sense of a blow and of a pushing away from the hard matter.

His dazed, staring eyes, his stultified vision galvanized into life; and he saw that, in the contorted fury of his movements, he had pushed himself away from the surface of a vast, round, dark-bodied metal monster, studded with row on row of glaring lights, like diamonds. The spaceship floated there in the velvet darkness, glowing like an immense jewel, quiescent but alive, enormously, vitally alive, bringing nostalgic and vivid suggestion of a thousand far-flung planets, and of an indomitable, boisterous life that had reached for the stars and grasped them. Bringing—hope!

The torpid tenor of his thoughts exploded into chaos. His mind, grooved through the uncounted ages to ultimate despair, soared up, up, insanely. Life surged from the bottom point of static to the swirling, irresistible height of dynamism, that jarred every atom of his scarlet, cylindrical body and his round, vicious head. His legs and arms glistened like tongues of living fire, as they twisted and writhed in the blaze of light from those dazzling portholes. His mouth, a gash in the centre of his hideous head, slavered a white frost that floated away in little frozen globules.

His brain couldn't hold the flame of that terrific hope. His mind kept dissolving, blurring. Through that blur he saw a thick vein of light form a circular bulge in the metallic surface of the ship. The bulge became a huge door that rotated open and tilted to one side. A flood of brilliance spilled out the great opening, followed by a dozen two-legged beings in transparent metal armour, dragging great floating machines.

Swiftly, the machines were concentrated around a dark projection on the ship's surface. Intolerable light flared up as what was obviously repair work proceeded at an alarming pace.

He was no longer falling away from the ship. The faint pressure of gravitational pull was drawing him down again—so slowly. Frantically, he adjusted his atomic structure to the fullest measure of attraction. But even his poorly responding brain could see that he would never make it.

The work was finished. The incandescent glare of atomic welders died to spluttering darkness. Machines were unclamped, floated toward the opening of the ship, down into it and out of sight. The two-legged beings scrambled after them. The vast, curved plain of metal was suddenly as deserted and lifeless as space itself.

Terror struck into Xtl. He'd have to fight, have to get there somehow. He couldn't let them get away now, when the whole universe was in his grasp—twenty-five short yards away. His letching arms reached out stupidly, as if he would hold the ship by sheer fury of need. His brain ached with a slow, rhythmical hurt. His mind spun toward a black, bottomless pit—then poised just before the final plunge.

The great door was slowing in its swift rotation. A solitary being squeezed through the ring of light and ran to the dark projection, just repaired. He picked up an instrument that gleamed weirdly, a tool of some kind forgotten, and started back toward the partly open lock.

He stopped. In the glow from the portholes, Xtl could see the other's face through the transparent armour. The face stared up at him, eyes wide, mouth open. Then the mouth moved rapidly, opening and shutting, apparently a form of communication with the others.

A moment later the door was rotating again, opening wide. A group of the beings came out, two of them mounted on the top of a large, metal-barred cage, steering it under power. He was to be captured.

Oddly, his brain felt no sense of lift, no soaring hope, none of that mind-inflaming ecstasy. It was as if a drug was dragging him down, down, into a black night of fatigue. Appalled, he fought off the enveloping stupor. He must hold to his senses. His race, that had attained the very threshold of ultimate knowledge, must live again.

The voice, a strained, unrecognizable voice, came to Commander Morton through the communicators in his transparent spacesuit: "How in the name of all the hells can anything live in intergalactic space?"

It seemed to the commander that the question made the little group of men crowd closer together. The proximity of the others made them feel easier. Then they suddenly grew aware of the impalpable yet *alive* weight of the inconceivable night that coiled about them, pressing down to the very blazing portholes.

For the first time in years, the immensity of that night squeezed icily into Morton's consciousness. Long familiarity had bred indifference into his very bones—but now, the incredible vastness of that blackness reaching a billion trillion years beyond the farthest frontiers of man stabbed into his mind, and brought an almost dismaying awareness. His deep voice, clattering into the communicators, split that scared silence like some harsh noise, startled him:

"Gunlie Lester, here's something for your astronomical-mathematical brain. Will you please give us the ratio of chance that blew out a driver of the *Beagle* at the exact point in space where that thing was floating? Take a few hours to work it out."

The astronomer replied immediately: "I don't have to think about it. The chance is unstatable in human arithmetic. It can't happen, mathematically speaking. Here we are, a shipload of human beings, stopping for repairs halfway between two galaxies—the first time we've ever made a trip outside of our own galaxy. Here we are, I say, a tiny point intersecting without prearrangement exactly the path of another, tinier point. Impossible, unless space is saturated with such—creatures!"

"I hope not," another man shuddered. "We ought to turn a mobile unit on anything that looks like that, on general principles."

The shudder seemed to run along the communicators. Commander Morton shook his great, lean body as if consciously trying to throw off the chill of it. His eyes on the manoeuvring cage above, he said:

"A regular blood-red devil spewed out of some fantastic nightmare; ugly as sin—and probably as harmless as our beautiful pussy last year was deadly. Smith, what do you think?"

The cadaverous-faced biologist said in his cold, logical voice: "This thing has arms and legs, a purely planetary evolution. If it is intelligent it will begin to react to environment the moment it is inside the cage. It may be a venerable old sage, meditating in the silence of distractionless space. Or it may be a young murderer, condemned to eternal exile, consumed with desire to sneak back home and resume the life he lived."

"I wish Korita had come out with us," said Pennons, the chief engineer, in his quiet, practical voice. "Korita's historical analysis of pussy last year gave us an advance idea of what we had to face and—"

"Korita speaking, Mr. Pennons," came the meticulously clear voice of the Japanese archæologist on the communicators. "Like many of the others, I have been listening to what is happening as a welcome break in this, the longest journey the spaceship *Beagle* has ever undertaken. But I am afraid analysis of the creature would be dangerous at this factless stage. In the case of pussy, we had the barren, foodless planet on which we lived, and the architectural realities of his crumbled city.

"Here we have a creature living in space a million years from the nearest planet, apparently without food, and without means of spatial locomotion. I suggest you make certain that you get him into the cage, and then study him—every action, every reaction. Take pictures of his internal organs working in the vacuum of space. Find out every possible thing about him, so that we shall know what we have aboard as soon as possible. Now, when we are fully staffed again and heading for a new galaxy for the first time in the history of man, we cannot afford to have anything go wrong, or anybody killed before we reach there. Thank you."

"And that," said Morton, "is sense. You've got your fluorite camera, Smith?"

"Attached to my suit," Smith acknowledged.

Morton who knew the capabilities of the mournful-looking biologist turned his attention back to the cage fifty feet away. He said in his deep, resonant voice: "Open the door as wide as possible, and drop over him. Don't let his hands grab the bars."

"Just a minute!" a guttural voice broke in. Morton turned questioningly to the big, plump German physicist. Von Grossen continued: "Let us not rush this capture, Commander Morton. It is true that I was not aboard last year when you had your encounter with the creature you persist in calling pussy. But when you returned to the base planet before embarking on the present voyage, the story you told to the world was not reassuring, not to me, anyway."

His hard, grey-dark face stared grimly at the others: "It is true that I can see no real objection to capturing this creature in a cage. But it happens that I am replacing a man who was killed by this— pussy. Therefore I speak for him when I say: Such a thing must never happen again."

Morton frowned, his face lined with doubt. "You put me in a spot, von Grossen. As human beings, we must take every possible precaution. As scientists, however, all is grist for our mill; everything must be investigated. There can be no thought of shunning danger before we even know it to be danger. If this voyage is to be ruled by fear, we might as well head for home now."

"Fear is not what I had in mind," said the physicist quietly. "But I believe in counting ten before acting."

Morton asked. "Any other objections?"

He felt oddly annoyed that there were none.

Xtl waited. His thoughts kept breaking up into little pieces of light and lightless—a chain of dazzle and dark—that somehow connected up with all the things he had ever known or thought. Visions of a long-dead planet trickled into his consciousness bringing a vague conceit—and a contempt of these creatures who thought to capture him.

Why, he could remember a time when his race had had spaceships a hundred times the size of this machine that swam below him. That was before they had dispensed completely with space travel, and just lived a quiet homey life building beauty from natural forces.

He watched, as the cage was driven toward him unerringly. There was nothing he could do, even had he wanted to. The gaping mouth of the large, metal-barred construction closed over him and snapped shut the moment he was inside.

Xtl clawed at the nearest bar, caught hold with grim strength. He clung there an instant, sick and dizzy with awful reaction. Safe! His mind expanded with all the violence of an exploding force. Free electrons discharged in dizzying swarms from the chaos of the spinning atom systems inside his brain and body, frantically seeking union with the other systems. He was safe—safe after quadrillions of years of sick despair, and on a material body with unlimited power to take him where he would to go. Safe when there was still time to carry out his sacred purpose. Or was he safe?

The cage was dropping toward the surface of the ship. His eyes became gleaming pools of caution, as they studied the men below. It was only too evident that he was to be examined. With a tremendous effort, stung by fear, he tried to push the clinging dullness from his brain, fought for alertness. An examination of him now would reveal his purpose, expose the precious objects concealed within his breast; and that must not be.

His steely-bright eyes flicked in anxious dismay over the dozen figures in transparent armour. Then his mind calmed. They were inferior creatures, obviously! Puny foes before his own remarkable power. Their very need of spacesuits proved their inability to adapt themselves to environment, proved they existed on a low plane of evolution. Yet he must not underestimate them. Here were keen brains, capable of creating and using mighty machines.

Each of the beings had weapons in holster at the side of his space armour—weapons with sparkling, translucent handles. He had noticed the same weapons in the holsters of the men at the top of the cage. That, then, would be his method if any of these creatures flashed a camera on him.

As the cage dropped into the belt of undiffused blackness between two portholes, Smith stepped forward with his camera—and Xtl jerked himself with effortless ease up the bars to the ceiling of the cage. The gash of his mouth in the centre of his round, smooth head was split in a silent snarl of fury at the unutterable bad luck that was forcing this move upon him. His vision snapped full on; and now he could see blurrily through the hard metal of the ceiling.

One arm, with its eight wirelike fingers, lashed out with inde-scribable swiftness at the ceiling, *through* it, and then he had a gun from the holster of one of the men.

He did not attempt to readjust its atomic structure as he had adjusted his arm. It was important that they should not guess that it was he who fired the gun. Straining in his awkward position, he aimed the weapon straight at Smith and the little group of men behind him—released the flaming power.

There was a flare of incandescent violence that blotted the men from view. A swirl of dazzling light coruscated virulently across the surface of the ship. And there was another light, too. A blue sparkle that told of automatic defence screens driving out from the armoured suits of the men.

In one continuous movement, Xtl released the gun, withdrew his hand; and, by the act, pushed himself to the floor. His immediate fear was gone. No sensitive camera film could have lived through the blaze of penetrating energy. And what was overwhelmingly more important—the gun was no good against himself. Nothing but a simple affair which employed the method of transmutation of one element to another, the process releasing one or two electrons from each atom system. It would require a dozen such guns to do damage to his body.

The group of men stood quite still; and Morton knew they were fighting, as he was, the blindness that lingered from the spray of violent light. Slowly, his eyes became adjusted; and then he could see again the curved metal on which he stood, and beyond that the brief, barren crest of the ship and the limitless miles of lightless, heatless space—dark, fathomless, unthinkable gulfs. There too, a blur among the blurs of shadows, stood the cage.

"I'm sorry, commander," one of the men on the cage apologized. "The ato-gun must have fallen out of my belt, and discharged."

"Impossible!" Smith's voice came to Morton, low and tense. "In this gravitation, it would take several minutes to fall from the holster, and it wouldn't discharge in any event from such a slight jar of landing."

"Maybe I knocked against it, sir, without noticing."

"Maybe!" Smith seemed to yield grudgingly to the explanation. "But I could almost swear that, just before the flare of light dazzled me, the creature moved. I admit it was too black to see more than the vaguest blur, but—"

"Smith," Morton said sharply, "what are you trying to prove?"

He saw the long-faced biologist hunch his narrow shoulders, as if pulling himself together. The biologist mumbled; "When you put it like that, I don't know. The truth is, I suppose, that I've never gotten over the way I insisted on keeping pussy alive, with such desperately tragic results. I suspect everything now, and—"

Morton stared in surprise. It was hard to realize that it was really Smith speaking—the scientist who, it had seemed sometimes in the past, was ready to sacrifice his own life and everybody else's if it meant adding a new, important fact to the science of biology. Morton found his voice at last:

"You were perfectly right in what you did! Until we realized the truth, you expressed the majority mind of this ship's company. The development of the situation in the case of pussy changed our opinion as well as your own, but it did not change our method of working by evidence alone. I say that we should continue to make such logic the basis of our work."

"Right. And beg your pardon, chief!" Smith was brisk-voiced again. "Crane, turn the cage light on, and let's see what we've got here."

To Morton, the silence that followed seemed like a sudden, oppressive weight, as the blaze of light showered down on Xtl crouching at the bottom of the cage. The almost metallic sheen of the cylindrical body, the eyes like coals of fire, the wirelike fingers and toes, the scarlet hideousness of it startled even these men who were accustomed to alien forms of life. He broke the spell of horror, half-breathlessly:

"He's probably very handsome—to himself!"

"If life is evolution," said Smith in a stiff voice, "and nothing evolves except for use, how can a creature living in space have highly developed legs and arms? Its insides should be interesting. But now—my camera's useless! That flare of energy would have the effect of tinting the electrified lens, and of course the film's ruined. Shall I get another?"

"N-n-no-o!" Morton's clean-cut, handsome face grew dark with a frown. "We've wasted a lot of time here; and after all, we can re-create vacuum of space conditions inside the ship's laboratory, and be travelling at top acceleration while we're doing it."

"Just a minute!" Von Grossen, the plump but hard-boiled physicist, spoke: "Let's get this straight. The Beagle is going to another galaxy on an exploration voyage—the first trip of the kind. Our business is to study life in this new system, but we're not taking any specimens, only pictures and notes—studies of the creatures in their various environments. If we're all so nervous about this thing, why are we taking it aboard?"

"Because"—Smith beat Morton to the reply—"we're not tied down to pictures and notes. There will, however, be millions of forms of life on every planet, and we shall be forced to the barest kind of record in most cases. This monster is different. In our fears we have almost forgotten that the existence of a creature capable of living in space is the most extraordinary thing we've ever run across. Even pussy, who could live without air, needed warmth of a kind, and would have found the absolute cold of space intolerable. If, as we suspect, this creature's natural habitat is not space, then we must find out why and how he came to be where he is. Speaking as a biologist—"

"I see," interrupted Morton drily, "that Smith is himself again." He directed a command at the men on the cage. "Take that monster inside, and put a wall of force around the cage. That should satisfy even the most cautious."

Xtl felt the faint throb of the motors of the cage. He saw the bars move, then grew conscious of a sharp, pleasant tingling sensation, brief physical activity within his body that stopped the workings of his mind for a bare second. Before he could think, there was the cage floor rising above him—and he was lying on the hard surface of the spaceship's outer shell.

With a snarl of black dismay that almost cut his face in two, he realized the truth. He had forgotten to readjust the atoms in his body after firing the gun. And now he had fallen through!

"Good Heaven!" Morton bellowed.

A scarlet streak of elongated body, a nightmare shadow in that braid of shadow and light, Xtl darted across the impenetrable heavy metal to the air lock. He jerked himself down into its dazzling depths. His adjusted body dissolved through the two other locks. And then he was at one end of a long, gleaming corridor—safe for the moment!

There would be searching for him: and—he knew with a cold, hardening resolve—these creatures would never trust alive a being who could slip through solid metal. Their reason would tell them he was a superbeing, unutterably dangerous to them.

One advantage only he had—they did not know the deadliness of his purpose.

Ten minutes later, Morton's grey eyes flicked questioningly over the stern faces of the men gathered in the great reception room. His huge and powerful body felt oddly rigid, as if his muscles could not quite relax. His voice was mellower, deeper, richer than normal:

"I am going to offer my resignation on the grounds that, for the second time under my leadership, an abnormal beast has gotten aboard this craft. I must assume that there is a basic lack in my mental make-up; for results, and not excuses, do count in this universe of ours; even apparently bad luck is rigorously bound up with character. I, therefore, suggest that Korita or von Grossen be named commander in my place. Korita because of the care he advocated, and von Grossen on the strength of his objection to taking any living specimens aboard—both are more fitted to hold the command than I am."

"The honourable commander has forgotten one thing," Korita said softly. "The creature was *not* carried into the ship. I admit it was our collective intention to bring him aboard, but it was he himself who entered. I suggest that, even if we had decided not to bring him into the interior, we could not have prevented his entry in view of his ability to slip through metal. It is absolutely absurd for Commander Morton to feel responsible."

Von Grossen heaved himself out of his chair. Now that he was out of his spacesuit, the physicist looked not so much plump as big and iron-hard. "And that goes for me all the way. I have not been long on this ship, but I have found Commander Morton to be a most able intellect and leader of men. So let us not waste time in useless self-reproach.

"In capturing this being we must first of all straighten our minds about him. He has arms and legs, this creature, yet floats in space, and remains alive. He allows himself to be caught in a cage, but knows all the time that the cage cannot hold him. Then he drops through the bottom of the cage, which is very silly if he doesn't want us to know that he can do it. Which means that he is a very foolish creature indeed, and we don't have to worry very much about him. There is a reason why intelligent living things make mistakes—a fundamental reason that should make it easy for us to analyse him right back to where he came from, and why he is here. Smith, analyse his biological make-up."

Smith stood up, lank and grim. "We've already discussed the obvious planetary origin of his hands and feet. The ability to live in space, however, is an abnormal development, having no connection with natural evolution, but is the product of brain power and science, pure and simple. I suggest that here is a member of a race that has solved the final secrets of biology; and, if I knew how we should even begin to start looking for a creature that can slip through walls, my advice would be: Hunt him down and kill him within an hour."

"Er!" Kellie, the sociologist, said. He was a bald-headed man with preternaturally intelligent eyes that gleamed owlishly from behind his pince-nez. "Er, any being who could fit himself to vacuum of space condition would be lord of the universe. His kind would dwell on every planet, clutter up every galactic system. Swarms of him would be floating in space, if space floating is what they go in for. Yet, we know for a fact that his race does not rule *our* galactic area. A paradox, which is worthy of investigation."

"I don't quite understand what you mean, Kellie!" Morton frowned.

"Simply, er, that a race which has solved the final secrets of biology must be millions, even billions of years in advance of man; and, as a pure sympodial—capable of adaptation to any environment—would, according to the lay of vital dynamics, expand to the farthest frontier of the universe, just as man is slowly pushing himself to the remotest planets."

"It is a contradiction," Morton agreed, "and would seem to prove that the creature is not a superior being. Korita, what is this thing's history?"

The Japanese scientist shrugged: "I'm afraid I can only be of the slightest assistance on present evidence. You know the prevailing theory: That life proceeds upwards by a series of cycles. Each cycle begins with the peasant, who is rooted to his bit of soil. The peasant comes to market; and slowly the market place transforms to a town, with ever less 'inward' connection to the earth. Then we have cities and nations, finally the soulless world cities and a devastating struggle for power—a series of frightful wars which sweep men back to the peasant stage. The question becomes: Is this creature in the peasant part of this particular cycle, or in the big city 'megalopolitan' era?"

Morton's voice slashed across the silence: "In view of our limited knowledge of this creature, what basic traits should we look for, supposing him to be in the big city stage?"

"He would be a cold, invincible intellect, formidable to the ultimate degree, undefeatable—except through circumstances. I refer to the kind of circumstances that made it impossible for us to prevent this beast entering our ship. Because of his great innate intelligence, he would make no errors of any kind."

"But he has already made an error!" von Grossen said in a silken voice. "He very foolishly fell through the bottom of the cage. It is the kind of blunder a peasant would make—"

"Suppose," Morton asked, "he were in the peasant stage?"

"Then," Korita replied, "his basic impulses would be much simpler. There would be first of all the desire to reproduce, to have a son, to know that his blood was being carried on. Assuming great fundamental intelligence, this impulse might, in the superior being, take the form of a fanatic drive toward race survival—"

He stopped, as half a dozen men came through the doorway. Morton said: "Finished, Pennons?"

The chief engineer nodded. Then in a warning voice: "It is absolutely essential that every man on the ship get into his rubberite suit, and wear rubberite gloves."

Morton explained grimly. "We've energized the walls around the bedrooms. There may be some delay in catching this creature, and we're taking no chances of being murdered in our beds, We—" Sharply: "What is it, Pennons?"

Pennons was staring at a small instrument in his hand; he said in a queer voice: "Are we all here, Morton?"

"Yes, except for four men guarding the engine room."

"Then... then something's caught in the wall of force. Quick— we must surround it."

To Xtl, returning from a brief exploration of the monster ship's interior, the shock was devastating, the surprise unutterable and complete.

One moment he was thinking complacently of the metal sections in the hold of the ship, where he would secrete his *guuls;* the next moment he was caught in the full sparkling fury of an energy screen.

His body writhed with an agony that blackened his brain. Thick clouds of free electrons rose up within him in that hell of pain, and flashed from system to system seeking union, only to be violently repelled by the tortured, madly spinning atom systems. For those long seconds, the wonderfully balanced instability of his structure nearly collapsed into an abyss of disintegration.

But the incredible genius that had created his marvellous body had fore-thought even this eventuality. Like lightning, his body endured readjustment after automatic readjustment, each new-built structure carrying the intolerable load for a fraction of a fraction of a second. And then, he had jerked back from the wall, and was safe.

In a flare of thought, his mind investigated the immediate pos-sibilities. Obviously, the men had rigged up this defence wall of force. It meant they would have an alarm system—and they would swoop down every corridor in an organized attempt to corner him.

Xtl's eyes were glowing pools of white fire as he realized the opportunity. He must catch one of these men, while they were scattered, investigate his *guul* properties, and use him for his first *guul*.

No time to waste. He darted into the nearest wall, a tall, gaudy, ungraceful streak, and, without pausing, sped through room after room, roughly parallel to a main corridor. His sensitive feet caught the vibrations of the approaching men; and through the wall his full vision followed the blurred figures rushing past. One, two, three, four—five—on this corridor. The fifth man was some distance behind the others.

Like a wraith, Xtl glided into the wall just ahead of the last man—and pounced forth in an irresistible charge. A rearing, fright-ful shape of glaring eyes and ghastly mouth, blood-red, metal-hard body, and four arms of fire that clutched with bitter strength at the human body.

The man tried to fight. His big form twisted, jerked; his lashing fists felt vaguely painful as they pounded desperately against the hard, sheeny crust of Xtl's body. And then, by sheer weight and ferocity, he was over-whelmed; the force of his fall jarring Xtl's sensitive frame.

The man was lying on his back, and Xtl watched curiously as the mouth opened and shut spasmodically. A tingling sensation sped along Xtl's feet, and his mouth opened in a snarl. Incapable though he was of hearing sounds, he realized that he was picking up the vibrations of a call for help.

He pounced forward, one great hand smashing at the man's mouth. Teeth broke, and crushed back into the throat. The body sagged. But the man was still alive, and conscious, as Xtl plunged two hands into the feebly writhing body.

The man ceased suddenly even that shadow of struggle, his widened eyes staring at the arms that vanished under his shirt, stirred around in his chest, stared in petrified terror at the monstrous blood-red cylindrical body that loomed over him, with its round bright eyes glaring at him as if they would see right through him.

It was a blurred picture the frantic Xtl saw. The inside of the man's body seemed solid flesh. He had to find an open space, or one that could be pressed open, so long as the pressing did not kill the man. He must have living flesh.

Hurry, hurry—His feet registered the vibrations of approaching footsteps—from one direction only, but coming swiftly, swiftly.

And then, just like that, it was all over. His searching fingers, briefly hardened to a state of semisolidity, touched the heart. The man heaved convulsively, shuddered, and slumped into death.

The next instant, Xtl discovered the stomach. For a moment; black dismay flooded him. Here was what he was searching for, and he had killed it, rendered it useless! He stared in cold fury at the stilled body, uncertain, alarmed.

Then suddenly his actions became deliberate, weighted with contempt. Never for an instant had he suspected these intelligent beings would die so easily. It changed, simplified everything. There was no need to be anything more than casually careful in dealing with them.

Two men with drawn ato-guns whipped around the nearest corner, and slid to a halt at the sight of the apparition that snarled at them across the dead body. Then, as they came out of their brief paralysis, Xtl stepped into the nearest wall, a blur of scarlet in that brightly lit corridor, gone on the instant. He felt the fury of the energy rays that tore futilely at the metal behind him.

His plan was quite clear now. He would capture half a dozen men, and make *guuls* of them. Then kill all the others, proceed on to the galactic system toward which the ship was heading, and take control of the first inhabited planet. After that, domination of the entire universe would be a matter of a short time only.

Commander Morton stood very stiffly there in the gleaming corridor, every muscle in his huge body like a taut wire. Only a dozen men were gathered round the dead body, but the audioscopes were on; nearly two hundred tense men throughout the ship were watching that scene. Morton's voice was only a whisper, but it cut across the silence like a whiplash.

"Well, doctor?"

Dr. Eggert rose up from his kneeling position beside the body, frowning.

"Heart failure."

"Heart failure!"

"All right, all right!" The doctor put up his hands as if to defend himself against physical attack. "I know his teeth look as if they've been smashed back into his brain, and I know Darjeeling's heart was perfect, but heart failure is what it looks like to me."

"I can believe it," a man said sourly. "When I came around that corner, and saw that thing, I nearly had heart failure myself."

"We're wasting time!" von Grossen's voice stabbed from behind Morton. "We can beat this fellow, but not by talking about him, and feeling sick every time he makes a move. If I'm next on the list of victims, I want to know that the best damned bunch of scientists in the system are not crying over my fate, but putting their best brains to the job of avenging my death."

"You're right," Smith said. "The trouble with us is, we've been permitting ourselves to feel inferior. He's only been on the ship about an hour but I can see now that some of us are going to get killed. Well, I accept my chance! But let's get organized for combat!"

Morton snapped: "Pennons, here's a problem. We've got about two square miles of wall and floor space in our twenty levels. How long will it take to energize every inch of it?"

The chief engineer stared at him, aghast; then answered swiftly: "I could sweep the ship and probably wreck it completely within an hour. I won't go into details. But uncontrolled energization is absolutely out. It would kill every living thing aboard—"

"Not everything!" von Grossen rejected. "Not the creature. Remember, that damn thing ran into a wall of force. Your instrument, Pennons, registered activity for several seconds. Several seconds! Let me show you what that means. The principle underlying his ability to slip through walls is simple enough. The atoms of his body slide through the empty spaces between the atoms of the walls. There is a basic electronic tension that holds a body together, which would have to be overcome, but apparently his race has solved the difficulty. A wall of force would increase those electronic tensions to a point where the atoms themselves would be emitting free electrons; and, theoretically, that should have a deadly effect on any interfering body. I'll wager he didn't like those few seconds he was in the wall—but the point is, he stood them."

Morton's strong face was hard: "You could feed more energy to those walls, couldn't you, Pennons?"

"N-no!" said Pennons reluctantly. "The walls couldn't stand it. They'd melt."

"*The walls couldn't stand it!*" a man gasped. "Man, man, do you know what you're making this creature out to be?"

Morton saw the consternation that leaped along that line of stern faces. Korita's thin, clear voice cut across that pregnant silence:

"Let us not forget, my honourable friends, that he did blunder into the wall of force, and recoiled in dismay, though apparently without damage to his person. I use the word 'blunder' with discretion. His action proves once again that he does make mistakes which, in turn, shows him to be something less than a superbeing—"

"Suppose," Morton barked, "he's a peasant of his cycle. What would be his chief intellectual characteristic?"

Korita replied almost crisply for one who usually spoke so slowly: "The inability to understand the full power of organization. He will think probably that all he has to fight in order to get control of this ship would be the men who are in it. His most instinctive reasoning would tend to discount the fact that we are part of a vast galactic civilization or organization, and that the spirit of that civilization is fighting in us. The mind of the true peasant is very individualistic, almost anarchic. His desire to reproduce is a form of egoism, to have his own blood particularly carried on. There can be no such thing as a peasant co-operative or organization. But this creature may want to have numbers of beings similar to himself beside him to help him with his fight. But, though there would be a loose union, they would fight as individuals, and not as a group."

"A loose union of those fire-eaters ought to be enough!" a crew member commented acidly. "I... a-a-a-a—"

His voice sagged. His lower jaw dropped two inches. His eyes, under Morton's gaze, took on a horribly goggled stare. The commander whipped around with an oath.

★

Xtl stood here, forbidding spectre from a scarlet hell, his eyes pools of blazing alertness. He knew with a vast contempt that he could plunge into the nearest wall before any gun could leap out at him in ravening fury. But he felt himself protected by another fact. These were intelligent beings. They would be more anxious to discover why he had deliberately come out of the wall than to kill him immediately. They might even consider it a friendly move; and, when they discovered differently, it would be too late.

His purpose, which was twofold, was simplicity itself. He had come for his first *guul*. By snatching that *guul* from their very midst, he would demoralize them thoroughly.

Morton felt a curious wave of unreality sweep over him, as he stood just behind von Grossen there in that glittering hallway, facing the tall, thick, cylindrical reality of Xtl. Instinctively, his fingers groped downward toward the sparkling, translucent handle of the ato-gun that protruded from his holster. He stopped himself, and said in a steady voice:

"Don't touch your guns. He can move like a flash; and he wouldn't be here if he thought we could draw on him. I'll take his opinion any day on that point. Besides, we can't risk failure. This may be our only chance!"

He continued in a swift, slightly higher, more urgent tone: "Every man listening in on the audioscopes get above and below and around this corridor. Bring up the heaviest portables, even some of the semiportables and burn the walls down. Cut a clear path all around this area, and have your beams sweep that space at narrow focus. Move!"

"Good boy, Morton!" Pennons' face appeared for an instant on the plate of the audioscope. "We'll be there—if you can stall that hellhound three minutes."

Korita's sibilant voice hissed out of the audioscope: "Morton, take this chance, but do not count on success. Notice that he has appeared once again before we have had time for a discussion. He is rushing us, whether intentionally or accidentally matters not, because the result is that we're on the run, scurrying this way and that, futilely. So far we have not clarified our thoughts. I am convinced the vast resources of this ship can defeat any creature—any single creature—that has ever existed, or that ever will exist, but only if we have time to use them—"

His voice blurred briefly in Morton's ears. Von Grossen had taken a notebook from his pocket, and was sketching rapidly. He tore the sheet loose, and stepped forward, handed it to the creature, who examined it curiously.

Von Grossen stepped back, and began to sketch again on the second page, with a swift deftness. This sheet he handed also the creature, who took one glance at it, and stepped back with a snarl that split his face. His eyes widened to blazing pools; one arm half reached forward toward von Grossen, then paused uncertainly.

"What the devil have you done?" Morton demanded his voice sounding on unnaturally shrill even to himself.

Von Grossen took several steps backward, until he stood level with Morton. To the commander's amazement, he was grinning:

"I've just shown him," the German physicist said softly, "how we can defeat him—neutronium alloy, of course and he—"

Too late, Morton stepped forward, instinctively trying to interpose his huge form in front of von Grossen. A blur of red swept by him. Something—a hand moving so fast that it was invisible—struck him a stunning blow, and knocked him spinning against the nearest wall. For an instant, his body threatened to collapse from sheer, dazed weakness. The world went black, then white, then black.

With appalling effort, he fought the weakness aside. The immense reservoir of strength in his magnificent body surged irresistibly forward; his knees stopped wavering, but his vision was still a crazy thing. As through a distorted glass, he saw that the thing was holding von Grossen in two fire-coloured arms. The two-hundred-and-ten-pound physicist gave one convulsive heave of dismay; and then seemed to accept the overpowering strength of those thin, hard muscles.

With a bellow, Morton clawed for his gun. And it was then that the maddest thing of all happened. The creature took a running dive, and vanished into the wall, still holding von Grossen. For an instant, it seemed to Morton like a crazy trick of vision. But there was only the smooth gleamingness of the wall, and eleven staring, perspiring men, seven of them with drawn weapons, which they fingered helplessly.

"We're lost!" a man whispered. "If he can adjust our atomic structure, and take us through walls, we can't fight him."

Morton chilled his heart to the dismay he read in that rough semicircle of faces. He said coldly:

"Your report, Pennons?"

There was a brief delay, then the engineer's lean leathery face, drawn with strain and effort, stared into the plate: "Nothing!" he replied succinctly. "Clay, one of my assistants, thinks he saw a flash of scarlet disappearing through a floor, going down. That's a clue of course. It means our search will be narrowed to the lower half of the ship. As for the rest, we were just lining up our units when it happened. You gave us only two minutes. We needed three!"

Morton nodded, his thoughtful mood interrupted by the abrupt realization that his fingers were shaking. With a muttered impreca-tion, he clenched them, and said icily:

"Korita has given us our cue—organization. The implications of that word must be fully thought out, and co-ordinated to the knowledge we have of the creature. Von Grossen, of course, has given us our defence—neutronium alloy."

"I don't follow the argument," interjected Zeller, the metallurgist.

It was Smith who explained: "The commander means that only two parts of the ship are composed of that incredibly dense metal, the outer shell and the engine room. If you had been with us when we first captured this creature, you would have noticed that, when the damned thing fell through the floor of the cage, it was stopped short by the hard metal of the ship's crust. The conclusion is obviously that it cannot slip through such metal; and the fact that it ran for the air lock is proof. The wonder is that we didn't think of it before."

Morton barked: "Therefore, to the heart of the ship—the engine room. And we won't go out of there till we've got a plan. Any other way, he'll run us ragged."

"What about von Grossen?" a man ventured.

Morton snapped harshly: "Don't make us think of von Grossen. Do you want us all to go crazy?"

In that vast room of vast machines, the men were dwarfs in *gigantica*. It was a world apart; and Morton, for the first time in years, felt the alien, abnormal tremendousness of it. His nerves jumped at each special burst of unholy blue light that sparkled and coruscated upon the great, glistening sweep of the ceiling. Blue light that was alive, pure energy that no eliminators, had ever been able to eliminate; no condensers absorb.

And there was something else that sawed on his nerves now. A sound—imprisoned in the very air! A thin hum of terrifying power, a vague rumble, the faintest, quivering reverberation of an inconceivable flow of energy.

Morton glanced at his watch, and stood up with an explosive sigh of relief. He swept up a small sheaf of notes from a metal desk. The silence of unsmiling men became the deeper, tenser silence of men who fixed him with their eyes. The commander began:

"This is the first breathing spell we've had since that creature came aboard less than—incredible as it may seem—less than two hours ago. I've been glancing through these notes you've given me, and I've divided them into two sections: those that can be discussed while we're putting into effect the purely mechanical plans for cornering the thing—these latter must be discussed now. There are two. First, Zeller!"

The metallurgist stepped forward, a brisk, middle-aged, young-looking man. He started: "The creature made no attempt to keep the drawings which von Grossen showed it—proof, incidentally that von Grossen was not seized because of the drawings. They fell on the floor; and I picked them up. I've been showing them around, so most of you know that the first drawing is a likeness of the creature stepping through a metal wall; and beside the wall is an enlarged atom system of the type of which the wall is composed—two hundred electrons arranged about the nucleus, forming a series of triangles.

"The second picture was a rough, unfinished but unmistakable single atom of neutronium alloy, with only eight hundred of the forty thousand electrons showing, but the design of each eighty electrons with their sixteen sides clearly indicated. That kind of language is intergalactic; and the creature understood the point instantly. He didn't like it, as we all saw by his actions; but apparently he had no intention of being thwarted; and perhaps saw the difficulty we might have in using such knowledge against him. Because, just as we cannot energize the walls of the whole ship—Pennons has said it would take days—so we have no materials to plate the ship throughout with neutronium alloy. The stuff is too rare.

"However, we have enough for me to build a suit of space armour, with which one of us could search for von Grossen, whom the thing is obviously hiding behind some wall. For the search, naturally, we'd use a fluorite camera. My assistant is already working out the suit, but we'd like suggestions—"

There were none; and, after a moment, Zeller disappeared into the machine shops adjoining the engine room. Morton's grim face relaxed slightly.

"For myself, I feel better knowing that, once the suit is built—in about an hour—the creature will have to keep moving von Grossen in order to prevent us from discovering the body. It's good to know that there's a chance of getting back one of the boldest minds aboard the ship."

"How do you know he's alive?" a man asked.

"Because the creature could have taken Darjeeling's dead body, but didn't. He wants us alive—Smith's notes have given us a possible clue to his purpose, but let that go now. Pennons, outline the plan you have—this is our main plan, gentlemen; and we stand or fall by it."

The chief engineer came forward; and it worried Morton to note that he was frowning blackly. His usually dynamic body lacked briskness and suggested uncertainty. The implications of the lack of confidence were mind-shaking. The mechanical wizard, the man who knew more about energy and its practical application that any other living human being—this man unsure of himself—

His voice added to Morton's dismay. It held a harsh, nasal tone that the commander had never heard from him in all the years he had known the man.

"My news isn't pleasant. To energize this ship under a controlled system would require about a hundred hours. There are approximately two square miles of floors and walls, mostly walls. And of course, as I said before, uncontrolled energization would be suicide.

"My plan is to energize the seventh level and the ninth, only the floors and not the walls. Our hope is this: so far the creature has made no organized attempt to kill us. Korita says that this is because he is a peasant, and does not fully realize the issues at stake. As a peasant he is more concerned with reproduction, though what form that is taking, and why he has captured von Grossen is a matter for our biologist. We know, as apparently he does not, that it's a case of destroy him, or he'll destroy us. Sooner or later, even a peasant will realize that killing us comes first, before anything else, and from that moment we're lost. Our chance is that he'll delay too long—a vague chance, but we must accept it because it is based on the only analysis of the creature that we have—Korita's! If he doesn't interfere with our work, then we'll trap him on the eighth level, between the two energized floors."

Somebody interjected with a swift question: "Why not energize the seventh and eighth levels, so that he'll be in hell the moment he starts down?"

"Because"—Pennons' eyes glittered with a hard, unpleasant light—"when he starts down, he'll have one of us with him. We want that man to have a chance for life. The whole plan is packed with danger. It will take about an hour and a half to prepare the floors for energizing."

His voice became a harsh, grating sound: "And during that ninety minutes we'll be absolutely helpless against him, except for our heavy service guns. It is not beyond the bounds of possibility that he will carry us off at the rate of one every three minutes."

"Thirty out of a hundred and eighty!" Morton cut in with a chill incisiveness. "One out of every six in this room. Do we take the chance? Those in favour raise their hands."

He noted with intense satisfaction that not one man's hand but was raised.

The reappearance of the men brought Xtl up to the seventh level with a rush. A vague anxiety pushed into his consciousness, but there was no real sense of doubt, not even a shadow of the mental sluggishness that had afflicted him at first. For long minutes, he was an abnormal shape that flitted like some evil monster from a forgotten hell through that wilderness of walls and corridors.

Twice he was seen; and ugly guns flashed at him—guns as different from the simple action ato-guns as life from death. He analysed them from their effects, the way they smashed down the walls, and made hard metal run like water. Heavy duty electronic guns these, discharging completely disintegrated atoms, a stream of pure electrons that sought union with stable matter in a coruscating fury of senseless desire.

He could face guns like that, but only for the barest second would the spinning atom system within his body carry that intolerable load. Even the biologists, who had perfected the Xtl race, had found their limitations in the hot, ravening energy of smashed atoms.

The important thing was; "What were the men doing with such determination? Obviously, when they shut themselves up in the impregnable engine room, they had conceived a plan—" With glittering, unwinking eyes, Xtl watched that plan take form.

In every corridor, men slaved over atomic furnaces, squat things of dead-black metal. From a hole in the top of each furnace, a white glare spewed up, blazing forth in uncontrollable ferocity at the ceilings; intolerable flares of living fire, dazzling almost beyond endurance to Xtl protected by a solid metal wall as well as by his superlatively conditioned body.

He could see that the men were half dazed by the devastating whiteness that beat against their vision. They wore their space armour with the ordinary transparent glassite electrically darkened. But no light metal armour could ward off the full effect of the deadly rays that sprayed, violent and untamed, in every direction.

Out of the furnaces rolled long dully glowing strips of some material, which were instantly snatched into the maw of machine tools, skillfully hacked into exactly measured sections, and slapped onto the floors. Not an inch of floor, Xtl noticed, escaped being inclosed in some way or another by these strips. And the moment the strips were laid, massive refrigerators hugged close to them, and froze the heat out of them.

His mind refused at first to accept the result of his observations. His brain persisted in searching for deeper purposes, for a cunning of vast and not easily discernible scope. Somewhere there must be a scheme that would explain the appalling effort the men were making. Slowly, he realized the truth.

There was nothing more. These beings were actually intending to attempt the building of walls of force throughout the entire ship under a strict system of controls—anything less, of course, was out of the question. They could not be so foolish as to think that a partial energization could have the faintest hope of success. If such hope smouldered, it was doomed to be snuffed out.

And total energization was equally impossible. Could they not realize that he would not permit such a thing; and that it would be a simple matter to follow them about, and tear loose their energization connections?

In cold contempt, Xtl dismissed the machinations of the men from his mind. They were only playing into his hands, making it easier for him to get the *guuls* he still needed.

He selected his next victim as carefully as he had selected von Grossen. He had discovered in the dead man—Darjeeling—that the stomach was the place he wanted; and the men with the largest stomachs were automatically on his list.

The action was simplicity itself. A cold, merciless survey of the situation from the safety of a wall, a deadly swift rush and—before a single beam could blaze out in sullen rage—he was gone with the writhing, struggling body.

It was simple to adjust his atomic structure the instant he was through a ceiling, and so break his fall on the floor beneath; then dissolve through the floor onto the level below in the same fashion. Into the vast hold of the ship, he half fell, half lowered himself.

The hold was familiar territory now to the sure-footed tread of his long-toed feet. He had explored the place briefly but thoroughly after he first boarded the ship. And the handling of von Grossen had given him the exact experience he needed for this man.

Unerringly, he headed across the dimly lit interior toward the far wall. Great packing cases piled up to the ceiling. Without pause, he leaped into them; and, by dexterous adjustment of his structure, found himself after a moment in a great pipe, big enough for him to stand upright—part of the miles of air-conditioning pipes in the vast ship.

It was dark by ordinary light, but to his full vision a vague twilight glow suffused the place. He saw the body of von Grossen, and deposited his new victim beside the physicist. Carefully now, he inserted one of his slender hands into his own breast; and removed one precious egg—deposited it into the stomach of the human being.

The man had ceased struggling, but Xtl waited for what he knew must happen. Slowly, the body began to stiffen, the muscles growing rigid. The man stirred; then, in evident panic, began to fight as he realized the paralysis that was stealing over him. But remorselessly Xtl held him down.

Abruptly, the chemical action was completed. The man lay motionless, every muscle stiff as a rock, a horrible thing of taut flesh.

There were no doubts now in Xtl's mind. Within a few hours, the eggs would be hatching inside each man's stomach; and in a few hours more the tiny replicas of himself would have eaten themselves to full size.

Grimly complacent, he darted up out of the hold. He needed more hatching places for his eggs, more *guuls*.

On the ninth level now, the men slaved. Waves of heat rolled along the corridor, a veritable inferno wind; even the refrigeration unit in each spacesuit was hard put to handle that furious, that deadly blast of superheated air. Men sweated in their suits, sick from the heat, dazed by the glare, labouring almost by instinct.

At last, Morton shut off his own furnace. "Thank Heaven, that's finished!" he exclaimed; then urgently: "Pennons, are you ready to put your plan into effect?"

"Ready, aye, ready!" came the engineer's dry rasp of a voice on the communicators. He finished even more harshly: "Four men gone and one to go. We've been lucky—but there is one to go!"

"Do you hear that, you spacehounds!" Morton barked. "One to go. One of us will be bait—and don't hold your guns in your hands. He must have the chance at that bait. Kellie, elaborate on those notes you gave me before. It will clear up something very important, and keep our minds off that damned thing."

"Er!" The cracked voice of the sociologist jarred the communicators. "Er, here is my reasoning. When we discovered the thing it was floating a million light-years from the nearest system, apparently without means of spatial locomotion. Picture that appalling distance, and then ask yourself how long it would require for an object to float it by pure chance. Gunlie Lester gave me my figures, so I wish he would tell you what he told me."

"Gunlie Lester speaking!" The voice of the astronomer sounded surprisingly brisk. "Most of you know the prevailing theory of the beginnings of the present universe: that it was formed by the disintegration of a *previous* universe several million million years ago, and that a few million million years hence our universe will complete its cycle in a torrent of explosions, and be replaced by another, which will develop from the maelstrom. As for Kellie's question, it is not at all impossible; in fact, it would require several million million years for a creature floating by pure chance to reach a point a million light-years from a planet. That is what you wanted, Kellie?"

"Er, yes. Most of you will recall my mentioning before that it was a paradox that a pure sympodial development, such as this creature, did not populate the entire universe. The answer is that, logically, if his race *should* have controlled the universe, then they *did* control it. We human beings have discovered that logic is the sole stable factor in the all; and we cannot shrink even from the most far-reaching conclusions that the mind may arrive at. This race did control the universe, but it was the previous universe they ruled, not our present one. Now, naturally, the creature intends that his race shall also dominate this universe."

"In short," Morton snapped, "we are faced with the survivor of the supreme race of a universe. There is no reason to assume that they did not arrive at our present level of progress any later than we did; and we've still got several million million years to go before our universe crashes into flaming death. Therefore, they are not only billions of years ahead of us, but millions of millions of years." His voice took on a strained note: "Frankly, it scares me. We're not doing enough. Our plans are too sketchy. We must have more information before we can hope to win against such a super-human monster. I'm very much afraid that—"

The shrill scream of a man protruded horribly into his words, and there came a gurgling "—got me... quick... ripping me out of my suit—"

The voice collapsed; and somebody shouted in frank dismay: "Good Heavens! That was Dack, my assistant!"

The world of ship became, for Morton, a long, shining corridor that persisted in blurring before his eyes. And it was suddenly as if he were looking, not out at it, but down into its depths—fearsome depths that made his brain reel.

Ages seemed to pass. But Morton, schooled now to abnormal calm, knew that only fractions of seconds were dragging by. Just as his nerves threatened to break, he heard a voice, Pennons' voice, cool, steady, yet almost unrecognizable:

"One!" said Pennons; and it sounded absolute mumbo-jumbo in that moment when out there another man was going through a hell of fear and torment.

"Two!" said Pennons, cold as ice.

Morton found himself staring curiously at his feet. Sparkling, brilliant, beautiful blue fire throbbed there. Little tendrils of that gorgeous flame reared up hungrily a few inches from his suit, as if baffled by some invisible force protecting the suit.

There was a distinct click in Morton's mind. Instantly, his brain jumped to full gear. In a flash of thought, he realized that Pennons had energized floors seven and nine. And that it was blue ferocity of the energization that was struggling to break through the full-driven screens of his space armour.

Through his communicators came the engineer's hiss of indrawn breath: "If I'm right," Pennons almost whispered, all the strength gone from his voice, "we've now got that—devil—cornered on the eighth floor."

"Then," barked Morton efficiently, "we'll carry on according to plan. Group one, follow me to the seventh floor."

The men behind Morton stopped short as he halted abruptly at the second corner. Sickly, he went forward, and stood staring at the human body that sagged against the floor, pasted to the metal by almost unbearably brilliant fingers of blue fire. His voice, when he spoke, was only a whisper, but it cut across the strain of silence like a whiplash:

"Pull him loose!"

Two men stepped gingerly forward, and touched the body. The blue fire leaped ravenously at them, straining with futile ferocity to break through the full-driven defence screens of their suits. The men jerked, and the unholy bonds snapped. They carried the body up the nearest stairs to the unenergized eighth level. The other men followed silently, and watched as the body was laid on the floor.

The lifeless thing continued to kick for several minutes, discharging torrents of energy, then gradually took on the quietness of natural death.

"I'm waiting for reports!" Morton said stiffly into his communicators.

Pennons' voice came. "The men are spread out over the eighth floor according to plan, taking continuous pictures with fluorite cameras. If he's anywhere on the floor, we'll get a picture of his swift-moving body; and then it will be a matter of energizing the floor piecemeal. It'll take about thirty minutes yet—"

And finally the report came: "Nothing!" Pennons' voice held an incredulous note tinged with dismay. "Morton, he's not here. It can only mean that he passed through the energized floor as easily as through ordinary metal. We know he must have gone through it because Dack's dead body was on *this* side."

Somebody said hopelessly: "And now what are we going to do?"

Morton didn't answer. It struck him abruptly, with a shock that tore away his breath, that he had no answer.

The silence in that shining corridor was a form of death. It pressed against Morton, a queer, murky, lightless thing. Death was written too in the faces that blurred around him, the cold, logical death expectancy of men who could see no way out.

Morton broke the silence: "I am willing to accept von Grossen's analysis of how the thing passes through metal. But he intimated the creature recoiled from the energized wall. Can anyone explain then—how?"

"Zeller speaking!" The brisk voice of the metallurgist came through the communicators. "I've finished the neutronium-alloy suit, and I've started my search at the bottom of the ship—I heard your question, Morton. To my mind, we missed one point the first time the creature struck the wall of force: The point is that he *was* in it. And what basic difference is there between being partially inside the wall, and actually passing through? He could pass through in less than a second. The first time, he touched the wall for several seconds, which probably means that, in his surprise, he recoiled and lost his balance. That must have made his position very unpleasant. The second time, however, he simply released poor Dack and passed on through with a minimum of discomfort."

"Hm-m-m!" Morton pondered. "That means he's still vulnerable to walls of force, provided we could keep him inside one for a long enough time. And that would mean complete energization of the ship which, in turn, would depend on his allowing us to make the connections without interference. I think he would interfere. He let us get away with energizing the two floors because he knew it didn't mean anything—and it gave him a good opportunity to kidnap some more men. Fortunately, he didn't grab off as many as we expected, though Heaven help those four."

Smith said grimly, his first words in a long time: "My firm opinion is that anything that would require more than two hours to complete will be fatal. We are dealing with a creature who has everything to gain by killing us, and obtaining control of the ship. Zeller, how long would it take to build neutronium-alloy suits for every man on this ship?"

"About two hundred hours," the metallurgist replied coolly, "mainly because I used up nearly all the available alloy for this one suit. We'd have to break down the walls of the ship, and build the alloy from an electronic base. We're not in the habit of carrying a lot of metal on this ship, as you know, because there's usually a planet a few minutes from anywhere. Now, we've still got a two weeks' trip either way."

"Then that's out!" frowned Smith blackly. He looked stunned. "And since the complete energization is out—we've got nothing else."

The usually lazy voice of Gourlay, the communications chief, snapped: "I don't see why those ways are out. We're still alive; and I suggest we get to work, and do as much as we can as soon as we can—everybody working first at making suits for the men who go out to prepare the walls for energizing. At least, that will protect them from being kidnapped."

"What makes you think," Smith asked coldly, "that the creature is not capable of smashing down neutronium alloy? As a superior being, his knowledge of physics should make it a simple matter for him to construct a beam that could destroy anything we have. Heaven knows there's plenty of tools lying in the various laboratories."

The two men glared at each other with the flashing, angry eyes of men whose nerves have been strained to the utmost limit. Before Morton could speak, Korita's sibilant voice cut across the tense silence: "I am inclined to agree with Smith. We are dealing with a being who must now know that he cannot allow us time for anything important. I agree with the commander when he says that the creature will interfere if we attempt to prepare the ship for complete controlled energization. The honourable gentlemen must not forget, however, that we are dealing with a creature whom we have decided is in the peasant stage of his particular cycle.

"Let me enlarge on that. Life is an ebb and flow. There is a full tide of glorious accomplishment, and a low tide of recuperation. For generations, centuries, the blood flows in the peasant, turgid, impure, gathering strength from the soil; and then it begins to grow, to expand, reaching finally for the remotest stars. At this point, amazingly enough, the blood grows weary; and, in this late megapolitan era, men no longer desire to prolong their race. Highly cultivated people regard having children as a question of pros and cons, and their general outlook on life is tinged with a noble scepticism.

"Nature, on the other hand, knows nothing of pro and con. You cannot reason with a peasant—and he cannot reason except as a peasant. His land and his son, or—to put a higher term to it—his property and his blood are sacred. If a bourgeoisie court orders him off his land, he fights blindly, ignorantly, for his own. It matters not to him that he may have accepted money for a mortgage. He only knows they're trying to take his property, to draw his roots from the soil where his blood has been nourished.

"Honourable sirs, here is my point: This creature cannot begin to imagine anyone else not feeling about his patch of home—his own property the way he does.

"But we... we can make such a sacrifice without suffering a spiritual collapse."

Every muscle in Morton's body grew taut, as he realized the implications. His exclamation was almost a whisper: "Korita, you've got it! It means sacrificing von Grossen and the others. It means sacrifice that makes my brain reel, but property is not sacred to us. And as for von Grossen and the other three"—his voice grew stern and hard, his eyes wide with a chill horror—"I didn't tell you about the notes that Smith gave me. I didn't tell you because he suggested a possible parallel with a certain species of wasp back home on the earth. The thought is so horrible that I think instantaneous death will come as a release to these bold men."

"The wasp!" A man gasped. "You're right, Morton. The sooner they're dead the better!"

"Then," Morton cried, "to the engine room. We—"

A swift, excited voice clamoured into his communicators; it was a long second before he recognized it as belonging to Zeller, the metallurgist:

"Morton—quick! Down to the hold! I've found them—in the air-conditioning pipe. The creature's here, and I'm holding him off as best I can. He's trying to sneak up on me through the walls. Hurry!"

Morton snapped orders with machine-gun precision, as the men swarmed toward the elevators: "Smith, take a dozen men and get Kent down from the bedrooms to the engine room. I'd almost forgotten about him and his broken leg! Pennons, take a hundred men to the engine room and make the preparations to carry out Korita's plan. The rest take the four heavy freight elevators and follow me!"

He finished in a ringing voice: "We won't kill him in the hold of course, unless he's gone stark mad. But the crisis has come! Things are breaking our way at last. And we've got him! We've got him!"

Xtl retreated reluctantly, sullenly, as the men carried off his four *guuls*. The first shrinking fear of defeat closed over his mind like the night that brooded beyond the inclosing walls of the ship. His impulse was to dash into their midst, a whirlwind of ferocity, and smash them. But those ugly, glittering weapons congealed that wild rage.

He retreated with a dismaying sense of disaster, conscious that he had lost the initiative. The men would discover his eggs now; and, in destroying them, would destroy his immediate chances of being reinforced by other Xtls. And, what was more, they were temporarily safe in the engine room.

His brain spun into a cold web of purpose. From this moment, he must kill, and kill only. It seemed suddenly incredible that he had thought first of reproduction, with everything else coming secondary, even his every other thought blurred by that subordination to his one flaming desire.

His proper action was preternaturally clear now. Not to get his *guuls* first, but to kill these dangerous enemies, to control the ship, then head for the nearest inhabited planet, where it would be a simple matter to find other, more stupid *guuls*.

To kill he must have an irresistible weapon, one that could smash—anything! And valuable time had already been wasted. After a moment's thought, he headed for the nearest laboratory, conscious of a burning urgency, unlike anything he had ever known.

As he worked—tall, nightmare body and hideous face bent intently over the gleaming metal of the queer-shaped mechanism— his sensitive feet grew aware of a difference in the symphony of vibrations that throbbed in discordant melody through the ship.

He paused, straightened, alert and tense; and realized what it was. The drive engines were silent. The monster ship of space had halted in its headlong flight, and was lying quiescent in the black deeps.

An abrupt, indefinable sense of urgency came to Xtl—an icy alarm. His long, black, wirelike fingers became flashing things as he made delicate connections, deftly and frantically.

Suddenly, he paused again. Through his brain pulsed a distinct sensation of something wrong, dangerously, desperately, terribly wrong. The muscles of his feet grew taut with straining. Abruptly, he knew what it was.

He could no longer feel the vibrations of the men. *They had left the ship!*

Xtl whirled from his nearly finished weapon, and plunged through the nearest wall. He knew his doom with a burning certainty that found hope only in the blackness of space.

Through deserted corridors he fled, slavering slit-faced hate, scarlet monster from ancient, incredibly ancient Glor. The gleaming walls seemed to mock him. The whole world of the great ship, which had promised so much, was now only the place where sudden intolerable hell would break loose in a devastating, irresistible torrent of energy.

He saw the air lock ahead—and flashed through the first section, then the second, the third—then he was out in space. There was a sense of increasing lightness as his body flung by momentum darted from the side of the ship, out into that blackest of black nights.

For a brief instant, his body glinted and flashed a startling scarlet, reflecting the dazzling light from the row on row of brilliant portholes.

The queerest thing happened then. The porthole lights snuffed out, and were replaced by a strange, unearthly blue glow, that flashed out from every square inch of that dark, sweeping plain of metal.

The blue glow faded, died. Some of the porthole lights came on again, flickering weakly, uncertainly; and then, as mighty engines recovered from that devastating flare of blue power, the lights already shining grew stronger. Others began to flash on.

Xtl was a hundred yards from the ship when he saw the first of the torpedolike craft dart out of the surrounding night, into an opening that yawned in the side of the mighty vessel. Four other dark craft followed, whipping down in swift arcs, their shapes blurred against the background of immensity, vaguely visible in the light that glowed now, strong and steady from the lighted portholes.

The opening shut; and—just like that—the ship vanished. One instant, it was there, a vast sphere of dark metal; the next he was staring through the space where it had been at a vague swirl of light, an enormous galaxy that swam beyond a gulf of a billion years.

Time dragged drearily toward infinity. Xtl sprawled moveless and unutterably hopeless on the bosom of endless night. He couldn't help thinking of the sturdy sons he might have had, and of the universe that was lost because of his mistakes. But it was the thought of the sons, of companionship, that really brought despair.

Morton watched the skillful fingers of the surgeon, as the electrified knife cut into the fourth man's stomach. The last egg was deposited in the bottom of the tall neutronium alloy vat.

The eggs were round, greyish objects, one of them slightly cracked.

As they watched, the crack widened; an ugly, round, scarlet head with tiny, beady eyes and a tiny slit of a mouth poked out. The head twisted on its short neck, and the eyes glittered up at them with a hard ferocity.

And then, with a swiftness that almost took them by surprise, it reared up and tried to run out of the vat, slid back—and dissolved into the flame that Morton poured down upon it.

Smith, licking his dry lips, said: "Suppose he'd got away, and dissolved into the nearest wall!"

Nobody said anything. They stood with intent eyes, staring into the vat. The eggs melted reluctantly, under the merciless fire of Morton's gun, and then burned with a queer, golden light.

"Ah," said Dr. Eggert; and attention turned to him, and the body of von Grossen, over which he was bending. "His muscles are beginning to relax, and his eyes are open and alive. I imagine he knows what's going on. It was a form of paralysis induced by the egg, and fading now that the egg is no longer present. Nothing fundamentally wrong. They'll all be O. K. shortly. What about the big fellow?"

Morton replied: "Zeller swears he saw a flash of red emerge from the main lock just as we swept the ship with uncontrolled energization. It must have been, because we haven't found his body. However, Pennons is out with half the men, taking pictures with fluorite cameras; and we'll know for certain in a few hours. Here he is now. Well, Pennons?"

The engineer strode in briskly, and placed a misshapen thing of metal on one of the tables. "Nothing definite to report yet—but I found this in the main physics laboratory. What do you make of it?"

Morton frowned down at the fragile-looking object with its intricate network of wires. There were three distinct tubes that might have been muzzles running into and through three small, round balls, that shone with a queer, silvery light. The light penetrated the table, making it as transparent as glassite. And, strangest of all, the balls irradiated, not heat, but cold.

Morton put his hands near, but the cold was of a mild, water-freezing variety, apparently harmless. He touched the metal ball. It felt as chilled metal might feel.

"I think we'd better leave this for our chief physicist to examine. Von Grossen ought to be up and around soon. You say you found it in the laboratory?"

Pennons nodded; and Morton carried on his thought: "Obviously, the creature was working on it, when he suspected that something was amiss—he must have suspected the truth, for he left the ship.

That seems to discount your theory, Korita. You said that, as a true peasant, he couldn't even imagine what we were going to do."

The Japanese historian smiled faintly through the fatigue that paled his face. "Honourable commander," he said politely, "a peasant can realize destructive intentions as easily as you or I. What he cannot do is bring himself to destroy his own property, or imagine others destroying theirs. We have no such limitations."

Pennons groaned: "I wish we had. Do you know that it will take us three months at least to get this ship properly repaired after thirty seconds of uncontrolled energization. For those thirty seconds, the ship created a field in space millions of times more intense than the energization output. I was afraid that—"

He stopped with a guilty look. Morton grinned: "Go ahead and finish what you were going to say. You were afraid the ship would be completely destroyed. Don't worry, Pennons, your previous statements as to the danger involved made us realize the risks we were taking; and we knew that our lifeboats could only be given partial antiacceleration; so we'd have been stranded here a million years from home."

A man said, thoughtfully: "Well, personally, I think there was nothing actually to fear. After all, he did belong to another universe, and there is a special rhythm to our present state of existence to which man is probably attuned. We have the advantage in this universe of momentum, which, I doubt, a creature from any other universe could hope to overcome. And in the world of man there is no just place for a creature that can even consider laying its eggs in the living flesh of other sensitive beings. All other intelligent life would unite against such a distinctly personal menace."

Smith shook his head: "There is no biological basis for your opinion, and therefore it falls in the category of 'things darkly spoken are darkly seen.' It dominated once, and it could dominate again. You assume far too readily that man is a paragon of justice, forgetting apparently that he lives on meat, enslaves his neighbours, murders his opponents, and obtains the most unholy sadistical joy from the agony of others. It is not impossible that we shall, in the course of our travels, meet other intelligent creatures far more worthy than man to rule the universe."

"By Heaven!" replied the other, "no creature is ever getting on board this ship again, no matter how harmless he looks. My nerves are all shot; and I'm not so good a man as I was when I first came aboard the *Beagle* two long years ago."

"You speak for us all!" said Morton.

MONSTER

John Christopher

John Christopher was the best known writing persona of British author Samuel Youd (1922–2012), who wrote some of the most popular science fiction of the 1950s and 1960s. He is remembered, at least amongst his adult novels, for The Death of Grass *(1956), an apocalyptic tale of the fall of civilization after a virus destroys all grass and grain crops. He produced another disaster novel in* The World in Winter *(1962) when the planet is devastated by a new Ice Age. In the 1960s Christopher turned to writing for a young-adult market and had considerable success with his Tripods sequence of novels, starting with* The White Mountains *(1967) where humanity is enslaved by aliens who, not unlike Wells's Martians, exist in their giant three-legged walking machines. The prize-winning* The Guardians *(1970) depicts a dystopian future of the mid-twenty-first century where Britain is divided between the overpopulated cities and the agrarian countryside and explores the concept of freedom. Early in his career Christopher wrote many short stories, some of the best collected as* The Twenty-Second Century *(1954), which includes the following.*

T HERE WAS A SWELL MOVING IN FROM THE DEEP. EVEN HERE in the Council Place where it was sheltered they could feel it and see the phosphorescence flickering under the quickening pulse of the waters. Out in the Deep the waters would be surging heavily. There would be damage on the outlying hydro-farms, and another bad harvest.

Dilwan, swimming in powerfully to the centre of the throng, could sense the mood of despair that hung over them. He looked down towards the mass of dark figures huddled on the sea-bed, and remembered what his father had told him of the last days of Serbena. Dilwan himself had been born during those days, when the harvests had failed for the last time and the giant sharks had breached the defences and torn a path of destruction through the doomed city. In a vague way he could even remember fragmentary details of the terror-fraught journey across the Deep to Kareeta. But most of what he remembered came from the stories his father had told him many seasons before. Of the deep, inky, non-phosphorescent blackness of the Deep. Of the huge forest of squids into which they had blundered, and where his mother had died. Of the flashing, bloody sorties of sharks, as they swept down on the tattered fugitives from Serbena. And, at last, of the sight of the walls of Kareeta, where they had found safety.

All that was ninety seasons ago. More than seventy seasons had passed since his father had been killed by the sharks while working on an outlying hydro-farm. In that time Kareeta, season by season, had slipped nearer to the doom that had overwhelmed her sister-city.

Each season the scavenger-fish preyed more openly on the hydro-fields, swooping down in the wake of the shark bands and laying waste acres of cultivated land. The two races had evolved a strange, menacing symbiosis; as though they were deliberately combining to exterminate the Kranaki and crush intelligence in the world of water. And they were only part of the doom, hanging more and more ominously over Kareeta. Each season the squids advanced more openly up the sides of the Deep. They had overwhelmed the whaling station at Purka. And the whales themselves were less and less tractable. Fewer returned to their pens each season. Those that did frequently turned on their Kranaki masters.

Finally, in the last thirty seasons, eruptions and land-quakes had occurred with greater and greater frequency, bringing with them swells and storms, splitting and laying waste the hydro-farms and shaking Kareeta itself. It seemed to the Kranaki that the end could not be long delayed. And with the end of Kareeta would come the end of their race. There was no other city to which the survivors could retreat. Since the fall of Serbena, Kareeta had been the only stronghold of the Kranaki.

Dilwan stopped swimming and allowed the current to carry him gently in to the place reserved for him on the dais. They had been waiting for him. He relaxed and listened. The President, Balakon, began speaking, slapping the water with his huge flippers into impulses that rippled out to the antennae of the waiting Kranaki.

He said: "The allotment of *pilner* will be halved from the begin-ning of next season. All the *pilner* crops in the hydro-fields to the north-west have been destroyed by the last eruption."

A sigh rippled round and in towards the dais, emanating from hundreds of flippers. Dilwan felt the shock; a realization of the desperate situation. Without *pilner* the Kranaki could not live.

On half their present allotment they would be perilously near to starvation.

Balakon went on. "In the last season over a hundred Kranaki have been killed; mostly by sharks, a few by squids, three by rebellious whales. Our numbers are now less than seven hundred. But even for seven hundred our harvests are too meagre. The fewer there are, the fewer we can spare for guards, and the more easily can the sharks break through to ravish the farms, and even the outskirts of the city itself. We must break this stranglehold if Kareeta is not to die."

He paused, waiting for the impulses of despair to die out of the water.

"I can remember," Balakon continued, "when the Kranaki held five great cities and numbered more than a hundred thousand. That was only eight hundred seasons ago. In the times of our grandfathers the Kranaki cities spread out in hundreds to the further seas; to the warm seas of the south and to the cold seas that stretched beyond to the ice. And round the cities, league after league, lay the hydro-farms, growing a multitude of crops that now are only a memory."

He stopped for a while, remembering. "When I was very young," he said, "I tasted *charang*. It had a lightness and warmth and beauty in it, so that your body felt as insubstantial as a floater when you had eaten it. It grew only in the cold beyond the warm, in the gardens of the city of Charbera, which died seven hundred seasons ago. There will be no more *charang*."

A current swept through the Council Place, stirring the tendrils of the Kranaki with thoughts of the storms swirling up from the Deep around them.

Balakon said: "In the days of our grandfathers Kranaki ruled from cold to warm and on to cold again; from the bottom of the

Deeps to the thin waters above. The whales came and went at our bidding; the sharks cowered away from us in the thin waters, and our ancestors hunted them for sport. We were supreme until—the Shock.

"You have all heard of it; of the days when the sea-bed crumbled beneath our cities and substances bubbled up, turning the water into thin, blindingly hot mist. Only in the far south and here in the north did a few cities survive; cities that have fallen one by one before the attack of the sharks and the squids, and the tremblings of the sea-bed. Now there is only Kareeta, and it seems impossible that Kareeta can survive another ten seasons."

The vibrations of despair rocked more violently through the waters of the Council Place. Dilwan, listening, realized that the calm pronouncements of Balakon were grimly reinforcing the sense of doom that hung over the Kranaki. Each must have known the end was near and hoped to be mistaken. Balakon spoke with a dreadful, inescapable authority. And yet Balakon himself had planned the one possible way of salvation. Now he went on, firmly over-riding the despair about him.

"It seems impossible," Balakon said, "but there is one chance of saving our race. For thousands of seasons, among the things that have dropped into our depths from the thin water, there have been some that were not dead fish but strange, artificial creations containing queerly-formed dead pygmies. It is in our history that these creations have changed throughout the seasons, becoming more complex as though fashioned by a race of growing culture and ingenuity. We thought for a long time that the pygmies who must have made them lived in the thin water, and that these, perhaps, were their funeral vessels, designed to carry their dead into what, to them, would be the mysterious depths below.

"For thousands of seasons our ancestors planned how they might establish contact with the pygmies, and perhaps help them in their struggles against their enemies. Some of their bodies that we found had had limbs torn by our own enemies, the sharks. But by ourselves we could not penetrate up into the thin water. It was not until a few hundred seasons before the Shock that Ralbaned, the great hydro-farmer, developed that new hard transparent coral of which Kareeta is built, and adapted it to the creation of pressure suits moulded to our shapes.

"Since then our adventurers have swum up through the thin water, and found a world of thin mist lying above it and learned that the pygmies live on the bed of that mist, using their strange vessels to cross the intervening waters. When the Shock came we were preparing to send large expeditions to meet them. Even since the Shock our adventurers have dared the thin waters and the blockade of sharks to see this strange world above us. And we have kept a watcher at our last outpost, Berdan.

"A tunnel leads up to Berdan, a tunnel which the sharks have not yet found. Once at Berdan our watchers are safe from them, for Berdan itself is surrounded on all sides by the air-bed on which the pygmies live. For a season at a time the watchers stay, burdened by pressure suits, trying to make contact with the pygmies. But as the watchers could only plunge into the mist for a fraction of time, they have always failed. The pygmies do not recognize them, except, perhaps, as a strange fish.

"Now, in the time of our greatest need, another hydro-farmer has found what may be the solution to our desperate plight. Dilwan, a native of lost Serbena, has found a means of lining the pressure suits with a new form of sponge. In the new pressure suit a Kranak can venture into the mist, protected from thinness by the coral, and from waterlessness by the sponge. At last we can meet the pygmies on their own air-bed! We will go to them, and they will help us against our mutual enemies, the sharks, and give us their strange, fashioned things to help on the hydro-farms, while we in turn teach them of all the richness that lies on the sea-bed for those that have the strength to take it. Nothing will be able to stand against the combined force of the Kranaki and the pygmies.

"But it will not be easy to penetrate the mist. Even with the new pressure suits it will be an agonizing adventure, only to be borne for a short time. We must send an emissary, who can first prove our intelligence to the pygmies. Dilwan, who made this venture possible, has asked to be allowed to go, and we have given permission. Dilwan! The future—the very existence of the Kranaki—depends on your mission. May the Ruler of the Deep attend you!"

Dilwan heard the chorusing vibrations.

"The Ruler of the Deep attend you!"

He felt inside himself the pride of the Kranaki, of the race that had once held the oceans to their furthest reaches. On him the future depended, and he would not fail them. Two of the Kranaki floated down to him, holding the artificially shaped coral that was to protect him from the thinness above. He wriggled into it, and when the head-piece had been pulled down the coral insects were set to work on the join, to seal them until his return. Only a small gap was left, so that water could continue to flood in round him. He would not seal this with coral until, at Berdan, he was ready to meet the pygmies.

Now, with powerful strokes, he swam above the council of Kranaki. For a moment he watched them, feeling their vibrations of hope and good-will beating even through the enclosing coral. Then, with a steady, powerful motion he was swimming away from

Kareeta. Six young Kranaki swam with him, spared from the desperately urgent need of the harvest to protect him against sharks until he should reach the mouth of the tunnel.

Half a dozen sharks eddied down, but sheered away quickly at the sight of the seven Kranaki. Dilwan felt a surge of vicious hatred against them, and their cowardly avoidance of battle except when they outnumbered the Kranaki by four or five to one. The hatred changed into triumph as he thought of his own mission, and how its success would put weapons into the hands of the Kranaki. We shall hunt them down, he thought with grim satisfaction, we and the pygmies. We shall hunt them until not a shark remains in the oceans. Even the small ones in the thin water we shall destroy. And the cities of the Kranaki shall rise again.

Roger Blaine groaned in more than spiritual anguish. The road seemed to be turning into a sticky river of molten lead. The front wheel of his bicycle was continually popping the bubbles of tar that swelled up in front of them. Ahead waves of heat shimmered up like a wall of mist between the loch and the forested hills. He felt as though he had been cycling for years through a section of Dante's Inferno. And Hilda, damn her, looked as cool and unperturbed as ever.

"Take it easy," he panted. "What are you using for power—atomic energy?"

His wife smiled sweetly at him. "Just ordinary muscle power, darling," she replied. "I told you you were getting too flabby. This sort of holiday is just what you need. Wait till I've had you up and down Ben Nevis a few times. You'll be a different man."

"I shan't last that long," he said gloomily. "Another hundred yards of this and I shall melt into a grease ball and evaporate. When I think of the things you told me about the cool Scottish valleys and lochs I feel that my faith in woman is shaken for ever."

Hilda smiled. "Hold on," she said. "It's less than a mile now to Invermoriston. I should hate to think of you melting away when almost in sniffing distance of a nice long, cool pint of beer. Contemplate the beauties of Ness and forget the heat. You might see the monster. As a qualified zoologist you could classify it. Think of it—*draco Blainensis!*"

Roger grunted. "Any monster with any sense would keep well under in this weather. Anyway, it's too early in the day, and the weather's too clear. For the creation of the Loch Ness monster you need a misty evening full of shadows, a preliminary oiling of good strong Scotch, and a Celtic imagination. Given those three you stand a chance of seeing monsters by the million."

"You sceptical scientists!" Hilda said. "Just because you haven't got their bones neatly docketed in the Natural History Museum in South Kensington, sea-monsters can't possibly exit. When it should be obvious that if they live at the bottom of the ocean you could never by any chance find their remains."

Roger mopped his sweating brow with a handkerchief. If anything it seemed to be getting a little hotter, absurd as that seemed.

"There are at least two very good reasons for disbelieving the Loch Ness monster story," he said wearily. "In the first place it is difficult to see how the monster could get along the Caledonian Canal from Inverness to the loch without being spotted, and no one has yet reported its presence in the Canal. In the second, if the monster lives, as you claim, at the bottom of the ocean, then the difference in pressure at the surface of the water would kill it immediately."

"Not valid," Hilda declared. "In the first place the monster might have been in the loch for hundreds of years, or there might be a subterranean entrance somewhere. And in the second, it might be a tough monster, able to withstand different pressures. There could be all sorts of reasons. You're just a dogmatic scientist. I hope the monster comes after you."

"I'll try the Scotch this evening and brush up my imagination," he promised.

"We'll see about that," his wife said grimly.

At last the road bent away from the loch, and the welcome sight of the Invermoriston Hotel lay before them. With surprising speed Roger parked his bicycle and disappeared into the parlour. When Hilda followed him she found him contemplating the remains of a pint of beer.

"Your watch was slow," he said reproachfully. "We almost didn't make it. It's a quarter to two."

"Lemonade would have been just as good for you," Hilda said, ignoring his instinctive shudder. "But I've good news for you. They have some room here. As it will probably be past three o'clock by the time we finish lunch I thought we might have a rest and set off for Fort Augustus in the morning. I think you've lost enough fat for one day."

Roger rolled his eyes up. "Saved at the eleventh hour," he murmured. "This calls for another drink."

Hilda watched the beer vanish.

"Come on," she said. "Lunch is ready. If we get it over quickly we can go for a ramble up the Moriston."

She dragged him away, protesting.

It was not until evening, however, that Hilda succeeded in getting him away from the hotel, and then he refused point-blank to walk up the winding Moriston, insisting instead on the shorter walk to the loch. And at Dalcataig Pier he determined on resting, developing a sudden passion for contemplation of the beauties of Ness. The scene was impressive. Behind them rose the hilly forests of Portclair and Invermoriston, dark, tossing green in the evening breeze. In front lay the purple loch and farther on the gently rising heights beyond Glen Albyn. The sun, which had set behind Portclair, was still lingering on the house-tops of Invermoriston.

A boat came in to Dalcataig Pier, and men got out, workers from the aluminium works on the other side of the loch. Roger and Hilda heard them talking excitedly as they passed:

"Och, Wullie McKay saw it. He said you couldna mistake it. It's the auld monster again. I ken fine we'll have the newspaper bodies doon with us again noo."

"There you are," Hilda said triumphantly. "It's back!"

Roger smiled the superior, irritating smile of one who knows better.

"Let's get back to the hotel," he said. "I want to stoke my imagination up."

As they were turning back from the Dalcataig they met a man running towards them. He called breathlessly:

"Tak heed! The monster's in the Moriston, wallowing like a whale. I'm off to the Pier for a gun."

There was no disputing his sincerity or sobriety. Without a word Roger and Hilda began to run towards the river Moriston. They reached the bridge and found all the inhabitants of the tiny village assembled on it.

Then they saw it, wallowing up the small river from the loch. A vast scaly neck rose from the water, upholding a long, flat head that peered dazedly about, as though the tranquil light of the Scottish twilight were too brilliant for it. Its body stretched behind, an impressive bulk tapering into flippers in parts. Just under the neck were two membranous tendrils, projecting stiffly like spears. It moved awkwardly up the river towards the bridge.

For a moment the villagers stayed, gazing at the invader in unbelief. Then they fled, panic-stricken, back to their houses. Hilda felt like joining them, but Roger was leaning so far forward over the bridge in his anxiety to take in all details of the monster that she felt obliged to hang on to his coat, in case he overbalanced and fell into the river.

The monster seemed to notice the villagers streaming away and made a move towards the bank, as though to follow them. But the pull of the water was too much for it, and it fell back defeated. Rolling in mid-stream, it lifted its head towards the bridge again, and saw the two people left on it. The long, scaly neck moved towards them. Hilda wanted to scream, but Roger was gazing at the approaching monster as though it were the Holy Grail. Her nose caught the thick, fishy smell of the sea. She stared at the broad, serpentine head and the gleaming eyes.

There was a cry from the south bank, and she saw the Scot they had passed on the road running towards them, waving a rifle.

"Ye're all richt!" he shouted. "Hauld on—I've got a bullet for it."

Roger shouted back frantically: "No, no! Don't shoot, for God's sake. *It's wearing a diving suit!*"

The Scot levelled his rifle.

"I'm no fashed if it's wearin' a kilt," he called. "It's not coming up the Moriston!"

The shot rang out above Roger's frantic appeals. The monster reared as a bullet hit it in the neck. There was a brief, high whistling as though a balloon were being deflated, and the long neck slumped forward into the water.

Roger dashed down to the bank and into the river, with Hilda following.

"It can't be dead," he muttered. "A single bullet can't stop an elephant, let alone a thing like this. Unless... I can't believe it."

The head had fallen sideways, so that it projected a little from the water. Roger bent over it, examining. After a moment he looked at Hilda, watching from the bank. The villagers had begun to swarm back, realizing the monster had been overthrown.

Roger said: "It's dead all right. Diagnosis—multiple internal ruptures. The same as we would have if suddenly transported into a vacuum. That shot merely punctured its protective covering."

Hilda said: "You mean..."

"That it was an intelligent being!" Roger finished. "I guessed it from the bridge when that fool was waving his gun about. God, what a waste!"

He climbed wearily out of the water.

"Maybe another one will follow it," Hilda said reassuringly. "The natives can be warned. Next time it will be different."

Roger looked back over the bridge. The villagers were clustered in excited groups looking down on the monster where it lay with the water washing over it.

"Maybe," he said. "If there is a next time."

The last quake had brought down several pillars of the Council Place. A strong current was flowing through Kareeta, brushing the phosphorescent organisms into startling lambency. Balakon looked round at the huddled Kranaki.

"We must still hope," he signalled. "A young, strong Kranak such as Dilwan could last a whole season in a pressure suit. Perhaps he is having difficulty in convincing the pygmies of the urgency of our plight. We must hope that he will come back. We have tried to duplicate the pressure suit he made, but the sponge does not breed true. We might stumble on it again tomorrow, or never. And the harvest is worse even than we had expected. Kareeta can only survive a few more seasons. We must hope Dilwan will come back."

The Kranaki huddled silently about the dais from which their leader spoke. High above circled a school of giant sharks, watching and waiting with timeless malignance.

RESIDENT PHYSICIAN

James White

In a career that lasted over forty years James White (1928–1999) produced a wide variety of novels and stories but is best remembered for his series featuring the Sector Twelve General Hospital, a huge space habitat run by and intended to look after all and every known alien species. The series, which began with the eponymous "Sector General" (1957), eventually ran to twelve books, starting with Hospital Station *(1962), and explored a remarkable diversity of creatures and problems, as the following story shows.*

White was born and lived in Belfast and worked initially in a tailoring firm before moving on to the aircraft industry. His first story was published in 1953 and he was a mainstay of the British science-fiction magazines for the next decade. Amongst his non-series novels are Second Ending *(serial, 1961), an end-of-the-world story with a bewildering restoration,* Open Prison *(serial, 1964) where human prisoners-of-war struggle for survival against alien overlords, and* The Watch Below *(1966) about how both humans and aliens survive after accidents under the sea. White was a gifted and ingenious writer who, having lived through the Troubles in Northern Ireland, never lost his belief in humanity.*

ONE

THE PATIENT BEING BROUGHT INTO THE OBSERVATION WARD was a large specimen—about one thousand pounds mass, Conway estimated—and resembled a giant, upright pear. Five thick, tentacular appendages grew from the narrow head section and a heavy apron of muscle at its base gave evidence of a snail-like, although not necessarily slow, method of locomotion. The whole body surface looked raw and lacerated, as though someone had been trying to take its skin off with a wire brush.

To Conway there was nothing very unusual about the physical aspect of the patient or its condition, six years in space Sector General Hospital, having accustomed him to much more startling sights, so he moved forward to make a preliminary examination. Immediately the Monitor Corps lieutenant who had accompanied the patient's trolley into the ward moved closer also. Conway tried to ignore the feeling of breath on the back of his neck and took a closer look at the patient.

Five large mouths were situated below the root of each tentacle, four being plentifully supplied with teeth and the other one housing the vocal apparatus. The tentacles themselves showed a high degree of specialization at their extremities; three of them were plainly manipulatory, one bore the patient's visual equipment and the remaining member terminated in a horn-tipped, bony mace. The head was featureless, being simply an osseus dome housing the patient's brain.

There wasn't much else to be seen from a superficial examination. Conway turned to get his deep probe gear, and walked on the Monitor officer's feet.

"Have you ever considered taking up medicine seriously, Lieutenant?" he said irritably.

The lieutenant reddened, his face making a horrible clash of colour against the dark green of his uniform collar. He said stiffly, "This patient is a criminal. It was found in circumstances which indicate that it killed and ate the other member of its ship's crew. It has been unconscious during the trip here, but I've been ordered to stand guard on it just in case. I'll try to stay out of your way, Doctor."

Conway swallowed, his eyes going to the vicious-looking, horny bludgeon with which, he had no doubt, the patient's species had battered their way to the top of their evolutionary tree. He said drily, "Don't try too hard, Lieutenant."

Using his eyes and a portable x-ray scanner Conway examined his patient thoroughly inside and out. He took several specimens, including sections of the affected skin, and sent them off to Pathology with three closely-written pages of covering notes. Then he stood back and scratched his head.

The patient was warm-blooded, oxygen-breathing, and had fairly normal gravity and pressure requirements which, when considered with the general shape of the beastie, put its physiological classification as EPLH. It seemed to be suffering from a well-developed and widespread epithelioma, the symptoms being so plain that he really should have begun treatment without waiting for the Path report. But a cancerous skin condition did not, ordinarily, render a patient deeply unconscious.

That could point to psychological complications, he knew, and in that case he would have to call in some specialized help. One of his telepathic colleagues was the obvious choice, if it hadn't been for the fact that telepaths could only rarely work minds that were not already telepathic and of the same species as themselves. Except for the very odd instance, telepathy had been found to be a strictly closed circuit form of communication. Which left his GLNO friend, the empath Dr. Prilicla...

Behind him the Lieutenant coughed gently and said, "When you've finished the examination. Doctor, O'Mara would like to see you."

Conway nodded. "I'm going to send someone to keep an eye on the patient," he said, grinning. "Guard them as well as you've guarded me."

Going through to the main ward Conway detailed an Earth-human nurse—a very good-looking Earth-human nurse—to duty in the observation ward. He could have sent in one of the Tralthan FGLIs, who belonged to a species with six legs and so built that beside one of them an Earthly elephant would have seemed a fragile, sylph-like creature, but he felt that he owed the Lieutenant something for his earlier bad manners.

Twenty minutes later, after three changes of protective armour and a trip through the chlorine section, a corridor belonging to the AUGL water-breathers and the ultra-refrigerated wards of the methane life-forms. Conway presented himself at the office of Major O'Mara.

As Chief Psychologist of a multi-environment hospital hanging in frigid blackness at the Galactic rim, he was responsible for the mental well-being of a Staff of ten thousand entities who were composed of eighty-seven different species. O'Mara was a very important man at Sector General. He was also, on his own admission, the most approachable man in the hospital. O'Mara was fond of saying that he didn't care who approached him or when, but if they hadn't a very good reason for pestering him with their silly little problems then they needn't expect to get away from him again unscathed. To O'Mara the medical staff were patients, and it was the generally held belief that the high level of stability among that variegated and often touchy bunch of e-ts was due to them being too scared of O'Mara to go mad. But today he was in an almost sociable mood.

"This will take more than five minutes so you'd better sit down, Doctor," he said sourly when Conway stopped before his desk. "I take it you've had a look at our cannibal?"

Conway nodded and sat down. Briefly he outlined his findings with regard to the EPLH patient, including his suspicion that there might be complications of a psychological nature. Ending, he asked, "Do you have any other information on its background, apart from the cannibalism?"

"Very little," said O'Mara. "It was found by a Monitor patrol vessel in a ship which, although undamaged, was broadcasting distress signals. Obviously it became too sick to operate the vessel. There was no other occupant, but because the EPLH was a new species to the rescue party they went over its ship with a fine-tooth comb, and found that there should have been another person aboard. They discovered this through a sort of ship's log cum personal diary kept on tape by the EPLH, and by study of the airlock tell-tales and similar protective gadgetry the details of which don't concern us at the moment. However, all the facts point to there being two entities aboard the ship, and the log tape suggests pretty strongly that the other one came to a sticky end at the hands, and teeth, of your patient."

O'Mara paused to toss a slim sheaf of papers on to his lap and Conway saw that it was a typescript of the relevant sections of the log. He had time only to discover that the EPLH's victim had been the ship's doctor, then O'Mara was talking again.

"We know nothing about its planet of origin," he said morosely, "except that it is somewhere in the other galaxy. However, with only one quarter of our own Galaxy explored, our chances of finding its home world are negligible—"

"How about the Ians," said Conway, "maybe they could help?"

The Ians belonged to a culture originating in the other galaxy which had planted a colony in the same sector of the home galaxy which contained the Hospital. They were an unusual species—classification GKNM—which went into a chrysalis stage at adolescence and metamorphosized from a ten-legged crawler into a beautiful, winged life-form. Conway had had one of them as a patient three months ago. The patient had been long since discharged, but the two GKNM doctors, who had originally come to help Conway with the patient, had remained at Sector General to study and teach.

"A Galaxy's a big place," said O'Mara with an obvious lack of enthusiasm, "but try them by all means. However, to get back to your patient, the biggest problem is going to come *after* you've cured it.

"You see, Doctor," he went on, "this particular beastie was found in circumstances which show pretty conclusively that it is guilty of an act which every intelligent species we know of considers a crime. As the Federation's police force among other things the Monitor Corps is supposed to take certain measures against criminals like this one. They are supposed to be tried, rehabilitated or punished as seems fit. But how can we give this criminal a fair trial when we know nothing at all about its background, a background which just might contain the possibility of extenuating circumstances? At the same time we can't just let it go free…"

"Why not?" said Conway. "Why not point it in the general direction from whence it came and administer a judicial kick in the pants?"

"Or why not let the patient die," O'Mara replied, smiling, "and save trouble all round?"

Conway didn't speak. O'Mara was using an unfair argument and they both knew it, but they also knew that nobody would be able to convince the Monitor enforcement section that curing the sick and punishing the malefactor were not of equal importance in the Scheme of Things.

"What I want you to do," O'Mara resumed. "is to find out all you can about the patient and its background after it comes to and during treatment. Knowing how soft-hearted, or soft-headed you are, I expect you will side with the patient during the cure and appoint yourself an unofficial counsel for the defence. Well, I won't mind that if in so doing you obtain the information which will enable us to summon a jury of its peers. Understood?"

Conway nodded.

O'Mara waited precisely three seconds, then said, "If you've nothing better to do than laze about in that chair…"

Immediately on leaving O'Mara's office Conway got in touch with Pathology and asked for the EPLA report to be sent to him before lunch. Then he invited the two Ian GKNMs to lunch and arranged for a consultation with Prilicla regarding the patient shortly afterwards. With these arrangements made he felt free to begin his rounds.

During the two hours which followed Conway had no time to think about his newest patient. He had fifty-three patients currently in his charge together with six doctors in various stages of training and a supporting staff of nurses, the patients and medical staff comprising eleven different physiological types. There were special instruments and procedures for examining these extra-terrestrial patients, and when he was accompanied by a trainee whose pressure and gravity requirements differed both from those of the patient to be examined and himself, then the 'routine' of his rounds could become an extraordinarily complicated business.

But Conway looked at all his patients, even those whose convalescence was well advanced or whose treatment could have been handled by a subordinate. He was well aware that this was a stupid practice which only served to give him a lot of unnecessary work, but the truth was promotion to a resident Senior Physician was still too recent for him to have become used to the large-scale delegation of responsibility. He foolishly kept on trying to do everything himself.

After rounds he was scheduled to give an initial midwifery lecture to a class of DBLF nurses. The DBLFs were furry, multipedal beings resembling outsize caterpillars and were native to the planet Kelgia. They also breathed the same atmospheric mixture as himself, which meant that he was able to do without a pressure suit. To this purely physical comfort was added the fact that talking about such elementary stuff as the reason for Kelgian females conceiving only once, in their lifetime and then producing quads who were invariably divided equally in sex, did not call for great concentration on his part. It left a large section of his mind free to worry about the alleged cannibal in his observation ward.

TWO

Half an hour later he was with the two Ian doctors in the Hospital's main dining hall—the one which catered for Tralthan, Kelgian, human and the various other warmblooded, oxygen-breathers on the Staff—eating the inevitable salad. This in itself did not bother Conway unduly, in fact, lettuce was downright appetizing compared with some of the things he had had to eat while playing host to other e-t colleagues, but he did not think that he would ever get used to the gale they created during lunch.

The GKNM denizens of Ia were a large, delicate, winged life-form who looked something like a dragonfly. To their rod-like but flexible bodies were attached four insectile legs, manipulators, the usual sensory organs and three tremendous sets of wings. Their table manners were not actually unpleasant—it was just that they did not sit down to dine, they hovered. Apparently eating while in flight aided their digestions as well as being pretty much a conditioned reflex with them.

Conway set the Path report on the table and placed the sugar bowl on top of it to keep it from blowing away. He said, "... You'll see from what I've just been reading to you that this appears to be a fairly simple case. Unusually so, I'd say, because the patient is remarkably clear of harmful bacteria of any type. Its symptoms indicate a form of epithelioma, that and nothing else, which makes its unconsciousness rather puzzling. But maybe some information on its planetary environment, sleeping periods and so on, would clarify things, and that is why I wanted to talk to you.

"We know that the patient comes from your galaxy. Can you tell me anything at all about its background?"

The GKNM on Conway's right drifted a few inches back from the table and said through its Translator, "I'm afraid I have not yet mastered the intricacies of your physiological classification system, Doctor. What does the patient look like?"

"Sorry, I forgot," said Conway. He was about to explain in detail what an EPLH was, then he began sketching on the back of the Path report instead. A few minutes later he held up the result and said, "It looks something like that."

Both Ians dropped to the floor.

Conway who had never known the GKNMs to stop either eating or flying during a meal was impressed by the reaction.

He said, "You know about them, then?"

The GKNM on the right made noises which Conway's Translator reproduced as a series of barks, the e-t equivalent of an attack of stuttering. Finally it said, "We know of them. We have never seen one of them, we do not know their planet of origin, and before this moment we were not sure that they had actual physical existence. They... they are gods, Doctor."

Another VIP...! thought Conway, with a sudden sinking feeling. His experience with VIP patients was that their cases were *never* simple. Even if the patient's condition was nothing serious there were invariably complications, none of which were medical.

"My colleague is being a little too emotional," the other GKNM broke in. Conway had never been able to see any physical difference between the two Ians, but somehow this one had the air of being a more cynical, world-weary dragonfly. "Perhaps I can tell you what little is known, and deduced, about them rather than enumerate all the things which are not..."

The species to which the patient belonged was not a numerous one, the Ian doctor went on to explain, but their sphere of influence in the other galaxy was tremendous. In the social and psychological sciences they were very well advanced, and individually their intelligence and mental capacity was enormous. For reasons known only to themselves they did not seek each other's company very often, and it was unheard of for more than one of them to be found on any planet at the same time for any lengthy period.

They were always the supreme ruler on the worlds they occupied. Sometimes it was a beneficent rule, sometimes harsh—but the harshness, when viewed with a century or so's hindsight, usually turned out to be beneficence in disguise. They used people, whole planetary populations, and even interplanetary cultures, purely as a means to solve the problems which they set themselves, and when the problem was solved they left. At least this was the impression received by not quite unbiased observers.

In a voice made fiat and emotionless only because of the process of translation the Ian went on, "... Legends seem to agree that one of them will land on a planet with nothing but its ship and a companion who is always of a different species. By using a combination of defensive science, psychology and sheer business acumen they overcome local prejudice and begin to amass wealth and power. The transition from local authority to absolute planetary rule is gradual, but then they have plenty of time. They are, of course, immortal."

Faintly, Conway heard his fork clattering on to the floor. It was a few minutes before he could steady either his hands or his mind.

There were a few extra-terrestrial species in the Federation who possessed very long life-spans, and most of the medically advanced cultures—Earth's included—had the means of extending life considerably with rejuvenation treatments. Immortality, however, was something they did *not* have, nor had they ever had the chance to study anyone who possessed it. Until now, that was. Now Conway had a patient to care for, and cure and, most of all, investigate.

Unless... but the GKNM was a doctor, and a doctor would not say immortal if he merely meant long-lived.

"Are you sure?" croaked Conway.

The Ian's answer took a long time because it included the detailing of a great many facts, theories and legends concerning these beings who were satisfied to rule nothing less than a planet apiece. At the end of it Conway was still not sure that his patient was immortal, but everything he had heard seemed to point that way.

Hesitantly, he said, "After what I've just heard perhaps I shouldn't ask but in your opinion are these beings capable of committing an act of murder and cannibalism—"

"No!" said one Ian.

"Never!" said the other.

There was, of course, no hint of emotion in the translated replies, but their sheer volume was enough to make everyone in the dining hall look up.

A few minutes later Conway was alone. The Ians had requested permission to see the legendary EPLH and then dashed off full of awe and eagerness. Ians were nice people, Conway thought, but at the same time it was his considered opinion that lettuce was fit only for rabbits. With great firmness he pushed his slightly mussed salad away from him and dialled for steak with double the usual accessories.

This promised to be a long, hard day.

When Conway returned to the observation ward the Ians had gone and the patient's condition was unchanged. The Lieutenant was still guarding the nurse on duty—closely—and was beginning to blush for some reason. Conway nodded gravely, dismissed the nurse and was giving the Path report a rereading when Dr. Prilicla arrived.

Prilicla was a spidery, fragile, low-gravity being of classification GLNO who had to wear G-nullifiers constantly to keep from being mashed flat by a gravity which most other species considered normal. Besides being a very competent doctor Prilicla was the most popular person in the hospital, because its empathic faculty made it nearly impossible for the little being to be disagreeable to anyone. And, although it also possessed a set of large, iridescent wings it sat down at mealtimes and ate spaghetti with a fork. Conway liked Prilicla a lot.

Conway briefly described the EPLH's condition and background as he saw it, then ended, "... I know you can't get much from an unconscious patient, but it would help me if you could—"

"There appears to be a misunderstanding here, Doctor," Prilicla broke in, using the form of words which was the nearest it ever came to telling someone they were wrong. "The patient is conscious..."

"*Get back!*"

Warned as much by Conway's emotional radiation at the thought of what the patient's boney club could do to Prilicla's egg-shell body as his words, the little GLNO skittered backwards out of range. The Lieutenant edged closer, his eyes on the still motionless tentacle which ended in that monstrous bludgeon. For several seconds nobody moved or spoke, while outwardly the patient remained unconscious. Finally Conway looked at Prilicla. He did not have to speak.

Prilicla said, "I detect emotional radiation of a type which emanates only from a mind which is consciously aware of itself. The mental processes themselves seem slow and, considering the physical size of the patient, weak. In detail, it is radiating feelings of danger, helplessness and confusion. There is also an indication of some overall sense of purpose."

Conway sighed.

"So it's playing 'possum," said the Lieutenant grimly, talking mostly to himself.

The fact that the patient was feigning unconsciousness worried Conway less than it did the Corpsman. In spite of the mass of diagnostic equipment available to him he subscribed firmly to the belief that a doctor's best guide to any malfunction was a communicative and co-operative patient. But how did one open a conversation with a being who was a near deity…?

"We… we are going to help you," he said awkwardly. "Do you understand what I'm saying?"

The patient remained motionless as before.

Prilicla said, "There is no indication that it heard you, Doctor."

"But if it's conscious…" Conway began, and ended the sentence with a helpless shrug.

He began assembling his instruments again and with Prilicla's help examined the EPLH again, paying special attention to the organs of sight and hearing. But there was no physical or emotional reaction while the examination was in progress, despite the flashing lights and a considerable amount of ungentle probing. Conway could see no evidence of physical malfunction in any of the sensory organs, yet the patient remained completely unaware of all outside stimulus. Physically it was unconscious, insensible to everything going on around it, except that Prilicla insisted that it wasn't.

What a crazy, mixed-up demi-god, thought Conway. Trust O'Mara to send him the weirdies. Aloud he said, "The only explanation I can see for this peculiar state of affairs is that the mind you are receiving has severed or blocked off contact with all its sensory equipment. The patient's condition is not the cause of this, therefore the trouble must have a psychological basis. I'd say the beastie is urgently in need of psychiatric assistance.

"However," he ended. "the head-shrinkers can operate more effectively on a patient who is physically well, so I think we should concentrate on clearing up this skin condition first…"

A specific had been developed at the hospital against epithelioma of the type affecting the patient, and Pathology had already stated that it was suited to the EPLH's metabolism and would produce no harmful side-effects. It took only a few minutes for Conway to measure out a test dosage and inject subcutaneously. Prilicla moved up beside him quickly to see the effect. This, they both knew, was one of the rare, rapid-action miracles of medicine—its effect would be apparent in a matter of seconds rather than hours or days.

Ten minutes later nothing at all had happened.

"A tough guy," said Conway, and injected the maximum safe dose.

Almost at once the skin in the area darkened and lost its dry, cracked look. The dark area widened perceptibly as they watched, and one of the tentacles twitched slightly.

"What's its mind doing?" said Conway.

"Much the same as before," Prilicla replied, "but with mounting anxiety apparent since the last injection. I detect feelings of a mind trying to make a decision… of making a decision…"

Prilicla began to tremble violently, a clear sign that the emotional radiation of the patient had intensified. Conway had his mouth open to put a question when a sharp, tearing sound dragged his attention back to the patient. The EPLH was heaving and throwing itself against its restraining harness. Two of the anchoring straps had parted and it had worked a tentacle free. The one with the club…

Conway ducked frantically, and avoided having his head knocked off by a fraction of an inch—he felt that ultimate in blunt instruments actually touch his hair. But the Lieutenant was not so lucky. At almost the end of its swing the boney mace thudded into his shoulder, throwing him across the tiny ward so hard that he almost bounced off the wall. Prilicla, with whom cowardice was a prime survival characteristic, was already clinging with its sucker-tipped legs to the ceiling, which was the only safe spot in the room.

From his position flat on the floor Conway heard other straps go and saw two more tentacles begin failing about. He knew that in a few minutes the patient would be completely free of the harness and able to move about the room at will. He scrambled quickly to his knees, crouched, then dived for the berserk EPLH. As he hung on tightly with his arms around its body just below the roots of the tentacles Conway was nearly deafened by a series of barking roars coming from the speaking orifice beside his ear. The noise translated as "Help me! Help me!" Simultaneously he saw the tentacle with the great, boney bludgeon at its tip swing downwards. There was a crash and a three-inch hollow appeared on the floor at the point where he had been lying a few seconds previously.

Tackling the patient the way he had done might have seemed foolhardy, but Conway had been trying to keep his head in more ways than one. Clinging tightly to the EPLH's body below the level of those madly swinging tentacles, Conway knew, was the next safest place in the room.

Then he saw the Lieutenant...

The Lieutenant had his back to the wall, half lying and half sitting up. One arm hung loosely at his side and in the other hand he held his gun, steadying it between his knees, and one eye was closed in a diabolical wink while the other sighted along the barrel. Conway shouted desperately for him to wait, but the noise from the patient drowned him out. At every instant Conway expected the flash and shock of exploding bullets. He felt paralysed with fear, he couldn't even let go.

Then suddenly it was all over. The patient slumped on to its side, twitched and became motionless. Holstering his unfired weapon the Lieutenant struggled to his feet. Conway extricated himself from the patient and Prilicla came down off the ceiling.

Awkardly, Conway said, "Uh. I suppose you couldn't shoot with me hanging on there?"

The Lieutenant shook his head. "I'm a good shot. Doctor, I could have hit it and missed you all right. But it kept shouting 'Help me' all the time. That sort of thing cramps a man's style…"

THREE

It was some twenty minutes later, after Prilicla had sent the Lieutenant away to have a cracked humerus set and Conway and the GLNO were fitting the patient with a much stronger harness, that they noticed the absence of the darker patch of skin. The patient's condition was now exactly the same as it had been before undergoing treatment. Apparently the hefty shot which Conway had administered had had only a temporary effect, and that was decidedly peculiar. It was in fact downright impossible.

From the moment Prilicla's emphatic faculty had been brought to bear on the case Conway had been sure that the root of the trouble was psychological. He also knew that a severely warped mind could do tremendous damage to the body which housed it. But this damage was on a purely physical level and its method of repair—the treatment developed and proved time and time again by Pathology—was a hard, physical fact also. And no mind, regardless of its power or degree of malfunction, should be able to ignore, to completely negate, a physical fact. The Universe had, after all, certain fixed laws.

So far as Conway could see there were only two possible explanations. Either the rules were being ignored because the Being who had made them had also the right to ignore them or somehow, someone—or some combination of circumstances or misread data—was pulling a fast one. Conway infinitely preferred the second theory because the first one was altogether too shattering to consider seriously. He desperately wanted to go on thinking of his patient with a small P...

Nevertheless, when he left the ward Conway paid a visit to the office of Captain Bryson, the Monitor Corps Chaplain, and consulted that officer at some length in a semi-professional capacity—Conway believed in carrying plenty of insurance. His next call was on Colonel Skempton, the officer in charge of Supply, Maintenance and Communications at the Hospital. There he requested complete copies of the patient's log—not just the sections relevant to the murder—together with any other background data available to be sent to his room. Then he went to the AUGL theatre to demonstrate operative techniques on submarine lifeforms, and before dinner he was able to work in two hours in the Pathology department during which he discovered quite a lot about his patient's immortality.

When he returned to his room there was a pile of typescript on his desk that was nearly two inches thick. Conway groaned, thinking of his six-hour recreation period and how he was going to spend it. The thought obtruded of how he would have *liked* to spend it, bringing with it a vivid picture of the very efficient and impossibly beautiful Nurse Murchison whom he had been dating regularly of late. But Murchison was currently with the FGLI Maternity Section and their free periods would not coincide for another two weeks.

In the present circumstances perhaps it was just as well, Conway thought, as he settled down for a good long read.

The Corpsmen who had examined the patient's ship had been unable to convert the EPLH's time units into the Earth- human scale with any accuracy, but they had been able to state quite definitely that many of the taped logs were several centuries old and a few of them dated back to two thousand years or more. Conway began with the oldest and sifted carefully through them until he came to the most recent. He discovered almost at once that they were not so much a series of taped diaries—the references to personal items were relatively rare—as a catalogue of memoranda, most of which was highly technical and very heavy going. The data relevant to the murder, which he studied last, was much more dramatic.

... *My physician is making me sick,* the final entry read, *it is killing me. I must do something. It is a bad physician for allowing me to become ill. Somehow I must get rid of it...*

Conway replaced the last sheet on its pile, sighed, and prepared to adopt a position more conducive to creative thinking; i.e. with his chair tipped far back, feet on desk and practically sitting on the back of his neck.

What a mess, he thought.

The separate pieces of the puzzle—or most of them, anyway— were available to him now and required only to be fitted together.

There was the patient's condition, not serious so far as the Hospital was concerned but definitely lethal if not treated. Then there was the data supplied by the two Ians regarding this God-like, power-hungry but essentially beneficent race and the companions—who were never of the same species—who always travelled or lived with them. These companions were subject to replacement because they grew old and died while the EPLHs did not. There were also the Path reports, both the first written one he had received before lunch and the later verbal one furnished during his two hours with Thornnastor, the FGLI Diagnostician-in-Charge of Pathology. It was Thornnastor's considered opinion that the EPLH patient was not a true immortal, and the Considered Opinion of a Diagnostician was as near to being a rock-hard certainty as made no difference. But while immortality had been ruled out for various physiological reasons, the tests had shown evidence of longevity or rejuvenation treatments of the unselective type.

Finally there had been the emotion readings furnished by Prilicla before and during their attempted treatment of the patient's skin condition. Prilicla had reported a steady radiation pattern of confusion, anxiety and helplessness. But when the EPLH had received its second injection it had gone berserk, and the blast of emotion exploding from its mind had, in Prilicla's own words, nearly fried the little empath's brains in their own ichor. Prilicla had been unable to get a detailed reading on such a violent eruption of emotion, mainly because it had been tuned to the earlier and more gentle level on which the patient had been radiating, but it agreed that there was evidence of instability of the schizoid type.

Conway wriggled deeper into his chair, closed his eyes and let the pieces of the puzzle slide gently into place.

It had begun on the planet where the EPLHs had been the domi-nant life-form. In the course of time they had achieved civilization which included interstellar flight and an advanced medical science. Their life-span, lengthy to begin with, was artificially extended so that a relatively short-lived species like the Ians could be forgiven for believing them to be immortal. But a high price had had to be paid for their longevity: reproduction of their kind, the normal urge towards immortality of race in a species of mortal individuals, would have been the first thing to go; then their civilization would have dissolved—been forced apart, rather—into a mass of star-travelling, rugged individualists, and finally there would have been the psychological rot which set in when the risk of purely physical deterioration had gone.

Poor demi-gods, thought Conway.

They avoided each other's company for the simple reason that they'd already had too much of it—century after century of each other's mannerisms, habits of speech, opinions and the sheer, utter boredom of looking at each other. They had set themselves vast, sociological problems—taking charge of backward or errant planetary cultures and dragging them up by their bootstraps, and similar large-scale philanthropies—because they had tremendous minds, they had plenty of time, they had constantly to fight against boredom and because basically they must have been nice people. And because part of the price of such longevity was an ever-growing fear of death, they had to have their own personal physicians—no doubt the most efficient practitioners of medicine known to them—constantly in attendance.

Only one piece of the puzzle refused to fit and that was the odd way in which the EPLH had negated his attempts to treat it, but

Conway had no doubt that that was a physiological detail which would soon become clear as well. The important thing was that he now knew how to proceed.

Not every condition responded to medication, despite Thornnastor's claims to the contrary, and he would have seen that surgery was indicated in the EPLH's case if the whole business had not been so be-fogged with considerations of who and what the patient was and what it was supposed to have done. The fact that the patient was a near-deity, a murderer and generally the type of being not to be trifled with were details which should not have concerned him.

Conway sighed and swung his feet to the floor. He was beginning to feel so comfortable that he decided he had better go to bed before he fell asleep.

Immediately after breakfast next day Conway began setting up things for the EPLH's operation. He ordered the necessary instruments and equipment sent to the observation ward, gave detailed instructions regarding its sterilization—the patient was supposed to have killed one doctor already for allowing it to become sick, and a dim view would be taken if another one was the cause of it catching something else because of faulty aseptic procedures—and requested the assistance of a Tralthan surgeon to help with the fine work. Then half an hour before he was due to start Conway called on O'Mara.

The Chief Psychologist listened to his report and intended course of action without comment until he had finished, then he said, "Conway, do you realize what could happen to this hospital if that thing got loose? And not just physically loose, I mean. It is seriously disturbed mentally, you say, if not downright psychotic. At the moment it is unconscious, but from what you tell me its grasp of the psychological sciences is such that it could have us eating out of its manipulatory appendage just by talking at us.

"I'm concerned as to what may happen when it wakes up."

It was the first time Conway had heard O'Mara confess to being worried about anything. Several years back when a runaway space-ship had crashed into the hospital, spreading havoc and confusion through sixteen levels, it was said that Major O'Mara had expressed a feeling of concern on that occasion also...

"I'm trying not to think about that," said Conway apologetically. "It just confuses the issue."

O'Mara took a deep breath and let it out slowly through his nose, a mannerism of his which could convey more than twenty scathing sentences. He said coldly, "Somebody should think about these things, Doctor. I trust you will have no objection to *me* observing the coming operation...?"

To what was nothing less than a politely worded order there could be no reply other than an equally polite, "Glad to have you, sir."

When they arrived in the observation ward the patient's "bed" had been raised to a comfortable operating height and the EPLH itself was strapped securely into position. The Tralthan had taken its place beside the recording and anaesthetizing gear and had one eye on the patient, one on its equipment and the other two directed towards Prilicla with whom it was discussing a particularly juicy piece of scandal which had come to light the previous day. As the two beings concerned were PVSJ chlorine-breathers the affair could have only an academic interest for them, but apparently their academic interest was intense. At the sight of O'Mara, however, the scandal-mongering ceased forthwith. Conway gave the signal to begin.

The anaesthetic was one of several which Pathology had pronounced safe for the EPLH life-form, and while it was being administered Conway found his mind going off at a tangent towards his Tralthan assistant.

Surgeons of that species were really two beings instead of one, a combination of FGLI and OTSB. Clinging to the leathery back of the lumbering, elephantine Tralthan was a diminutive and nearly mindless being who lived in symbiosis with it. At first glance the OTSB looked like a furry ball with a long ponytail sprouting from it, but a closer look showed that the ponytail was composed of scores of fine manipulators most of which incorporated sensitive visual organs. Because of the *rapport* which existed between the Tralthan and its symbiote the FGLI-OTSB combination were the finest surgeons in the Galaxy. Not all Tralthans chose to link up with a symbiote, but FGLI medics wore them like a badge of office.

Suddenly the OTSB scurried along its host's back and huddled atop the dome-like head between the eye-stalks, its tail hanging down towards the patient and fanning out stiffly. The Tralthan was ready to begin.

"You will observe that this is a surface condition only," Conway said, for the benefit of the recording equipment, "and that the whole skin area looks dead, dried-up and on the point of flaking off. During the removal of the first skin samples no difficulty was encountered, but later specimens resisted removal to a certain extent and the reason was discovered to be a tiny rootlet, approximately one quarter of an inch long and invisible to the naked eye. My naked eye, that is. So it seems clear that the condition is about to enter a new phase. The disease is beginning to dig in rather than remain on the surface, and the more promptly we act the better."

Conway gave the reference numbers of the Path reports and his own preliminary notes on the case, then went on. "... As the patient, for reasons which are at the moment unclear, does not respond to medication I propose surgical removal of the affected tissue, irrigation, cleansing and replacement with surrogate skin. A Tralthan-guided OTSB will be used to insure that the rootlets are also excised. Except for the considerable area to be covered, which will make this a long job, the procedure is straightforward—"

"Excuse me. Doctors," Prilicla broke in, "the patient is still conscious."

An argument, polite only on Prilicla's side, broke out between the Tralthan and the little empath. Prilicla held that the EPLH was thinking thoughts and radiating emotions and the other maintained that it had enough of the anaesthetic in its system to render it completely insensible to everything for at least six hours. Conway broke in just as the argument was becoming personal.

"We've had this trouble before," he said irritably. "The patient has been physically unconscious, except for a few minutes yesterday, since its arrival, yet Prilicla detected the presence of rational thought processes. Now the same effect is present while it is under anaesthetic. I don't know how to explain this, it will probably require a surgical investigation of its brain structure to do so, and that is something which will have to wait. The important thing at the moment is that it is physically incapable of movement or of feeling pain. Now shall we begin?"

To Prilicla he added, "Keep listening just in case…"

For about twenty minutes they worked in silence, although the procedure did not require a high degree of concentration. It was rather like weeding a garden, except that everything which grew was a weed and had to be removed one plant at a time. He would peel back an affected area of skin, the OTSB's hair-thin appendages would investigate, probe and detach the rootlets, and he would peel back another tiny segment. Conway was looking forward to the most tedious operation of his career.

Prilicla said, "I detect increasing anxiety linked with a strengthening sense of purpose. The anxiety is becoming intense..."

Conway grunted. He could think of no other comment to make.

Five minutes later the Tralthan said, "We will have to slow down, Doctor. We are at a section where the roots are much deeper..."

Two minutes later Conway said, "But I can *see* them! How deep are they now?"

"Four inches," replied the Tralthan. "And Doctor, they are visibly lengthening as we work."

"But that's impossible!" Conway burst out; then, "We'll move to another area."

He felt the sweat begin to trickle down his forehead and just beside him Prilicla's gangling, fragile body began to quiver—but not at anything the patient was thinking. Conway's own emotional radiation just then was not a pleasant thing, because in the new area and in the two chosen at random after that the result was the same. Roots from the flaking pieces of skin were burrowing deeper as they watched.

"Withdraw," said Conway harshly.

For a long time nobody spoke. Prilicla was shaking as if a high wind was blowing in the ward. The Tralthan was fussing with its equipment, all four of its eyes focussed on one unimportant knob. O'Mara was looking intently at Conway, also calculatingly and with a large amount of sympathy in his steady grey eyes. The sympathy was because he could recognize when a man was genuinely in a spot and the calculation was due to his trying to work out whether the trouble was Conway's fault or not.

"What happened, Doctor?" he said gently.

Conway shook his head angrily. "I don't know. Yesterday the patient did not respond to medication, today it won't respond to surgery. It's reactions to anything we try to do for it are crazy, impossible! And now our attempt to relieve its condition surgically has triggered off—something—which will send those roots deep enough to penetrate vital organs in a matter of minutes if their present rate of growth is maintained, and you know what that means..."

"The patient's sense of anxiety is diminishing," Prilicla reported. "It is still engaged in purposeful thinking."

The Tralthan joined in then. It said, "I have noticed a peculiar fact about those root-like tendrils which join the diseased flakes of skin with the body. My symbiote has extremely sensitive vision, you will understand, and it reports that the tendrils seem to be rooted at each end, so that it is impossible to tell whether the growth is attacking the body or the body is deliberately holding on to the growth."

Conway shook his head distractedly. The case was full of mad contradictions and outright impossibilities. To begin with no patient, no matter how fouled up mentally, should be able to negate the effects of a drug powerful enough to bring about a complete cure within half an hour, and all within a few minutes. And the natural order of things was for a being with a diseased area of skin to slough it off and replace it with new tissue, not hang on to it grimly no matter what. It was a baffling, hopeless case.

Yet when the patient had arrived it had seemed a simple, straightforward case—Conway had felt more concern regarding the patient's background than its condition, whose cure he had considered a routine matter. But somewhere along the way he had missed something, Conway was sure, and because of this sin of omission the patient would probably die during the next few hours. Maybe he had made a snap diagnosis, been too sure of himself, been criminally careless.

It was pretty horrible to lose a patient at any time, and at Sector General losing a patient was an extremely rare occurrence. But to lose one whose condition no hospital anywhere in the civilized galaxy would have considered as being serious... Conway swore luridly, but stopped because he hadn't the words to describe how he felt about himself.

"Take it easy, son."

That was O'Mara, squeezing his arm and talking like a father. Normally O'Mara was a bad-tempered, bull-voiced and unapproachable tyrant who, when one went to him for help, sat making sarcastic remarks while the person concerned squirmed and shamefacedly solved his own problems. His present uncharacteristic behaviour proved something, Conway thought bitterly. It proved that Conway had a problem which Conway could not solve himself.

But in O'Mara's expression there was something more than just concern for Conway, and it was probably that deep down the psychologist was a little glad that things had turned out as they did. Conway meant no reflection on O'Mara's character, because he knew that if the Major had been in his position he would have tried as hard if not harder to cure the patient, and would have felt just as badly about the outcome. But at the same time the Chief Psychologist must have been desperately worried about the possibility of a being of great and unknown powers, who was also mentally unbalanced, being turned loose on the Hospital. In addition O'Mara might also be wondering if, beside a conscious and alive EPLH, he would look like a small and untutored boy...

"Let's try taking it from the top again," O'Mara said, breaking in on his thoughts. "Is there anything you've found in the patient's background that might point to it wanting to destroy itself?"

"*No!*" said Conway vehemently. "To the contrary! It would want desperately to live. It was taking unselective rejuvenation treatments, which means that the complete cell-structure of its body was regenerated periodically. As the process of storing memory is a product of ageing in the brain cells, this would practically wipe its mind clean after every treatment..."

"That's why those taped logs resembled technical memoranda," O'Mara put in. "That's exactly what they were. Still, I prefer our own method of rejuvenation even though we won't live so long, regenerating damaged organs only and allowing the brain to remain untouched..."

"I know," Conway broke in, wondering why the usually taciturn O'Mara had become so talkative. Was he trying to simplify the problem by making him state it in non-professional terms? "But the effect of continued longevity treatments, as you know yourself, is to give the possessor an increasing fear of dying. Despite loneliness, boredom and an altogether unnatural existence, the fear grows steadily with the passage of time. That is why it always travelled with its own private physician, it was desperately afraid of sickness or an accident befalling it between treatments, and that is why I can sympathize to a certain extent with its feelings when the doctor who was supposed to keep it well allowed it to get sick, although the business of eating it afterwards—"

"So you are on its side," said O'Mara drily.

"It could make a good plea of self-defence," Conway retorted.

"But I was saying that it was desperately afraid of dying, so that it would be constantly trying to get a better, more efficient doctor for itself... Oh!"

"Oh, what?" said O'Mara.

It was Prilicla, the emotion sensitive who replied. It said, "Doctor Conway has just had an idea."

"What is it, you young whelp? There's no need to be so damn secretive...!" O'Mara's voice had lost its gentle fatherly tone, and there was a gleam in his eye which said that he was glad that gentleness was no longer necessary. "What *is* wrong with the patient?"

Feeling happy and excited and at the same time very much unsure of himself, Conway stumbled across to the intercom and ordered some very unusual equipment, checked again that the patient was so thoroughly strapped down that it would be unable to move a muscle, then he said, "My guess is that the patient is perfectly sane and we've been blinding ourselves with psychological red herrings. Basically, the trouble is something it ate."

"I had a bet with myself you would say that sometime during this case," said O'Mara. He looked sick.

The equipment arrived—a slender, pointed wooden stake and a mechanism which would drive it downwards at any required angle and controlled speeds. With the Tralthan's help Conway set it up and moved it into position. He chose a part of the patient's body which contained several vital organs which were, however, protected by nearly six inches of musculature and adipose, then he set the stake in motion. It was just touching the skin and descending at the rate of approximately two inches per hour.

"What the blazes is going on?" stormed O'Mara. "Do you think the patient is a vampire or something!"

"Of course not," Conway replied. "I'm using a wooden stake to give the patient a better chance of defending itself. You wouldn't expect it to stop a steel one, would you." He motioned the Tralthan forward and together they watched the area where the stake was entering the EPLH's body. Every few minutes Prilicla reported on the emotional radiation. O'Mara paced up and down, occasionally muttering to himself.

The point had penetrated almost a quarter of an inch when Conway noticed the first coarsening and thickening of the skin. It was taking place in a roughly circular area, about four inches in diameter, whose centre was the wound created by the stake. Conway's scanner showed a spongy, fibrous growth forming under the skin to a depth of half an inch. Visibly the growth thickened and grew opaque to his scanner's current setting, and within ten minutes it had become a hard, bony plate. The stake had begun to bend alarmingly and was on the point of snapping.

"I'd say the defences are now concentrated at this one point," Conway said, trying to keep his voice steady, "so we'd better have it out."

Conway and the Tralthan rapidly incised around and undercut the newly-formed bony plate, which was immediately transferred into a sterile, covered receptacle. Quickly preparing a shot—a not quite maximum dose of the specific he had tried the previous day—Conway injected, then went back to helping the Tralthan with the repair work on the wound. This was routine work and took about fifteen minutes, and when it was finished there could be no doubt at all that the patient was responding favourably to treatment.

Over the congratulations of the Tralthan and the horrible threats of O'Mara—the Chief Psychologist wanted some questions answered, fast—Prilicla said. "You have effected a cure, Doctor, but the patient's anxiety level has markedly increased. It is almost frantic."

Conway shook his head, grinning. "The patient is heavily anaestheticized and cannot feel anything. However, I agree that at this present moment..." He nodded towards the sterile container. "... its personal physician must be feeling pretty bad."

In the container the excised bone had begun to soften and leak a faintly purplish liquid. The liquid was rippling and sloshing gently about at the bottom of the container as if it had a mind of its own. Which was, in fact, the case...

Conway was in O'Mara's office winding up his report on the EPLH and the Major was being highly complimentary in a language which at times made the compliments indistinguishable from insults. But this was O'Mara's way, Conway was beginning to realize, and the Chief Psychologist was polite and sympathetic only when he was professionally concerned about a person.

He was still asking questions.

"... An intelligent, amoebic life-form, an organized collection of submicroscopic, virus-type cells, would make the most efficient doctor obtainable," said Conway in reply to one of them. "It would reside within its patient and, given the necessary data, control any disease or organic malfunction from the inside. To a being who is pathologically afraid of dying it must have seemed perfect. And it was, too, because the trouble which developed was not really the doctor's fault. It came about through the patient's ignorance of its own physiological background.

"The way I see it," Conway went on, "the patient had been taking its rejuvenation treatments at an early stage of its biological life-time. I mean that it did not wait until middle or old age before regenerating itself. But on this occasion, either because it forgot or was careless or had been working on a problem which took longer than usual, it aged more than it had previously and acquired this skin condition. Pathology says that this was probably a common complaint with this race, and the normal course would be for the EPLH to slough off the affected skin and carry on as usual. But our patient, because the type of its rejuvenation treatment caused memory damage, did not know this, so its personal physician did not know it either."

Conway continued, "This, er, resident physician knew very little about the medical background of its patient-host's body, but its motto must have been to maintain the *status quo* at all costs. When pieces of its patient's body threatened to break away it held on to them, not realizing that this could have been a normal occurrence like losing hair or a reptile periodically shedding its skin, especially as its master would have insisted that the occurrence was not natural. A pretty fierce struggle must have developed between the patient's body processes and its Doctor, with the patient's mind also ranged against its doctor. Because of this the doctor had to render the patient unconscious the better to do what it considered to be the right thing.

"When we gave it the test shots the doctor neutralized them. They were a foreign substance being introduced into its patient's body, you see. And you know what happened when we tried surgical removal. It was only when we threatened underlying vital organs with that stake, forcing the doctor to defend its patient at that one point..."

"When you began asking for wooden stakes," said O'Mara drily, "I thought of putting *you* in a tight harness."

Conway grinned. He said, "I'm recommending that the EPLH takes his doctor back. Now that Pathology has given it a fuller understanding of its employer's medical and physiological history it should be the ultimate in personal physicians, and the EPLH is smart enough to see that."

O'Mara smiled in return. "And I was worried about what it might do when it became conscious. But it turned out to be a very friendly, likeable type. Quite charming, in fact"

As Conway rose and turned to go he said slyly, "That's because it's such a good psychologist. It is pleasant to people *all* the time..."

He managed to get the door shut behind him before the paperweight hit it.

PERSONAL MONSTER

Idris Seabright

Idris Seabright was the pseudonym of Margaret St. Clair (1911–1995) but her identity was kept hidden for years. St. Clair had been writing well crafted and often satirical science fiction for the pulps since 1946, and continued to be published in a variety of magazines. But in 1950, with the launch of the more literary Magazine of Fantasy & Science Fiction, *St. Clair created the Seabright alias for her more sophisticated and polished stories. Many were fantasy but they included some dark science fiction such as the following. She continued to write steadily through to the end of the 1950s, turning more to novels in the 1960s, but then faded away. Apart from a few stray stories she was almost forgotten. There were several collections of her work, notably* The Best of Margaret St. Clair *(1985) and her 1963 novel* The Sign of the Labrys, *set underground after Earth has been devastated by a plague, has been reprinted. A volume of her Seabright stories is long overdue.*

THE THING IN THE ASH PIT WAS, TO BABS HOFFMEIER, AN agonizing disgrace. More than anything else in the world, she wanted to keep its existence concealed from her mother and her dad. But the need for secrecy did not apply to other children. She could show the thing to them. She took Neenie around behind the house, back in the bushes where the old ash pit was, without shame.

Neenie climbed up on the fence Mr. Hoffmeier had built around the pit, and looked down at the monster. She was a little afraid, but not much. With the candid selfishness of childhood, she recognized that the thing in the ash pit was Babs's problem exclusively. Provided she stayed away from direct physical contact with it, it wouldn't hurt *her*.

"How're you gonna feed it while you're at camp?" she asked, teetering precariously. "Two whole weeks?"

Babs shook her head. "I don' know. And if I don' feed it, mom and dad will find out I've got it, for sure. If it gets hungry. Maybe I could feed it a lot just before I go…. But I'm scared."

"It sure is a mean-looking old thing," Neenie replied obliquely. "It looks like the head off a great big baby. Or like a great big, big eye. How does it eat, anyhow?"

"You want to watch?" Babs said. "It's kind of funny."

She opened the package of stew meat—she had bought it with the last of her allowance—and picked up a red, flabby chunk. She clambered up on the fence beside Neenie, and leaned out over it. Daintily she dropped the cube of meat on the monster's thin-skinned pink upper surface.

It is impossible to say what did happen to the meat. The pink membrane did not appear to fold up around it, or to open to take it in. The meat was gone, that was all, as soon as it touched the membrane. There wasn't even a lump to show where it had been.

"Jeepers!". Neenie said. "That was as quick as—as wet the bed!" She giggled rather nervously.

"Um-hum. I bet it could eat up a whole chicken—a whole turkey, even—and not show it. It could eat it up right at once."

By common consent they got down from the fence and seated themselves on the dusty ground a few yards away from the ash pit, in the shade of the shrubbery. "Where'd it come from?" Neenie asked.

"Up there." Babs pointed to a part of the sky in which, if it had been dark, Arcturus would have been visible. "It told me so."

"Oh. Like a comic book." Neenie didn't care for comic books. She lost interest perceptibly.

"How'd you get it, though?" she asked after a moment.

"I... I came out to the ash pit one evening, and there it was, just the way it is now. It told me—it can tell you things inside your head, without talking—it told me I'd have to take care of it. Or it would tell mother and dad. Back where it comes from, people like me—little girls—have to take care of it. Some of the grown-ups make them."

"Yeah, but..." Something in Babs' demeanour aroused Neenie's curiosity. She said, "Why'd it come to you, though? There are lots and lots of little girls."

Babs turned her face away. One brown pigtail hung down between her and Neenie. She said, very quickly, "I broke the cut glass vase mother said she got at her wedding. An' I threw the pieces out here, in the ash pit, because nobody puts ashes in it any more or comes here. An' when mother said I must have broke it, I said I hadn't. She switched me to make me tell, and I still wouldn't. An' daddy said he'd slap my face if I was lying. So I said I wasn't. An' then they both said they didn't know *what* could have happened to that vase."

There was a silence. Neenie broke off a sprig of privet and chewed on it absently. Then she said, "Maybe they had it come to you. Like Santa Claus, I mean. Only the other way round. Because you were bad."

"Unh-unh." Babs was positive. "They wouldn' do a thing like that. Mother'd switch me and dad would slap me. But they wouldn' make me have a thing like *that*."

"You're 'dopted," Neenie said doubtfully.

"Oh, sure, I'm 'dopted," Babs answered with a touch of hauteur. "But that doesn't make any difference. They just *wouldn't*."

Neenie chewed some more on her privet sprig. "Maybe you ought to tell them," she said slowly. "Tell them about how that old thing came and you have to take care of it. Maybe they could think up a way to get rid of it."

Babs' face puckered up. "I can't. I just can't. I don't want them to know. Having that old thing makes me feel so bad!" She had begun to cry.

"Lying about that glass vase you broke must have been awful bad to make you get a mean big thing like that," Neenie said virtuously.

Babs stopped crying. She raised her face and looked at Neenie. "Big deal!" she said spitefully. "Big schlemiel! I guess we can't all be as good as you are."

Neenie sniffed. "I haven' got a thing in an ash pit to take care of. *Anyway*."

"You will have," Babs said dangerously. She leaned forward. "You and everybody else. *All* the other little girls will. One of these days."

Neenie sat very still. Her little brown face looked pinched and frightened. "How do you know that?" she asked in a wobbling voice.

"It told me," Babs answered positively. "It's going to have babies, a lot of babies, mighty soon. Hundreds and hundreds of them. And then all the little girls will have things to take care of. Just like mine. You too. Everybody will."

Neenie sat quiet a minute longer. Then she got up, brushing dust from the skirt of her faded-blue denim dress. "I have to go home now," she said. She walked rapidly toward the front of the Hoffmeier house.

When she was almost at the kitchen windows she began to run.

Babs looked after her with spiteful satisfaction. But when Neenie was out of sight her face grew worried again. She'd be leaving for girl scout camp in four days. Her allowance was all spent; there was less than a dollar in her piggy bank. What was she going to do?

Albert Pike jumped out of the box car a little before the freight train drew into the station. He was wearing a pair of painters' overalls, a cloth jacket, and a pair of shoes. Nothing else at all. In one pocket he had a can of lye and in the other a knife. The lye and the knife stood for the same thing in his mind—a particular kind of power. They were both nice things to have.

He made a wide detour around the station. A block and a half up the street from it there was a small, clean restaurant. He went in and ordered coffee and apple pie. The waitress thought he was an awfully nice-looking old man.

When he had finished his lunch he walked along the street slowly until he saw a flash of greenery ahead. His face brightened. It was a park, and where there was a park there was pretty sure to be a playground. A playground meant children. Albert Pike liked children *very* much.

Babs woke on Tuesday, morning feeling sick with anxiety. She was to go to camp tomorrow; she had shaken the last penny out of her piggy bank; she hadn't any idea how she could keep the monster in the ash pit quiet for fourteen days.

For a moment she experimented hopefully with the idea of being *really* sick, too sick to go to camp. But her mother was never sympathetic toward physical illness. If she thought Babs was ailing she'd probably send her off to camp a day early, on the theory that fresh air and exercise would be the best treatment for her. And if she discovered that Babs was only playing sick she'd switch her legs good and hard. No, being sick wouldn't help.

After breakfast Babs went out to the garage and scrabbled around, trying to find something she could get the deposit back on at the store. Two dusty Pepsi-Cola bottles were the only refundable objects she could locate. Behind them, in a corner of the garage with a tarpaulin thrown over it, she found something that puzzled her considerably.

It was a heap of curving, silvery pieces of very heavy metal. It looked as if the pieces fitted together to make something shaped like an egg, but they were so heavy that Babs couldn't try them around and be sure.

She puzzled over the pieces for quite a long time, glad to have something to think about besides the thing in the ash pit. They looked as if they might be worth something, but they were too heavy for her to load in her wagon and take to the junk yard. Where had they come from? She was almost positive they hadn't been there the last time she had looked in the garage.

A little before noon she took the two Pepsi-Cola bottles to the grocery. She got four cents for them.

By 3 o'clock in the afternoon she was desperate. She tiptoed into the kitchen, very quiet and quick, and opened the refrigerator. She wasn't supposed to open it.

At the back of the bottom shelf there was a big beef roast, rolled up and tied with pieces of string. The grocery boy had brought it just a little while ago. Mrs. Hoffmeier was going to have it for supper that night. It must weigh six or seven pounds.

Babs twisted her fingers together. But she was already in such a fix that it didn't matter much, and they might not even suspect her. Grown-ups might think a little girl would break a cut glass vase and lie about it, but they wouldn't think she would steal a big piece of raw meat.... Of course taking it would be wrong.... It was a big piece; it could even last the thing in the ash pit the two whole weeks. Babs put her hands in the refrigerator and lifted out the meat.

"What on earth do you think you're doing?" her mother's voice said.

Babs spun round. Her heart was pounding so hard she was afraid she was going to be sick. How had her mother known she was in the kitchen? Mrs. Hoffmeier always wore crepe-soled shoes, so it was no wonder Babs hadn't heard her coming. But how had she known where Babs was?

"Put it right back," her mother went on severely. She looked down at Babs, frowning. She was a tall woman with puffy flesh and very light brown eyes. "I don't know what you're thinking of, to want raw meat. You'll have to wait until supper time."

She frowned at Babs a moment longer. Then she took the roast from her hands and thrust it back into the refrigerator. She closed the door.

Babs stared at the blank white enamel. Suddenly she couldn't stand it any longer. Neenie had said maybe she ought to tell her parents; she'd tell her mother. Nothing could be worse than this. They might punish her, but your *mother* had to help you, no matter how bad you'd been. She couldn't stand having the thing in the ash pit any more.

"Mommie," she said, "please, mommie, I—help me, I—"

"Barbara, there's something I want to warn you about," her mother cut in loudly and rapidly. It sounded to Babs almost as if she was trying to keep her from saying what she had to say. "I want you to take this seriously, do you understand?"

Babs's mouth stayed open. Her mother bent down until their two faces were almost touching. Her breath had its usual metallic smell. "I don't want to frighten you," she said, "but I've been hearing over the radio about a little boy who… It's terrible, he was burned with… Well, never mind, but I want you to promise me that if somebody offers you candy, or a soda, or ice cream if you go with him, you'll say no. Do you understand? Candy, or a soda, or anything like that. You must say no and run away. You're not to go with the man."

Babs was frightened. The strange words, the tone in which they were spoken, most of all the yellowish gleam in her mother's light eyes, seemed to her uncanny and horrible. "All right," she whispered. "I won't."

"Very well." Mrs. Hoffmeier straightened up. "Thank goodness you're going to camp tomorrow," she said, sighing. "I won't have to worry about you there. Was there something you wanted to speak to me about?"

Babs shook her head violently. "Unh-unh. No."

"All right, then. Run along and play. And remember what I warned you about."

Babs nodded. She wanted to get away. She unhooked the screen door and ran out into the back yard.

Her run slowed to a stumbling walk. There was no use in going to the ash pit to see if it was still there, the way she had so often in the first days. The thing wasn't so very hungry yet—she'd given it a good meal last night. But it was getting hungrier.

Misery overcame her. She crawled in under the bushes, into the hot, twiggy, sun-dappled darkness, and lay there for a long time, crying. She cried until her hair was wet and her ears tickled. At last she hadn't any more tears left to cry.

The sun was still up when she came out, but it was getting along to supper time. She made a wide detour around the ash pit, opened the back gate, and stepped out into the alley—not quite an alley, not yet a street—on which the Hoffmeier house backed. She'd go see what Neenie was doing. She hadn't seen her all day.

Neenie's house was almost a block away. Babs hadn't gone half the distance when she saw an old man, with paint on his clothes, walking toward her.

"Hello," he said when he got up to her. He had a kind voice. "What's a little girl like you doing out by herself when it's going, to be dark pretty soon? Ain't it almost dinner time?"

Babs didn't like his saying *ain't*, but she thought he was a nice man. "I'm going to my girl friend's house. Neenie," she said.

"And your face is all dirty," the old man said. He gathered up a fold of his jacket and wiped her cheek with it. The cloth was rough and he wiped too hard. Babs whimpered.

"Did I hurt you?" he asked. He sounded surprised. "Well, now... I'll tell you. I'll give you a dollar if you'll take a little walk with me instead of going to Neenie's house."

Her mother's warning recurred to Babs briefly. But this wasn't what her mother had meant. Money wasn't candy or a soda or ice cream. And a dollar would buy quite a lot of meat. "All right," she said.

He took her hand. His hand was warm, and slippery with sweat. "Come on," he said. He started walking rather fast in the direction from which Babs had come.

"When will you give me the dollar?" Babs asked when they had gone a few steps.

"When we get there."

"Where are we going? How far is it?"

"To the park. I'll show you something nice." He began pulling her along. Babs knew the park, but she didn't like his pulling her. "I want the dollar now," she said.

"You can't have it." He sounded cross. "As soon as we get to the park." He tightened his grip on her hand.

He wasn't her mother or her daddy, she didn't have to mind him. They were almost opposite the Hoffmeier gate. Babs didn't like him very much; maybe he never would give her the dollar. "I don't want to go," she said.

"You come on!"

For a moment Babs was quiet. Then she pulled as hard as she could against his hand. Even then she wouldn't have been able to manage it, except that his hand was so wet. She jerked loose. The gate was ajar. She darted through it into the Hoffmeier yard.

He yelled something at her—short words that she had never heard before and didn't understand—and then ran after her. Until then she hadn't been really afraid. She had run away from him, but not basically because she was afraid. But his pursuit of her into the yard filled her with an intense, paralysing fear. Her legs turned to wood.

She stumbled on for a few yards, sobbing. She tried to call "Mommie! Help!" but her throat wouldn't let the words out. She couldn't run any further. Her legs wouldn't go.

She collapsed on her knees near the clump of bushes where she had cried for so long earlier that day. With a last effort she rolled back into it.

She could hear the slap of his feet. He wasn't running very fast. He was talking to himself in a soft, angry voice with words that sounded like they came out of the Bible. The noise of his feet got nearer. Then it went away a little. He had gone around on the other side of the ash pit.

It never entered Babs' head that now was the time for her to make a run for the house. She couldn't have, anyhow. She lay stricken in the bushes while he fumbled about in twigs and shrubbery, always talking in the same soft, angry voice.

He was getting nearer. Oh, if she could only die. If her heart would only stop beating. Then there was a creak. After a moment Babs realized that the old man must have climbed up on the ash pit fence. He must be looking down in the pit for her.

Another creak. Babs' eyes were shut so tight the eyelids hurt, but she knew he was leaning far out over the pit, looking at the thing in it. Silence. Then, in the loudest voice she had heard him use yet, "Iniquity," he said.

His voice strengthened. "The iniquity of the monster of the pit," he said. "Sinning. He delighteth in stripes, yea in the pit he delighteth. Whom he loveth he tormenteth, and great shall be his reward. Chastiseth. Beloved. The pain of the angels glorifies the Lord."

The words were horrifying, and yet Babs felt somehow less afraid, as if the contact between her two terrors had neutralized them reciprocally. She wriggled around very cautiously until she was facing the ash pit. She looked.

Um-hum. Yes. It was just the way she had thought it was. It was getting dark, but not too dark for her to see the old man bending out over the ash pit. He was doing something to his hand. Cutting it? With a knife.

"If thine hand offend thee, pluck it out," he said, still in the same loud voice. He gave a sort of whimper. "That the stone may be wet with blood."

He leaned way, way out and shook his hand. The fence creaked. She thought she saw dark drops fall.

He was crazy, *crazy*. At the thought the terror seemed to withdraw from Babs' limbs, leaving them free, and to come to an acute, icy focus around her heart. She gnawed her wrist for a moment. Then she darted out of the bushes and pushed hard against the legs of Albert Pike.

Babs didn't know what happened next. She had closed her eyes when she started her rush, and when she got them open again it was all over. It was almost too dark for her to see anything anyhow.

She walked a few steps away from the ash pit and sank down upon the ground. She was still sitting crouched there when the back door opened and her mother's voice called, "Bar-bra! Supper's ready!" from the house.

After the first few days, Babs enjoyed girl scout camp. The events of Tuesday night receded, and even the agonizing responsibility she had felt for her personal monster seemed far away. If she thought, about the thing in the ash pit at all, it was with an easy assumption that it had had enough to eat to last it for quite a long while. The counsellors at the camp were real, real cool; she liked Miss Ash, who taught basketry and beadwork, best. But they were all nice.

Guilt for the disposal of Albert Pike never entered her head.

She went back home on Wednesday. Her mother met her at the station. Babs would have liked to hug her, for she was glad to see her, but her mother never liked to hug. She gave Babs a brief kiss on the cheek and led her to the car.

Babs was used to talking without her mother answering, and she chattered away during most of the drive home even though Mrs. Hoffmeier said nothing at all. Babs ran down finally and sat with her hands in her lap, but she still wasn't anxious. The thing in the ash pit was still a good many blocks away.

The trees had come out all green while she was gone.

Her mother drove the car into the Hoffmeier garage with expert ease. It was a big car. Babs' father was fond of saying that it was too big, a gas-eater, and he wished he'd never saddled himself with it. One night Babs had waked up to go to the toilet. On the way back she'd gone over to the bedroom window and looked out of it. It was a fine bright night. She'd seen the car floating up above the top of the garage, and Mrs. Hoffmeier, who was in the driver's seat, leaning out and saying something to Mr. Hoffmeier on the ground below. That must have been a dream, though Babs hadn't felt like she was dreaming. But it *was* an awfully big car.

Mrs. Hoffmeier got Babs's suitcase out of the back of the car. "I'll unpack your things, Barbara," she said. "Run along and play. But don't go far. Your father and I want to have a serious talk with you as soon as he gets, home."

Babs' heart gave a terrific bound. Her latent fear was suddenly wide awake. They wanted to have a serious talk with her—that meant she had done something bad. Had they found out about the thing in the ash pit while she was away at camp?

She looked up at her mother anxiously, but Mrs. Hoffmeier's face was as blank and impersonal as a mask. Only the white gleam of her very light eyes showed that she might be angry. But Babs couldn't be sure.

"Run along and play," Mrs. Hoffmeier repeated. She picked up the suitcase and started toward the front door with it. "But don't be long."

Babs could hardly wait until she'd gone in the house before she ran around to the ash pit. She climbed up on the fence. She looked down into it.

There wasn't anything there.

Babs was so surprised she nearly fell off the fence. She clutched at the rail and looked over once more. No, nothing. There was nothing there.

That wasn't quite true. The pieces of cut glass vase Babs had put in the pit two months ago were still there, and there was a part of a heavy tin can on the bottom, and some shiny marks, like snail tracks, on the sides. But nothing else. The big pink thing like the head of an enormous baby, the big pink thing like a six-foot eye—it was gone.

Babs sat down in the shade of a privet bush. She broke off a piece of privet and poked at the gap in her front teeth with it. The thing in the pit had seemed as permanent and solid as her own flesh to her; she couldn't form any idea of what had happened to it.

Finally she decided that it must have over-eaten itself. That crazy old man had been pretty big; the thing in the pit had had so much to eat all at once that it had burst. (Babs, naturally, knew nothing about the can of lye Albert Pike had been carrying in one hip pocket.) Yes, that must be it.

She drew a deep breath. Now that she knew what had happened she felt lots better. For a moment she sat hugging her knees. Then she got to her feet.

It was over. She'd never have to think about the thing in the ash pit again. It had killed itself, filled its big stomach up so full it had burst. It had been nothing but a big old stomach bag anyway.

She began to smile. She looked around her, smiling, at the house, the bushes, the ash pit, the trees. It was as if she'd never seen any of them before. She opened the back gate and started down the alley toward Neenie's house at a run. She wanted to tell Neenie all about camp. She kept yelling, "Neenie! Neenie! I'm back!" all the way.

Her parents were waiting for her in the living room. They were standing side by side. They must have been talking; Babs' mother looked upset.

Mr. Hoffmeier looked a good deal like Mrs. Hoffmeier. He had the same white flesh and very, very light brown eyes. His breath even had the same metallic smell. But he was taller than she was and a lot more thin. Babs had always been more afraid of Mr. Hoffmeier than of his wife.

"Sit down," he said. His face was expressionless. He cleared his throat. "Barbara, you've been very bad."

Babs licked her lips. Her knees felt so weak she was glad she was sitting down. She didn't know what she had done, but she was afraid. "Father, I—"

"Very bad," he repeated. His eyes looked almost white. "I never heard of a little girl doing what you've done. I don't understand how you did it. How did you kill your glannanth?"

A stab of perplexity shot through the haze of Babs' intimidation and guilt. What was he talking about? *She* hadn't killed anything.

He couldn't mean the thing in the pit—it was gone, sure, but she hadn't done it. "I don' know what you mean," she said weakly. "What's a glannan?" She twisted in her chair.

Mr. Hoffmeier bent over her. "You do know," he said insistently. "What did you do to the glannanth out in the ash pit?"

"... I didn' do *anything*."

"What difference does it make?" Mrs. Hoffmeier cut in from where she was standing by the window. She laughed bitterly. "After we came so far! Ruined, ruined! Nothing but bad news! It will take years—" She controlled herself. "Be careful with her, Rysan," she said anxiously. "I don't think she *does* know how she did it. But she may be dangerous."

"Yes. But I'd like—"

"There's the signal now," Mrs. Hoffmeier said sharply. "Don't you hear it?"

Babs hadn't heard anything. The Hoffmeiers exchanged glances. They had withdrawn their attention so completely from Babs that she felt they no longer knew she was in the room. Mrs. Hoffmeier said something in a language that might be French—it wasn't English, anyway. Then, side by side, almost running, they started toward the rear of the house.

Babs heard the back door slam. She shifted in her chair. She had been sweating so much that the seat under her was sticky and damp.

For a moment she felt so sick at her stomach she thought she was going to throw up. It wasn't because she'd been scared, either; this was like the time she'd been up in an express elevator. It felt like her stomach had suddenly lost weight.

The nausea passed, but it wasn't until nearly fifteen minutes later that Babs got up courage enough to leave her chair and go through the house looking for the Hoffmeiers.

They weren't in any of the rooms, and when she went out to the garage they weren't there either, and the car was gone.

Babs came back in the house. She pinched her lower lip for a moment and then went in her own room. Her suitcase was lying on the bed, with the lid back, but Mrs. Hoffmeier hadn't unpacked it.

Babs got her Storybook doll out of the bottom drawer of her dresser and put it in the suitcase. It made the suitcase a little full, but she managed to get the catches fastened. She pulled the suitcase off the bed and lugged it through the house to the back yard, where her coaster wagon was. She loaded the suitcase on the wagon.

She'd go stay with Neenie tonight. Maybe she'd stay there always. Neenie's mother would be glad to have her, she thought; she was always saying she wished she had another little girl. And it didn't look like Mr. and Mrs. Hoffmeier would be coming back.

Humming "Old MacDonald Had A Farm" and pulling the coaster wagon after her, Babs started down the alley toward Neenie's house.

ALIEN INVASION

Marcia Kamien

Marcia Kamien (b. 1933) toyed briefly with science fiction in the early 1950s before moving on. She had taken a degree in journalism at Syracuse University where she was editor-in-chief of the college's humour magazine The Syracusan. *After graduating she worked as a copywriter and later an in-house editor at Holt, Rinehart, Winston whilst producing the occasional story. She later collaborated with Rose Novak under the alias Marcia Rose producing several romance novels but here, from 1954, is a romance of a very different kind.*

Pain gripped Riva, pain worse than anything she had ever experienced before. It's true, she thought, it's all true. But her mind shrank away from the thought, leaving her a blank, save for terrible pain.

Two doctors entered the room silently and when one of them spoke to her, it was with a start of surprise that she opened her eyes and saw, instead of a red wall of hurt, their kind faces, and beyond them, the window looking out upon the calm countryside.

"Riva," the doctor said, "tell me every time there is a pain."

"It's true, then," she whispered. The doctor nodded; and she whimpered a little. "But—how? Why?" The face above her where she lay on the hospital bed was still kind, but there was no answer in the eyes. Riva turned her head away.

How had it happened? Nine months before she had felt a strange sensation inside her, in the night. She had thought nothing of it. And then, the lump growing in her abdomen, growing steadily. But she, an unmarried woman, an intelligent scientist with no emotional ties...

However, there was life in her womb, life that would not be ignored... life that squirmed and kicked inside her and demanded care. She had gone to the doctor; there were many tests. And then the gentle voice of the medical man, saying:

"And you're sure you have had no—ah—romantic interludes?"

"Absolutely positive!" she had snapped.

"In that case..." and his hands moved out expressively, "...I have no explanation for the fact that you will give birth in three or four months."

And that had been that. Now here she was in a Maternity Hospital waiting for whatever it was to be born. As she grimaced with pain and nodded to the waiting doctor, she turned her thoughts away from the horror that the child within her might not be a...child.

"You must be awake. Answer me." The voice was strange cold, foreign.

Riva shuddered beneath the blankets and turned her face away from the voice. It would not be denied. "You can't escape me, Riva. Answer!" She raised her head, but there was no one in the room. She looked around wildly.

"You can't see me."

"Who are you?"

"Never mind who we are right now. The child lives?" It wasn't until then that she turned to look into the basket by her bed. Then she screamed.

"Hush, Riva," the voice commanded, but it was gentler now. "Tell me about the child. It lives, doesn't it?"

"Yes." Yes, it lived, it breathed... but half monster! "How?" she whispered in agony.

"We are a scientifically advanced world. And we have ways. But a dying world, Riva. Strange diseases, taking our women from us. Terrible heat, burning our food, our live-stock.

"This is an experiment," tire voice continued. "We cannot breathe your air. But a child, a mixture of your lungs and our lungs, might be able to survive. A child with our instincts. Do you understand?"

Riva nodded, then said: "Yes." She was beginning to understand. Aliens, coming to her world, in the form of their monster children. To take over this world.

"To take over," she murmured aloud, clenching her fists.

"No, Riva," the voice said, calmly and almost soft, "we don't want to take over. But a world that has gone so far, done so much, been so good. Ah, Riva, ours is a world which must not entirely die and be lost. We nova shortly. When you look up at the sky you will see us, burning like a bright, brief flame. And then we will be gone to eternity." The voice stopped for an instant and Riva thought, wonderingly, he speaks like a poet, this alien. He feels so strongly, but so gently.

"We will try to send books and films by rocket, but we can only guess if they will survive..." Again the alien broke off his train of thought and added, more briskly, "The child, Riva, is it female?"

She looked.

"Yes."

There was a sigh of relief. "Riva, there is not much time... Please listen to me. We chose you because of your intelligence. Because you would listen and perhaps, understand a little. She is not so different from you. Look at her closely and love her. You will love her, because she is yours!" Then, he added, And mine, Riva. I am a great scientist. She will be very intelligent."

She was calmer now. The voice was still soft, calm and she thought—intelligent. She knew they would try this again, now; and that her own people would destroy these poor little creatures as soon as they were born, or maybe before. In the meantime, she would converse with the alien. As a scientist, she owed her people the information. And now she felt almost exhilarated and listened quietly while the alien man spoke to her and, later, left.

Then she turned and looked the infant over carefully. The poor thing was a mixture. It had her hair, her eyes... but the mouth was misshapen and there was an arm missing and the skin was like the belly of a dead animal, so pale and colourless it was.

The doctor walked in and smiled, seeing her so calm.

"Ah then everything is peaceful." He glanced at the basket and cleared his throat carefully. "I must admit," he started, "I was amazed—"

"Aliens," she said shortly, "I don't know how they do it, but they could be stopped. I speak to one of them. I'll find out. They must be very intelligent."

The doctor touched the baby with a careful finger. "Poor deformed thing," he muttered. "You will try to forget this, Riva. We'll have it destroyed, now that these aliens—have made contact." He touched the child again.

Riva said nothing, looking down at the baby.

"Did they say who they are?" the doctor asked.

Riva looked at the infant, then the doctor, and took a deep breath. "Do not destroy that child."

The doctor's head came up with a jerk.

"No," she insisted. "That child is mine. Anyone else may do as they wish; I shall take a chance. Perhaps... perhaps, she will be much like her—father."

The doctor stared at her. He spluttered. "Of course... you're right... of course..."

Riva smiled at him a little.

"Yes," she said, addressing the baby in the basket. "I shall take a chance on you, little Half-One, on you and your world. And I shall call you by the name your father called himself. A strange name, but yours."

Rival's hand was soft on the infant's head.

"I name you," she said, ignoring the doctor, "Earthman." Then, she added, "And may you love the planet your father called Venus as much as I."

THE WITNESS

Eric Frank Russell

Eric Frank Russell (1905–1978) was a close rival to Arthur C. Clarke as Britain's leading writing of science fiction during the 1940s and 1950s. His career began in 1937, his earliest stories being in imitation of Stanley G. Weinbaum, but he also had a fascination for the theories of Charles Fort, that we were all the property of an alien race that watched over us and possibly influenced our lives. He channelled these ideas into the novel Sinister Barrier *which, by chance, led the first issue of* Unknown, *the new companion magazine to* Astounding SF, *in 1939. The novel, which finally appeared in book form in 1943, was extremely popular and Russell utilized Fortean theories again in* Dreadful Sanctuary *(serial, 1948) where something is clearly stopping mankind's attempts to venture into space.*

Russell had a mischievous sense of humour, which is evident in the following story. His typically British story "Allamagoosa" (1955) surprisingly won him the Hugo Award for that year's best short fiction. His output, especially in the 1950s, was relentless and his short fiction was collected in Deep Space *(1954),* Far Stars *(1961),* Dark Tides *(1962) and the linked series,* Men, Martians and Machines *(1955). Other novels include* Three to Conquer *(1956),* Wasp *(1957) and* Next of Kin *(1959). He more or less stopped writing in 1965 and gradually dropped out of favour but, as the following story shows, his ideas are every bit as relevant today.*

N O COURT IN HISTORY HAD DRAWN SO MUCH WORLD ATTEN-
tion. Six television cameras swivelled slowly as they followed
red and black-robed legal lights parading solemnly to their seats.
Ten microphones sent the creaking of shoes and rustling of papers
over national networks in both hemispheres. Two hundred reporters and special correspondents filled a gallery reserved for them
alone. Forty representatives of cultural organizations stared across
the court at twice their number of governmental and diplomatic
officials sitting blank-faced and impassive.

Tradition had gone by the board; procedure resembled nothing familiar to the average lawyer, for this was a special occasion
devised to suit a special case. Technique had been adapted to cope
with a new and extraordinary culprit, while the dignity of justice
was upheld by means of stagy trimmings.

There were five judges and no jury, but a billion citizens were
in their homes watching and listening, determined to ensure fair
play. Ideas of what constituted fair play were as varied as the unseen
audience, and most of them unreasoning, purely emotional. A
minority of spectators hoped for life, many lusted for death, while
the waverers compromised in favour of arbitrary expulsion, each
according to how he had been influenced by the vast flood of col-
ourful and bigoted propaganda preceding this event.

The judges took their places with the casual unconcern of
those too old and deeply sunk in wisdom to notice the limelight.
A hush fell, broken only by the ticking of the large clock over their
rostrum. It was the hour of ten in the morning of May 17, 1977.

The microphones sent the ticking around the world. The cameras showed the judges, the clock, and finally settled on the centre of all this attention: the creature in the defendant's box.

Six months ago this latter object had been the sensation of the century, the focal point of a few wild hopes and many wilder fears. Since then it had appeared so often on video screens, magazine and newspaper pages, that the public sense of amazement had departed, while the hopes and fears remained. It had slowly degenerated to a cartoon character contemptuously dubbed "Spike," depicted as halfway between a hopelessly malformed imbecile and the crafty emissary of a craftier other-world enemy. Familiarity had bred contempt, but not enough of it to kill the fears.

Its name was Maeth and it came from some planet in the region of Procyon. Three feet high, bright green, with feet that were mere pads, and stubby limbs fitted with suckers and cilia, it was covered in spiky protrusions and looked somewhat like an educated cactus. Except for its eyes, great golden eyes that looked upon men in naive expectation of mercy, because it had never done anyone any harm. A toad, a wistful toad, with jewels in its head.

Pompously, a black gowned official announced, "This special court, held by international agreement, and convened within the area of jurisdiction of the Federal Government of the United States of America, is now in session! Silence!"

The middle judge glanced at his fellows, adjusted his spectacles, peered gravely at the toad, or cactus, or whatever it might be. "Maeth of Procyon, we are given to understand that you can neither hear nor speak, but can comprehend us telepathically and respond visually."

Cameras focused as Maeth turned to the blackboard immediately behind him and chalked one word. "Yes."

"You are accused," the judge went on, "generally of illegal entry into this world known as Earth and specifically into the United States of America. Do you plead guilty or not guilty?"

"How else can one enter?" enquired Maeth, in bold white letters.

The judge frowned. "Kindly answer my question."

"Not guilty."

"You have been provided, with defending counsel—have you any objection to him?"

"Blessed be the peacemaker."

Few relished that crack. It smacked of the Devil quoting Scripture.

Making a sign, the judge leaned back, polished his glasses. Adjusting the robes on his shoulders, the prosecuting attorney came to his feet. He was tall, hatchet-faced, sharp-eyed.

"First witness!"

A thin, reedy man came out the well of the court, took his chair, sat uncomfortably, with fidgeting hands.

"Name?"

"Samuel Nall."

"You farm outside Danville?"

"Yes, sir. I—."

"Do not call me 'sir'. Just reply to my questions. It was upon your farm that this creature made its landing?"

"Your Honours, I object!" Mr. Defender stood up, a fat, florid man, but deceptively nimble-witted. "My client is a person, not a creature. It should therefore be referred to as the defendant."

"Objection overruled," snapped the middle judge. "Proceed, Mr. Prosecutor."

"It was upon your farm that this *creature* landed?"

"Yes," said Samuel Nall, staring pridefully at the cameras. "It come down all of a sudden and—"

"Confine yourself to the question. The arrival was accompanied by much destruction?"

"Yes."

"How much?"

"Two barns and a lot of crops. I'm down three thousand dollars."

"Did this *creature* show any remorse?"

"None." Nall scowled across the court. "Acted like it couldn't care less."

Mr. Prosecutor seated himself, throwing a mock smile at the fat man. "Your witness."

Standing up, the latter eyed Nall benevolently and enquired, "Were these barns of yours octagonal towers with walls having movable louvres and with barometrically-controlled roofs?"

Nall waggled his eyebrows and uttered a faint, "Huh?"

"Never mind. Dismiss that query and answer me this one: were your crops composed of foozles and bi-coloured merkins?"

In desperation, Nall said, "It was ripe barley."

"Dear me! Barley—how strange! Don't you know what foozles and merkins are? Wouldn't you recognize them if you saw them?"

"I reckon not," admitted Farmer Nall, with much reluctance.

"Permit me to observe that you seem singularly lacking in perceptive faculties," remarked Mr. Defender, tartly. "Indeed, I am really sorry for you. Can you detect sorrow in my face?"

"I dunno," said Nall, feeling that his throne before the cameras was becoming somehow like a bed of nails.

"In other words, you cannot recognize remorse when you see it?"

"Objection!" roared Mr. Prosecutor, coming up crimson. "The witness cannot reasonably be expected—." He stopped as his opponent sat down. Recovering swiftly, he growled, "Next witness!"

Number two was big, beefy, clad in blue, and had all the assurance of one long familiar with courts and the tedious processes of the law.

"Name?"

"Joseph Higginson."

"You are an officer of Danville police?"

"Correct."

"You were summoned by the first witness?"

"I was."

Mr. Prosecutor wore the smile of one in complete command of circumstances as he went on, "Discovering what had occurred, you tried to apprehend the cause of it, did you not?"

"I sure did." Officer Higginson turned his head, threw a scowl at the golden eyes pleading in the box.

"And what happened?"

"It paralysed me with a look."

The judge on the left interjected, "You appear to have recovered. How extensive was this paralysis, and how long did it last?"

"It was complete, Your Honour, but it wore off after a couple of hours."

"By which time," said Mr. Prosecutor, taking over again, "this outlandish object had made good its escape?"

Lugubriously, "Yes."

"It therefore obstructed a police officer in the execution of his duty, assaulted a police officer, and resisted arrest?"

"It did," agreed Higginson, with emphasis.

"Your witness." Mr. Prosecutor seated himself, well satisfied.

Mr. Defender arose, hooked thumbs in vest-holes, and enquired with disarming amiability, "You can recognize another police official when you see him?"

"Naturally."

"Very well. There is one at present seated in the public section. Kindly point him out for the benefit of this court."

Higginson looked carefully over the small audience which represented in person the vaster audience beyond. Cameras swung in imitation of his search. Judges, reporters, officials, all looked the same way.

"He must be in plain clothes," declared Higginson, giving up.

The middle judge interposed mildly, "This court can hardly accept witness's inability to recognize a plain clothes officer as evidence."

"No, Your Honour," agreed Mr. Defender. His plump features registered frustration and disappointment which gladdened the heart of his watching opponent. Then, satisfied that the other had reached the heights, he plunged him to the depths by brightening and adding, "But the said official is in full uniform."

Mr. Prosecutor changed faces like swapping masks. Higginson got a crick in the neck as he took in the audience again.

"Olive-drab with red trimmings," Mr. Defender went on. "He is a Provost Marshal of the Corps of Military Police."

"You didn't tell me that," Higginson pointed out. He was openly aggrieved.

"Did you tell the defendant that you were a police officer?"

The witness reddened, opened his mouth, closed it, gazed appealingly at the prosecuting attorney.

"Answer the question!" insisted a judge.

"No, I did not tell it."

"Why not?"

Mopping his forehead, Higginson said in hoarse tones, "Didn't think it was necessary. It was obvious, wasn't it?"

"It is for me to put the questions; for you to provide the answers. Do you agree that the Provost Marshal is obvious?"

"Objection!" Mr. Prosecutor waved for attention. "Opinions are not evidence."

"Sustained!" responded the middle judge. He eyed defending attorney over his glasses. "This court takes cognizance of the fact that there was no need for witness to offer vocally any information available to defendant telepathically. Proceed with your examination."

Mr. Defender returned his attention to Higginson and asked "Precisely what were you doing at the moment you were paralysed?"

"Aiming my gun."

"And about to fire?"

"Yes."

"At the defendant?"

"Yes."

"Is it your habit to fire first and ask questions afterward?"

"The witness's habits are not relevant," put in the middle judge. He looked at Higginson. "You may ignore that question."

Officer Higginson grinned his satisfaction and duly ignored it.

"From what range were you about to fire?" pursued defending attorney.

"Fifty or sixty yards."

"So far? You are an excellent marksman?"

Higginson nodded, without pride, and warily. The plump man, he had decided, was a distinct pain in the neck.

"About what time do you hope to get home for supper?"

Caught on one foot by this sudden shift of attack, the witness gaped and said, "Maybe midnight."

"Your wife will be happy to know that. Were it not for the radio and video, you could not have told her vocally, could you?"

"I can't bawl from here to Dansville," assured Higginson, slightly sarcastic.

"Of course not. Such a distance is completely beyond range of the unaided human voice." Mr. Defender rubbed his chin, mused awhile, suddenly demanded, "Can you bawl *telepathically* for fifty to sixty yards?"

No reply.

"Or is your mental limit in keeping with what the defendant assures me to be the normal limit of twenty-five to thirty yards?"

Higginson screwed up his eyes and said nothing.

"Don't you know?"

"A pity!" commented Mr. Defender, shaking his head sadly and taking a seat.

The third witness was a swarthy, olive-skinned character who stared sullenly at his boots while the prosecuting attorney got to work.

"Name?"

"Dominic Lolordo." He gave it in an undertone as if reluctant to have it coupled with his image on the video.

"You operate a sea-food restaurant."

"Yes."

"Do you recognize the creature in that box?"

His eyes slid sidewise. "Yes."

"In what circumstances did you last see it?"

"In my joint, after hours."

"It had forced an entrance, had it not shortly before dawn, and it awakened you while plundering the place?"

"That's correct."

"You did not try to catch it?"

Lolordo made a face. "Catch that? *Look* at it!"

"Appearance alone would not deter you if you were being robbed," Mr. Prosecutor suggested meaningly. "Surely there was something else?"

"It had walked in through the window," said Lolordo, his voice rising considerably. "Right through the window leaving a hole its own shape. It went out the same way, making another hole. No broken glass around, no splinters, nothing. What can you do with a green nightmare that walks through glass as if it wasn't there?"

"Seeing this demonstration of supernormal powers, you ran for assistance?"

"You bet!"

"But it came too late? This unscrupulous plunderer had gone?"

"Yes."

The questioner handed over with a gesture, and defending attorney began.

"You assert that you were plundered? Of what?"

"Stuff."

"That is not an answer."

"Ain't it?" Lolordo yawned with exaggerated disinterest.

The middle judge bent forward, frowning heavily. "Does the witness desire to be committed for contempt?"

"Lobsters and oysters," said Lolordo, hurriedly and with bad grace.

"In other words, a square meal?" enquired Mr. Defender.

"If that's what you want to call it."

"Was it being consumed as if the defendant were ravenously hungry?"

"I didn't stick around to see. I took one look and went on my way—fast."

"So that if defendant picked up enough of your thoughts to realize that a felonious act had been committed, there was no opportunity to apologize or make restitution?"

No reply.

"And, in any case, your departing thoughts were violently hostile?"

"I wasn't hot-footing for a bouquet," assured Lolordo.

Mr. Defender said to the judges, "This witness is impertinent. I have no further use for him."

The judges conferred, and the middle one decided coldly, "The witness will be detained within the precincts of this court until the case has been decided."

Lolordo stamped away from his seat, glowering right and left.

"Fourth witness!"

The chair was taken by a middle-aged, dapper man who resembled the movie notion of a bank president or an eminent surgeon. He could have been cast equally well for either part.

"Name?"

"Winthrop Allain."

"You are a resident professor of zoology, are you not?" enquired the prosecuting attorney.

"That is correct."

"You recognize the creature in the box?"

"I ought to. I have been in close communication with it for many weeks."

Mr. Prosecutor made an impatient gesture. "In what circumstances did you first encounter it?"

An answer to that one seemed unnecessary. The whole world knew the circumstances, had been told them time and time again with many fanciful frills.

Nevertheless, Allain responded, "It appeared in the zoo some two hours after closing time. How it got there I don't know."

"It was snooping around, seeing all there was to see, making mental note of everything?"

Hesitantly, "Well—."

"Was it or was it not looking over the place?"

"It certainly saw a good bit of the zoo before the keepers discovered it, but—."

"Please do not embellish your answers, Professor Allain," said Mr. Prosecutor, firmly. "Let us continue: owing to the great furore created by this strange object's arrival and subsequent exploits, your keepers had no difficulty in recognizing it?"

"None at all. They reported to me at once."

"What did you do then?"

"I attended to the matter myself. I found it a warm and comfortable apartment in the unused section of the Reptile House."

The entire court along with the cameras peered respectfully at the expert who could treat such an occasion with such nonchalance.

"How did you achieve that without suffering paralysis, disintegration or some other unnatural fate?" Mr. Prosecutor's voice had a touch of acid. "Did you graciously extend a cordial invitation?"

The witness, drily, "Precisely!"

"There is a time and place for humour, Professor," reproved Mr. Prosecutor, with some severity. "However, the court understands that you classified this nightmarish entity as a reptile and managed to put it in its proper place."

"Nonsense! The Reptile House was immediately available, convenient and acceptable. The defendant is unclassifiable."

Dismissing that with a contemptuous gesture, the prosecuting attorney went on, "You are not prepared to tell this court by what

means you overcame this creature's menacing powers and succeeded in trapping it?"

"I did not trap it. I knew it was sentient and treated it as such."

"If we can rely upon the evidence of other witnesses," said Mr.
Prosecutor, tartly, "you were fortunate to have any choice about
the matter. Why did this caricature permit you to make the contact
it denied to others?"

"Because it recognized my mind as of a type accustomed to
dealing with non-human forms. With considerable logic it assumed
that contact with me would be far easier than with any others."

"With considerable logic," echoed prosecuting attorney, turning
toward the judges. "I ask Your Honours to make especial note of
that remark, bearing in mind that the witness has a distinguished
status." He returned his attention to Allain. "By that, you mean it
is intelligent?"

"Indubitably!"

"You have had many weeks in which to study the mind of this
unwanted invader. Just how intelligent would you say it is?"

"As much so as we are, though in a different way."

"Do you consider this sample to be fairly representative of its race?"

"I have no reason to suppose otherwise."

"Which race, therefore, equals us in brain-power?"

"Very probably." Professor Allain rubbed his chin and mused a
moment. "Yes, insofar as one can relate things which are not the
same, I'd say they are our intellectual equals."

"Perhaps our superiors, not only in brains, but also in numbers?"
persisted Mr. Prosecutor.

"I don't know. I doubt it."

"The possibility, cannot be ruled out?"

"Such data as is available is far from sufficient and therefore I—."

"Do not evade my question. There is a possibility, no matter how remote, that the life-form represented by this monster now standing before us is the direst menace humanity has ever been called upon to face?"

"Anything can be construed as a menace if you insist, but—."

"*A menace*, yes or no?"

The middle judge interjected profoundly, "Witness cannot be required to provide a positive answer to a hypothetical question."

Not fazed in the least, Mr. Prosecutor bowed. "Very well, Your Honour, I will put it differently." He resumed with Allain. "In your expert estimation, is the intelligence quotient of this life-form high enough to enable it to conquer, subdue and enslave humanity if it so desired?"

"I do not know."

"That is your only answer?"

"I'm afraid so."

"It is quite satisfactory," commented Mr. Prosecutor, throwing a significant look through the cameras at the unseen but billion-strong jury, "inasmuch as it admits the possibility of peril, extreme peril."

"I did not say that," protested Allain.

"Neither have you said the contrary," retorted the other. He seated himself, confident and pleased. "Your witness."

Mr. Defender began heavily, "Professor Allain, have your various hand-outs concerning the defendant been reported factually?"

"Without exception, they have been grossly distorted," said Allain, grimly. He cast a cold look at the big group of reporters who grinned back arrogantly.

"Defendant has repeatedly been described as a spy who must receive drastic treatment lest worse befall. Does your data support that theory?"

"No."

"What status do you assign to the defendant?"

"A refugee," said Allain.

"It is impossible for the defendant's motives to be hostile?"

"Nothing is impossible," said Professor Allain, honest though the heavens fall. "The smartest of us can be fooled. But I don't think I am fooled. That is my opinion, for what it is worth."

Mr. Defender sighed, "As I have been reminded, opinions are not evidence." He sat down murmuring. "Most unfortunate! Most unfortunate!"

"Fifth witness!"

"Tenth witness!"

"Sixteenth witness!"

That one, number sixteen, ended the prosecution's roster. Four or five times as many witnesses could have been produced, but these were the pick of the bunch. They had something cogent to offer, something calculated to help the public to decide once and for all—at least with its prejudices if not with its brains—whether gallivanting life-forms were to be tolerated or given the bum's rush, or worse. The question at issue was the ephemeral one of public safety, and it was for the public to say whether or not they were going to take any risks. With this in mind, the evidence of the sixteen made a formidable indictment against the queer, golden-eyed thing on trial for its liberty or even its life.

Conscious that he was leading on points, Mr. Prosecutor came erect, gazed authoritatively at the defendant.

"Just why did you come to this world?"

"To escape my own."

"Do you expect us to believe that?"

"I expect nothing," chalked Maeth laboriously. "I merely hope."

"You hope for what?"

"For kindness."

It disconcerted the questioner. Left with no room for a telling retort, he was silent a moment while he sought another angle.

"Then your own world did not please you? What was wrong with it?"

"Everything," responded Maeth.

"Meaning you were a misfit?"

"Yes."

"Nevertheless you view *this* world as a suitable dumping-ground for misfits?"

No reply.

"I suggest that your plea is nonsense, your whole story a sheer fabrication. I suggest that your motives in coming here are deeper and darker than you dare admit. I will go further and put it to you that you do not come even from the region of Procyon, but from somewhere a good deal nearer, such as Mars."

Still no reply.

"Are you aware that astronautical engineers have subjected your damaged ship to long and careful examination and made a report on it?"

Maeth stood there, pathetically patient, eyes looking into the distance as if in search of peace, and said nothing.

"Are you aware that they have reported that while your vessel is far in advance of anything yet developed by us, and while it is undoubtedly capable of travelling far outside this solar system, it is not able to reach Alpha Centauri, much less Procyon?"

"That is true," wrote Maeth on the board.

"Yet you maintain that you came from the region of Procyon?"

"Yes."

The prosecuting attorney spread despairing hands. "You have heard defendant, Your Honours. His ship cannot reach here from Procyon. All the same, it came from Procyon. This creature cannot manage to be consistent, either because it is dimwitted or, more probably, an ineffectual liar. I therefore see little purpose in continuing my—."

"I rode on a rock," scrawled Maeth.

"There!" Mr. Prosecutor pointed sardonically at the blackboard. "Defendant rode on a rock. That is the escape from a self-created impasse—a rock, no less!" He frowned at the box. "You must have ridden a long, long way."

"I did."

"So you sat your ship on this rock and saved fuel by letting it carry you many millions of miles? Have you any idea of the mathematical odds against finding a wandering asteroid in any section of space?"

"They are very large," admitted Maeth.

"Yet you discovered the very asteroid to bring you all the way here? Most astonishing spacemanship, is it not?"

"It did not bring me all the way. It brought me most of the way."

"All right," agreed Mr. Prosecutor, with airy contempt. "Ninety-nine millions instead of one hundred millions or what-ever the distance is supposed to be. It is still amazing."

"Moreover," continued Maeth, writing steadily, "I did not select one to bring me here, as you imply. I thankfully used the only visible rock to take me anywhere. I had no specific destination. I fled into the void at random, putting my trust in the fates."

"So some other rock might have borne you some place else, might it not?"

"Or no place at all," Maeth put morbidly. "The fates were kind."

"Don't be too sure of that." Mr. Prosecutor hooked thumbs in vest pockets and studied the other with sinister expression. "If your real purposes, your real motives are in fact those which have been attributed to you by our ever-alert news-services, it is to be expected that you would have a cover-up story replete with plausibility. You have given this court such a story but have offered no concrete evidence in proof. We are left with nothing but your unsupported word—and the word of an ill-formed alien, an unknown quantity, at that!" He paused, ended, "Can you not submit to this court something more material than a series of bald assertations?"

"I have no way of combating disbelief," wrote Maeth, slowly and tiredly, "except with trust."

Mr. Prosecutor countered that one by striking hard and ruthlessly. "How many others of your kind are now upon this world, following their dastardly designs while you distract attention by posing in the full glare of publicity?"

The court, the hidden audience, had not thought of that. Half a dozen reporters quietly kicked themselves for not having conceived it first and played it up for all it was worth. It had been assumed from the beginning that the alien in their hands was the only one on the planet. Yet there might well be more, a dozen, a hundred, hiding in the less frequented places, skulking in the shadows, biding their time. People stared at each other and fidgeted uneasily.

"I came alone," Maeth put on the board.

"I accept that statement. It may be the only truthful one you have made. Experts report that your vessel is a single-seater scout, so obviously you came in it alone. But how many other vessels came about the same time?"

"None."

"It would be a comfort to think so," remarked Mr. Prosecutor, thereby discomforting his listeners. "Doubtless, your world has many other ships, much larger and more powerful than yours?"

"Many," admitted Maeth. "But they can go no farther or faster. They can only bear greater loads."

"How did you come by your own ship?"

"I stole it."

"Indeed?" The prosecuting attorney raised his eyebrows, gave a little laugh. "A self-confessed thief!" He assumed an air of broad-minded understanding. "It is expected, of course, that one would suffer less by confessing to theft rather than espionage." He let that sink in before attempting another hard blow. "Would you care to tell us how many other bold and adventurous males are ready or making ready to follow your path to conquest?"

Defending attorney stood up and said, "I advise my client not to answer."

His opponent waved him down, turned to the judges. "Your Honour, I am ready to state my case."

They consulted the clock, talked in undertones between themselves, then said, "Proceed."

The speech for the prosecution was able, devastating and long. It reviewed the evidence, drew dark conclusions, implied many things from which the hidden audience could draw other and still darker conclusions. This is not to say that Mr. Prosecutor had any real hatred of or fear of the stranger at the gate; it was merely that he was doing his specialized job with ability that was considerable.

"This case, with its own new and peculiar routine," he reminded, "will go down in legal annals. As from today it will constitute a precedent by which we shall determine our attitude toward future visitors from space. And the final arbiters of that attitude will be *you*, the members of the general public, who will reap the reward of outside alliances or"—he paused, hardened his voice—"suffer the sorrows of other-world enmities. Allow me to emphasize that the rewards can be small, pitifully small—while the sorrows can be immense!"

Clearing his throat, he had a sip of water, started to get into his stride. "In trying to decide what should be done for the best we have no basis for forming conclusions other than that provided by the fantastic example who will be the subject of your verdict."

Turning, he stared at Maeth while he went on. "This creature has not been put on oath because we know of no oath binding upon it. Its ethics—if any—are its own, having little in common with ours. All we do know is that its far-fetched and highly imaginative story places such a strain upon human credulity that any one of us might be forgiven for deeming it a shameless liar."

Maeth's large eyes closed in pain, but Mr. Prosecutor went determinedly on. "While the question of its truthfulness or lack of same may remain a matter for speculation, we do have some evidence based upon fact. We know, for instance, that it has no respect for property or the law, which forms of respect are the very foundation-stones of the civilization we have builded through the centuries and intend to preserve against all comers."

He overdid it there. Maeth was too small, too wide-eyed and alone to fit the part of a ruthless destroyer of civilizations. Nevertheless, the picture would serve to sway opinions. Some thousands, probably millions, would argue that when in doubt it is best to play safe.

"A thief. More than that: a self-admitted thief who steals not only from us but also from his own," declared the prosecuting attorney, quite unconscious of switching his pronoun from neuter to male.

"A destroyer, and an intelligent one, possibly the forerunner of a host of destroyers. I say that advisedly, for where one can go an army can follow." Dismissing the question of whence said army was going to get its flock of trans-cosmic asteroids, he added, "A dozen armies!"

His voice rising and falling, hardening and softening, he played expertly upon the emotions of his listeners as a master would play on a giant organ, appealing to world patriotism, pandering to parochialism, justifying prejudices, enlarging fears—fear of self, fear of others, fear of the strange in shape, fear of tomorrow, fear of the unknown. Solemnity, ridicule, sonorousness, sarcasm, all were weapons in his vocal armoury.

"He," Mr. Prosecutor said, pointing at Maeth and still using the male pronoun, "he pleads for admission as a citizen of this world. Do we take him with all his faults and follies, with all his super-normal powers and eccentric aptitudes, with all his hidden motives that may become clear only when it is too late? Or, if indeed he be as pure and innocent as he would have us believe, would it not be better to inflict upon him a grave injustice rather than court infinitely greater injustices to a great number?"

Challengingly he stared around. "If we take him, as a refugee, who will have him? Who will accept the society of a creature with which the average human has no joint understanding?" He gave a short, sharp laugh. "Oh, yes, there have been requests for the pleasure of his company. Incredible as it may seem, there are people who want him."

Holding up a letter for all to see, he continued, "This person offers him a home. Why? Well, the writer claims that he himself was a spiky thing in Procyon during his eighth incarnation." He tossed the letter on his desk. "The crackpots are always with us.

Fortunately, the course of human history will be decided by calmly reasoning citizens and not by incurable nuts."

For a further half hour he carried on, a constant flow of words which concluded with, "In human affairs there is a swift end for the human spy, quick riddance for the suspected spy. I can conceive of no reason why any alien form deserves treatment more merciful than that which we accord to fellow humans. Here, we have before us one who at very least is an undesirable character, at most the first espionage agent of a formidable enemy. It is the prosecution's case that you have to consider *only* whether it is in the best interest of public safety that he be rewarded with death or with summary expulsion into the space from which he came. The weight of evidence rules out all other alternatives. You will not have failed to note that the witnesses who have appeared are overwhelmingly for the prosecution. Is it not remarkable that there is not one witness for the defence?" He waited to give it time to sink home, then drove it further by repeating, "Not one!"

Another sip of water, after which he seated himself, carefully smoothed the legs of his pants.

One thing seemed fairly clear: Maeth was a stinker.

Mr. Defender created a mild stir right at the start by rising and saying, "Your Honours, the defence does not intend to state its case."

The judges peered at him as if he were a sight ten times more strange than his own client. They pawed papers, talked together in whispers.

In due time the middle one enquired, "By that, do you mean that you surrender to verdict by public poll?"

"Eventually, of course, Your Honour, but not just yet. I wish to produce evidence for my side and will be content to let my case rest on that."

"Proceed," ordered the judge, frowning doubtfully.

Addressing Maeth, the defending attorney said, "On your home world all are like you, namely, telepathic and non-vocal?"

"Yes, everyone."

"They share a common neural band, or, to put it more simply, they think with a communal mind?"

"Yes."

"That is the essential feature in which your home world differs from this one of ours: that its people share a racial mind, thinking common thoughts?"

"Yes," chalked Maeth.

"Tell this court about your parents."

Maeth's eyes closed a moment, as if the mind behind them had gone far, far away.

"My parents were freaks of nature. They drifted from the common band until they had almost lost contact with the race-mind."

"That was something the race-mind could not tolerate?" asked Mr. Defender gently.

"No."

"So they were killed—*for having minds of their own?*"

A long pause and a slow, "Yes." The scrawl on the board was thin, shaky, barely decipherable.

"As you would have been had you not fled in sheer desperation?"

"Yes."

Mr. Defender eyed the judges. "I would like to put further questions to the fourth witness."

They signed agreement, and Professor Allain found his way back to the chair.

"Professor, as an expert who has made a long, personal study of my client, will you tell this court whether defendant is old or young."

"Young," said Allain promptly.

"Very young?"

"Fairly young," Allain responded. "Not quite an adult."

"Thank you." Mr. Defender let his mild, guileless gaze roam over the court. There was nothing in his plump features to warn them of the coming wallop. In quieter tones, he asked, "Male or female?"

"Female," said Allain.

A reporter dropped a book. That was the only sound for most of a minute. Then came a deep indrawn hiss of breath, a rapid ticking as cameras traversed to focus on Maeth, a running murmur of surprise from one end of the court to the other.

Back of the gallery, the most pungent cartoonist of the day tore up his latest effort, a sketch of defendant strapped to a rocket hellbent for the Moon. It was captioned "Spike's Hike." What could one call it—him—*her*, now? Spikina? He raked his hair, sought a new tack, knowing that there was none. You just can't crucify a small and lonely female.

Mr. Prosecutor sat with firmed lips and the fatalistic air of one who has had eighty per cent of the ground snatched from under his feet. He knew his public. He could estimate their reaction to within ten thousand votes, plus or minus.

All stared at the golden eyes. They were still large, but somehow had become soft and luminous in a way not noticed before. You could see that now. Having been told, you could really *see* that they were feminine. And in some peculiar, inexplicable manner the outlines around them had become subdued, less outlandish, even vaguely and remotely human!

With effective technique, the defending attorney gave them plenty of time to stew their thoughts before carefully he struck again.

"Your Honours, there is one witness for my side."

Mr. Prosecutor rocked back, stared searchingly around the court. The judges polished their glasses, looked around also. One of them motioned to a court official who promptly bawled in stentorian tones.

"Defence witness!"

It shuttled around the great room in echoing murmurs. "Defence witness! There is a witness for the defence!"

A bald-headed little man came self-consciously from the public section, bearing a large envelope. Reaching the chair, he did not take it himself, but instead placed upon it a photograph blown up to four feet by three.

Court and cameras gave the picture no more than the briefest glance, for it was instantly recognizable. A lady holding a lamp.

Rising with a disapproving frown, the prosecuting attorney complained, "Your Honours, if my learned opponent is permitted to treat the Statue of Liberty as a witness he will thereby bring into ridicule the proceedings of this—."

A judge waved him down with the acid comment, "The bench is fully capable of asserting the dignity of this court." He shifted his attention to Mr. Defender, eyeing him over the tops of his glasses. "A witness may be defined as one able to assist the jury in arriving at a just conclusion."

"I am aware of that, Your Honour," assured Mr. Defender, not in the least disturbed.

"Very well." The judge leaned back, slightly baffled. "Let the court hear witness's statement."

Mr. Defender signed to the little man who immediately produced another large photograph and placed it over the first.

This was of the enormous plinth, with Liberty's bronze skirt-drapes barely visible at its top. There were words on the plinth, written bold and large. Some in the court gave the picture only another swift look, since they knew the words by heart, but others read them right through, once, twice, even three times.

Many had never seen the words before, including some who had passed near by them twice daily, for years. Cameras picked up the words, transmitted them pictorially to millions to whom they were new. An announcer recited them over the radio.

> *Send me your tired, your poor,*
> *Your huddled masses yearning to breathe free.*
> *The wretched refuse of your teeming shore,*
> *Send these, the homeless, tempest-tost to me—*
> *I lift my Lamp beside the Golden Door.*

In the deep, heart-searching silence that followed nobody noticed that Mr. Defender had bowed deeply to the judges and resumed his seat. The defence rested, having nothing more to add.

Midnight. A large stone cell with a metal grille, a bed, a table, two chairs and a radio in one corner. Maeth and the plump man sat there conversing, examining correspondence, watching the clock.

"The opposition picked a sloppy one with that crackpot's letter," remarked Mr. Defender. He could not refrain from expressing himself vocally though he knew full well that the other was hearing only the thoughts within his mind. He tapped a heavy forefinger on the bunch of missives at which they had been looking. "I could easily have countered him with this bunch written from a week ago to way back. But what was the use? They prove nothing except that all people don't think alike."

He sighed, stretched his arms wide and yawned, had his twentieth or thirtieth look at the clock, picked up another letter. "Listen to this one." He read it aloud.

"My son, aged thirteen, keeps pestering us to offer your client a home for at least a little while. I really don't know whether we are being wise in giving way to him, but we shall certainly suffer if we don't. We have a spare room here, and if your client is clean about the house and don't mind a bit of steam around on washdays—."

His voice petered out as he had to yawn again. "They say it will be six in the morning before this public poll is complete. Bet you it's at least eight o'clock and maybe ten. They're always late with these things." He jerked around in vain effort to make himself more comfortable in his hard chair. "However, I'm staying with you until we've seen this through, one way or the other. And don't kid yourself I'm the only friend you've got." He pointed to the letters. "You've plenty there, and none of them certifiable."

Maeth ceased perusal of a note in uneven, spidery writing, reached for pencil and paper and scribbled, "Allain did not teach me enough words. What is a 'veteran'?" Having had it explained, she said, "I like this writer best. He has been hurt. If I am freed I will accept his invitation."

"Let me see." Taking the note, Mr. Defender read it, murmuring, "Um... um..." as he went along. He handed it back. "The choice is yours. You'll have something in common, anyway, since you'll both be coping with a cock-eyed world." Throwing a glance at the wall, he added, "That clock has gone into a crawl. It's going to take us a week to get to morning."

Somebody opened the grille with a jangle of keys, and Mr. Prosecutor came in. Grinning at his rival, he said, "Al, you sure make it tough for yourself in clink—you don't even use the comforts provided."

"Meaning what?"

"The radio."

Mr. Defender gave a disdainful sniff. "Darn the radio. Noise, noise, noise. We've been busy reading—in peace and quiet." Sudden suspicion flooded his ample features. "What have we missed on the radio, if anything?"

"The midnight news." Mr. Prosecutor leaned on the edge of the table, still grinning. "They have thrown up the poll."

"They can't do that!" The defending attorney stood up, flushed with anger. "It was by international agreement that this case was—"

"They can do it in certain circumstances," interrupted the other. "Which are that a torrent of votes overwhelmingly in favour of your client has already made further counting a waste of time." He turned to Maeth, finished, "Just between you and me, Funny-face, I was never more happy to lose a fight."

The man in the back room was nearing middle age, prematurely grey, and had long slender fingers that were sensitive tools. He was listening to the radio when the door-bell rang. There was no video in the room, only the radio softly playing a Polynesian melody. The bell jarred through the music, causing him to switch off and come upright. Very deliberately he moved around the room, through the door and into the passage.

Strange for anyone to call in the early evening. Not often that people came then. The mailman occasionally turned up in the morning and one or two tradesmen toward midday. Rarely did somebody appear later, all too rarely. He was not expecting a visitor, either.

He trod gently along the passage toward the front door, his feet silent on the thick carpet, his right hand brushing the wall.

There was something mighty queer about this summons because as he neared the door he conceived the weird, notion that he knew in advance who was waiting outside. The picture crept into his mind, shadowy but discernible, as if insinuated by some means he could not define, as if hopefully projected by one of those beyond the door. It was a picture of a big, plump, confident man accompanied by something small, all green and golden.

Despite past trials and stern testings which had made him what he was today, his nerves were passably good and he was not subject to delusions, or had not yet developed a tendency to delusions. So he was puzzled, even a little upset by preconceptions without any basis. He had never known a big, heavy man such as his brain was picturing, not even in other more normal days. As for the second one…

Here and there, of course, are people with greatly sharpened senses, with odd aptitudes developed to an extreme. That was to be expected, for the fates were kind and provided compensations. Without them, it would be hard to get around. But he knew his own, and they included none like this.

His fingers, usually so precise, fumbled badly as they sought the door-latch, almost as if they had temporarily forgotten where it was placed. Then, finding it, they began to turn the lock, and at that point a thin piping voice came into his mind as clearly as a tinkling bell.

"Open please—*I am your eyes!*"

STORY SOURCES

The following gives the first publication details for each story and the sources used. They are listed in alphabetical order of author.

"The Dragon of St. Paul's" by Reginald Bacchus and C. Ranger-Gull, first published in *The Ludgate*, April 1899.

"The Monster from Nowhere" by Nelson S. Bond, first published in *Fantastic Adventures*, July 1939.

"De Profundis" by Coutts Brisbane, first published in *The Red Magazine*, 15 November 1914.

"Monster" by John Christopher, first published in *Science Fantasy*, Spring 1950.

"King Kong" by Draycott M. Dell & Edgar Wallace, first published in *Boys' Magazine*, 28 October 1933.

"Alien Invasion" by Marcia Kamien, first published in *Universe Science Fiction*, March 1954.

"In Amundsen's Tent" by John Martin Leahy, first published in *Weird Tales*, January 1928.

"Dagon" by H. P. Lovecraft, first published in *The Vagrant*, November 1919.

"The Cloud-Men" by Owen Oliver, first published in *Munsey's Magazine*, August 1911.

"The Witness" by Eric Frank Russell, first published in *Other Worlds Science Stories*, September 1951.

"Personal Monster" by Idris Seabright, first published in *The Magazine of Fantasy & Science Fiction*, September 1955.

"Discord in Scarlet" by A. E. van Vogt, first published in *Astounding Science Fiction*, December 1939.

"The War of the Worlds" by H. G. Wells, abridged version, first published in *The Strand Magazine*, February 1920.

"Resident Physician" by James White, first published in *New Worlds*, September 1961.

'It's a hazardous experiment,' they all said, 'putting in new and untried machinery.'

Caution – beware the menace of the machine: a man is murdered by an automaton built for playing chess; a computer system designed to arbitrate justice develops a taste for iron-fisted, fatal rulings; an AI wreaks havoc on society after removing all censorship from an early form of the internet.

Assembled with pieces by SF giants such as Isaac Asimov and Brian W Aldiss as well as the less familiar but no less influential input of earlier science fiction pioneers, this new collection of classic tales contains telling lessons for humankind's gradual march towards life alongside the thinking machine.

The voice which came back through a clamour of noise greater than any before was that of a stranger; it was hysterical, raging futilely into the void. "The sun's blown up!"

Join humanity on the brink of destruction in fourteen doom-laden tales exploring our fixation with how and when our end will come, selected from the SF magazines and rare literary journals of the British Library collection.

Illustrating the whole gamut of apocalyptic fiction from cosmic calamities to self-inflicted nuclear annihilation, this explosive new selection also includes accounts of post-apocalyptic worlds from the speculative warnings of the 1890s to Ray Bradbury's poignant vision of a silent planet after the last echoes of humanity have died away.

In 1925 Muriel Jaeger, dissatisfied with the unrealistic utopian stories of H.G. Wells and Edward Bellamy, set out to explore 'The Question Mark' of what a future society might look like if human nature were truthfully represented.

Her hero, disgruntled office worker Guy, is pitched 200 years into a future London where each citizen is offered free education and a personal 'power-box' granting access to communication, transportation and entertainment. To Guy, the great challenges facing society seem solved, but its inhabitants tell a different story of fractured life in this supposed utopia.

Preceding the publication of Huxley's *Brave New World* by five years, *The Question Mark* is a significant cornerstone in the foundation of the dystopia genre, and an impressive work of literary science fiction.

BRITISH LIBRARY SCIENCE FICTION CLASSICS

We welcome any suggestions, corrections or feedback you may have, and will aim to respond to all items addressed to the following:

The Editor (Science Fiction Classics)
British Library Publishing
The British Library
96 Euston Road
London, NW1 2DB

We also welcome enquiries through our Twitter account, @BL_Publishing.